The Little Angel

Rosie GOODWIN
The Little Angel

ZAFFRE

First published in Great Britain in 2017 by
ZAFFRE PUBLISHING
80–81 Wimpole St, London W1G 9RE
www.zaffrebooks.co.uk

A CIP catalogue record for this book is available from the British Library.

ISBN: 978-1-785-76234-5
Also available as an ebook

3 5 7 9 10 8 6 4 2

Typeset in Simoncini Garamond 12/16.5pt by
Palimpsest Book Production Limited, Falkirk, Stirlingshire

Printed and bound by Clays Ltd, St Ives Plc

Zaffre Publishing is an imprint of Bonnier Zaffre,
a Bonnier Publishing company
www.bonnierzaffre.co.uk
www.bonnierpublishing.co.uk

In loving memory of Doreen Brownson
22nd December 1925 – 20th January 2017

A beloved Aunt missed by everyone that knew her.

To live in hearts we leave behind is not to die

Monday's child is fair of face.

Prologue

'Excuse me, Mrs Branning, but I reckon I just heard sommat outside the front door.'

Sunday paused in the hallway to glance at the maid. She had been about to enter the dining room to join her husband and her mother for dinner, but now she asked, 'What sort of thing did you hear, Em'ly?'

The young lass had only recently joined the staff at Treetops Children's Home from the Nuneaton Union Workhouse and she was as nervy as a kitten.

'Please, ma'am, it . . . it sounded like a knock – but it's late an' I'm scared to answer the door.' The girl blinked furiously and began to twist her apron into a tight ball.

Sunday smiled at her kindly. 'In that case we'd best check what it was, hadn't we? We'll do it together – how's that?'

Striding across to the large double oak doors in a swish of skirts she swung one open – to be met by an icy blast of wind. It was dark as pitch outside and the grass on the lawns, or what could be seen of it in the light spilling out from the hallway, was stiff with hoar frost, each blade seemingly standing to attention and sparkling like diamonds.

'I can't see anyone or anything amiss,' Sunday remarked, her teeth chattering as she peered into the darkness.

1

'But I *'eard* it, ma'am – I did, 'onest!'

'Perhaps it was just the soughing of the wind?' That was the trouble with old houses, Sunday thought. They were draughty places. The wind seemed to find every opening there was, and sometimes it could be so fierce it rattled the windowframes. However, she ventured a little further out onto the top step all the same, wanting to put the girl's mind at rest.

'No, I still can't hear anything,' she said, and was just about to turn away when something caught her eye. Lying against one of the tall stone pillars was a tiny bundle wrapped tightly in a large blanket.

'There *is* something here – you were right, Em'ly,' she called to the wide-eyed maid, and as she bent to lift it, another voice wafted out from the hallway.

'Where on earth is that wife of mine, Em'ly? Cook will be after us if she's not allowed to serve the dinner very soon.'

'I'm here, Tom.' Gently lifting the bundle and holding it tight to her chest, Sunday hurried back into the warmth of the hallway while Em'ly quickly closed the door shut behind them to keep out the cold.

As Tom approached to see what was going on, Sunday's heart flipped at the sight of him, just as it always did. Tom was now twenty-eight years old and the couple had been married for almost seven years, but she still loved him as much, if not more than she had on the day they had wed. With his expressive deep brown eyes and thick dark hair, he no longer resembled the skinny lad she had met so long ago. He had grown into a tall, handsome man and Sunday counted herself a very fortunate woman indeed. Her only regret was that, as yet, they had not had a child of their own. Still, the home for foundlings that they ran with the help of her mother, Lady Lavinia Huntley, ensured that she was never short of the company of babies and children, and as Lavinia often pointed out, there was still plenty of time for Sunday to give her a grandchild. She was only twenty-six years old, after all.

2

'So what's this that's been left on the doorstep then?' Tom twitched the blanket aside and they all gasped as they looked down into a pair of deep brown eyes. 'My God . . . it's a baby!'

'Yes, another one,' Sunday sighed, for this wasn't the first infant they had found abandoned on the steps of Treetops Children's Home.

'But we ain't got room fer any more, ma'am,' Em'ly fretted.

'Oh, I have a feeling we could fit just one more little one in,' Tom told her, noting the dreamy look on his wife's face. Sunday was busy crooning to the baby and drinking in the sight of the dear little bundle in her arms. 'Run up and fetch Cissie from the nursery for me, would you, Em'ly? I dare say this little boy or girl will want feeding before very much longer.'

The young lass scuttled away and it was then that Tom noticed the edge of a large brown envelope protruding from the blanket. He plucked it free, noting that it looked to be very good quality stationery, and as Sunday looked on he tore it open and removed a single sheet of paper.

'What does it say?' she asked, so Tom obligingly began to read aloud.

To whom it may concern

It has been brought to my attention that you provide a safe and wholesome refuge for babies and children who are unable to live with their own families. I applaud you for this and with regret have to ask you most earnestly if you would do the same for this child. She was born yesterday and her name is Katherine. You will find a sum of money within the envelope that is intended to provide her with all she needs for the near future. Please rest assured that there will be more to follow at regular intervals.

With sincere thanks and kind regards.

Tom then rummaged in the envelope and produced a wad of bank-notes that made both his and his wife's eyes bulge.

'So it's a little girl – I shall call her Kitty,' Sunday breathed as her eyes returned to the perfect little face. She was easily the most beautiful baby she had ever seen, and a mass of dark hair lay about her head like a tiny halo.

At that moment, Em'ly came clattering down the stairs, closely followed by Cissie Jenkins, who was in charge of the babies' nursery. Cissie was heavily pregnant with her third child and was huffing and puffing by the time she reached them.

'Not another one!' She shook her head resignedly. 'Ah well, it's only a little scrap of a thing. I dare say it can sleep at the bottom of one of the other babies' cots till I get my George to fit an extra one into the nursery. That's if – an' I presume you are – lettin' it stay?'

Sunday gave her a guilty grin. 'Yes, we can't turn her away. It's a little girl and her name is Katherine but we're going to call her Kitty.'

'Hmm, well, that's a nice straightforward enough sort o' name,' Cissie said approvingly, then leaning over she remarked, 'Lordie, but she's a pretty little thing, ain't she?'

'She certainly is. She was born yesterday, wasn't she – and what is it they say? Monday's child is fair of face!'

With that, Cissie took the child from Sunday's arms and headed back to the nursery with her.

'I'll be up to help you just as soon as dinner is over,' Sunday called out.

'Take yer time,' Cissie answered, and Sunday watched her climb the stairs until she and the precious new addition to Treetops Children's Home were out of sight.

Once in the dining room, Sunday found that she had quite lost her appetite, and Lavinia and Tom exchanged an amused glance. Knowing her as they did, they were both aware that she was longing to get her hands on the baby again.

4

'Now come along and eat something, darling,' her mother urged. 'You'll be up in the nursery soon enough.'

Sunday flushed and dutifully lifted her knife and fork. Despite the fact that she and her mother had been unaware of each other's existence for the first sixteen years of her life, they were as close as could be now – and sometimes Sunday was sure that her mother could read her like a book.

'Sorry, I was just thinking of the newest addition,' she said.

'I'm sure you were, dear, but Cissie is more than capable.'

Knowing that she was right, Sunday forced herself to eat some of the food on her plate but her eyes kept straying to the ceiling.

'Judging by the quality of the blanket the baby was wrapped in and the amount of money that was left to pay for her keep, I wouldn't mind betting she's of good stock,' Tom commented as he lifted a forkful of tender roast beef to his mouth. Nothing ever seemed to put Tom off his food. 'I wouldn't mind betting that wad amounts to more than we get from our sponsors for a whole year.'

'You may well be right,' Sunday said, 'although I haven't counted it yet.'

The second dessert was cleared away and she shot upstairs to the nursery quarters without even waiting for coffee to be served.

The whole of the second storey had been given over to the eight foundlings they cared for – nine now, including baby Kitty. The first three babies had come at intervals during the year the home had opened, and were now cheerful, robust children. First had come Benjamin, a happy-go-lucky little lad with a mind of his own who had stolen Sunday's heart the second she set eyes on him. Two months later he had been joined by Edwina, and a month after that, Marianne, affectionately known as Annie. Over the next six years, five other babies had found a home at Treetops and each of them was loved – but somehow, as Sunday pounded up the grand staircase, lifting her skirts in a most unladylike manner, she

5

had a feeling that little Kitty was going to be very important to her.

She found Zillah, her mother's devoted maid, and Cissie, her own dear friend, just tucking the babies into their cots and settling them for the night.

'How is she?' she asked immediately and Zillah grinned as she pointed towards the furthest cot. She had no need to ask which baby Sunday was enquiring after.

'She's had a bath, not that she needed one as she was clean as a whistle. And she took a bottle lovely – every last drop, in fact. She looks to be a healthy little mite to me. She's fast asleep already, top to toe with yon Maggie now.' Margaret was now six months old and had been the youngest of the foundlings until Kitty had arrived so unexpectedly.

As Sunday leaned over the cot she itched to lift the new arrival and give her a cuddle, but she knew that Zillah and Cissie would not appreciate it if she were to wake her. Between them, the two women had the nursery running like clockwork and Sunday didn't know how she would manage without them.

Further along the second-floor landing were three more rooms, a bedroom for the slightly older boys and another for the girls. The children ranged in age from two to seven and were always into some sort of mischief. The final room had been transformed into a schoolroom where Mrs Verity Lockett, a very close friend of the family, as well as the local vicar's wife, came to teach the younger ones their lessons each weekday for three hours in the afternoon. The older children attended the local board school, and always went to Sunday School. Sunday was very protective of all her charges and would have loved to keep them at Treetops, where she knew they were safe, for ever.

Now as she gazed down on the sleeping baby she felt a surge of love towards her. With her long eyelashes resting on her plump, rosy cheeks, Kitty looked just like a little angel. Each of the children in Sunday's care had been deprived of the love of their natural mother for various reasons, just as she herself had in her formative years, and this and her yearning for a child of her own made every single one of them so very precious to her.

Chapter One

April 1900

'Now then, Maggie, that wasn't very nice, was it?' Cissie scolded. 'Say sorry to Kitty this minute else it'll be bed for you tonight wi' no supper, me girl!'

Three-year-old Maggie pouted and crossed her arms as her chin rose defiantly. 'Shan't!' she muttered as she glared at Kitty. She knew, as all the children did, that Cissie's bark was far worse than her bite.

Cissie meanwhile had hurried across to Kitty and lifted her to her feet. 'There, pet,' she soothed as she brushed the grass from the child's skirts. 'It was very naughty of Maggie to trip you up like that, wasn't it?'

Kitty stuck her thumb in her mouth and lowered her head. She was used to Maggie bullying her and didn't take much notice of her any more, unless she really hurt her, which she did whenever she got the opportunity. For some reason, Maggie had always been jealous of Kitty. There were only six months between them in age but they were as different as chalk from cheese. Maggie was stockily built with mousy-brown straight hair and grey eyes – she was quite a plain child really – whereas Kitty was already developing into a beauty. She was quite daintily built and her deep brunette hair hung in shimmering curls to her shoulders; her soft brown eyes seemed

8

to reflect her mood, for they could change from amber to almost black when she was upset; and her skin was like porcelain. All the staff did their utmost to treat each of the children the same, but it was clear that Kitty was a favourite, for her sweet nature matched her looks.

Unfortunately, Maggie's temperament wasn't much better than her looks and she tried Cissie's patience sorely. On being reprimanded, the child had run off in a temper and almost reached the edge of the lawn when Sunday suddenly appeared from the rose garden and caught hold of her.

'Whoa there, where's the fire?' she asked as she looked down into the sulky little face.

'Cissie is pickin' on me again,' Maggie whined, throwing a dark look at the woman across her shoulder.

'Now I'm sure that isn't true,' Sunday answered patiently. 'What did you do?'

'Nothin'!' Maggie sniffed indignantly. 'She reckons I tripped Kitty up but I never did. She fell over me foot.'

'I see. Your foot just happened to be in the way, did it?' Sunday was well aware how spiteful Maggie could be to Kitty, but she was also very aware that she was only three years old, so she made allowances for her. 'Well, she looks all right now, so let's just hope it doesn't happen again, shall we?'

Without answering, Maggie stalked off, making for the swing that George, Cissie's husband, had tied to the branch of the big oak tree. Heaving a sigh, Sunday went to join Cissie, who was watching the children play, with her own youngest son, Johnny, sitting close to her.

'I see madam's been at it again,' Cissie said, nodding towards Maggie as Sunday sat down on the grass beside her.

'Hmm, so I believe,' Sunday answered. 'I do wish those two could get on better.'

'Well, happen they're only babies as yet. No doubt they'll make friends as they get a bit older. And because they're so close in age they're bound to vie for attention.' The words had barely left Cissie's lips when Kitty came toddling towards them, none the worse for her fall, to hand Sunday a small bunch of daisies she had plucked from the grass.

'Thank you, sweetheart.' Sunday took them and drew the child onto her lap, burying her face in the little girl's thick dark curls. At the same moment, Ben, who was now eleven years old, flopped down onto the grass beside her. For most of the time he was Kitty's protector and he had saved her from any number of spats with Maggie.

He's growing up so fast, Sunday thought to herself. He was almost as tall as she was now and already showed signs of turning into a very comely young man. His hair was thick and the colour of ripe corn, and his eyes were a lovely deep blue colour. Sunday felt a pang of regret as she realised that, in not too many years' time, he would be ready to fly the nest and make his own way in the world. She had tried her best to ensure that he and all the other children at the Home enjoyed the stability that she herself had lacked in her early years in the workhouse. But because Ben had been the first foundling she and Tom had taken in, he too had a special place in her heart and she dreaded the day when she would have to let him go. Not that he'd shown any inclination to leave as yet, fortunately. Ben loved nothing more than helping George and Tom with any odd jobs that needed doing when he wasn't attending the local school, and deep inside, Sunday secretly hoped that he might want to stay with them. They would be able to afford to pay him a small wage, if that was what he chose to do. Goodness knows, there was always more than enough to keep everyone busy about the house and grounds, and another pair of hands would be more than welcome. But that was still a few years in the future.

It was only recently that Sunday had realised what a wrench it was going to be when the first of her foundlings grew up and left, but for now she pushed the thought away and turned her attention back to the children gambolling about on the lawn like spring lambs. *Life is almost perfect*, she found herself thinking. The location of Treetops Children's Home was idyllic. It nestled close to Hartshill Hayes, a well-known Warwickshire beauty spot. The Hayes consisted of over 137 acres of unspoiled forest, and the view from the top on a clear day was breathtaking: you could see many of the neighbouring counties. In the summer, Sunday and Tom and their brood, and many local families enjoyed picnics there and the children would romp amongst the trees. *Perhaps one day I shall have a child of my very own to join them*, Sunday mused wistfully, but for now she was grateful for the ones in her care, particularly Ben and Kitty. She hadn't included Maggie in her thoughts, she noted guiltily – but then Maggie was a particularly needy little girl, which was perhaps what made her so difficult to love.

The spring and summer of 1900 passed in the blink of an eye, and before they knew it they were into winter and the first Christmas of this new millennium was fast approaching. Sunday was spending every spare minute she had shopping for Christmas presents for the children with her mother and planning special activities. Christmas was always a joyous occasion at the Home. Already Mrs Rose, the plump and motherly cook, had a number of Christmas puddings soaking in brandy and a row of rich fruit cakes had been made weeks ago and were ready to be iced. Like many of the staff, Tabitha Rose had worked there since Treetops had opened as a home for foundlings. She and her late husband, Fred, who had been a hard-working miner at the Haunchwood pit, had never been blessed with children of their own and so working at the Home had fulfilled a need in her and she spoiled the children shamelessly. Sunday regularly scolded her for slipping treats to them between meals although there was always a forgiving twinkle in her eye when she did so, well aware that her words went in one ear and out of the other. The way Mrs Rose saw it, Sunday was little more than a child herself, and so she spoiled her too.

The rest of the staff consisted of Mrs Brewer, the efficient housekeeper, who kept the house running in an orderly fashion, and Laura the laundry maid who somehow managed to plough her way through mountains of washing and ironing each week without complaint. Laura was in her late twenties and also lived in. Her parents had been only too glad to let her leave home and live at Treetops as Laura was, as her mother termed it, 'a little slow'. For all that she was a pleasant-natured young woman and another great favourite with the children. Bessie, the general maid, was the one responsible for cleaning the house and lighting the fires each morning, and she shared a bedroom in the servants' quarters with Laura, whom she had taken under her wing. Then there was Jessie, the kitchen maid who assisted Mrs Rose. Finally, the two girls Em'ly and Ruth served the meals and in between helped out with anything that needed doing as well as acting as the parlour maids. Both Em'ly and Jessie lived in the village and turned in for work each morning bright and early. Sunday, Lavinia, Cissie and Zillah cared for the children, while the men tackled the outside jobs, kept the gardens tidy and did any repairs that were required in the house, so all in all for most of the time the Home ran harmoniously and Sunday was content.

On the fourteenth of December, Kitty celebrated her fourth birthday. She rose that morning with her face aglow with excitement. As a special treat, Sunday had promised to take her into town and she was looking forward to it immensely.

She came step by step down the flight of stairs and went into the dining room, where her eyes shone to see the small pile of presents waiting for her on the breakfast table. Maggie watched her enviously. Her own fourth birthday in June felt so long ago.

'Come on, darling, open them up,' Sunday encouraged and Kitty happily did as she was told. There were a number of small gifts from the staff, including a game of Spillikins, some marbles and a tin of toffees with a dog on the front, who looked just like Barney, the golden labrador at the Home. But it was the present from Sunday and Lady Huntley that made the child's eyes pop. The beautiful doll with a china face and eyes that opened and shut was the one that she had admired in the toyshop window, the last time they had gone into town.

'Oh, she's lovely, thank you!' The child was almost crying with delight as she cuddled the doll to her while the adults looked on indulgently. 'I shall call her Annabelle.'

'That's a silly name,' Maggie declared immediately and Sunday frowned at her.

'That's quite enough, Maggie. You don't want to spoil Kitty's birthday for her, do you?'

Maggie sniffed and crossed her arms. That was exactly what she wanted to do although she didn't say it, of course. She just wished that someone would come along and take Kitty away so that *she* could be the baby of the family again. Only the year before, a childless couple had come along wishing to offer Kitty a home with them but Sunday had refused – and eventually they had gone away with a little boy called Alfred, who had only been at the Home for a week and was now the apple of their eyes. They hadn't even looked at Maggie. Everyone made a fuss of Kitty, and the way the other little girl saw it, it wasn't fair! Just because Kitty was pretty! Ben adored her too, although even at her tender age, Maggie would have laid down her life for him. Sinking down further in her seat, tears filled her eyes as she stared at the birthday girl. Bessie had mentioned that Kitty would be going into town with Sunday and

13

Tom in his new motor car later that day, but they hadn't taken Maggie into town when it was *her* birthday! She conveniently didn't recall the reason why: that she had been ill in bed with a cold!

Then Sunday shocked her somewhat when she suggested, 'Why don't you come into town with us, Maggie? You were too poorly to come when it was your birthday but I'm sure Kitty wouldn't mind you joining us today.'

Kitty smiled her agreement, for she wasn't one to bear a grudge, and Maggie wrestled with her conflicting thoughts. She didn't really want to be in Kitty's company for a second longer than she had to be – she just wanted to have Sunday all to herself – but if she didn't go along she would be cutting off her nose to spite her face.

'All right,' she agreed reluctantly.

'Good!' Sunday smiled. 'Then let's all get this lovely breakfast eaten and then we'll be on our way.'

Over the next few minutes the piles of bacon, eggs and sausages disappeared at an alarming rate and when the meal was over Sunday ushered Kitty and Maggie upstairs to put their Sunday-best clothes on. Maggie's coat and bonnet were made of a fine wool in a dark navy-blue colour, which suited her colouring, while Kitty's were made in an identical wool and design in bright red that set off her dark eyes and hair to perfection.

'There!' Sunday sighed with satisfaction as she tied the ribbons of Kitty's bonnet beneath her chin while Maggie stood to one side, scuffing her best shoes on the ground. 'You both look beautiful. Now let's go and see if Tom has brought the car around to the front, shall we?'

She took their hands and led them downstairs, one on either side of her, to find Tom standing proudly beside his new toy, explaining how it worked yet again to Ben, who was totally enthralled with it. It was a Daimler shooting brake, which had been manufactured in Coventry three years before.

'It's six horsepower, with twin cylinders and a four-speed gearbox,'

14

she heard Tom tell the boy as they peered in at the engine as if it was the best invention on earth. Then, spotting his wife, Tom grinned sheepishly. 'Sorry, love. I was just running over a few things with Ben.'

Sunday said tartly, 'I should think he knows it all by now, the amount of time you two spend playing with this contraption.' She was secretly still rather afraid of it and much preferred the horse and trap, but Tom asked for so little that she hadn't found it in her to deny him it.

Ben meanwhile had spotted Kitty, and bending down to her level, he chucked her under the chin, saying, 'My, don't we look smart today, eh? Off into town for a birthday treat, are we?'

Kitty nodded. She was clutching the small bird he had carved for her as a present for her birthday and his chest swelled with pride as he noticed. 'Right, well, I hadn't better hold you up.' He glanced up at the grey sky. 'I wouldn't be surprised if we didn't have snow sometime soon. I reckon I can smell it.'

Sunday gave him a playful punch on the arm. 'Oh, you and your weather forecasting,' she teased, although truthfully she was forced to admit that nine times out of ten he was right in his predictions. They then settled the two little girls into the back seat, placed a warm rug over their legs and seconds later they were whizzing off down the drive as Sunday hung on to her hat.

'You're looking rather lovely today, pet,' Tom remarked, daring to take his eyes off the road for a moment to admire Sunday's new outfit. The days of the crinoline were gone and now women were favouring a longer, straighter skirt, with a small train at the back.

Sunday flushed with pleasure. She was wearing a light brown and cream heavy silk day dress with a darker brown coat over the top of it and a large hat boasting feathers that had been dyed to match her outfit. For most of the time she didn't have the inclination to worry about changing fashions but Lavinia had insisted she should have this one as a treat – and Sunday loved it.

'Thank you, sir,' she answered coyly, smiling prettily at him. 'You don't look so bad yourself.'

In the back seat, Kitty giggled and Maggie grinned too as the car motored on.

Soon they were strolling amongst the market stalls in Nuneaton town centre, enjoying the hustle and bustle. Kitty took Sunday's hand and hauled her in the direction of the cattle market, followed by Tom and Maggie. She loved the atmosphere there and was fascinated by all the animals that were for sale. The little group wandered amongst the pens as red-faced farmers bartered noisily over chickens and cows and sheep.

Eventually Sunday told them: 'It's time to say goodbye to the animals, girls. I have a few things I need to get for Cook, then if you're both very good I'll take you to the tea rooms for an ice cream. How about that?' Even Maggie looked momentarily happy at the prospect of such a treat and the four of them hurried on their way, their faces rosy with the cold.

However, people repeatedly stopped to tell Kitty what a pretty little girl she was. Ignoring Maggie, they commented on her lovely hair and her striking eyes or stared at her admiringly – and soon Maggie's happy mood had soured. It didn't matter where they went, it was always the same, and the attention that Kitty attracted only made the other girl feel all the more desperate for someone to love *her*, for deep inside she was feeling very vulnerable and alone. Even so, she enjoyed the shopping trip and the visit to the tea rooms and so she was in a slightly mellower frame of mind by the time they all returned to Treetops.

'I do worry about the way Maggie seems to be so envious of Kitty,' Sunday confided to Tom as they were getting ready for bed. She was sitting at her dressing table brushing out her long fair hair

16

as he lay in bed propped against the pillows watching her. Even though they had now been married for a good ten years he still couldn't get enough of her and adored the very ground she walked on.

'The problem is that even though they're both very young, Maggie has already realised that Kitty is prettier than her,' he answered, and Sunday nodded as she paused with the brush still in her hand. 'And,' he added cautiously, 'I know you don't mean to do it, my love, but you do rather tend to favour Kitty.'

'I'm afraid you're right,' she said, and her voice was rueful. 'I must try harder with Maggie but she makes it so difficult at times. And other times I think Kitty is just too pretty for her own good and it worries me. I fear that when she's older, men will be drawn to her like moths to a flame.'

'That's a long way in the future,' Tom said. 'We'll worry about that when we come to it, but for now . . . why don't you come to bed and get your old man warm?'

Sunday laid down the hairbrush and approached the bed, only too willing to do as she was asked.

Chapter Two

It was almost five years to the day since they had found Kitty on the doorstep when Em'ly tapped on the drawing-room door to tell Sunday, 'This was left outside, missus. I heard the sound of a motor car in the distance an' I peeked out, and that was when I saw it lyin' there.'

Sunday glanced at the large brown envelope and instantly guessed what it was. Each year in December, a similar envelope containing a sum of money had been left there. This year she had spent most of the month peeping out of the front windows, hoping to catch a glimpse of whoever it was that had left it – but once again she had somehow missed them.

Tom looked at her and quipped, 'Seems they've evaded you again.' Then, taking the envelope from her, he opened it and let out a silent whistle at the banknotes enclosed inside. 'This is far too much for one child's keep,' he said. 'Perhaps we should start to put it away for Kitty for when she's older?'

Sunday had been thinking much the same thing herself, and was relieved to learn that Tom was of the same mind. 'I think that's an excellent idea, but I can't understand how I missed them *again*.' Her eyes strayed back to the window and she sighed with frustration.

'But you haven't been able to stand there every minute,' her husband pointed out. 'And I dare say whoever it is will make themselves known when the time is right.'

'I suppose so,' she agreed, but she couldn't help but be curious. Whoever it was who was paying such a large sum of money for Kitty's expenses must truly care about her. The trouble was, Sunday dreaded the day when they might well turn up and take Kitty back, because she had come to love the child as her own. Even so, now was not the time to fret about it, she decided. Christmas was racing towards them and there were the rest of the children to think about, so she left Tom to put the money away in the safe and went about her business.

'Now calm down, you lot, else this tree is goin' to be ruined. We can't all get to it at once,' Cissie scolded. Earlier in the day, Tom and George had taken the pony and trap into town and arrived home with the biggest Christmas tree any of them had ever seen. Now it stood in a large bucket of earth in the entrance hall and the children were keen to decorate it. The trouble was, they were attacking it from all sides, jostling each other, and Cissie was getting harassed. Thankfully, just then, Em'ly appeared to tell them, 'Come on, all of you, dinner is served. Into the dinin' room now afore it gets cold.'

There was a mad exodus as the children immediately discarded the ornaments they were holding and headed off as if they hadn't eaten for a month.

'Phew!' Cissie sighed with relief and looked up at Sunday, who was balancing rather precariously on a stepladder in order to decorate the top of the tree. It was only inches from the high ceiling and like Cissie she was feeling a bit on edge. She just hoped no one let Barney the labrador out of the boot room where he'd been put to keep him from 'helping'. The cats would no doubt come and investigate. One year, they had pulled the entire tree down.

'Aren't you going for your dinner, pet?' Sunday asked Kitty as she tentatively descended the ladder. The child was standing observing the tree with her thumb jammed in her mouth.

'I wanted to wait for you,' she said.

As Sunday's feet landed on the ground the child took her hand and Sunday's heart melted as she felt the warm tiny fingers in her own. She suffered all manner of guilt feelings about the love she felt about Kitty; after all, she had always promised herself that every child in her care should be treated equally – but try as she might, she couldn't stop herself from having a soft spot for this little one. There was something about her that was just so appealing. True, she grew prettier with every month that passed, but it wasn't just her looks that made her so lovable, it was her character too. The little girl rarely complained about anything, even Maggie's sulks. This worried Sunday, for she was aware that she wouldn't always be there to protect her, and Kitty's passive nature meant that others might easily take advantage of her. She had often remarked on this to Tom, but he waved aside her concerns. 'That's a long way off,' he would tell her – and she supposed he was right.

Now she and Cissie headed for the dining room with Kitty walking sedately between them and found themselves amidst noisy and less than organised chaos. A scrimmage, in fact. Kitty instantly skipped off to claim the seat at the side of Ben. Maggie had already positioned herself on the other side of him and she made a face at Kitty as Ben affectionately tousled Kitty's shining dark hair. The children were all highly excited about the delivery of the tree and the fact that Christmas was almost upon them, and they were so noisy that the four adults could barely make themselves heard above the laughter and chatting.

'Bloody 'ell, I reckon I can feel a headache comin' on,' Cissie groaned as she began to ladle vegetables from a large tureen onto the nearest children's plates.

'At least they're happy.' Sunday winked at her as she served the children at the other end of the table and eventually when their plates were full, they quietened a little in order to wolf down their food. The way they saw it, the sooner the meal was over the sooner they could get back to decorating the tree – hence the food disappeared at an amazing rate.

'So much fer tryin' to teach 'em good table manners,' Cissie remarked as she helped herself to a succulent piece of roast pork and crackling, and popped it into her mouth.

Sunday didn't comment. As well as Christmas, she had other things on her mind. Exciting, wonderful things that she daren't even think about too deeply. Her monthly course was now two weeks late and she was praying that at last she might be carrying the longed-for baby. She hadn't mentioned it to Tom as yet. The way she saw it, there was no sense in raising his hopes until she was sure – but she had confided in Cissie, who was almost as excited as she was. The roast pork dinner was followed by Mrs Rose's delicious jam roly-poly and jugs of thick creamy custard, which again disappeared at an alarming rate.

'May we stay up to finish decorating the tree before we have our baths?' one little boy asked Sunday's mother hopefully and after glancing at her daughter, Lavinia Huntley smiled.

'I should think so, just so long as you promise to go up as soon as it's finished,' she agreed.

The children were then excused from the table and they raced off for the boxes of baubles in the hall again, leaving the adults to enjoy their coffee in peace.

'Em'ly, make sure none of them tries to climb the stepladder!' Sunday shouted after her, as the girl shepherded the smaller children into the corridor. Em'ly nodded and closed the door as Cissie leaned back in her seat.

'Eeh, they've fair worn me out today,' she yawned. 'If they're this excited now, goodness knows what they'll be like come Christmas morning!'

'I thought I'd carry on with wrapping some more of the presents

21

this evening when they've all gone up to bed,' Lavinia said as she poured herself more coffee. 'Are there any volunteers to help?'

'Well, much as I'd like to, I can't. I have me own brood to get to bed,' Cissie said. 'George is lookin' after 'em at the moment, but they won't go to sleep without me bein' there.' Cissie, George and their brood lived happily in Primrose Cottage, which lay in the grounds of Treetops Manor.

Tom hastily made his excuses too but Sunday offered, 'I'll help. I quite like wrapping presents as it happens.'

'Huh! It's a complete waste o' time if yer ask me,' Cissie snorted. 'The first thing they do is rip 'em open.'

'Yes, but opening the present and not knowing what's inside is half the pleasure,' Sunday argued. Then, 'Are we going to let them open them first thing Christmas morning or when we get back from church?'

'Well, seeing as their stockings are going to be hanging on the end of their beds I think you'll have a bit of a job on to try and make them wait,' Lavinia chuckled. 'Although I dare say you could put them all under the tree and hand them out when we get back from church. That way, they'd have no choice but to wait.'

A heated debate then took place about what they should do. Lavinia and Tom thought it best for the children to open their stockings in their rooms. Sunday was keen to see them all open their presents downstairs, but eventually she was outvoted and it was decided that the children should hang their stockings on the ends of their beds as they had on previous years.

'Makes sense to me,' Cissie muttered, spooning sugar into her coffee. 'It's allus worked that way before.'

Sunday shrugged, conceding that her old friend was right.

An hour later, the tree was finally finished and stood in all its somewhat haphazard splendour. The tiny candles clipped to the branches in their tin holders were twinkling. Zillah had lit them, but had warned the children in no uncertain terms that they must *never* attempt to light them if there wasn't an adult present. Now the children gazed at the sight in awe and Sunday felt a lump rise in her throat as she watched their faces. At times like this she was more determined than ever to try and make their childhoods as happy as she could, unlike her own, with its terrifying memories. She only wished that she could take in even more orphans, but she knew that to do that would not be fair on the ones who already lived here.

'All right, children, it's really time for your baths now.' Sunday clapped her hands and tried to ignore the disappointed young faces. 'Don't worry,' she said kindly, 'the tree will still be here tomorrow.'

And so somewhat reluctantly, the children began to file up the stairs.

At 10 p.m. Sunday retired to use the bathroom and was devastated to find that once again, her hopes of having a child of her own had come to nothing. Her monthly course had started.

When she entered the bedroom, Tom immediately noticed her downcast face and guessed what had caused it. She reacted the same way every month.

'It'll happen in its own time, pet,' he assured her gently, taking her in his arms and planting a tender kiss on her sweet-smelling hair. 'And it's not as if we haven't already got a rook of children to pour our love onto, is it?'

'I know that.' Sunday sniffed to hold the tears at bay. 'But I so want to give you your very own child.'

'Do you know what? So long as I have you, I don't care.' He gave her a squeeze. 'A baby would be a bonus but it's you that matters the most to me.' And as she stared up into his expressive, deep brown eyes, she saw that he meant every single word he said.

On Christmas morning Treetops Children's Home was a hive of activity and excitement. When the children woke, whoops of delight echoed around the house as they opened the stockings they had hung at the end of their beds and which Santa Claus had filled, during the night while they slept.

'They sound happy enough.' Tom grinned as he buttoned his shirt in their bedroom. Barney had caught the excitement and was barking loudly.

'They certainly do.' Sunday fastened the last of the pins into her hair and patted it into place before suggesting, 'Should we go and be bombarded, then?'

'I can't think of anything nicer.' He held his arm out to his wife and after hooking hers through it they ventured out onto the landing.

'Sunday, Tom, look what Santa left for me! A wooden train. How did he know it was just what I wanted?' Little Zeke hurtled towards them clutching the precious gift to his chest as Tom winked and tapped the side of his nose.

'Ah well now, he must have got that letter you sent to him, and even if he didn't, he's magic, see? He knows just what every child wants.'

The little fellow nodded and toddled away hugging his treasure and almost colliding with Zillah as she came out of the nursery.

'I've had a job to get them dressed this morning,' she chuckled. 'I think we can safely say they're all happy with their presents. Even young Maggie has a smile on her face.'

'Hallelujah! Long may it last,' Tom said comically as Sunday playfully punched his arm.

'Come along you,' she scolded with a giggle. 'We have to get the children in to breakfast or we'll be late for church.' And on that happy note they set off for the dining room.

The rest of the day was almost magical, as Sunday remarked to her husband when they finally retired to their room that evening. The morning service conducted by the Reverend Lockett at Chilvers

24

Coton Church had been beautiful, and when it started to snow as they made their way home, the children were thrilled to bits.

'Will we be allowed to get the sledges out?' they cried. 'Please, Tom!'

'Yes, if the snow lies deep enough,' he had agreed indulgently.

They arrived home to the appetising smell of roast goose and once seated at the enormous table they had all done justice to Cook's wonderful meal. It began with a thin leek soup accompanied by fresh-baked crusty bread, and was followed by roast goose, Cook's home-made sage and onion stuffing and crispy roast potatoes, along with a selection of vegetables. Finally, they were served with an enormous Christmas pudding, which to their delight was brought into the dining room with flames licking around it from the brandy which Tom had lit with a spill from the fire.

Once the Christmas dinner was over, the adults organised a number of games to keep the children happy. The boys continuously crossed to the window, delighted to see that the snow had indeed begun to settle and they all sat and planned where they would take the sledges the next day. Eventually they had all come flocking in for their Christmas tea and Sunday and Tom were shocked to see how the children tucked in again after what they had eaten at dinnertime.

'I'm sure they all have hollow legs,' Lavinia commented with a grin.

Because it was Christmas Day the children were allowed to stay up a little longer that evening, and when a band of carol singers walked down the drive and came to stand outside the front doors, singing the best-loved carols beneath the gently falling snow, the children were enchanted. The group were invited in for warm mince pies and a glass of Cook's hot punch, and by the time they departed there were more than a few of the children yawning. Some had even fallen asleep on the chairs.

'Come on, missie.' Tom lifted Kitty, who was snoring softly, to carry her to her room and for the first time that day, Maggie's face fell.

'Come on, sweetheart, I'll help you get ready for bed,' Sunday said, offering her hand, and Maggie reluctantly took it. 'I'll tell you what, just for this once, seeing as it's Christmas Day, I'll let you off having a wash this evening,' Sunday told the silent little girl. 'We'll just slip your nightdress on, tuck you in and I'll tell you a story, eh? How does that sound?'

Slightly mollified, Maggie nodded but she kept her eyes fixed on Tom who was cradling Kitty in his arms as he mounted the stairs as if she weighed no more than a feather. Maggie wished now that she had pretended to fall asleep and then perhaps Tom would have carried her up to bed too, but at least Sunday was holding her hand. They found Cissie and Zillah already in the children's rooms trying to bring some sort of order into bedtime, but today nobody minded and at last all the children were safely tucked in and fast asleep.

'I think we adults ought to go down now and treat ourselves to a glass of port,' Lavinia suggested, and they were all only too happy to agree. It would be the perfect end to a perfect day.

Chapter Three

There were only three days to go before the New Year when Zillah came down with a fever and was confined to her bed. Lavinia flew into a panic.

'She hasn't been looking well for some time,' she fretted. 'And I blame myself. She's no spring chicken any more and I should have made her slow down.'

'Huh!' Sunday snorted. 'That would have taken some doing. You know what's she's like, bless her, she's always on the go and thrives on it.' Knowing how close her mother was to her former maid, she felt sorry for her. Zillah had been like a mother to Lavinia and had gone through some of the darkest times of her young mistress's life with her. Now Lavinia wrung her hands in dismay to see her beloved friend so ill and wondered why the doctor was taking so long to arrive.

'He should have been here by now,' she said, crossing to the drawing-room window for the tenth time in as many minutes.

'I'm sure when he does turn up he'll just say that she's come down with a chill,' Sunday placated her but Lavinia didn't even appear to hear her as she paced restlessly about like a caged animal.

Tom was sitting smoking his pipe and trying to read the newspaper in one of the comfortable wing chairs that stood at either side of the fireplace; his stockinged feet were stretched out to the fire that was roaring up the chimney. This was his favourite room in the

27

house, one of the very few forbidden to the children. Elegant, heavily fringed pelmets framed the deep-red velvet curtains that hung at the long windows overlooking the garden, and Turkish carpets were scattered about the polished parquet floor, giving it a cosy feel. Gold damask wallpaper gleamed on the walls. Sunday had chosen every single thing in this room shortly after she had come to live at Treetops Manor, and Tom knew that she loved it too, although today her thoughts were too full of Zillah to notice it. But then that was women for you – they always seemed to be worrying about something or another whereas he was very calm and tended to let the world go by. All Tom wanted was a quiet life and he was sure that Zillah would be all right. His wife and mother-in-law were just getting themselves into a flummox over nothing.

'He's here!' Lavinia's voice interrupted his thoughts as she saw Doctor Cushion's pony and trap coming down the drive. She raced for the door with Sunday close behind her, leaving him to read his newspaper in peace.

When Sunday came back into the room an hour or so later, one glance at her face told him that something was seriously amiss. She was as white as a ghost.

'The doctor thinks that Zillah may have pneumonia,' she told him croakily and he was shocked. He hadn't realised how ill she was.

'Are they moving her to the hospital?' he enquired.

Sunday's head wagged from side to side. 'No, he thinks it's too cold to move her. She's better here, he reckons, and there are enough of us to look after her.'

'Of course.' Tom stood and took his wife in his arms and gave her a gentle hug. 'Is there anything I can do?'

'Not really. My mother will be doing most of the nursing. She insists on it, and the doctor is going to call by every day.'

'Strangely enough, I was just reading in the newspaper that Queen Victoria is ill as well. She's at Osborne House on the Isle of Wight, but then she is eighty-one years old. I'm surprised she's lasted this long without Prince Albert. Did you know it's almost forty years since he died?' He was trying to take Sunday's mind off Zillah's situation but it wasn't working, and soon enough she was off again to see if there was anything that Zillah needed.

Peering from the window, Tom was just in time to see the doctor climbing into the trap, holding his medical bag, and for a few seconds he watched the children, who were all warmly wrapped up, playing out in the snow. They had built an enormous snowman and the boys were having a snowball fight, oblivious to how poorly Zillah was. *I shall have to get them to keep the noise down when they come inside*, he thought, then quietly left the room to go about his chores. It would be time to call the children in for their midday meal soon and no doubt a little help wouldn't come amiss in the kitchen. He wondered then if he should speak to Sunday about cancelling the big party they had planned for New Year's Eve, but then he thought perhaps he should look on the bright side. It was still a few days away and Zillah could well be on the mend by then.

Later that day, Em'ly answered the doorbell to find a well-dressed couple standing on the doorstep.

'We do apologise for coming unannounced. I realise we should have written and made an appointment,' the gentleman said sheepishly, removing his hat. 'But my wife and I wondered if it might be possible to see Mrs Branning?'

'Oh.' Em'ly glanced worriedly towards the stairs. Sunday was upstairs with Zillah and probably wouldn't want any distractions. But then the couple looked very respectable, so she ushered them into the drawing room, telling them, 'I'll just go and see if Mrs Branning is available.'

'Thank you, my dear.' The woman smiled at her nervously as Em'ly flitted away.

'Who is it?' Sunday asked impatiently when Em'ly tiptoed into Zillah's room to tell her about the unexpected visitors. Sunday had just ordered her mother to go and have a lie-down, and she didn't want to leave Zillah alone.

The young girl shrugged. 'They didn't say, but they look quite well-to-do and they were so polite I didn't like to send them away, especially when they've come here in the snow. Happen it's sommat important?'

'Oh, very well. I suppose I can spare them a few minutes, but will you wait here with Zillah until I get back?'

'Of course.' Em'ly took Sunday's seat when she rose and taking the damp sponge from her hand she continued to gently bathe Zillah's burning forehead.

Once out on the landing, Sunday shook out her skirt and patted her hair into place before making her way down to the drawing room.

'Good afternoon.' She held out her hand. 'How may I help you?'

The couple looked genuinely surprised. They had expected Mrs Branning to be much older. The man swiftly shook her hand and explained the purpose of their visit.

'My wife and I heard of your establishment and wondered if you ever allowed any of the orphans in your care to be homed with families?'

It appeared that Treetops' reputation as a foundling home was spreading, Sunday thought to herself.

'Well, it's not impossible,' she said cautiously. 'But you must appreciate that I insist on stringent checks being carried out first. Are you looking to offer a child a home?'

The man glanced at his wife. 'Well, yes, if it was possible. But do forgive me, Mrs Branning. We haven't formally introduced ourselves. This is my wife, Stella, and my name is Victor Dawes. I own a number of shops in Nuneaton but we live in Witherley, not too far away at all as the crow flies.'

Sunday inclined her head. She was aware of one of his shops at least. Dawes Hardware. She had purchased a great number of things from there over the years.

Mr Dawes then licked his lips anxiously, and as he again glanced at his wife, Sunday saw tears spring to the woman's eyes and her heart softened. She was a pretty woman, small and delicate, with deep brown hair and blue eyes. Sunday judged the couple to be somewhere in their mid- to late thirties.

'The thing is, we had a lovely daughter . . .' He stopped momentarily to clear his throat. 'But unfortunately she died during the measles epidemic a few years ago.' It was obviously painful for him to talk about it but he forced himself to go on. 'Recently my wife was again with child but sadly she lost it early in the pregnancy and was very ill. The doctor advised us then that it would be harmful to her to attempt to have any more children. Hence our presence here.'

'I see – but if it is a baby you were hoping for, I'm afraid I couldn't help you,' Sunday told him gently. 'The youngest of our children are four years old now, ranging to their teens.'

'Oh, it needn't be a baby,' Stella Dawes told her hastily, speaking for the first time. 'A four-year-old would be wonderful. In fact, we passed the most delightful-looking little girl as we motored down the drive. She was dressed in a red coat and had the most beautiful dark hair. I was quite enchanted with her.'

Sunday's heart lurched. 'That would be Kitty,' she told her. 'And I'm afraid she isn't one of the children who I could allow to leave.' Just the thought of losing Kitty, even to such a lovely couple, made Sunday feel physically sick.

'Oh, I see.'

Trying to ignore the disappointment on the woman's face, Sunday told them, 'But we do have a number of other children who might be suitable. Of course, I would need you to produce some references and I would also need to visit your home to ensure that it would be suitable for a child. Would that be possible?'

'Oh yes,' they said simultaneously.

'Then that's what we shall do.' Sunday forced a smile. She had no wish to be rude but she was keen to get back to Zillah now. 'Perhaps while you get the references together we could delay the visit for a week or two? A member of the family is very ill at the moment and I'm afraid I couldn't spare the time to take things further just yet. I do hope you understand,' she added.

'Of course, and we hope that the patient will soon be on the mend. We shall look forward to hearing from you shortly then.' Mr Dawes again shook her hand and gave her a card with his address on, and Sunday personally saw the couple to the front door before rushing back to Zillah's side.

'They took a keen interest in Kitty,' Sunday told Tom that evening as they sat together enjoying a mug of cocoa when all the children were fast asleep, worn out by their frolics in the snow.

'And what did you tell them about her?' he asked.

Sunday fiddled with the fringes on the tablecloth so she could avoid his eyes. 'I just explained that I couldn't let her go,' she said defensively. 'Well I couldn't, could I? Not when someone is paying us to look after her.'

'As it happens you're quite right,' he agreed. 'But you know you should prepare yourself, because one of these days whoever that someone is might just come along to claim her back.'

Sunday was only too well aware of that possibility but didn't allow herself to dwell on it, for how would she cope, if someone were to take Kitty away from her?

Rising from her seat, she told him, 'I'd best go up and take over from my mother for a while. That's if I can persuade her to leave Zillah.'

'Of course.' And as he watched her leave the room, his heart ached for his wife.

Chapter Four

The next day, 30 December, it was decided that the New Year's Eve party they had planned would have to be cancelled. Zillah was no better – in fact, her condition had deteriorated – and so George and Tom set off in the snow to inform the guests personally as Lavinia and Sunday took it in turns to sit with the sick woman. Lavinia was so worried about her beloved friend that she looked almost as frail as the invalid did – and now Sunday was concerned about her mother too.

'Please go and rest, Mother. You're going to be ill too at this rate,' she pleaded, but Lavinia took no notice.

'I'm fine,' she assured her daughter, her eyes never leaving Zillah's face. Zillah had been delirious since the evening before. 'I need to be here when she wakes up.'

If she wakes up, Sunday found herself thinking but she didn't voice her fears. Her mother was frightened enough as it was.

'Dr Cushion seems to think that if this fever breaks, she might start to recover,' Lavinia said then, but as she said it she knew that she was clutching at straws. In actual fact, the doctor had appeared to be very concerned when he had left less than an hour earlier. So much so that he had promised to come in later that afternoon to check on Zillah again.

'In that case I shall go and fetch you a tray up,' Sunday told her. 'You haven't eaten or drunk a thing today.' And with that she swept from the room with her mother's protests ringing in her ears. It felt strangely quiet as she descended the stairs. The older children were playing outside in the snow and the younger ones were being entertained by Em'ly and Cissie in the library where their noise wouldn't disturb Zillah. Normally they would be racing around the hall and along the corridors, and Sunday found the silence ominous.

Down in the kitchen, Mrs Rose quickly made up a tray of sandwiches and a pot of tea for Lavinia. She also added a thick wedge of her delicious sponge cake, oozing jam and cream, but Sunday doubted that her mother would even touch it. Still, it was worth a try.

'I don't know what we're supposed to do with all this food I made for the party,' Mrs Rose lamented, gesturing towards the laden tables. 'I dare say it'll all go to waste now. There's far too much for us to eat.'

'Then pack up what you don't want and I'll get George and Tom to deliver it to the workhouse,' Sunday said sensibly. 'I know the children there will be really glad of so many treats.'

'What a good idea!' Cook looked slightly happier now. 'I'll do just that – but how is Zillah?'

'Not good,' Sunday confided with a tired frown. 'We can't seem to get this fever to break and the doctor says he's going to come back later this afternoon to look at her again.'

Cook's lips wobbled. She was very fond of Zillah – as they all were – but all they could do was pray that she would recover.

'And what about the couple that came to see you earlier?' she asked then. There wasn't much slipped past Tabitha Rose.

'They're interested in giving one of the children a home with them.'

Cook sniffed. 'So why don't they go and choose one of the poor little mites from the workhouse then?' Cook spoiled all the children and, like Sunday herself, hated the thought of any of them leaving Treetops.

'I don't know and I'm not even going to think about it for now,' Sunday said wearily. 'All I care about at present is Zillah. I know that the children are going to be disappointed that we've had to cancel the party too. I'd better go and tell them and explain why.' She wasn't looking forward to it.

'I'll tell you what. I'll do a little party in here for them,' Mrs Rose offered good-naturedly. 'The kitchen is far enough away not to disturb Zillah and it's better than nothing at all. I'm sure Em'ly and Bessie will help to keep them occupied. We'll do it late tomorrow afternoon, and with luck, by the time it's finished they'll be worn out and ready for bed. You just concentrate on Zillah and leave everything to me.'

'You're such a treasure, Mrs Rose,' Sunday told her gratefully, then leaving the kitchen she hurried back to the sick room.

The party Cook organised for the children on New Year's Eve turned out to be a roaring success but upstairs, things didn't improve for Zillah. She was dangerously ill. Each rasping breath she took was an effort for her now and Lavinia was almost beside herself with grief and worry. She and Zillah had been through so much together that she couldn't imagine life without her.

Cissie, Sunday and Tom had all begged her to go to her room for a rest while they sat with the invalid, but Lavinia refused to leave her side.

'I want to be here when she wakes up,' she insisted – and miraculously Zillah did just that as it was approaching midnight.

She suddenly opened her eyes and as they settled on Lavinia, who was clutching her hand tightly, she gave her a beautiful smile.

'Ah . . . there you are, pet.'

'Of course I'm here. Where else would I be?' Lavinia choked

back tears and stared down at the beloved woman she had come to regard as a mother.

'Are you sure you've forgiven me for what I did to you and Sunday?' Zillah asked suddenly. Her voice was little more than a whisper now, but her tone was urgent.

'You know I have.' Lavinia gently kissed the hot damp fingers as a solitary tear trickled down her cheek.

'Then I can go and meet my maker with a clear conscience.'

'You're not going anywhere. I need you – do you hear me?'

Zillah gave a sad smile. 'No, pet,' she gasped. 'You have your daughter and a whole family of little ones to care for now, and that's just as it should be. But I want you to know . . . I've loved you like my own daughter, and I only kept you from yours to try and protect you both . . . God bless you.'

Lavinia opened her mouth to protest but Zillah had already lapsed into sleep again. A cold hand closed around her heart, and she wondered if Zillah was preparing herself for her final journey. From that moment on, she just sat there willing her beloved Zillah to live – but all the time she could feel her inexorably, unstoppably, slipping away.

Zillah finally passed away on the fourteenth of January and the whole household was plunged into mourning. The funeral was arranged for the following week, the twenty-second, and on that day, it wasn't only the residents of Treetops Children's Home who grieved but the whole country, for it was announced that the Queen had also died that morning at Osborne House, surrounded by her family.

'Why does everyone keep crying?' Kitty asked innocently as Sunday was helping her to dress.

'It's because Zillah has gone, darling,' she replied.

'But where has she gone?'

'She's gone to be an angel in heaven.'

Kitty gravely thought about this for a moment before asking, 'Will she be able to come back and see us?'

'I'm afraid not.' Sunday swallowed the huge lump in her throat.

Tears welled in the child's eyes and spilled over onto her cheeks. 'But why can't she? We all love her so.'

'Yes, we do,' Sunday gulped. 'But Zillah was very poorly indeed, so God decided to call her home so that she wouldn't be poorly any more.'

Kitty pouted. 'Then I think he's very mean. *This* is Zillah's home.'

Unable to go on with the conversation for fear of breaking down, Sunday gently patted her bottom and turned her towards the door, saying, 'Why don't you go down to breakfast like a good girl. You don't want the others to eat all the porridge up, do you?'

Kitty instantly did as she was told. She loved Cook's thick creamy porridge and she didn't want to miss out.

Once she was gone, Sunday folded her little nightgown up and tucked it under her pillow before making her way slowly downstairs. It would be time to start getting ready for the funeral soon and she wasn't looking forward to it one little bit. Em'ly and Bessie were already carrying the food Cook had prepared into the dining room for any of the mourners who might wish to come back to the house after the burial, so this morning the children were all eating in the kitchen. This would be one day that Sunday would be very glad to get over with.

The following week, Sunday and Tom finally visited the Dawes family in the nearby village of Witherley, and when they turned into the drive leading to their home they were very pleasantly surprised. A large sign announced THE GABLES, with an arrow pointing the way.

'Why, it's almost as big as Treetops,' Sunday commented. 'I didn't expect anything quite so grand.'

Tom nodded as he steered the car along the drive beneath a canopy of leafless trees. 'Well, everyone knows that Victor Dawes is a wealthy businessman so it stands to reason that he's going to have a nice house.'

And it was a nice house. A large, rambling redbrick building, it was covered in a profusion of ivy and Virginia creeper, which made it look welcoming. The large windows on either side of the impressive front doors were glinting in the early-morning sunshine and the grounds surrounding it looked extensive.

When Tom had parked the car, the couple ascended the steps leading to the front door, which was opened almost immediately by a fresh-faced, fair-haired young maid in a starched white apron and cap. She had obviously been told to expect them.

'Mr and Mrs Branning?' she asked with a nervous smile.

When Tom and Sunday nodded, she ushered them into the hall out of the cold, saying, 'The master and mistress are expecting you.' She then helped them off with their hats and coats and after hanging them up, went on, 'They told me to show you straight into the drawing room. Would you come this way, please?'

They followed her along a corridor that smelled of beeswax polish. Everything Sunday looked at was gleaming with not a single thing out of place and she couldn't help grinning to herself. It was certainly a far cry from Treetops, which was lovely but very much lived-in.

Once the maid had announced them and shown them into the drawing room, Mr and Mrs Dawes rose to greet them. Mrs Dawes was clearly anxious about the visit and flitted about the room like a butterfly, plumping up the cushions on the chairs and rearranging the expensive-looking china ornaments on the shelf.

'I'm sure you'll find our home is suitable for a child,' she gabbled, and Sunday smiled at her.

'You have a beautiful house,' she said in an attempt to put her at ease.

Mrs Dawes rang the bell for the maid. 'We'll have tea before I show you around, shall we?' she twittered.

Once Mrs Dawes had placed the order and the maid had gone away again, Sunday commented, 'Your house is so immaculate. Are you sure you won't mind a child messing it up? I'm afraid all our children are very untidy. It's quite usual for us to find toys scattered everywhere and in the most unlikely of places.'

'Oh, I wouldn't mind at all,' Mrs Dawes said immediately.

An awkward silence followed until the maid returned with the tea. Mrs Dawes poured them all a cup, and when they'd finished she asked, 'Would you like to see the room the child would sleep in now?'

'Yes, we would, thank you.' Sunday rose from her seat, glad of a chance to escape the strained silence and Tom rose with her. Mr and Mrs Dawes personally showed them the way upstairs and again Sunday noticed that everywhere was pristine. There seemed to be an army of maids scurrying about the place like little ants all with dusters in their hands, and Sunday feared that if she stood still they might start to polish her. She also noticed that they kept their eyes downcast as they passed their mistress. What was it – deference or fear?

'Here we are.' Mrs Dawes stopped outside a door on the first-floor landing and flinging it open, she beckoned them in.

At a glance, Sunday and Tom saw that it was indeed a very beautiful room – and one that had been furnished and decorated for a little girl. The carpet and the curtains were a pale lilac colour, and dollies and teddy bears in regimentally straight rows were placed on the chairs strategically set out around the room. A four-poster bed trimmed with lace drapes took centre stage, and there was a pretty rosewood wardrobe, ornately carved, with a matching chest of drawers and dressing table. An enormous doll's house stood against one wall. Even the tiny furniture inside it was neat as a new pin. On another wall was a large bookshelf full of beautifully illustrated fairy stories. Sunday couldn't help but think that any little girl would love this room – and yet for some reason that she couldn't quite put her finger on, she felt uneasy. Even so, now that she had seen the house she could find no valid reason to stop the Dawes from taking a child, so she began to question them.

'I assume after seeing this room that you wish to take in a little girl?'

'Oh yes, if it is possible,' Stella Dawes answered as she wrung her hands. 'We would prefer a little girl, wouldn't we, Victor?' She addressed her husband as if for support.

'If that's what you have your heart set on, my dear,' he answered indulgently.

'Hmm, well as it happens I do have a child in the age bracket you would prefer,' Sunday admitted. 'It couldn't be Kitty, the little girl you saw when you visited us.' Then, feeling that she needed to offer some explanation she hurried on, 'We are paid to care for her and feel sure that her guardian, although they haven't made themselves known to us as yet, will come to claim her some day. But I do have another little girl. Her name is Margaret, but we call her Maggie and she's almost the same age as Kitty.'

'Oh!' Mrs Dawes clapped her hands together, her eyes alight. 'Could we perhaps come and meet her?'

'Of course. I would expect you to visit her a few times before you made your decision,' Sunday answered. She was feeling very agitated. Maggie could be a complete nuisance for most of the time but even so, Sunday was very attached to all the children in her care and found it hard to contemplate letting go of any of them, even Maggie. Sensing this, Tom reached out and held her trembling hand in his big, warm paw.

40

'When may we come?' the woman asked.

'Perhaps tomorrow afternoon?' Sunday suggested.

'Oh, yes please! We could manage that, couldn't we, darling?' Stella Dawes turned to her husband.

'Certainly,' he agreed, and they all then made their way back downstairs. Once they had arranged a time, the couple saw Sunday and Tom to the front door and said their goodbyes. Tom helped Sunday up into the Daimler then collected the starting handle, and going round to the front of the car, he inserted it and gave it a few hefty swings until the engine purred into life. Then they were off as the Dawes waved to them.

As he steered the car towards home, he commented, 'You're very quiet, pet.'

Sunday sighed. 'Sorry, I just feel . . . Oh, I don't know. What did *you* think of them?'

'I thought they were quite charming, so stop worrying,' he chided gently. He knew how much his wife cared about the children in their care and how hard it would be for her to let one of them go, but even so he believed it would be in the child's best interest.

'Hmm, I'm not so sure now,' Sunday answered, hanging on to her hat. 'Didn't you feel they were a little . . . reserved?' she shouted above the roar of the engine, wishing again that they'd come in the pony and trap. It was almost impossible to have a conversation in this dratted automobile.

'What?' Tom shouted back and Sunday lapsed into silence. Perhaps it would be better to wait until they got home to voice her concerns.

Chapter Five

Em'ly met them at the door and took their hats and coats when they arrived back at Treetops. Seeing the look on their faces, she said, 'I'll go and fetch you a nice cup of tea, shall I? You look frozen through.'

Sunday couldn't help but notice the difference between her staff and those at the Daweses' house in Witherley. Here it was hard to distinguish who was the mistress and who was the maid, which was just as Sunday liked it. But at the other house, it had struck her how all the staff crept about like shadows – as if they were afraid of bringing Mrs Dawes's wrath down upon their heads. Could it be that the woman wasn't quite as meek and mild as she made out?

As if he could read her mind, Tom stepped over to the fire and said, 'All right then, madam, out with it! There's obviously something worrying you.'

Sunday frowned as she gazed out of the window at the few children who had ventured out into the snow. The whole house was still in mourning for Zillah and it was unusually quiet.

'You . . . you don't think that Mr and Mrs Dawes are just trying to replace their dead daughter, do you?'

Tom looked shocked. 'What a terrible thing to say,' he scolded gently. 'You of all people should know how strong a woman's urge is to have a child.' The second the words had left his lips, he could have bitten his tongue out as Sunday's face fell and tears started to her eyes.

'Oh, pet, I didn't mean that how it came out,' he apologised, crossing to her and placing his arm about her shoulders.

She forced a smile. 'It's all right. It's probably just me being silly. Go and park your car up then come back and have some tea. You'll only fret if you leave it outside.'

Tom hesitated then nodded and left the room. He'd had the doors taken off one of the stables so that the car could be parked under cover. Left alone, Sunday wandered over to the fire and stared into the flickering flames. The references the Daweses had produced from some very influential people had been faultless. They all said what a wonderful mother they thought Stella Dawes would make. The house had been beautiful too and yet . . . Sunday sighed, wondering why something didn't feel quite right. Also, Mr Dawes made her feel uneasy – not that he had said a single word out of place. But then with an effort she gave herself a mental shake. *You're just jealous because you've cared for Maggie since she was a baby*, she told herself. *Come on, admit it!* Of course the child deserved the chance to be a part of a normal family! Feeling slightly better, she poured out the tea and waited for Tom to return.

The following afternoon, when the Daweses were shown into the drawing room, Sunday sat opposite them, her hands folded primly in her lap, trying to ignore the shrieks of laughter coming from the hall.

'I do apologise for the noise,' she told her visitors. 'Now that the snow has started to thaw we thought it best if the children played inside today. I'm afraid they can be rather boisterous.'

Tom was standing by her side. Normally he would leave things like this to his wife and her mother, but Lavinia was still in deep mourning for Zillah and he felt that Sunday might need a little support.

'Should I bring Maggie in for you to meet her?' he suggested.

Stella Dawes nodded excitedly. Tom strode to the door and after peering up and down the corridor he spotted Maggie playing with a dolly on the bottom stair.

'Ah, Maggie, pet. Come and meet Mr and Mrs Dawes,' he encouraged.

Maggie was surprised. She wasn't usually invited to meet the guests but she did as she was told all the same and, carrying her doll, she headed for Tom, who gave her a wink and led her by the hand into the drawing room.

Mrs Dawes had risen and was standing in front of the fireplace, watching the door avidly for her first glimpse of the child who might become her daughter. However, her reaction wasn't at all what Sunday had hoped for. In fact, her face fell when confronted with the little girl.

'Mrs Dawes, this is Margaret, or Maggie as we call her. Maggie, this is Mr and Mrs Dawes.' Tom introduced them and Maggie smiled at the woman. She thought the pearl-coloured silk day dress the lady was wearing was very pretty and so was she.

'How do you do, ma'am,' Maggie said politely as she had been taught.

At last Mrs Dawes moved towards her with her hand outstretched. 'How do you do, Margar . . . I mean Maggie.' *What a plain little girl*, she was thinking as she stared at the child's mousy brown hair and plump figure. But then she supposed she could always force a few curls if she tied rags in her hair each evening and the child would soon lose a little weight if they were to cut out cakes and treats. She would certainly be much easier on the eye then. And as this was the only child she was being offered . . .

Maggie was waiting, looking puzzled, as the woman continued to stare at her. The child was completely oblivious as to why she

44

was there, so Sunday quickly stepped in and explained. 'We visited Mr and Mrs Dawes a short time ago, Maggie dear, and when we told them what a good girl you could be, they expressed a wish to meet you. Isn't that nice?'

Maggie's little face was transformed then when she flashed the woman a smile and stuck her chest out. No one had ever come to see her before, as far as she could remember, and it made her feel very special. Usually when they had visitors they spent their time fawning over Kitty.

'I can count to ten,' she told Mrs Dawes solemnly and was rewarded when the woman dropped to her level.

'Well, what a clever girl you are,' she praised her and Sunday sighed with relief. It appeared that the awkward introductions were over.

'Why don't you stay and have a chat to Mr and Mrs Dawes while Sunday and I go and fetch a tray of tea, eh?' Tom suggested then, the soul of tact.

Maggie nodded happily enough so he took his wife's elbow and steered her out of the room.

'What did you have to go and do that for?' Sunday hissed when they were in the hallway.

'Stands to common sense they need to get used to each other,' he pointed out. 'And they're not going to feel completely at ease with us hovering over them, are they?'

'I suppose not,' Sunday admitted grudgingly. 'But we'll only leave them for ten minutes. That should be long enough for them to decide whether they want her or not.'

Tom frogmarched her off to the kitchen to sit by the roaring range and chat to Cook, and for now Maggie and the Daweses were left in peace.

Sunday paced up and down like a cat on hot bricks until Tom eventually said, 'Right, I think we could go back in now.'

They re-entered the drawing room, carrying a tray, to find Maggie and Mr Dawes in conversation while Mrs Dawes looked on from her seat by the fire.

'Ah, Maggie here was just telling me all about the cats you have and Barney the dog. I've always fancied having a dog myself but I haven't been able to persuade Stella up to now.'

His wife visibly shuddered at the thought. 'They're such *smelly*, dirty creatures,' she said, giving Sunday another thing to worry about.

'Oh, what a shame you feel that way,' Sunday said sweetly as she strained the tea into the cups. She had brought out her favourite tea-set, which had been a wedding present from Mrs Spooner, the dear soul she had gone to work for when she eventually left the workhouse. It was made of very fine bone china with delicate blue forget-me-nots hand-painted all over it. 'Maggie is *very* fond of animals,' she ended with emphasis.

Mrs Dawes had the grace to blush as Sunday turned her attention to Maggie, saying, 'Why don't you go back to play now, pet? I think I saw Ben looking for you.'

At the mention of Ben, Maggie was off like a shot. Once they were alone again Sunday asked the couple, 'So, what did you think of her?'

Mr Dawes glanced at his wife before saying cautiously, 'I thought she was a delightful child. What did you think, dear?'

'I think she would be very happy with us,' she answered, then addressing Sunday and Tom: 'Would you consider letting us take her? I can assure you she would want for nothing.'

Sunday still had a bad feeling about this – some gut instinct that warned her things were not quite as they should be . . . and yet outwardly she had no reason to deny them.

'If you are quite sure? You must appreciate this is a very serious decision. It would do Maggie irreparable harm if you were to take her then change your mind.'

'That won't happen, I assure you. If she comes to us she will have a home for life,' Mrs Dawes promised. 'Now what do we do next?'

'I think perhaps we should talk to Maggie again first and see how she feels about it. However, I suppose there's no time like the present if you've really made up your mind. Are you sure you wouldn't like a little more time to think about it?'

The couple both shook their heads. They appeared to be of one mind. Sunday nodded at Tom, asking, 'Would you mind asking Maggie to step inside again, love?'

'Of course not.' Tom disappeared to return minutes later with Maggie, who was wondering what was going on by now. Why did Sunday and Tom keep wanting her to spend time with their visitors? They hadn't asked any of the other children to meet them.

'Ah, here you are again, pet.' Sunday forced a note of joviality into her voice as she patted the seat at the side of her. 'I have something to tell you. Come and sit here by me.'

Maggie obediently did as she was told as Sunday cleared her throat and began, 'The thing is, Mr and Mrs Dawes here are looking for a little girl to go and live with them, and as it happens they've taken a great shine to you.'

'To *me*?' Maggie looked astounded. Most of the people who visited always fell in love with Kitty because she was the prettiest. She then surveyed the couple solemnly and a big smile broke out on her face. 'So if I came to live with you, would you be my mummy and daddy?'

'Yes, I suppose we would,' Mrs Dawes answered. 'Do you think you might like that?'

Maggie thought about it for a minute. It would mean leaving Sunday and Tom and all her friends, but then it would be lovely to have a real mummy and daddy of her very own. As she thought of it she began to tremble with excitement, but then as it began to sink in she asked, 'Would I be able to come back and see everybody sometimes?'

47

It was Mr Dawes who answered with a smile, 'I don't see why not. We don't live all that far away, as it happens.'

'Hmm.' Maggie imagined how jealous Kitty would be when she told her that the Daweses had chosen her and she beamed. 'In that case I think I'd like that.'

Sunday suddenly panicked. Everything was happening a little too quickly for her liking.

'Perhaps Tom and I could take you to visit Mr and Mrs Daweses' home so that you can see it before you make up your mind?' she intervened.

'All right.' Maggie frowned then as something occurred to her. 'Will I share my bedroom? And do you have a dog?'

Again, it was Mr Dawes who answered. 'Yes, you will have your very own room and no, we don't have a dog at the minute but I dare say we could get you one.' He knew that his wife wouldn't be very keen on that idea, but if it made the child happy, the way he saw it, it was a small price to pay.

'In that case, I'd like to come and see your house,' Maggie informed him, then bursting to tell Kitty and the others the exciting news she skipped from the room leaving the grown-ups to arrange the visit.

Chapter Six

Maggie could hardly wait to impart her exciting news to the rest of the children, but if she had been hoping for jealous tantrums she was sadly disappointed.

'A new mummy and daddy?' said Kitty, who was cuddling her birthday doll, Annabelle. 'That's nice for you.'

Maggie was put out at her reaction. 'It's better than nice. They chose me because they liked me the best,' she said with tears in her eyes. 'And I'm going to have a bedroom all to myself and Mr Dawes – I mean my new daddy – said I could have a dog too!'

'That's nice,' Kitty repeated as Ben approached them.

'What's this I'm hearin' then?' he enquired of Maggie, ruffling her hair. She hastily told him and he whistled through his teeth. 'Well, that's brilliant, ain't it? I hope you'll be happy, little 'un.'

'Of *course* I shall be happy,' Maggie answered waspishly, knocking her wobbly front tooth back into place with her tongue. She was hoping it would come out soon because Sunday had told her that when it did, if she left it under her pillow, the tooth fairies would come and take it and leave her a new shiny penny. She hoped they knew their way to her new home. At four and a half years old she really had no comprehension of the enormity of what was about to happen to her. She was due to move from everything and everyone that was familiar to her! However, for now she could only gloat

49

because the Daweses had chosen her to be their little girl rather than Kitty.

Ben knew that Maggie could be a right little madam when she wanted to be, but he still had a soft spot for her and would miss her when she went.

'So when will you be leaving us then?' he asked, and eyes still firmly fixed on Kitty, Maggie shrugged.

'Don't know yet. Sunday and Tom are taking me for a visit to my new home first, then I s'ppose I'll go.'

He bent to give her a little squeeze. 'That's grand then . . . but we'll miss you.'

This from her idol brought tears springing to Maggie's eyes. It was just beginning to sink in now, that she really *was* going to live in a new house – and suddenly she felt a little apprehensive. What if she didn't like living with her new family? Would Sunday and Tom let her come home? And Treetops *was* the only home she'd ever known up to now. She would even miss Kitty, although she wouldn't tell her that. Feeling suddenly deflated, the little girl turned about and went to cadge another biscuit off Cook.

Two days later, Maggie set off with Sunday and Tom in the big motor car. The rest of the children and the staff had been informed that she might be leaving them, and some of them stood on the steps to wave them off, making Maggie feel very important. She nestled down onto the back seat of the Daimler with a warm rug tucked firmly about her legs and sat back to enjoy the ride.

Her first sight of the Daweses' home impressed her and she wished that Kitty were there to see it. In fact, she found herself almost wishing that Kitty could come with her. It certainly looked very grand and there seemed to be a whole army of gardeners working in the grounds.

The door was opened by a straight-faced woman with a hooked nose who wore a chatelaine about her waist containing a number of keys that jingled musically when she moved. She reminded Maggie of a scary witch.

'Come in,' she said in a clipped voice with no word of welcome. 'Mr and Mrs Dawes are expecting you.' She looked down on Maggie then, and the child shrank into Sunday's side.

'She must be the housekeeper,' Sunday whispered to Maggie as they followed her across the hallway. Maggie's eyes were like saucers as she gazed around at the spotlessly clean and tidy house. It was a far cry from Treetops, with its homely atmosphere, and it was very grand.

'Ah, Margaret, here you are,' Mrs Dawes said with a smile when the housekeeper had shown them into the drawing room. 'Hello, Mr and Mrs Branning. Do sit down, I've ordered coffee for us all. Do you like coffee, Margaret? Or perhaps you would prefer some milk?'

'I like coffee,' Maggie answered, her voice little more than a squeak. Then as the grown-ups began to chat she surveyed the room, thinking again how tidy it was and how quiet. It was never quiet at Treetops – and again, little doubts began to creep in. Who would she have to play with here? She suddenly became aware of Mr Dawes watching her, and when she had caught his eye he winked at her.

'How about you, me and Tom go out to the stables to see the horses while the ladies have a chat?' he asked kindly.

Maggie willingly took the hand he offered.

'Now don't go letting her get into a state,' his wife warned when they had all reached the door. 'I know what you're like when you get around those horses of yours.'

'I wouldn't dream of it, dear.' There was a twinkle in his eye when he winked at Maggie again and, heartened, she gladly escaped with him.

After an enthralling half-hour spent giving sugar lumps to the horses and being nuzzled by their velvety noses, which made her giggle, Maggie was given a tour of the house by Stella and shown the bedroom that was to be hers. Her eyes instantly lit on the doll's house and crossing to it she began to finger the tiny dolls and the perfectly carved miniature furniture inside it.

'Oh, do be careful with that, dear,' Stella Dawes said worriedly. 'That has been in my family for some time and I'd hate it to be damaged.'

What was the point of putting such a lovely thing in a small child's room and expecting her not to touch it? Sunday thought crossly. It was like putting a dish of strawberries down in front of a donkey and telling him not to eat them, but she held her tongue. She had wrestled with herself over the last few days but had finally decided that apart from the little niggles of doubt she had had about Mr and Mrs Dawes – probably quite unfounded – there was nothing to suggest that Maggie wouldn't be perfectly happy here. Little Arthur, whom she had placed with a new family, was thriving happily, so she must give Maggie the same chance.

Maggie meanwhile moved away from the doll's house and began to examine the rest of the room. She lifted some of the books from the shelves to inspect them before going to have a bounce on the beautiful four-poster bed and Sunday stifled a grin as she noticed Mrs Dawes following her about, putting everything back as it had been. Maggie would certainly be getting a few lessons in tidiness by the look of it, but this was no bad thing. She and the other adults tended to let the children get away with murder, back at Treetops.

Eventually they all made their way back downstairs and while Mr Dawes and Tom kept Maggie entertained with one of the books they had brought down with them, Sunday and Mrs Dawes had a discussion and it was decided that Maggie could move in with them the following weekend. After more coffee and biscuits, Tom, Sunday and Maggie departed.

'My bedroom is *gigantic*!' Maggie boasted to the other children when they arrived back at the Home. 'An' it's got *so* many toys in there. Dolls, books, games *an'* a great big doll's house with little people inside. I'm to have me own nanny too,' she went on importantly. 'That's someone who is there to take care o' me – *just me!*'

Some of the others sighed enviously. It really did sound like Maggie was going to live the life of Riley! Kitty herself wasn't the least bit jealous. She was quite happy where she was and wouldn't have given a thank you to be taken away from her beloved Sunday and Tom. As far as she was concerned they were her family and she wouldn't have swapped them for all the tea in China.

'So when are you goin'?' piped up seven-year-old Edwina and Maggie stuck her chest out.

'This weekend. Sunday has already asked Cissie to start packin' me clothes.'

But then suddenly the gong sounded for dinner and there was no more time for boasting as the children all surged towards the dining room.

On Saturday morning, Cissie carried Maggie's little case down to the hallway and sniffed tears away as she placed it at the side of the door. The night before, they had had a little leaving party for Maggie, and Cissie was sad at the thought of her going.

'But she'll only be a couple of miles away,' Tom had reminded her and Sunday earlier that day. 'It's not as if she's going to the other side of the world.'

'I know that,' Sunday had huffed. 'But she won't be our responsibility any more, will she?'

At this, Tom had shaken his head and gone to lose himself in the stable block. Women could be funny creatures, that was for sure – not that he'd change his Sunday for the world!

As the time for the Daweses to arrive approached, the children and the staff began to assemble in the hallway to say their goodbyes. Even Lavinia, who had barely left her room since Zillah's passing, made an appearance.

'Be sure to come and see us sometimes,' she said as she bent to plant a kiss on Maggie's plump little cheek. Mrs Rose was the next to say goodbye, followed by Em'ly, Jessie, the housekeeper Mrs Brewer, Bessie and even Laura the laundry maid. It was the turn of the children then but Maggie showed no emotion about leaving them. She was just really excited about going to her new family now and glad that Kitty was there to see it. George and Cissie's children arrived then to add their good wishes to the others, and they had barely done so when the clatter of the door knocker echoed around the hall.

'That'll be Mr and Mrs Dawes!' Em'ly said all of a flap as she hurried away to answer it. Sunday meanwhile hurriedly placed Maggie's best bonnet on her head and tied the ribbons beneath her chin.

'You be happy now,' she whispered in a choky voice as she fought back tears, but then Stella and Victor were inside and she extended her hand to each of them in turn. 'Maggie's all ready to go and her case with her clothes in is just there,' she told them in an overly bright voice. She felt as if her heart was breaking, but knew that she must give Maggie this chance of having a family she could call her very own. The trouble was, letting go was always so very hard.

'Oh, she needn't bother bringing them,' Mrs Dawes answered airily. 'Pass them on to one of the others. I have all new clothes waiting for her at home.'

Maggie looked at Kitty with her nose in the air, as if to say, 'See how lucky I am?' But Kitty merely smiled as she ran forward to give the girl a final hug.

'I shall miss you,' she whispered in Maggie's ear and the latter's eyes suddenly filled with tears. She knew that she hadn't always been kind to Kitty because she was envious of how pretty she was, and now she wished that she had been nicer to her.

Mrs Dawes took Maggie's hand then and marched her towards the front door.

'But won't you stay for tea?' Sunday asked, suddenly in a panic.

'No we won't, if you don't mind,' Mrs Dawes replied. 'Margaret's new nanny is anxious to meet her and I think perhaps it's best for her if we just go and get the parting over with, rather than prolonging it, don't you?'

Lavinia had come to place her arm through Sunday's now and feeling her daughter's pain, she answered for her. 'Yes, Mrs Dawes. I think you are probably right. Take good care of her and remember, we are here if you should need us. Goodbye.'

Maggie suddenly didn't feel quite so confident about leaving behind the only people she had ever cared about, but she took the woman's hand and after a brief wave she went off and never even looked back.

'There then. Let's hope that's another child that has found a happy home,' Lavinia said warmly.

Sunday gave one last anxious look at the door before dutifully following her mother and husband into the morning room to discuss plans for the day ahead.

Over the next three months Treetops gradually settled back into some sort of normality as the people who lived there resigned themselves to their dear Zillah's death. Even Lavinia seemed to have accepted it now and gradually began to come out of her shell. Little had been seen of Maggie until one day, as she was walking through the marketplace, intent on purchasing new under-garments for Marianne and Kitty, who both seemed to have grown a good deal recently, Sunday saw a woman in a dove-grey uniform coming towards her clutching the hand of a small girl. For an instant she didn't take much notice of them, but something familiar about the child make her look again – and when she did, the breath caught in her throat.

'Maggie?' As they drew abreast of her the woman paused and frowned at Sunday as Maggie looked up at her from dull eyes. She had lost a great deal of weight and her usual lank hair was now a mass of ringlets tied up with a red ribbon. 'H-how are you, pet?'

The woman said repressively, 'Do you know this person, Margaret?'

The little girl nodded meekly, not at all as the Maggie Sunday remembered would have done.

'Yes, Nanny. This is Sunday, the lady I used to live with before I went to live with Mr and . . . Mother and Father.'

'Ah, I see.' Then addressing Sunday, the woman said, 'You must be Mrs Branning?'

Sunday inclined her head, hardly able to take her eyes off Maggie. She looked so different. 'Yes, yes, I am and it's lovely to see Maggie again. We were rather hoping she might come and visit us all at Treetops.'

'So I understand. But the master and mistress felt it best to give her time to settle in first,' the nanny answered pompously.

'And how is she settling in?' Sunday asked, taking an instant dislike to the woman. She seemed so cold and impersonal.

'Margaret, as we prefer her to be known, is doing very well – all things considered,' the woman replied.

'What things?' Sunday asked boldly. The longer she spent in this woman's company the less she liked her, and Maggie was so quiet, not at all her usual cheeky little self.

'Well, the fact that she is a foundling and has only ever lived in a children's home all her life. Of course, living within a civilised family will take some adjusting to.'

'I can assure you we are *very* civilised at Treetops Manor,' Sunday

56

snorted, deeply offended, and the woman had the good grace to look slightly embarrassed.

'No offence intended, I assure you, Mrs Branning. But now we really must be going. The mistress won't like it if we are late back.'

Ignoring her, Sunday bent to Maggie's level and gave her a reassuring smile. The child had picked up on the chilly atmosphere and looked worried.

'So how are you, pet?'

After a quick glance at the nanny, Maggie answered politely, 'I am very well, thank you.'

'Good.' But Sunday was far from pleased. Why wasn't Maggie being her normal, natural outspoken self? The child seemed like a stranger.

'I'm sorry, Mrs Branning, but we really *must* be going,' the stern-faced woman repeated, and realising that she had no valid excuse to detain them, Sunday rose.

'Of course. Good day. And, Maggie, do ask Mr and Mrs Dawes to bring you to visit us soon. We would all love to see you.'

The child nodded expressionlessly before being hauled away, and all Sunday could do was stare after her in bemusement.

Chapter Seven

Sunday arrived home to total chaos as usual. Verity Lockett was just leaving after teaching the children, and let loose from the schoolroom they were rampaging about. Their laughter was echoing down the hallway as they surged towards the door, keen to get out into the fresh air. Barney was barking wildly, adding to the mayhem. A huge golden labrador, he was a firm favourite with the children and was like Tom's shadow. They had found him wandering about the grounds shortly after they got married and had taken him in, and ever since, everyone in the household had spoiled him shamelessly. The cats, who lived in the kitchen, had come there the same way and Sunday remembered laughing when Tom had once suggested they should put up a sign saying HOME FOR WAIFS AND STRAYS. ANY LEGGED VARIETY WELCOME.

'Hello, Sunday,' the children chorused as they flooded past her out into the spring sunshine with Barney in hot pursuit, his tail wagging furiously.

'Phew, I thought I was going to get trampled in the rush, for a moment there,' Sunday commented to Verity. When Sunday was growing up in the workhouse, Verity had been the only person to ever show Sunday any real kindness or affection. Sunday would never forget that and she loved the woman dearly. Poor Verity was Zillah's niece – the two had been very close, and Verity had taken

58

her aunt's death very badly. Now, however, she laughed as she drew on her gloves and took her hat from Em'ly.

'George has the trap outside and he just offered to run you home,' Sunday told her just as Tom emerged from his office to join them.

'Wonderful.' Verity was pleased. 'Edgar has some parish meeting or another tonight in the church hall so I could do with getting home a little early. See you the same time tomorrow, Sunday.' She was gone then with a breezy wave of the hand.

Sunday took Tom's elbow and almost dragged him into the drawing room. She couldn't wait to tell him the news.

'I bumped into Maggie today. She was in the marketplace with her nanny.'

'Well, that was nice then,' Tom said. 'How did she look?'

Sunday began to pace, a sure sign that she was agitated. 'It's not so much how she looked that disturbed me as how she acted.'

Tom took a seat. 'What do you mean?'

'She just seemed so . . . oh, I don't know – quiet, I suppose, and not herself at all. And she's lost an awful lot of weight.'

'Isn't it normal for very young children to lose their baby weight as they grow a little older? And let's be honest, Maggie was a chunky little thing. Losing a little weight won't hurt her, surely?'

Seeing the twinkle in her husband's eye, Sunday grew annoyed. 'Oh, I know what you're thinking,' she snapped. 'That I'm just looking for things to worry about, but I tell you – something isn't right with her.'

'You're like a mother hen worrying about her chick,' he teased as he crossed to give her an affectionate hug. 'I'm sure if there had been any concerns, Mr and Mrs Dawes would have been in touch with us.'

'It was something about her eyes . . . as if her spirit had been broken,' Sunday went on, ignoring his comment. 'Almost as if she was afraid to speak without the nanny's permission. Ugh, she was a tartar!'

'In that case, I suggest we employ her to come here for a few days a week. She might be able to get our unruly lot into some sort of order. Now for goodness sake stop fretting, will you? Maggie will be fine, I'm sure.'

Sunday snuggled against his broad chest. No doubt Tom was right. She had to give Maggie a chance to settle in her new home with no interference from her, but it was always so hard to stand back . . .

'Ben, I miss Maggie.' Kitty was watching Ben scythe the grass on the front lawn, an art he had perfected and greatly enjoyed doing.

'Do you, little 'un? Well, that's understandable. You spent a lot o' time together, even if she was a pain for most of it.' He laid down the scythe and swiped his forearm across his sweating forehead. It had taken him a long time to persuade Tom to let him learn to scythe. Tom had felt he was too young to be trusted with such a dangerous tool but Ben had proved him wrong and was now almost as proficient as Tom was at the job.

If truth be told, Ben missed Maggie too. She'd been an annoying little chit for the majority of the time but she had possessed some saving graces. Her leaving had also brought home to him how vulnerable they all were. He regarded Treetops as his home, but when the Daweses had taken Maggie away it came to him that he and the rest of the youngsters there were merely being cared for by Tom and Sunday. They weren't really his family, so who was to say that someone wouldn't come along and offer to give him a home? Would he be allowed to refuse? He knew that now he was growing bigger and stronger he might be an asset to a farmer, and if truth be told he wasn't averse to working on a farm. He loved

60

being outdoors in the fresh air, yet the thought of leaving Sunday and Tom, who were the closest to a family he had ever had, filled him with dread. Of course, he would have to leave Treetops one day and make his own way in the world, but for now he preferred not to think of it.

'Perhaps we could ask Sunday or Tom if they could arrange for you to visit Maggie? Or perhaps she could come here to see us?' he suggested then, seeing Kitty's dejected little face.

Because they were all aware that she was missing Maggie, they had spoiled her, and it was beginning to show a little in her attitude. Kitty had finally realised just how very pretty she was and was now extremely good at using her looks to get what she wanted. A little pout or the glimmer of a tear in her eye could have Sunday jumping to please her, a fact that worried Tom slightly, as Ben was aware. Only the day before, he had overheard Tom telling her, 'You're over-indulging that child, pet, and it's not doing her a bit o' good.'

Shame-faced, she had nodded. 'I suppose I do spoil her a little,' she'd admitted. 'But now that you've pointed it out, I shall stop.'

Ben didn't think there was much chance of that happening and now he lifted the scythe to resume his work, saying, 'Off you go then. This is very sharp and I wouldn't like you to get hurt.'

Knowing that she was being dismissed, Kitty wandered away with her doll Annabelle tucked firmly beneath her arm and Ben was thoughtful as he watched her go.

It was the middle of April when Sunday suddenly suggested, 'Why don't we pack a picnic and take the children for a walk in the woods? It's such a lovely day, it's a shame to waste it.'

Tom, who had his head stuck in a newspaper, sighed to himself.

He had just been snatching a few minutes before returning to the list of jobs that never seemed to get any shorter, but he agreed all the same.

'All right then. But only for a couple of hours, mind. There's still a lot of work to do in the orchard if we're to get the best of the crops when they come. I was hoping to finish pruning the apple trees today, and there's still a mass of weeding waiting to be done in the vegetable garden. George is out there now working on it even as we speak.'

He laid down his paper as Sunday rushed off to the kitchen to organise a picnic hamper and round the children up, and within half an hour they set off with the younger ones racing ahead laughing and shouting. Hartshill Hayes was always a beautiful place to stroll in, but in the spring it took on a magical quality. Beneath the canopy of trees was a carpet of bluebells for as far as the eye could see . . . and the smell of the flowers was heady.

Sunday often told the little ones stories about the fairies who played in the woods and today Kitty ran up to her, her dark hair glinting with golden lights in the dappled sun that managed to break through the canopy of branches overhead.

'Will we see any fairies today, Sunday?' she asked innocently.

Sunday raised a finger to her lips before whispering, 'You just might if you're very quiet, but if you're noisy and they hear you coming, they'll hide.'

Big brown eyes as wide as saucers stared back at her before Kitty turned abruptly about and hurried off to try and shush the other children.

Sunday's heart swelled with love for the child as she watched her go. She knew that Tom was right and she shouldn't spoil her the way she did, but it was hard not to.

Eventually they came to a break in the trees and emerged onto the bank. The fields and hedgerows stretched away into the distance like a patchwork quilt of multicoloured shades of green. There was nothing to be heard but the sound of birdsong and the children's laughter, and Sunday sighed with contentment.

'It doesn't get much better than this, does it?' she said and Tom nodded in agreement as he spread a blanket on the ground and began to unpack the hamper. There were three bottles of lemonade, freshly made that morning, and a number of hard-boiled eggs, small cakes and biscuits.

'I shan't pack too much, else the children won't want their dinner tonight,' Mrs Rose had told Sunday firmly.

The children tucked into the treats, their appetites sharpened by the romp in the fresh air, and it was then that two people emerged from the trees. Sunday didn't take too much notice of them, since it just looked like a mother and her small daughter, but as they drew closer she realised with a start that it was Maggie with her nanny.

Kitty spotted her friend at the same moment and before anyone could stop her she had scampered across to them to say hello.

'Tom, look – it's Maggie,' Sunday hissed.

Kitty had reached them by then and Sunday could see her chatting animatedly.

'So it is.' Tom rose from the blanket and brushed the crumbs from his trousers before strolling casually across to join them, with Sunday in hot pursuit.

'Good afternoon, Maggie. Good afternoon, er . . .'

'It's Blake. Miss Blake,' the poker-faced woman informed him. 'I am Margaret's nanny.'

'How do you do.' Tom held his hand out and the woman had no choice but to shake it without appearing to be very rude.

'I'm very well, thank you,' she replied stiffly, and Sunday and Tom then turned their attention to Maggie, who was standing quite still at the side of her.

'So how are you, pet?' Tom asked with a warm smile.

'She's very well,' the woman answered for her as Maggie kept her eyes downcast.

'Well, if you'd like to come over there to the blanket, there are some biscuits left and some of Mrs Rose's special lemonade. You always liked that, didn't you?'

'Thank you, but Margaret will be having her evening meal when we get back and she is not permitted to eat between meals.'

Again, the woman spoke for her and Tom began to wonder if Maggie had lost her tongue. Now he could see what Sunday had meant the last time she had bumped into her in town. Maggie had indeed lost quite a lot of weight; in fact, she looked rather thin now although he noted she glanced longingly towards the picnic basket. Maggie had always loved her food.

'It's time we were heading for home now,' the nanny stated and without a word Maggie nodded.

Tom was shocked. At one time, Maggie would have screamed blue murder if asked to do anything she didn't want to do. But now she stood like a little shadow of her former self. Like Sunday, he thought it was almost as if she'd had the spirit knocked out of her. She was immaculately dressed though and spotlessly clean. Too clean, Tom found himself thinking. She looked like a little doll. For the first time, he wondered if he and Sunday had done right, allowing her to go and live with Mr and Mrs Dawes, but he wouldn't admit that to his wife. She was worried enough about the little girl as it was.

'Now say goodbye, Margaret,' Miss Blake instructed sharply.

'Goodbye,' Maggie said woodenly to no one in particular and then the woman took her hand and they strode away without a backward glance.

'I didn't like that lady. She's mean!' Kitty declared, jamming her thumb into her mouth, and although they couldn't say it, both Tom and Sunday were inclined to agree with her. It had taken all Sunday's willpower not to snatch the little girl up into her arms and run for home with her, but of course, common sense had prevailed. She had entrusted Maggie to the Daweses' care and now she had to stand by her decision, although she still missed the little girl dreadfully and fretted about her every single day.

With a heavy sigh, Sunday herded the children together and they set off for home themselves then in a much more subdued mood than the one in which they had started out.

Chapter Eight

December 1908

'I can't understand it,' Sunday confided to Cissie as they sat together in the kitchen enjoying a mid-afternoon cup of tea. 'This is the first year that we've received no money for Kitty's care and she was twelve almost a week ago now. What do you think it might mean? Don't misunderstand me, Tom and I don't want the money for ourselves. In fact, we've been saving it for her for a number of years now, and she has quite a little nest egg stashed away as it happens.'

Cissie shrugged. She too thought it was strange. The money had usually been left as regular as clockwork. 'Perhaps they're just late paying it?' she suggested as she took a gulp of her tea and wiggled her swollen feet out of her shoes. She had been on her feet since early that morning and was glad of a breather.

'That's what Tom said, but I have a feeling there's more to it than that.'

'Oh, here we go,' Cissie teased her. 'Lookin' for problems where there are none again.'

'I am *not*,' Sunday said defensively. 'I just can't help thinking it's a sign of something, that's all.'

Beyond the kitchen door they could hear the sounds of the piano in the day room. A music teacher came in twice a week now to teach those who were interested in learning to play. In the drawing room, Kitty was having her singing lesson from Miss Lark, an aptly named private tutor, and the sound of her sweet voice echoed down the hallway.

There had been many changes in Treetops Manor during the last eight years. Mrs Tabitha Rose, their beloved cook, had retired some time ago to go and live with her daughter in Manchester. Mrs Cotton, a widow from the town, a round merry soul who Tom often teased and who could make a complete meal out of next to nothing, had taken her place. Shy young Em'ly had also left, to be married, and now Ethel, another young lass from the parish of Coton, who had come highly recommended by Mrs Lockett, had taken on her role. She was a plain, dumpy girl, but what she lacked in looks she more than made up for in personality and she was already a great favourite with the children. Edwina and Marianne, two of the first foundlings that Sunday and Tom had ever cared for, had also left, Marianne to be a governess to a solicitor's children in Kenilworth and Edwina to an apprenticeship with a seamstress in the town. Ben, however, had remained and was now a fine strapping lad of nineteen who had proved himself to be invaluable to Tom and George. He would tackle any job big or small that needed doing and so more than earned the wage he was now paid each month.

Cissie and George still lived in Primrose Cottage, where they were very happy. In truth, apart from sleeping there they spent very little time in it, as they all ate with the family at Treetops, but Cissie loved it with a passion. She, like Sunday, had grown up in the Nuneaton Union Workhouse, with all its privations, and she adored the cottage. It was her little palace and it gleamed inside and out and from top to bottom. Sunday and Tom had officially given it and the small plot of land it stood on to Cissie and George, and for the first time in her life Cissie now had somewhere to call her own. The roof was thickly thatched to withstand rain, snow and sunshine, and each room boasted a small leaded window. Lavinia had given them some fine pieces of furniture that had been stored in the attic. Some might have said that the intricately carved pieces made of solid mahogany and rosewood were too grand for a humble cottage, but Cissie loved them and had polished them with beeswax until you could see your face in them. All in all, Primrose Cottage was Cissie's haven. Her oldest son, Jim, had recently become a merchant seaman and had sailed off to see the world, leaving his mother to cry copious tears. Rebecca, her middle child, had joined the staff at Treetops. There never seemed to be enough hands to do everything that needed doing as well as look after the children, so her help was invaluable. Johnny, Cissie and George's youngest, who was now eleven years old, joined in lessons with the other children at the Home.

There had still been no sign of Sunday's longed-for baby despite her praying each month that this might change. Lavinia often told her that if she didn't worry about it so much and relaxed that it just might happen, but after twenty years of marriage, it seemed unlikely. Sunday had, however, found a certain solace in the last two foundlings that they had taken in – Sophie and Michael. They were both now two years old and doted on by the older children and the staff alike. And then she still had Kitty and Ben, of course, so she was happy enough, although from time to time she still thought of Maggie with a sense of loss.

Lavinia seemed to be very happy too, of late, and Sunday wondered whether it might have something to do with a certain Mr Dewhurst, a widower who had recently joined the board of guardians at the workhouse. She had said as much to Tom one day after breakfast when her mother had gone off for a meeting looking very fetching indeed in a new outfit and hat in the very latest style and with a twinkle in her eye.

'You're nothing but a little matchmaker,' he had teased her and Sunday had not bothered to deny it. The way she saw it, her mother deserved to be happy and if the handsome widower was the one who could make her so, then she certainly would raise no objections.

Finishing her last mouthful of toast and home-made blackberry jam, Sunday stood up and looked towards the window. 'It's gone very quiet and grey,' she remarked, staring up at the sky.

'It has that.' Cissie drained her cup and reluctantly got up from the table, forcing her feet back into her shoes. 'George reckons we'll have snow afore much longer so the children will be wanting the sleds out then. Despite meself I allus think there's something quite magical about a white Christmas.'

'You old romantic you,' Sunday chuckled, then leaving Cissie to her chores she went through the green baize door into the corridor just as Miss Lark emerged from the room where she had been giving Kitty her singing lesson.

'Ah, Mrs Branning,' she twittered and Sunday had to make a conscious effort not to laugh. Everything about the tiny little woman reminded her of a little bird, like her name. 'Kitty is doing *extraordinarily* well. I was only saying to Mrs Lockett the other day I think she's ready to join the church choir now – if you have no objections. She really does have the voice of an angel.'

She blinked her faded blue eyes, and as her hand rose to pat her grey hair, which was coiled in a plait around the crown of her head, Sunday was once again reminded of a little bird about to take flight. One of these days she was sure that Miss Lark would sprout wings.

'I have no objections at all,' she replied, managing to keep a straight face. 'I shall speak to Verity about it at the earliest opportunity.'

Just then, Kitty came tearing out of the room only to skid to a halt when she saw Sunday and Miss Lark talking.

'Sorry!' She gave a smile that would have melted ice and Sunday bit her lip. The girl was so pretty that sometimes it frightened her. Whenever they went into town or out and about, people commented on her hair, or her perfect skin, or her eyes. Sunday had loved it when Kitty was little, but now that the girl was growing, she worried about what sort of attention she might attract from men. Still, she told herself, that wouldn't be for a while yet and feeling happier, she then went off to fetch Miss Lark her fee as the teacher prepared to leave. On opening the front door for the little lady, she spied a familiar brown envelope, propped against the pillar where they had found the baby Kitty all those years ago.

Christmas that year was a joyous occasion and so was the party that Sunday and Tom held at Treetops on New Year's Eve. Sunday's only regret was that Mr and Mrs Dawes had declined their invitation, saying that they had already made previous arrangements, which meant that yet again Sunday would not get to spend time with Maggie. She saw very little of her apart from the few occasions when she had gone to the church in Mancetter that the Daweses attended, just to get a glimpse of the girl. On those occasions, Maggie had greeted her stiltedly, without warmth, and now Sunday was resigned to the fact that the girl was gone from her for good. Her loss still affected her in her quieter moments and she still worried about the child, but she had finally accepted that there was nothing to be done about it.

On New Year's Eve, the older children were allowed to stay up late after the younger ones had been tucked safely into bed, and when Kitty came downstairs in the new velvet plum-coloured dress she had had for Christmas, she looked truly stunning. Her long dark hair had been brushed till it shone and hung down her back like a silken cloak, while her skin glowed and her beautiful dark eyes sparkled with excitement.

'Will we be allowed to have a little wine?' she asked cheekily as Sunday and Tom prepared to greet the first of their guests.

'No, you most certainly will not, young lady,' Sunday retorted, then weakening a little when she saw the disappointment on the girl's face, she whispered, 'Well . . . perhaps just a little sip when we see the New Year in, if you stay awake that long.'

'Oh, I shall!' Kitty flashed a smile at her then scampered away in a most unladylike manner to root Ben out to show him her new finery.

In the drawing room, which had been cleared of furniture, a band Tom had hired for the evening was tuning up, and in the day room a buffet fit for a king was laid out on tables that seemed to almost groan beneath their weight of food.

The guests began to arrive, Mr Dewhurst amongst them, and Sunday nudged Tom meaningfully as her mother started to blush like a schoolgirl as the kindly gentleman made a beeline for her, gave a stiff little bow and kissed her hand.

'I don't think I've seen my mother look that happy since Zillah died,' she whispered. Tom heartily agreed with her. 'I think we ought to invite him to dinner once we get tonight over with,' she said.

'Then when dinner is done we can make our excuses and disappear and give them a little time alone,' he whispered back.

Sunday giggled, thinking what an excellent idea that was, but then more guests were arriving and she turned her attention to them. Soon the house was heaving with people and the air was fragrant with the women's perfumes. They flitted about like gaily-coloured butterflies in gowns all the colours of the rainbow, and their jewels flashed in the light from the chandeliers. The men strutted around like penguins in their dicky bows, smart black dinner suits and fancy waistcoats, and within no time at all everyone was clearly having a wonderful time. The band was playing, the dance floor was full of couples and Kitty, who was standing in a corner with Ben, remarked wonderingly, 'Don't the ladies look beautiful, Ben?'

He stared at her strangely for a moment before replying, 'Aye, they do – but none of 'em is as pretty as you, Kitty.'

71

Astounded, she stared back up at him, with her mouth gaping open. She had worshipped Ben for as far back as she could remember – and now here he was paying her a compliment. She blushed and fluttered her eyelashes. Even at her tender age, Kitty was beginning to realise that she could twist the opposite sex around her little finger with just a smile. But then Sunday was bearing down on them with a glass of lemonade in her hand for Kitty. She had decided against allowing the girl to try a sip of wine. At nineteen, Ben was now permitted to drink beer. He didn't much care for the fancy short drinks.

'Are you both having a good time?' she asked, and both heads nodded vigorously. 'Good – well, you keep your eye on her for me, Ben, while I go and find my husband.'

She melted away into the guests and it was then that Kitty asked, 'Shall we have a dance?'

Ben almost choked on his drink. 'What – to this? It's a waltz an' I wouldn't have a clue how to do it.' He looked petrified at the very thought of it.

'We only have to watch what everyone else is doing.' Kitty was used to getting her own way and after putting her drink down on a small table she grabbed Ben's hand and dragged him onto the dance floor.

In actual fact, he soon discovered that it wasn't quite as difficult as it looked. He just had to sort of shuffle about and Kitty went with him. They made an amusing couple, he so tall and the child barely up to his shoulder, and people smiled as they glided past. Kitty's hair was loose about her shoulders and it gleamed in the light. Her new dress set off her dark beauty to perfection.

The pair were breathless and giggling by the time the waltz finished and Kitty knew she would never forget this night for as long as she lived. It was her very first taste of a real grown-ups' party but she prayed it would be the first of many. It was nice to see all the admiring glances she was attracting from men and women alike and it made her feel happy. Even so, by the time eleven o'clock approached she was drooping somewhat, and much to Ben's amusement, she gave a very unladylike yawn.

'Tired are yer, little 'un?' he asked indulgently and Kitty blinked. He was talking to her as if she was a little girl again now.

'Not at all,' she retorted with a toss of her head. 'That just sort of slipped out.' She then flounced away to the kitchen to cool off a little. It had got very stuffy with so many bodies floating about.

Shortly before midnight everyone gathered in the hallway and listened quietly as the old grandfather clock chimed twelve times and welcomed in the New Year of 1909. Then suddenly everyone was kissing each other and Kitty found herself being grabbed by all and sundry. Her cheeks were quite wet by the time everyone had done and she was happy to slink off to bed unnoticed. She was so tired that she merely slung her lovely new dress across the bottom of the bed and slid between the cold cotton sheets in her petticoats. She didn't even bother to brush her hair, she was far too tired – but, eeh . . . it had been a grand night. And she fell asleep with a broad smile on her face!

Chapter Nine

It took the staff of Treetops two whole days to put the house back to rights following the party, and on the third day everyone was tired. The snow had held off so far but it was bitterly cold, the wind was almost gale force, and each night a thick hoar frost coated the grass and the surrounding trees.

Sunday, who felt that she was coming down with a cold, decided that she would have an easy day by the fire as the rest of the staff were entertaining the children. She had only just settled into the fireside chair, however, when there was a tap on the door. She had been just about to start *Daniel Deronda* by George Eliot, a local novelist. It was one of the books Tom had bought her for Christmas and she'd been looking forward to reading it.

'Come in,' she called.

Bessie, the general maid, almost tumbled into the room, clearly very distressed. 'Oh, missus, you'd best come straight away,' she babbled. 'It's the master – he's had a bad fall in the stableyard.'

Flinging the book down, Sunday exploded from the room, holding her skirt high so that it wouldn't hinder her. She fairly flew through the hallways, and as she raced out into the back yard the bitterly cold air seemed to suck the air from her lungs. From there it took seconds to reach the stable block where she found Ben and George hanging over Tom who was a ghastly white colour as he lay on the ground clutching his leg.

'I had a bit of a fall, pet,' he gasped, trying to put a brave front on but at a glance Sunday could see that it was much more than that. Below the knee his trouser leg was soaked with blood and his leg was twisted at an unnatural angle.

'He were exercisin' Major and just bringin' him back to the stables when the 'oss slipped on the frosty cobbles an' unseated him,' George explained. 'Luckily I reckon Major has only sprained a ligament but we'll have to get the vet out to look at him.'

At that moment, much as she loved the horses, Sunday's concerns were all for Tom who was clearly in agony, and she had to force herself to stay outwardly calm although she felt sick with fear.

'Ben, help us get Tom into the house then take the car into town and fetch the doctor as soon as you can.' She was trying not to panic but she couldn't prevent her hands from trembling. 'You could ask the vet to call and look at Major at the same time,' she ended.

George turned and hared off into the stable block to fetch a door they could lie Tom on as Sunday dropped to her knees at the side of him regardless of the mess it would make of her smart silk skirt.

'I don't know, I can't leave you alone for a minute,' she chided him but her voice was heavy with tears. He was clearly in tremendous pain though he was valiantly trying to hide it from her.

Once George returned with the door he and Ben lifted the injured man as carefully as they could onto it but Tom couldn't help but scream with pain. Between them they carried him back through the house and into the drawing room, with Sunday clinging to his hand, then Ben raced off intent on fetching the doctor as quickly as he could.

Alerted by all the noise, Lavinia had come downstairs, and seeing that Sunday was almost beside herself with fear she instantly took control of the situation.

'We're going to need scissors to cut his trouser leg and hot water and clean cloths, plenty of them,' she said. 'Off you go now, chop-chop! Panicking isn't going to help.'

Tom's eyes were rolling back in his head by then and he seemed to be barely aware that they were even there as Sunday rushed off to do as she was told.

'Right,' Lavinia told her when she returned. 'I'm going to cut this trouser leg straight up now. Hold his hand. It's going to hurt, I'm afraid.'

As gently as she could she began to cut through the material but she had hardly reached his knee when the full extent of his injuries became evident and Sunday almost swooned with shock. His leg from the knee down was already swollen to twice its size and a bone stuck grotesquely through the skin as blood pumped from the wound.

'Pass me a cloth quickly – we have to stem this flow of blood,' Lavinia ordered. Once Sunday had done as she was told, Lavinia then tore the cloth into long strips and tied it above the knee as tightly as she could in a tourniquet, to try and stem the bleeding. Sweat stood out on her forehead. Tom then screamed once more before lapsing into merciful unconsciousness. Lavinia then propped the injured leg on a small pile of cloths, to keep it elevated.

'Right – we'll try and clean him up a little now,' she said, fully in control of the situation. It was just as well, for Sunday was a gibbering wreck. The women made him as comfortable as they possibly could, then after ensuring that he was well covered and the drawing-room fire was blazing fiercely, all they could do was wait for Ben to return.

At last, after almost an hour, Ben appeared with Dr Cushion close on his heels. Tom was still unconscious and after seeing the extent of his injury the doctor declared it was just as well.

'We shall need to get him to hospital,' he told them. 'They are going to have to put the bone back in place and splint it, and it will require a number of stitches. Hopefully he will stay asleep until it's done, otherwise he's going to be in agony, poor chap.'

'But he will be all right, won't he?' Sunday asked, her voice quavering.

'It all depends, my dear Mrs Branning,' the man said. 'His injuries are not life-threatening but it could be that he'll lose his leg. Let's wait and see what the surgeon has to say about it, shall we?'

At that moment, the door to the drawing room inched open and Kitty's anxious little face appeared. Her eyes went straight to Tom and the doctor hastily pulled the blanket across his injured leg.

'Is Tom going to be all right?' she asked, much as Sunday had done only seconds before.

'Of course he is, pet.' Sunday hurried over to her and forced a watery smile. 'We just have to get him to hospital so the doctors there can make him better, so you run along to Cissie, eh?'

Seeing the blood that had seeped through the blanket, Kitty began to cry. She could still clearly remember how upset they had all been when Zillah had died, and now she was terrified that Tom was going to die too.

'But *I* want to go to the hospital with him,' she wailed, afraid to let him out of her sight. Tom was the nearest thing to a father that she had ever known.

Ben and George had already lifted the door on which Tom was still lying and as they strode out to the car with it, it was all Sunday could do to persuade Kitty to let them do what had to be done.

'Come on now, sweetheart,' she encouraged chokily as Kitty clung to her blood-stained skirts. 'You wouldn't want Tom to go to the hospital without me, would you? I need you to stay here and be brave for me and I'll tell you what's happening when I get back, I promise.'

Thankfully, Cissie appeared then and after gentle coaxing led the distraught child away to the kitchen. One of Mrs Cotton's fresh-baked scones always made everything seem better.

Meanwhile, oblivious to the state she was in, Sunday lifted her skirts, snatched up a coat and chased after Ben and George.

It was late that evening when she returned home to Treetops Manor looking pale and drained. Cissie and the staff were waiting for her.

'How is he?' they all chorused as she stepped through the door.

'Well, his leg has been set and he's been stitched up,' she was able to inform them. 'Now we just have to pray that he doesn't get an infection. The surgeon said it was one of the worst breaks he had ever seen.'

'Right, we'd best get something hot inside you,' Mrs Cotton said bossily, taking matters into her own hands. 'I've got a nice pan of beef stew and dumplings keeping warm for you. And I don't want no excuses, mind. If you don't eat we'll end up with two invalids on our hands.'

Knowing it would be pointless to argue, Sunday nodded before asking Cissie, 'How is Kitty? She was very upset when we left.'

Cissie, who was keen to get back to Primrose Cottage now that she knew there was no more she could do, shrugged. 'Frightened and tearful, but she'll be fine. Children are a lot more resilient than you think. Soon as she knows he's on the mend you can take her to visit him and she'll be right as rain. But now if there's nothing you need, I'd best be off. George took Johnny over to the cottage some time ago. They'll think I've got lost.' She pecked Sunday on the cheek then and hurried away as Sunday reluctantly went to face her beef stew. Eating was the last thing on her mind.

For the rest of that week, Kitty stayed constantly at Sunday's side apart from when Sunday went to visit Tom at the hospital. It was as if she was afraid to let her only remaining 'parent' out of her sight. Thankfully, the swelling on Tom's leg had gone down and he appeared to be on the mend although he was still in a great deal of pain and fretting about how Sunday would manage without him at Treetops.

'Nobody is indispensable,' she reminded him as she straightened the covers on his bed, and he almost growled with frustration. Tom had never been one to laze about and it was going sorely against the grain. And then on the following day when Sunday entered the ward she was concerned to see that the curtains were drawn about his bed. The ward sister instantly drew her to one side.

'I'm afraid Mr Branning has developed an infection,' she told Sunday. 'The doctor is in with him now.'

Sunday paled. 'Will they be able to cure it?' she asked in a wobbly voice.

The woman shook her head, setting her starched white cap swaying on her iron-grey hair. 'Of course we shall do everything within our power, but now I think you should prepare yourself. If we can't beat the infection it looks more than likely that the surgeon will have to amputate his leg below the knee.'

'NO!' Sunday's objection echoed down the ward, alarming the other patients. Tom had always been such an active man; she knew how much he would hate being a cripple. 'You must ensure that doesn't happen,' she said with a new-found strength. 'My husband is only young, and to lose his leg would break him, I know it. Now, I would like to go and see him, if you please – and the doctor!'

The sister, who was not used to having her authority flouted, stared open-mouthed as with her back as stiff as a broom handle, Sunday strode off down the ward.

'Now, doctor,' she said, startling the man as she barged through the curtains. 'I want your assurance that my husband will receive the very best drugs that are available to fight this infection. If you

79

cannot provide them then tell me who can and I will make sure he gets them.'

The doctor peered at her over the top of the tiny gold spectacles that were perched on the end of his nose and smiled grudgingly before barking at a small fair-haired nurse: 'Go and get me a dish with disinfectant in, nurse. *Strong* disinfectant! I shall bathe this wound myself throughout the day. And you, young man' – he smiled grimly at Tom – 'had better grit your teeth because this is going to hurt like hell. Better than losing your leg though, eh? I shall have this bathed every hour on the hour. There's nothing so fine as a drop of fine disinfectant, but it'll sting.'

Sunday took her place at the side of her husband and while the doctor cleaned the wound, Tom gripped her hand and screwed his eyes tight shut.

'Visiting time is over now, Mrs Branning,' the frosty-faced ward sister informed her sometime later, but Tom was running a very high temperature and Sunday had no intention of leaving him.

'I am well aware of that, sister,' she answered. 'But I'm staying with my husband until his temperature comes down a little.'

The ward sister glanced at the doctor, who had just returned to cleanse Tom's wound again, and was incensed to see a small grin playing at the corners of his mouth.

'I'm sure you won't mind Mrs Branning staying a little longer, will you, sister?' he said coaxingly and she positively bristled although she didn't argue with him.

'I suppose not, just so long as you keep the curtains pulled around the bed,' she said tightly. 'It really wouldn't do to let the rest of the visitors see that we are setting a precedent with Mrs Branning. Rules are made for a reason and the whole of the ward would be in chaos in no time and Matron would be breathing down my neck.'

From Sunday's determined stance it was more than clear, however, that in order to get her to leave they would have to forcibly evict

80

her. The sister went off in a huff then and Sunday turned her attention back to Tom.

It was late that evening before she got home again to find Kitty waiting for her in the hallway in her nightgown.

'She wouldn't go to bed until you got back,' Cissie whispered as Sunday put her arm about the girl's shoulders and gave her a gentle hug.

'We've had a little setback,' she told them truthfully. 'Tom has developed an infection but the doctors have it in hand and I'm sure he'll be fine.' Her arm actually ached from all the hours she had spent bathing his forehead with cold water, but already her efforts appeared to be paying off, for he had not been quite so hot when she had finally left him, and a pleasant young nurse who had come on night duty had promised that she would continue her efforts throughout the night.

It was almost a week later when Sunday arrived at the hospital one day to find the doctor waiting for her with wonderful news.

'Your husband is mending nicely now, although I have to warn you, he may well always have a limp and that leg will never be as strong as it was. Despite that, he is fit enough to come home tomorrow.'

Sunday could hardly wait to share her good news with everyone at Treetops, and again the house took on a party atmosphere as they prepared for his return. The crisis was over and soon Tom would be back where he belonged. Kitty flew into her arms when she heard the good news and Sunday was shocked to see how tall she was growing. *You'll be a young lady soon*, she found herself thinking and wondered where all the years had gone.

Chapter Ten

March 1914

It was a bright sunny day early in March when Kitty entered the drawing room following her singing lessons to tell Sunday, 'There's a lady at the door asking to see Tom.'

'Oh? Did she say who she was?' Sunday asked curiously, looking up from the housekeeping ledgers that she checked each month for Mrs Brewer. She had never come across a single discrepancy but the woman still insisted she should check them.

Kitty shook her head. 'No, but Tom is out in the manège. I saw him with the new pony on a training lead. Shall I ask him to come in?'

Although Tom's leg had healed, just as the doctor had predicted, he now had quite a severe limp and was no longer able to tackle some of the jobs he had used to do. Nowadays much to his frustration he was having to occupy himself with lighter duties, although he was building up a good reputation for being a talented horse-breeder. Riding the horses and driving his beloved car were a couple of things he could still do without putting too much pressure on his weak leg.

Kitty was now seventeen years old and right up until her sixteenth birthday the money for her keep had been left in the porch, more or less regularly every December, although Sunday had never once managed to get a glimpse of the person who left it there. Kitty had turned into a stunning young woman. She was tall and slim and carried herself with a grace that made Sunday sigh with envy. Like Ben, who was now George's right-hand man, Kitty too had asked to stay on at Treetops and Sunday couldn't envisage a life without her although she knew that one day some handsome young blade would come along and sweep her off her feet.

'If you would please, pet,' Sunday answered now. 'And on your way through, would you ask the visitor to come in here?'

'Of course.'

Once Kitty had left the room, Sunday leaned back in her chair and absently gazed out of the window. She saw a car rattling down the drive and smiled. It was Mr Dewhurst who had recently become betrothed to her mother – and not before time, the way Sunday saw it. They had been 'walking out together', as Lavinia termed it, for a few years now and Sunday hoped they wouldn't leave it too much longer before they finally became man and wife.

Her thoughts were interrupted when there was a tap at the door and the mistress of the workhouse popped her head around it.

'Ah, Mrs Conway, how lovely to see you, do come in,' Sunday encouraged, then glimpsing Ethel in the hallway over the woman's shoulder she ordered two mugs of hot chocolate and ushered the visitor to the chair by the fire. These early March mornings could still be nippy and Tom's leg pained him when he got cold, so she ensured the fires were always lit.

'How can I help you?' she asked then. Mrs Conway and her mother were friends and knew each other well, but Sunday had never known the woman to visit before although she was most welcome.

'Actually, I came because of this, dear.' The woman began to delve into a voluminous bag and after a few moments she extracted a rather crumpled envelope. 'This came to the workhouse two days ago; it's addressed to your husband. I'm sorry I couldn't get it to you before.'

'To Tom?' Sunday took the envelope and turned it over. It was indeed addressed to him, care of the Nuneaton Union Workhouse although the postmark was smudged and quite indistinguishable. But who would be writing to him there? It was many years since he had left. Nevertheless, she thanked the woman for delivering the letter and they went on to talk about the new bathrooms that were being installed at the workhouse. It was all very exciting and as Sunday listened to Mrs Conway's enthusiasm she couldn't help wishing that this kindly soul had been the mistress there when she and Tom had been in residence instead of the evil Miss Frost.

Ethel wheeled a trolley in with a selection of Cook's fresh baked biscuits and a large pot of hot chocolate, and the two women continued to chat amiably until Mrs Conway reluctantly declared, 'Well, I really should be going, dear.'

'Oh please, let Ben give you a lift back,' Sunday said. 'He's going into town anyway and it's hardly out of his way.'

'In that case thank you kindly, dear.' Mrs Conway chuckled. 'I must admit the walk was a little farther than I'd thought and I'm not getting any younger. I dare say I shall pay for all this exercise tomorrow.'

They said their goodbyes, and after propping Tom's letter on the mantelshelf, Sunday went back to what she had been doing before her guest arrived. It was after lunch when she and Tom were sitting enjoying a few moments of peace and quiet before she remembered it again, and jumping up from her seat she carried it across to him.

'A letter for me, delivered to the workhouse?' He was bemused as he stared at the envelope. 'I wonder who it could be from.'

'Well, why don't you open it and find out?'

He slit the envelope and extracted a sheet of paper and as he began to read, Sunday heard him gasp.

'What is it?' she asked, concerned. 'Is it bad news?'

'I . . . I don't know what to make of it,' he muttered, then holding it out to her he urged, 'Read it for yourself.'

Sunday took the paper from his shaking fingers and bent her head to the neat writing on the page.

Dear Tom,

I fear this may come as something of a shock to you after all these years, but as my days on this earth are now numbered I felt I had to share with you the terrible secret I have been forced to keep all this time – and I hope you will find it in your heart to forgive me.

It seems so long ago since you worked for my father and I have never forgotten the times you and I spent together, although I always knew deep down that your heart belonged to another. My own heart was broken when you left, although I lay no blame at your door. What we shared was beautiful but you never told me that it would be for always and I accepted it for what it was. However, shortly after you had gone I realised that I was carrying your child.

I was in a predicament. My father was, as you know, a kind but stern man and knowing that he would be deeply ashamed if he found out, I ran away and travelled to your home town. It took some time to find out where you were living – in a little house in Shepperton Street – but I also discovered that you were now reunited with the girl you loved and I didn't wish to cause you pain. And so I took a job and worked right up until our child's birth and then, God forgive me, I left the baby on the steps of the workhouse – the very same one that you had told me about. The child was a little boy. I called him Benjamin and pinned his name to his shawl.

I stayed in the town for some while after that, by which time you had married. And then I discovered that you and your wife had taken the child to live in the foundling home that you had opened, and I thanked God that at least my darling boy would know one of his parents. I then returned home and told my father that I had run away to find you. He accepted this but I never married and I often think of you and our son and pray that you are both healthy and happy.

By the time you read this I shall be gone to meet my maker. Whether or not you decide to acknowledge the boy, or the man as he will be now, as your own, will be up to you and your wife – but at least I have salved my conscience by telling you the truth and hope that you will not think badly of me.

Affectionately yours,
Cecile Randle

Sunday stared up at Tom with her emotions in a whirl. This couldn't be true, surely? And yet as she began to work out the dates in her mind, everything fitted together like the pieces of a jigsaw. The child must have been conceived when Tom had run away from Mrs Spooner's following his sister Daisy's death.

'So Ben is your *son*?'

Tom looked away from the confusion and the pain in his wife's eyes. 'It would appear so, but I swear to you I never had an inkling.'

'And you remember this Cecile?'

He nodded. 'Yes. I briefly worked for her father and we . . . well, we sort of came together a few times. I was in a very dark place in my mind, as you know, and I was hurting and not thinking straight. But I never dreamed that I had left the poor girl carrying a child.'

They both lapsed into silence for a while as they tried to digest what they had just discovered until Kitty poked her head around the door to ask, 'Are you ready to start exercising the horses now, Tom?' She stopped abruptly as she saw the looks on their faces.

'Is anything wrong?' she asked, and pulling himself together with an effort, Tom managed a weak smile.

'No, pet, everything is fine. You go on out and start. I'll be with you in a moment or two.' Kitty, with Tom's careful training, was now an accomplished horsewoman.

Tom heaved himself out of the chair. 'Can we, err . . . speak about this later on when all the young 'uns are in bed? We can decide what we're going to do about it then.' He stared anxiously at his wife's pale face.

'Yes, of course.' But she avoided his eyes and for the first time in their marriage Tom felt as if a chasm had opened up between them. Half of him, now that he was getting used to the information, was delighted to know that Ben was his son. After all, he was a fine upright chap, the sort any father would be proud of. But the other half of him was worried about how this earth-shaking news would affect Sunday. She was bound to feel hurt to know that he'd had a previous relationship with another girl, especially as that girl had given birth to his child when she herself had never been able to get in the family way. Would she feel jealous and resentful of Ben? he wondered. It was all very confusing and worrying.

With a sigh, he left the room, leaving Sunday to her own jumbled thoughts. Tears pricked sharp as needles at the back of her eyes. She supposed she should be pleased that now they had some legal claim to Ben, for hadn't they loved and cared for him since he was a tiny baby? And yet she couldn't get the picture of Tom with another woman out of her mind. And what were they supposed to do now? Should they tell Ben that, unknown to all of them, his natural father had brought him up? How would *he* react to the news? Would he be upset – or ecstatic? A headache began to throb behind her eyes.

The atmosphere between Sunday and Tom was strained that evening and Kitty, who was very astute, immediately picked up on it.

'Are you two all right?' she asked innocently as they all sat over steaming bowls of Cook's leek and potato soup and fresh baked bread.

'Oh yes, pet, I just have a bit of a headache, that's all. In fact, I'm not really hungry so if you'll excuse me I shall go and lie down for a while.' With that Sunday rose from the table and left the room without even a glance in her husband's direction.

Tom watched her go with a worried expression on his face. He'd been in an agony of indecision all afternoon as to what he should do, and found that he could barely bring himself to look at Ben. Through no fault of his own the poor lad had grown up knowing neither of his natural parents, and when he discovered the truth – if Tom decided to tell him, that was – how was he going to react? He could understand Sunday feeling shaken or jealous even – but it wasn't as if they had been together when he'd had his brief affair with Cecile, was it? Once she'd got used to the idea she'd be pleased for him, surely? Tom himself was already beginning to feel a tingle of excitement. He had a son, his very own son – and that was something to celebrate, wasn't it, however the lad had come about?

'Are you going to swish that soup around your dish all night, Tom?' Ben asked, interrupting his thoughts. 'You haven't touched a drop and it must be stone cold now. Are you not feeling well either?'

'What? . . . Oh, I'm fine, thanks. But I think I'll just pop upstairs and see how Sunday is, if you'll excuse me?'

As the door closed behind him Ben and Kitty exchanged glances and shrugged before going on with their meal.

Sunday was standing at the window staring out into the darkening night when Tom entered their bedroom. The grounds of Treetops were a haven for the local wildlife and she often stood there watching the muntjacs, foxes and rabbits on the lawns and the squirrels in the trees. But tonight, he could tell that she wasn't really seeing anything. Her mind was no doubt full of the latest developments and how they should handle the situation.

'I've been thinking,' she mused as she heard Tom come to stand behind her. 'I think you should tell Ben about the letter and let him know who he is.'

'Really? You wouldn't mind?' Tom couldn't stop the joy from showing on his face as she turned to face him, appearing calm although inside she was in turmoil.

'The girl must have held you in very high regard and cared for you deeply to do what she did. She could have gone to you and told you of her condition so that you would do the right thing and marry her, but she didn't. Ben is your son . . . probably the only one you will ever have, so he should be acknowledged as such.' The words were threatening to choke her but she forced herself to go on. 'He deserves to know about his true parentage.'

Then, when Tom went to embrace her, she sidestepped him, lifted the fluffy towels Bessie had laid ready on the end of the bed and went and locked herself away in the bathroom, leaving Tom to chew on his lip as he watched her go. Once there, her chin drooped to her chest and she sobbed, broken-heartedly.

Chapter Eleven

'What do you think is wrong with Sunday and Tom?' Kitty asked Ben two days later as he helped her to saddle her horse in the stable. 'I don't know if you've noticed but they're still being very cool towards one another. It isn't like them, is it?'

'Yes, I have noticed and no, it isn't like them.' Ben tightened the straps on the saddle. 'Perhaps they've had a tiff?'

'Sunday and Tom?' Kitty snorted. 'I shouldn't think so. I've never known them to argue before. Still, I suppose there's a first time for everything. If that's the case, it's a matter of least said soonest mended.'

Ben cupped his hands then and when Kitty placed her foot onto them he hoisted her up into the saddle, thinking how beautiful she looked in her dark green riding habit. But then Kitty looked beautiful in anything. She had turned into a remarkably pretty young woman and he and Tom regularly had to fight off would-be suitors, much to Kitty's amusement. He felt colour stain his cheeks and quickly lowered his head as she edged her mount out into the stableyard. When had his feelings for her developed? he wondered. They just seemed to have crept up on him all of a sudden and now, instead of seeing her as a nuisance little sister, he found himself looking at her through the eyes of a would-be lover. As she rode out into the bright early morning, the sun caught her hair and it gleamed like spun copper, making his heart do funny little cartwheels.

But then she gently dug her heels into the horse's flank and was off, galloping away down the drive with the wind in her hair, as free as a bird.

'Ben.'

He turned to see Tom crossing the yard towards him.

'Could I have a word . . . in private?'

Ben tensed. Tom looked very solemn and he wondered if he had done something wrong.

'Perhaps we could go into the library. We won't be disturbed in there,' Tom said, and with a nod, Ben followed him back to the house. As they entered the hall they almost bumped into Sunday who had her arms full of clean bedlinen that she was taking upstairs. She gave Ben a polite smile, but hurried on without even glancing at Tom. The young man felt apprehensive. He sensed that Tom was about to tell him something he wouldn't like to hear.

With the library door firmly closed, Tom joined his arms behind his back and began to pace to and fro as Ben looked on bewildered. And then Tom suddenly stopped and delved in his pocket to withdraw a rather wrinkled envelope.

'This came for me very recently,' he told Ben. 'I think you should read it.'

Ben had no idea why Tom should wish him to see his private mail, but he obediently took it and began to read the letter in front of him.

'Phew!' he muttered when he was done. 'So you had a child that you never even knew about by another girl. It must have come as a real shock! No wonder Sunday's been looking a bit preoccupied. And what a coincidence that the child's name was Ben, eh?' And then as comprehension suddenly dawned he gripped the back of the nearest chair until his knuckles bled white.

'The child . . . Ben – it was *me*, wasn't it?'

Tom nodded as the two stared at each other, neither of them quite knowing what to say or do. It was Tom who finally broke the silence when he muttered thickly, 'I can't think of anyone I would rather call my son. I'm right proud of you and right sorry that I didn't know about any of this before. Can you forgive me?'

Ben reeled for a moment at the enormity of what Tom was telling him. He had a father! *A father!* It was hard to take in, but eventually he answered chokily, 'There's nothing to forgive. How could you be blamed for something you didn't even know about? But . . . it's nice to know now who my parents are – or in my mother's case, were, God rest her soul. It were clearly very hard from what she says in this letter for her to leave me at the workhouse.'

'Her father would never have allowed her to keep a child who was born the wrong side o' the blanket,' Tom tried to explain. 'He was a good man but very God-fearing, and he would have died of shame if his only daughter had presented him with an illegitimate grandchild. But if only she had told me I would have stood by her and given you my name.'

'And then you wouldn't have married Sunday and you would never have been truly happy,' Ben pointed out. 'My mother understood that, and so she did what she thought was best. I wish I could have met her,' he said wistfully. 'She sounds as if she was a nice person.'

'She was a lovely person,' Tom agreed. 'And I'm ashamed now to think I left her in such a predicament. I was so fond of her, but I could never love her, you see? Not the way Cecile deserved to be loved. It was always Sunday, but she was there and I was mourning Daisy, my sister who had died . . . and somehow we . . . Well, it just sort of happened. I suppose we were both looking for comfort.'

'There's no point in whipping yourself,' Ben said, and Tom admired the maturity of his reaction. 'You ended up bringing me up, after all, didn't you? I've always looked on you as a father, so things needn't change that much. But how does Sunday feel about all this? I mean, she makes no secret of the fact that she's always

92

wanted children of her own. It must be hard for her to know that you already have a son.'

'I think she's finding it strange,' Tom admitted. 'But she doesn't blame you. She's always loved you, since the day we fetched you from the workhouse. I think knowing that I have fathered a child is just making her feel rather inadequate but she'll come to terms with it. As a matter of fact, it was Sunday herself who encouraged me to tell you about all this. So, all I can say now is . . . Welcome to the family, son. I'm going to make it all up to you, you just see if I don't.'

He took Ben's hand then and shook it as the two men stared at each other with happy tears in their eyes. And all the time Tom was thinking, *Why didn't I see the resemblance before?* Ben had dark hair just like his, his eyes were the same colour as his, and they were of a similar height. Eeh, there was no doubt about it, life had some funny cards up her sleeve, so she did!

That evening when Sunday climbed into bed beside him she asked, 'How did Ben take the news?' They'd had little time to talk as two of the younger children were recovering from chickenpox so she had spent the majority of the day looking after them up in the nursery.

'As you'd expect,' Tom responded, turning over to her and leaning up on one elbow. 'He was shocked, as we were – but pleased, I think. At least the lad knows where he came from now.'

'Good.' Sunday tossed her long plait across her shoulder and turned her back on Tom as she struggled to keep a check on her emotions. Tears were never far away at present. 'Then I'm very pleased for you both. You have a legitimate heir now when anything happens to us.'

Tom frowned as she dimmed the oil lamp and lay as far away

from him as was possible, then there was only silence save for the sound of an owl in the branches of the cedar tree outside the bedroom window.

'Things are looking bad abroad,' Tom commented the following week as he sat reading the newspaper after breakfast. 'There's a lot of unrest. I wouldn't be surprised if we didn't end up at war with Germany.' He always read the newspapers religiously from cover to cover each day and was very well informed about world events.

'Why should trouble abroad affect us?' Sunday asked as she poured herself another cup of tea.

'War has a way o' suckin' different countries in, but I hope I'm wrong,' Tom commented distractedly, but then brightening his tone he asked, 'An' what have you got planned for today, pet?'

Sunday was still a little reticent with him although she had officially welcomed Ben into the family and told him that she was proud to be his stepmother. But Tom was missing the free and easy, all-enveloping warmth they had shared before the revelation about Ben. *Still, give her time to get used to things*, he told himself, *they're bound to come right in the end.*

'I'm taking all the children into town to have their photographs taken,' Sunday informed him. 'I thought it would be nice to have one of all of them together on the mantelshelf and I'm told the new photographic studio in town uses all the latest equipment.'

'That's if you can get the little ones to sit still for long enough,' he quipped. Normally, Sunday would have giggled but today she just shrugged.

'I can only do my best,' she answered primly, and pulling her gloves on she swept from the room leaving Tom to sigh and wonder how much longer this cold shoulder treatment was going to go on for.

The day was actually a huge success although the handsome young photographer almost drooled over Kitty when he saw her and could hardly take his eyes off her – a fact which Kitty quickly latched on to.

'Have you ever thought of being a photographic model?' he asked as Kitty flirted and batted her long dark eyelashes at him.

'No, she has *not* thought of being a model and no, she is definitely *not* interested!' Sunday interrupted him sternly and Kitty giggled as she then ushered all the children outside and towards the ice-cream parlour. They had all been promised a treat if they behaved, and they had . . . well, most of them had.

'You know, I wouldn't mind being a model,' Kitty mused when they were all seated in the parlour with huge ice-cream sundaes in front of them.

Sunday almost choked as she glared at the girl. 'Don't be ridiculous! It's not respectable,' she snapped. 'You could be taken advantage of.' And then as a squabble broke out amongst two of the younger children about whose sundae was the biggest, she turned her attention to them and the subject was dropped.

It was late afternoon by the time they trooped down the drive leading to Treetops and the children were somewhat subdued. It had been a long walk from the town and they were tired.

At the door, Cissie informed her that her mother had gone out for the evening with Mr Dewhurst and that there was a visitor waiting in the drawing room for her with Tom.

'Who is it?' Sunday asked as she took the hat pin out of her hat and removed it, along with her coat, which was whisked away by Ethel.

'No idea, pet.' Cissie shrugged, then she ushered the children off to wash their hands before going in for their supper.

Sunday had been looking forward to a nice quiet evening with her feet up and the chance to start on *The Return of Sherlock Holmes*. Her feet were throbbing as it happened and she could hardly wait to get her shoes off, but she supposed she should go and see who the visitor was, first. As far as she knew, they hadn't been expecting anyone. As she headed for the drawing room, the appetising smell of Mrs Cotton's beef stew and dumplings wafted up to her and her stomach grumbled. Apart from the ice cream in town she'd had little to eat today and she'd just realised how hungry she was. Still, first things first, she thought and plastering a polite smile on her face she entered the drawing room.

Her eyes were instantly drawn to a neat and tidy-looking little woman sitting in one of the fireside chairs. Her clothes were very respectable but they put Sunday in mind of something a governess or a nanny might wear. She certainly didn't look to be dressed like a lady and her grey hair, coiled simply at the nape of her neck, was not at all styled as a lady's might be.

'Ah, Sunday, here you are.'

At a glance Sunday saw that Tom was looking concerned and the smile froze on her face as the woman rose to greet her.

'Good afternoon, Mrs Branning. I'm Miss Fox – Phyllis Fox.' The woman had a London accent – Sunday recognised the sound of it from her holiday there, aged fifteen, and also from the weekend she and Tom had spent in the city when London had hosted the Summer Olympics in 1908. They'd had a wonderful time. But what could this woman want with them?

'How do you do, Miss Fox,' Sunday answered, somewhat bemused. And then as she noted the way Tom was fidgeting a cold finger ran up and down her spine.

'Miss Fox has come because . . .' Tom seemed reluctant to go on '. . . because of Kitty.'

'What – our Kitty?' Sunday's eyebrows disappeared into her hairline. 'But what could Kitty possibly have to do with you?' she asked.

'I'm the one who has brought the money for her keep each year,' the kind-faced woman told her. 'And of course you'll have noticed

96

that there wasn't an envelope this Christmas past, and you must have wondered why. The long and the short of it is, her mother is now in a position to have her back.'

Giddy from the shock, Sunday swayed, and Tom rushed forward to catch her and help her into the nearest chair. Inside, her heart was crying, *No, no, I can't lose Kitty!* Little by little she felt as if her life was falling apart. First she had lost Maggie, then her special loving relationship with Tom, and now it looked as if Kitty was to be taken from her too. Just the thought of it was almost more than she could bear.

Chapter Twelve

'Would you care to explain yourself?' After managing to pull herself together with an incredible effort, Sunday eyed the woman coldly. 'You can't just expect to turn up here out of the blue saying Kitty's mother suddenly wants her back after all this time. You could be anyone, for all we know!'

Miss Fox began to delve into her handbag and after a moment she produced a list of all the dates when she had left the money for Kitty's keep, along with the correct sums.

'I've also got her birth certificate here, although her mother called her Katherine. You'll see it's all legal like, if you care to look, Mrs Branning.'

Sunday took it from her with shaking fingers and was forced to admit it did look official. It read: *Father Unknown*; and the mother was: *Ruby Smith, Professional Singer*. Before she could look for an address, Miss Fox took it from her and replaced it in her bag, which she closed with a snap.

'But our Kitty is a young woman now and she's lived here all her life,' Sunday said with a note of desperation in her voice. 'I doubt very much indeed if she will wish to leave Treetops. This is her home.'

'Perhaps she herself should be allowed to make that decision, my dear,' the woman replied and it was then that Tom stepped in. He could see how upset Sunday was becoming, just as he had feared. She adored Kitty and always had.

'I'll go and fetch her. You sit still, pet.' And then he was gone, his limp pronounced as it always was when he became agitated. He found Kitty down in the kitchen having a game of cards at the table with Ben.

'Kitty, love,' he began hesitantly, 'you have a visitor in the drawing room. Would you like to come and meet her?'

Kitty looked intrigued. 'A visitor? For *me*?' She grinned at Ben, laid her cards down, then skipped ahead of Tom up the stairs towards the drawing room. She rarely got visitors and wondered who it could be.

When they entered the room the little woman's hand flew to her mouth and she gasped, 'Lordie, you look so like your mother, my dear! You gave me a rare old turn when you came in then.'

'M . . . my *mother*?' Kitty's heart began to pound. All her life she had yearned to know who her mother was, and she had always dreamed that one day, she would come and fetch her. Kitty knew she was pretty, and so she had always assumed that her mother would be too – and now here was this older woman confirming it.

'What's going on?' she asked Sunday then, and slowly Sunday began to explain.

'This is Miss Fox. She works for your mother and says that your mother is now in a position where she can offer you a home with her. Of course, you don't *have* to go,' Sunday said as Kitty stared incredulously. 'You're quite old enough to make your own mind up. I just wonder why your mother wants you back all of a sudden and after all this time. Why, Miss Fox hasn't even told us where she lives!'

'Don't you worry about that, my dear,' Miss Fox stated, smiling at Kitty. 'The thing is, your mother wasn't in a position to keep you when you were born because she wasn't wed. Your father was wed all right – but to someone else, see? He was a well-known politician in London. Your mother wanted to keep you, of course she did, but it was decided it would be best for all concerned – yourself included – if you were to be fostered out. It would have caused too much of a scandal if she'd kept you. Now at that time we had a young maid working for us who came from round these parts, and it was she who told us about the Treetops Children's Home. So the day after you were born I brought you all the way here on the train, all bundled up you were in the December cold. It did my poor old back not a bit of good, I don't mind telling you. So I left you on the step outside, then I banged on the door good and hard, then I watched from behind that big tree on the lawn till you came out, Mrs Branning, along of a maid. So I knew you were safe and in good hands, Katherine. I've brought the money each year since then, but last year your father sadly passed away and so Ruby realised that there was nothing to stop her having you with her now.'

Kitty's eyes were on stalks. 'Is that my mother's name – Ruby? And where does she live?'

'Yes, Ruby Smith is her name and she has a fine house in Chelsea which your father bought for her,' the woman informed her solemnly. 'Your mother is a well-known singer in the music halls. She's sung with the best during her time on stage and that's the truth. Her stage name is Ruby Darling.'

'Oh!' To Sunday's horror, Kitty appeared excited. 'And you say I look like her?'

The woman nodded. 'The spit out of her mouth and that's the truth, though she's a bit older now, of course, and not in the best of health. She'd like you to come back with me on the train and live with her so that you can both get to know each other before it's too late. But not tonight, of course. I've got myself a room in a lodging house in town and I'll be going back to London tomorrow afternoon if you've a mind to come with me.'

'I think Kitty needs some more time to make up her mind. This isn't a decision to be made at the drop of a hat,' Sunday butted in

100

desperately, but already she saw the stars in the girl's eyes and knew that she was losing her.

Feeling torn in two, Kitty looked from Sunday to Miss Fox, then taking a deep breath she said shakily, 'Sunday, forgive me but this is a chance to meet my *real* mother, so I feel I must take it. You do understand, don't you? It's what I've always dreamed of, and the chance might never come again.'

Sunday felt as if someone had punched her in the stomach as she stared at the girl from stricken eyes. She had loved her as her own since the moment she had clapped eyes on her as a tiny baby – and yet she did understand, for during the years that she and her own birth mother had been parted, hadn't she too dreamed of being reunited with her, one glorious day? Even so, she wasn't prepared to let the girl go without a fight.

'How do we know you're who you say you are?' she challenged Miss Fox. 'You haven't even given us a proper address.'

The woman said kindly, feeling her pain, 'But I've already shown you documents to prove that I am who I say I am, Mrs Branning. Kitty is returning home at last. The address is hers to give you. I'm sure she'll forward it to you just as soon as she's settled in.'

Tom placed his hand gently on his wife's arm, and seeing the warning in his eyes, Sunday felt deflated.

'You have to let Kitty make up her own mind, lass,' he told her.

She could only nod; words failed her for now as Kitty turned back to the woman with that same excited gleam in her eyes.

'So what will happen tomorrow?' the girl asked.

Tom hastily stepped in there. 'I dare say we could take you to the railway station to meet Miss Fox there, if she tells us what time the train leaves and if you're quite sure that is what you want.'

Kitty glanced at the woman, who nodded.

'That would be most helpful, thank you. Our train leaves at 3.30 p.m. so that should give Kitty plenty of time to pack, although she doesn't need to bring too much. I'm sure her mother will want to take her shopping for some new things.'

'Is she rich?' There was so much that Kitty wanted to ask but she didn't like to in front of Sunday.

The woman smiled. 'Let's just say she is comfortably off,' she suggested and with that Kitty had to be content.

Satisfied that she had done what she had come to do, Miss Fox rose then and held her hand out to Sunday, who took it tremulously. She daren't say so much as a word for fear of bursting into tears.

'Thank you for all you've done for the girl, Mrs Branning,' Miss Fox said. 'I know her mother appreciates it. And I must say, from what I've seen of her she's a credit to you. But now I'll wish you goodbye and leave young Kitty here to get on with her packing. Good day to you.'

Tom escorted her from the room as Sunday was left trembling like a leaf in the wind. It was then that the enormity of what had just happened hit Kitty and she too began to shake. She was going to meet her mother!

'I, err . . . I'd better go and tell Ben what's happened,' she said, and Sunday nodded as the girl left the room.

'You'll never guess who that was!' Kitty told Ben breathlessly when she burst into the basement kitchen. He was still seated at the table where she had left him and he looked at her, eager to know what had made her look so happy.

'It was a lady called Miss Fox. She lives in London – *with my mother* – and tomorrow I am going to live with her – *my mother!* Can you believe it?'

Both Mrs Cotton the cook, who was sitting in the chair at the side of the fire with a cup of tea in her hand, and Ben stared at Kitty as if she had lost her senses so hurriedly she told them what had transpired. When she was done, Ben whistled through his teeth.

'Crikey, what with what's happened to me and now you finding

102

your real mother, it's hard to guess what might happen next. But I'm happy for you, Kitty – although I'll miss you. We all will.'

Kitty's smile vanished as she stared at the dear familiar faces. They had all been her family up until now and she knew that she would miss them too. Ben in particular. But then this was an opportunity not to be missed. It wasn't every day that you were offered the chance to live with your real family, so she knew that she must grasp it with both hands.

'I shall miss you too,' she told Ben. 'But I shall write to you, and as soon as I'm settled you could perhaps come for a visit. London isn't so very far away on the train, is it?'

'I suppose not,' he answered, then surprised her when he rose abruptly and said, 'Right, well, I'd best get on. I've work to do and I dare say you have a lot of packing to get on with so I'll leave you to it and see you later.'

'He's hurting, lass,' Dora Cotton said as she saw the distress on Kitty's face. 'He's pleased for you – we all will be – but it won't stop the pain of seeing you go.'

Kitty gave her a quick hug, then made her way upstairs. She would need to sort out what she wanted to take with her and there seemed no sense in delaying. This time tomorrow she would be gone, possibly for good. It was a sobering thought, for although she was eager to meet her natural mother she was sad to be leaving Treetops and Sunday and Tom, who had been like parents to her – the best any child could have wished for.

After seeing Miss Fox out and into the car, with George at the wheel to drive her to her digs for tonight, Tom went back to the sitting room where he found Sunday sitting with tears streaming down her face. She found it strange that at one time she would never allow herself to cry, since she had learned at a very young age that tears got her nowhere in the workhouse, and yet recently it seemed to be all she had done – but only when Tom wasn't there to see her. Today, however, she couldn't seem to stop herself.

Tom tried to take her in his arms to comfort her, but she shrugged him off and moved away. He sighed. She even kept to her own side of the bed now instead of cuddling into him as she had used to, and he wondered if things would ever go back to the way they were before they had discovered that Ben was his son.

'She'll be all right,' he assured her. 'Kitty is tougher than she looks and we'll keep in close touch with her. She can always come home if things don't work out in London.'

'Of course.' Sunday answered him as if she were talking to a mere acquaintance and Tom's frustration grew although he didn't say anything.

'I must go and sort out some luggage for her,' Sunday said then, after drying her cheeks on a scrap of lace handkerchief. 'It wouldn't do for her to arrive at her mother's with shabby bags. I shall give her the two I bought last year.'

He didn't respond. Sunday clearly didn't expect him to, and then she left the room without another word, leaving Tom with a heavy heart. They had lost poor little Maggie, and now they were about to lose Kitty, the girl he had loved since she had come into his care. These days, he had seriously begun to wonder if he had lost his wife too.

Chapter Thirteen

Kitty stood staring at the rabbits playing on the lawn from her bedroom window. Behind her, the smart leather travelling bags that Sunday had gifted to her stood packed and ready to go, and it hit her afresh that this would be the last time she would ever look out upon this beloved view. Sunday had never made a secret of the fact that Kitty was a foundling and yet strangely, although she had fantasised about her mother coming for her, the girl had never felt that she had missed out on love. At Treetops, she had been a part of one great big happy family. She stared at the woods rolling away into the distance and the spring flowers that were peeping from beneath the hedgerows as if she was trying to commit every tiny detail to her mind. It was doubtful there would be such wide-open spaces and panoramic views in London. She would probably have to find a park to stroll in if she wished to see a green space. But then she shook herself. She was going to meet her birth mother – and that would make up for everything she was leaving behind, surely? Already she could picture them arm in arm making up for all the lost time.

A tap on the door interrupted her thoughts and Ben stepped into the room, his face solemn.

'I've come to take your bags downstairs if you've finished packing and to tell you that Tom has brought the car around to the front door. He says that you'll be leaving in ten minutes.'

'Very well. I've just got to put my coat and my hat on.'

He nodded, then lifting the bags he quietly left the room as Kitty sat down in front of the dressing-table mirror to secure her hat with a pin. She was wearing her newest outfit, which had been made by the local seamstress to a pattern that the woman had assured her was the very latest fashion. It consisted of a long, dark green skirt that hung straight at the front and had a slight train at the back. With it she wore a lace-frilled white blouse with a high ruffled neckline and wide sleeves, and over the top of that she donned a short jacket cinched in at the waist with a flared peplum. The jacket was made of the same material as the skirt, trimmed with cream cord, as was the wide-brimmed hat, which also boasted some long cream feathers which floated about each time she turned her head.

With the jacket buttoned and the hat firmly in place Kitty looked in the mirror for one last time and was pleased with what she saw. With her hair combed into a neat chignon on the back of her head she felt extremely grown up and hoped her mother would approve of her when they met. But first there were the goodbyes here to get through and she wasn't looking forward to that one little bit. Still, it could not be postponed so, bracing herself, she picked up her small bag and sailed from the room and down the wide staircase.

She was surprised and touched to find the entire household waiting for her in the hallway. The children, ranging from the youngest to the eldest, were all there, as well as the staff, who were all teary-eyed.

Kitty kissed the children one by one, and then each member of staff stepped forward and she kissed them too, with a large lump in her throat.

'You look after yourself now,' Cook said solemnly, wiping her eyes on her huge white apron and then she was gently nudging the girl towards the door, where Kitty paused to take one last peek at the familiar surroundings.

Tom and Ben were already outside waiting for her with her bags strapped securely to the rear of the car. Sunday was in the back waiting and so the men climbed into the front seats after Tom had settled her beside Sunday. And then they were off and everyone stood on the steps waving until the car turned out of the drive and they were lost from sight.

This was turning out to be far more difficult than Kitty had imagined it would be and she had no doubt it would be harder still when she had to say goodbye to Sunday, Tom and Ben. It was as they were driving along that Sunday slipped a thick envelope into her hand, telling her, 'I want you to tuck this away in your bag, and when you get to your destination put it somewhere safe. There's a large sum of money in there that we've been saving for you over the years – so that if ever you should need to, you will always be able to get home to us.' It was the money that she and Tom had saved for Kitty each year from the money that had been left for her keep. She was also given a tiny gold locket on a slender gold chain and Kitty knew that she would treasure it forever.

Kitty rammed the envelope and the box containing the locket deep into her bag before giving Sunday a grateful smile. Just for a fleeting moment their eyes met and she knew that she should say thank you – but she was too full to speak now that the time for parting was drawing close. She knew how fortunate she had been to have Sunday and Tom as her guardians and she would never forget them . . . and so she merely clung to Sunday's hand.

There was so much that Kitty wanted to say and yet the words lodged in her throat, and she was wise enough to know that the worst was still yet to come when they arrived at the station. She stared at the back of Ben's head, noting the way his hair blew in the wind and his broad shoulders. And it was then it hit her like a bolt of lightning. She was starting to have feelings for him, and not those of a sister for a brother as they had used to be! Perhaps if she had stayed at Treetops they might have come together one day? She would never know now.

Emotions churning, she started to have second thoughts. Everything had happened so fast. Perhaps she should have waited, given herself time to be sure that this was what she wanted? But no, of course it was. As much as she loved Sunday and Tom, she was also aware that they were very protective of her, to the point that she felt stifled sometimes. Why, a young man only had to look at her and Tom would usher her away like a mother hen would usher her chicks away from a fox. At least in London she would have freedom. And if her mother was as famous in the music halls as Miss Fox had told her she was, then she was sure to know some very exciting people. Kitty could just see herself attending balls in fabulous gowns on the arms of dashing young gentlemen who would all be vying for her attention. She smiled to herself – but then as another thought occurred to her, it turned into a frown. What if Miss Fox's visit had been nothing more than a cruel joke? What if they arrived at the station to find she wasn't there? How foolish she would look then if she had to return to Treetops with her tail between her legs.

They were almost there now and Kitty leaned anxiously to one side so that she could see across Ben's shoulder. The large hand on the big clock above the station entrance was ticking away the minutes. It was almost twenty past three. And then as Tom pulled up in front of the doors, Miss Fox suddenly emerged, glancing this way and that. She looked exactly as she had the day before and Kitty let out her breath on a sigh of relief.

Once the car was parked they piled out of it, and when Tom had untied Kitty's luggage they all went to meet Miss Fox.

'Good afternoon,' she greeted them civilly, and then she said to Kitty, 'I thought you might change your mind, my dear.'

When Kitty shook her head, she turned about and they followed her onto the platform. There were just seven minutes to go now until the train was due and Kitty's hands began to shake.

Ben was the first to give her a self-conscious hug. 'You take care now,' he muttered thickly and Kitty beamed up at him with tears trembling on her lovely dark lashes.

It was Tom's turn then and he simply held her close for a second before stepping away from her, blinking rapidly. And now there was only Sunday left and she began to cry, great tearing sobs that shook her whole body as she hugged Kitty to her.

'Just remember, we will always be here for you, do you hear?'

Kitty nodded, her own cheeks wet as behind them the sound of the train chugging towards the station could be heard. It bore down on them like some great fire-breathing dragon and drew to a halt in a hiss of steam and smoke that surrounded them like fog.

The guard was rushing along opening doors and people were emerging as others climbed aboard, but still Kitty and Sunday clung together until Miss Fox said quietly, 'We'd best be getting aboard now.'

One last kiss and then Miss Fox was edging Kitty towards the carriage door as Tom lifted their bags aboard. The guard was slamming the doors and once he had shut theirs Kitty let down the window and hung out, suddenly panicking.

'*I'll write often*,' she shouted above the roar of the engine.

'Just make sure you do, and forward us your address as soon as you're settled in,' Sunday called back. She still felt uneasy at allowing Kitty to go off into the great unknown, even though she had always known in her heart that this day would come. But then the guard blew his whistle and the train chugged into life again.

Kitty could see the three of them standing on the platform waving furiously and she waved back as the train picked up speed and bore her away from everything that was familiar. Soon her Treetops family were nothing but tiny specks in the distance. Luckily they had a carriage all to themselves so there was no one but Miss Fox to see Kitty's tears.

'Now then,' the little woman said brightly, delving into her bag, 'I had the lady at my lodging house make us a few sandwiches for the journey. Would you like one? They look quite tasty as it happens. Cheese and home-made chutney, I believe she said they were.'

'No, thank you.'

Kitty dabbed at her cheeks with a handkerchief and soon her home town was far behind her. It was then that she began to feel more optimistic. After all, London wasn't so very far away and she could always come back to visit them all. Better still, they could come and visit her. What fun she could have, showing them around London.

'Is my mother's house very big?' she asked then and with a mouthful of sandwich, Miss Fox nodded.

'Quite big, and it's in one of the finest roads in Chelsea. She has a maid and a cook . . . and me, of course. Then there's the laundry maid and the housekeeper. She used to have a groom who saw to the horses too, but she let him go a while back. Cabs are two a penny in London so we had no real need of our own carriage.'

'And what do you do for my mother? Are you her lady's maid?' Kitty had so many questions that she wanted to ask.

Miss Fox swallowed the food in her mouth. 'I'm not quite sure what I'd be classed as really,' she replied vaguely. 'I've been with your mother so long now, I dare say you'd call me her companion.'

'And is she *very* beautiful?'

'Oh, she's still a fine-looking woman right enough, although she's just turned forty so she's not exactly in the first flush of youth any more. But once upon a time, you'd not mention her name anywhere in London without it being known. She was one of the darlings of the music halls. Every time she went on stage she'd arrive back at her dressing room to find bottles of champagne, jewels and huge bouquets from her many admirers waiting for her. And oh . . . she had the voice of an angel.' Miss Fox smiled reminiscently.

'I like singing too,' Kitty informed her proudly. 'I must get that from her.'

'No doubt you do,' the woman agreed.

'And my father? Was he well known too? I believe you said he was a politician.'

Miss Fox looked a little uncomfortable. 'He was, and he worshipped the very ground that your mother walked on for years.' She cleared her throat. 'I'm sure he would have wanted to keep you, under other circumstances,' she ended lamely.

'I see – but then if he wanted me so much and cared so deeply for my mother, why didn't he divorce his wife and marry her?'

Miss Fox sighed. 'You ask a lot of questions, don't you, young Kitty? But the answer to that is he didn't dare. His widow is a very rich and powerful woman from a very good family and she would have seen him crawl in the gutter if he'd done that to her.'

Kitty nodded absently as she tried to get her head around everything. She was quiet for a time – much to Miss Fox's relief – staring from the window at the towns and countryside they were passing through. And all the time she was acutely aware that every mile they travelled brought her closer to her mother . . . and her excitement began to mount again.

After what seemed like an eternity the train finally chugged into Euston and Kitty felt as if she'd been transported to another world as she stared at the platform from the carriage window. She had travelled to Southend-on-Sea and Skegness with Sunday and Tom and the other children for summer holidays, but neither of those places had been anything like this. Here everything was hustle and bustle, with people milling about everywhere. There were women in uniform, nannies and governesses shepherding children around, and maids, and other ladies in smart outfits and fashionable hats. The gentlemen, she noted, were rushing about as if they hadn't a minute to live. She felt overwhelmed.

'It's very busy, isn't it?' she commented with a nervous smile and Miss Fox laughed.

'If you think this is busy, you should see it when everyone finishes work,' she said. 'Why, the platforms are so packed sometimes with

111

people trying to get their trains home that you can hardly put a pea between 'em. But pick up your bags now and we'll hail a cab to take us the rest of the way. Been to London before, have you, dear?'

Kitty shook her head as they alighted from the train, and she made sure to keep close as Miss Fox marched along. It occurred to her then that she still hadn't actually asked for her mother's full address. Sunday and Tom hadn't got it either: they had simply been told that Ruby Smith lived somewhere in Chelsea, so it was imperative that she didn't lose Miss Fox now.

Kitty had thought the station was busy but when they emerged onto the main road, her mouth gaped open and she looked around with alarm. Everywhere was positively teeming with people and the road was full of traffic. There were motor cars, horse-drawn carriages, trams and omnibuses crammed with passengers.

Miss Fox took her life in her hands by stepping into the busy road and holding her hand up to hail a cab. Within seconds one had drawn into the kerb and after pushing Kitty and the bags inside it, Miss Fox had a hasty word with the driver, then joined her.

'How far away is my mother's house?' Kitty asked as she settled back against the worn leather squabs. The sawdust on the floor was dirty and smelled quite strongly but she supposed it was better than walking.

'A couple of miles, I should say.' Miss Fox yawned then. It had been a long couple of days and she was beginning to tire now. She would be grateful to get home.

Kitty then began to stare from the window looking for the landmarks that she had only ever seen in books, and she became so engrossed that the journey was over in no time.

'We're in the King's Road in Chelsea now, almost there,' Miss Fox informed her and sure enough, soon afterwards they drew up in front of a very smart-looking townhouse. After climbing out of the cab, Miss Fox paid the driver while Kitty stared at what was to become her new home. The swirly writing above the front door read BRUNSWICK VILLA.

The house was one in a long terrace of dwellings that seemed to stretch up into the sky forever. White-painted railings with steps going down to what Kitty supposed must be the basement kitchen ran all along one side of it, and grander, marble steps led up to a door that was painted a bright cherry red. It all looked very grand, but at the moment the house was the last thing on Kitty's mind. She was about to meet her birth mother – and that knowledge was quite daunting. But she had come this far and there was no going back now. So after taking a deep breath, she followed Miss Fox sedately up the steps with her young heart in her mouth.

Chapter Fourteen

'Ah, Mabel. In the drawing room, is she?' Miss Fox asked the neatly dressed little maid who opened the door to them as she handed over her hat and began to unbutton her coat.

'Yes, ma'am,' Mabel replied politely, eyeing Kitty curiously. Kitty looked to be about sixteen or seventeen and was quite pretty with dark brown hair and brown eyes.

'Well, don't just stand there, my girl,' Miss Fox told Kitty bossily. 'Take your hat and coat off, and look as if you're staying.'

Kitty immediately did as she was told, her hands shaking as she tried to undo her buttons. Suddenly she was all fingers and thumbs. At last she handed the coat and hat to Mabel, who hung them on a large, solid coat-stand to one side of the door. 'Shall I fetch you both a tray of tea, Miss Fox, to keep you going until dinnertime?'

'Yes, please.' The woman smiled at her and when the maid had shot away she asked Kitty, 'All ready to meet her then, are you?'

'I . . . I think so.'

With a nod Miss Fox set off down the hallway and as she followed her, Kitty stared about her in wonder. This house was nowhere near as big as Treetops, but it was certainly much, much grander. The walls were lined with expensive wallpaper, and the black and white tiles on the floor had been polished to a mirror-like shine. Nothing like the ones back at home that were always covered in little foot-prints despite the staff's best efforts to keep them clean, Kitty

114

thought. Huge oil paintings and mirrors in heavy gilt frames hung on the walls, and an enormous vase of lilies placed on a spindly-legged table scented the air as she brushed past it. Then Miss Fox stopped abruptly and after giving Kitty an encouraging smile she opened a door and stepped into a room that was even more luxuriously furnished than the hallway. However, it wasn't the furniture that Kitty's eyes fastened on but the woman reclining on a chaise longue that stood to one side of an imposing marble fireplace.

We are so alike, that could be me in twenty years' time, Kitty thought. The woman was just short of being plump – rounded was the word that occurred to Kitty – and her hair was almost exactly the same shade as hers, as were her eyes.

Kitty hadn't quite known how to react but the woman rose immediately and held out a well-manicured hand that was as soft as swansdown. That hand had clearly never done a day's hard work in the whole of its life and Kitty was a little disappointed. She had expected a cuddle at least.

'So you are my little Katherine. All grown up now,' the woman said as she took Kitty's hand in her own.

'She likes to be called Kitty,' Miss Fox informed her and the woman nodded. Her hair hung loose about her shoulders in thick waves, and close up Kitty saw that there were a few grey streaks in it. There were fine lines about her eyes and mouth too, on closer inspection, but even so their likeness to each other was undeniable.

Ruby was dressed in a pink floaty peignoir trimmed with white feathers that wafted about her as she moved, and her feet were clad in dainty jewelled house slippers. The heavy scent of French perfume moved with her like a cloud, and Kitty noticed that her lips were painted red, showing off her straight white teeth to perfection, and there was rouge on her cheeks. But she had no more time to study her because her mother was drawing her towards the chaise longue to sit beside her. Kitty couldn't help but compare her to Sunday, who was always rushing about doing something. And the house was completely different to the homely Treetops too. Kitty felt almost afraid of disturbing the silken cushions here.

'It must have been a shock when Foxy came for you as she did?' Then, smiling, Ruby apologised. 'Sorry, Foxy is my pet name for Miss Fox.'

'Yes, it was a bit of a shock,' Kitty admitted. Her mother's voice had a musical quality to it and she was quite bemused by her.

'A nice one, I hope?' Ruby's laughter tinkled about the room and Kitty found herself smiling. Miss Fox had told her that men had used to flock to her mother like bees to a honey pot and now she could understand why. She was totally enchanting and everything about her was so feminine. 'And has Foxy told you why I couldn't have you here before?' If truth be told, she had only agreed to claim the girl after abandoning her so long ago because of Miss Fox's constant nagging. But at least she was old enough to be sent out to work now should the need arise and she also saw Kitty as someone who might care for her in her old age when Miss Fox was gone. The fact that she was pretty was a bonus. There were many men who would be willing to pay to be seen out and about with such a presentable young woman on their arm.

Kitty nodded.

'Well, at least you are here now and we have so much catching up to do. We shall go shopping for new clothes for you at the very earliest opportunity. And of course, you will want to see all the sights – Buckingham Palace, the Tower of London and Westminster Abbey to name but a few. We're going to have such fun, you and I, you just wait and see. There is only one thing . . .' She pouted then, reminding Kitty of Maggie when they were tiny playmates. 'I have a favour to ask of you. Do you think you could call me Ruby instead of Mother? It would make you so much easier to explain, you see? I can tell people you are my sister's daughter and that you've recently become orphaned.'

Kitty felt a sharp stab of disappointment and hurt. She was finally

116

reunited with her real mother and now here she was asking her to call her Ruby and pretend that she was her niece! But then grudgingly she could see that it would indeed make things much simpler for Ruby, so she nodded; she didn't really feel that she had much choice.

'Very well, if that is what you'd prefer,' she said stiffly.

'*Shame* on you, Ruby!' Miss Fox suddenly scolded. 'This poor girl's just found her mother and already you're asking her to call you by another title!'

'Oh, Foxy, don't be angry with me,' Ruby implored with tears sparkling becomingly on her lashes and instantly Miss Fox softened.

'Oh very well. If you're going to turn on the tears . . .' she said grumpily. 'But now I'm heading off to the kitchen to see what's for supper. Would you like me to show you to your room, young Kitty, while I'm at it? You'll probably want to have a bit of a wash and brush up after your journey before we sit down to eat.'

Kitty glanced at her mother for permission and when the woman gave an almost imperceptible nod she rose and followed Miss Fox from the room. When they'd gone, Ruby reached for the box of fine chocolates she had been enjoying before they arrived.

As Kitty followed Miss Fox up a wide curving staircase she couldn't help but feel a little flat. Her mother was every bit as beautiful as she had always imagined she would be, but her greeting had lacked real affection. Kitty had always dreamed that when they finally met, there would be tears and hugs – and the fact that her mother had asked her to call her Ruby or 'Aunt' had also hurt, although she supposed she could understand the reasons behind it. It would be very difficult for Ruby to present everyone she knew with a daughter they had never even known existed, whereas presenting them with a niece was far more believable.

They reached a long landing and turning to the left, Miss Fox threw open a door and said, 'This will be your room, dear. I hope you will find it comfortable.'

Kitty's eyes shone with pleasure as she looked around. This was truly a room fit for a princess. The wallpaper was pink and white, the heavily fringed curtains were a deep pink, even the rugs on the floor were pink – but the bedspread on the magnificent four-poster bed was patterned with roses. There was a dressing table boasting a large mirror with a dainty little stool in front of it, and also an armoire and two chests of drawers in the same wood. Kitty thought it might be rosewood but wasn't sure. She loved it nonetheless. The same pink curtains that hung at the window framed the bed and it was just the prettiest room she had ever seen.

'I think you'll find Mabel has unpacked your things and put everything away for you,' Miss Fox told her.

Kitty looked shocked. 'But I could have done that myself.'

'No need to while you're here, young lady. That's what we have maids for,' Miss Fox told her with a grin.

Kitty shook her head. She had received the best of care back at Treetops but was used to helping out. All of the children had been given little jobs to do when they reached a certain age, since Sunday and Tom always believed it was a good lesson towards their independence. Now being waited on was going to take some getting used to. What was she going to do with her time?

'Right, well, I'll leave you to settle in. I'll come and call you when dinner is ready,' Miss Fox told her. 'Then after dinner I'll show you round so you know where each room is. The bathroom is next door but one along the corridor, and you'll find fresh towels and everything you need in there.' She added: 'I know it's a lot to take in, dear, but you'll soon get used to our ways.'

'Thank you.' Kitty watched the kindly little woman flit away then sank down onto the end of her bed feeling totally overwhelmed. She had an idea that this new life was going to take quite a bit of getting used to.

At that moment, back at Treetops, Sunday was standing in the middle of Kitty's room crying quietly. It was the only place she could come where she felt close to her now. Both Kitty and Ben had always been special to her, but since the revelation that Ben was Tom's son she hadn't been able to come to terms with it. She knew that she should, but her emotions were still all over the place. It wasn't Ben's fault that her husband had fathered him, of course, and the young man was still as caring towards her as ever, but for some reason now she found herself holding him at arm's length. She was doing exactly the same to Tom. They hadn't lain together since the letter informing them of Ben's natural mother had arrived, although Tom had tried to love her on numerous occasions. Somehow the closeness they had shared was gone and she feared it might never return. Now on top of that she had lost Kitty too, the little girl she had adored since the second she saw her, and she felt as if her world was falling apart.

For some long time now Sunday had resigned herself to the fact that she would never bear any children of her own, but having Ben and Kitty to pour her love into had been a huge consolation. And now in different ways they were both gone. She knew that Ben was feeling Kitty's going too. Ever since they had arrived back from the station the light seemed to have gone from his eyes and he had found any job he could to keep himself occupied. A noise behind her made her whirl about to find Tom watching her with a worried expression on his face.

'Come away out of here, pet,' he encouraged, feeling her pain. 'We'll go down an' see what the children are up to, eh?' He held his hand out to her but ignoring it, she swiped the tears from her face with the back of her hand and straightened up.

'I'm quite all right,' she said coldly and with that she stalked past him, leaving him there to stare after her wondering, as she herself had, if they would ever be the same again.

True to her word an hour or so later, Miss Fox tapped on Kitty's bedroom door and on entering the room she smiled at her approvingly.

Kitty had only brought three outfits and an assortment of underclothes with her as Miss Fox had advised her. There was the outfit she had travelled in, plus another blouse and skirt that was suitable for daytime wear, and the dress she was wearing now, which was one of her newer ones. It was made of a fine ivory silk. Sunday had always felt that young ladies looked their best in pastel colours and this dress certainly set off Kitty's dark beauty to perfection. It had a modestly low lace-trimmed neckline and short lace sleeves, with a tight waist that flared into a slightly wider skirt at the front with a small train at the back. Other than the lace it had no adornments whatsoever but it was the simplicity of it set against Kitty's dark hair and flawless skin that made it so stunning.

'Why you look a perfect treat.' Miss Fox beamed at her then confided, 'Your mother has informed the staff that you've come to live with us and told them all that you are her niece – so from now on you're to address her as Aunt or Ruby. Can you remember to do that?'

Kitty felt a slight flush rise to her cheeks. 'Yes, I think so,' she said.

'Good, then we'll go down now.'

Kitty followed her back downstairs and into a beautiful dining room where a long, highly polished mahogany table was set for three people. A silver candelabra was placed in the centre of it and the candles made the silver cutlery and the cut-glass wine goblets sparkle. It all looked very grand just for three people and Kitty wondered if the staff went to all this trouble every day.

They had only been in the room for a matter of minutes when Ruby made her entrance. She looked as if she was about to go out to the theatre rather than have dinner at home. Her gown in a pale sea-green satin made a pleasing swishing noise every time she walked, and the bodice of it was heavily embroidered with sequins and pearls. Her hair had been swept up onto her head and fell in loose curls about her shoulders, and there were diamond earrings dangling from her ears and a matching necklace clasped about her neck. Her fingers were covered in rings fashioned from different gems that flashed all the colours of the rainbow, and Kitty was in awe of her. Even more so now she could see why she had acquired the male following that Miss Fox had told her about. Her mother might well be approaching middle age, but she was still a remarkably attractive woman.

'Why, you look quite charming,' she told Kitty in her beautiful musical voice. 'Do sit here next to me and I'll ring the bell for the maid to begin serving us.'

Somewhat self-consciously Kitty took a seat at the side of her, gazing with alarm at the array of cutlery laid out at her place-setting. There were so many different knives and forks. Which ones was she supposed to use? She decided to wait and see which ones her mother and Miss Fox picked up first. That would be the safest way.

'Now I'm trying to think what I ordered for this evening,' Ruby said, spreading the starched white napkin across her lap. Then smiling at Kitty, she explained, 'I give my menu to the cook at the beginning of each week. I believe I ordered wild mushroom soup finished with cream to start with, this evening.'

Again, Kitty was shocked. She had assumed that all this pomp and ceremony was in honour of her arrival – but it sounded as if they dined this way every day. It was a far cry from Treetops where the food was plain but wholesome.

Just then, a maid bustled in dressed in a pretty lace-trimmed apron and mob-cap and placed a large silver tureen in the centre of the table. After a nod from Ruby she removed the lid and began to ladle the soup into their dishes. It certainly smelled lovely and the bread rolls that were served with it were still warm from the oven. Kitty suddenly realised how hungry she was. It had been a long time since she had shared Miss Fox's sandwiches on the train and after watching which spoon to use she tucked in with relish.

As soon as they were finished the dishes were efficiently whisked away and yet more silver salvers were laid down the centre of the table.

'Mm, one of my favourites,' Ruby trilled, clapping her hands together much as a child might have done at the sight of a treat. 'Roast beef with all the trimmings. Crushed potatoes and a selection of vegetables.'

She began to load her plate and soon they were all eating. And silence reigned save for the sound of the cutlery on the plates. Kitty noticed that her mother had quite a voracious appetite but when she began to load her plate yet again with seconds, Miss Fox frowned at her.

'Now, Ruby, what have I told you? You're pleasantly plump at present, but carry on like this and you'll turn to fat.'

Ruby pouted. 'Oh, Foxy, you can be *so* cutting,' she whined. 'You know how I enjoy my food. Would you begrudge me a little pleasure?'

'All I'm saying is, you have a booking at the Prince of Wales Theatre next week, and you want to fit into that expensive gown you've bought, don't you?'

Feeling a bit uncomfortable, Kitty kept her eyes fixed on her plate. No one would have believed to hear the two of them that Miss Fox was Ruby's employee. She spoke to her as a mother would to an errant child, but then Miss Fox had told her that she had been with her for many years so that probably explained it. However, Kitty did wonder what kind of a world she had stumbled into. Her life at Treetops seemed very far away.

When dessert was served Kitty already felt as if she was about to burst – but it looked so delicious that she knew she would have to try some.

'Sugar-glazed lemon tart with champagne sorbet,' her mother

purred. Her eyes glinted greedily and heedless of what Miss Fox had said she again had second helpings.

By the time they had finished the rich dessert Kitty realised guiltily that she had probably eaten more at this one meal than she would have in a whole day back at home. She felt slightly queasy, so when the maid then carried in a huge board with an enormous selection of cheeses on it, many of which Kitty had never seen before, she said, 'Just a cup of coffee for me, please.'

'Nonsense,' Ruby giggled girlishly. 'There's nothing wrong with a healthy appetite,' although as she said it she was eyeing Kitty's slim figure enviously. By now the girl was eager for the meal to be over. She really wanted to spend some time with her mother and get to know her.

But that hope was dashed when Miss Fox asked, 'What time is your visitor expected, Ruby?'

The way she emphasised the word *visitor* made Kitty think that she was less than pleased about whoever it was that would be calling.

Glancing at the clock, Ruby gasped, 'Oh my goodness, he will be here in less than an hour! I must go and get ready. Do excuse me, dear Kitty. We'll go shopping tomorrow and we'll have *such* fun. I can hardly wait! Meantime I'm sure Foxy will entertain you. Good night.' And with that she daintily wiped the crumbs from her mouth and hurried from the room in a swish of silken skirts.

Kitty felt decidedly cheated. It should have been their first evening together but instead she would have to spend it with her mother's companion because Ruby had chosen to make other plans. Homesickness swept through her and she had to stifle the urge to cry. All in all, her mother's welcome had been nothing like she had hoped and dreamed it would be . . . but then Kitty told herself that it must be just as strange for her mother as it was for her, so things would surely improve as they became better acquainted? Even so, it was hard to swallow her disappointment.

Chapter Fifteen

The sound of traffic on the street outside her bedroom window the next morning woke Kitty and for a second she lay there feeling disorientated. And then as the events of the day before came back to her and she realised where she was, she swung her legs over the side of the bed and hurried across to the window. Drawing aside the curtains, she stared out at a sea of rooftops. London was nowhere near as glamorous by day as it was by night, and compared to the vast open spaces she was used to she felt quite hemmed in. Below, a stream of vehicles moved to and fro, and she watched as one of the cab horses deposited a pile of dung on the road. A scruffy little urchin boy carrying a bucket and shovel hastily scooped it up and set off along the road like a greyhound as she wrinkled her nose in disgust. Whatever could he want that for? She would ask Miss Fox over breakfast, although it wasn't really a topic to discuss at a mealtime. She was still standing there when there was a tap on the door. Mabel appeared and smiled at her brightly.

'I've brought you a jug of hot water, miss,' she said chirpily. 'And your aunt said to ask you if you needed any help with dressing or with your hair?'

Kitty giggled. 'Thank you, Mabel, but no, I shan't need any help. I'm very capable of dressing myself.'

'Right you are, miss. Miss Fox said to tell you that breakfast will be in half an hour in the dining room. It'll be just you and her. Your aunt is having her breakfast in bed on a tray.'

Once again, Kitty felt slightly downcast. Surely her mother could have made an effort just this once? It was to have been the first breakfast they had ever shared together, after all! Even so she smiled politely and Mabel hurried away after asking, 'Will you find your own way down, miss?'

'Yes, I'm sure I can remember the way,' Kitty told her. The evening before, Miss Fox had taken her on a tour of the whole house, and Kitty had been amazed to discover how large it was. There was a huge garden at the back of it too, but it had been too dark to see much of it by the time they got around to that, so Kitty determined that after breakfast she would go outside and explore. As she washed and dressed, her spirits lifted again and she found herself singing. She was feeling a little like a fish out of water at present but her mother had promised that they would go on a shopping trip today so things were bound to improve.

She found her way down to the dining room with no trouble, amused to note that any of the staff she met bobbed their knee to her as she passed. It was almost like being royalty and Kitty quite enjoyed it.

Miss Fox was already in the dining room when she entered and on her second cup of tea, and she greeted Kitty with a warm smile. 'Ah, here you are, pet. Did you sleep all right with that racket going on outside? Must be a far cry from what you're used to.'

'I did eventually,' Kitty told her. 'Once I'd got used to the noise of the traffic. You're right – it was so quiet at Treetops. I'm going to have to get used to being in London.'

Miss Fox nodded in understanding. 'Help yourself to a cup of tea and anything you fancy,' she instructed. 'The breakfast is laid out on the sideboard.'

Kitty was dazed by the amount of food that had been set out just for the two of them. She was sure there was almost enough there to feed everyone back at home. There was crispy bacon and juicy sausages, fried whole tomatoes, mushrooms, devilled kidneys, a platter of freshly fried eggs, slices of toast and dishes of various jams and marmalade as well as orange juice, a jug of coffee and a pot of tea.

'Phew!' Kitty was over-faced with so much food. 'I only usually have some toast at breakfast-time.'

Miss Fox grinned. 'You have whatever you want. The staff will polish that lot off no doubt when it goes back to the kitchen. I've told Ruby time and time again to cut down – but will she listen? All this waste wasn't a problem when she had a string of admirers to pay the bills, but now . . .' Realising she had said too much she promptly changed the subject as Kitty helped herself to some toast and a cup of tea. In truth, she still felt full up from the night before and could never imagine being hungry again.

'So you're off out shopping today, are you, young lady?'

Kitty nodded enthusiastically. 'I believe so. What time do you think my moth . . . I mean my aunt will be ready?'

'Huh!' Miss Fox snorted. 'I doubt you'll set off till after lunch at the earliest. She was entertaining till all hours so she's having a lie-in this morning. Mind you, she has a lie-in most days. Then when she does get up there's her beauty regime to be gone through. She won't set foot outside the door till she's looking her best. And then she may be rehearsing her songs.'

Kitty nibbled at her toast. 'I see, and does she go out often?'

'As often as someone will take her, but the gentlemen callers are getting a bit thinner on the ground now. As I said, I keep telling her we need to start cutting back a bit. Making some economies. I mean, look at this place.' She spread her hands and tutted loudly. 'What do the two of us – well, the three of us now – want all this space for? And so many staff! We don't need half of them to my way of thinking – but will she have it? No, she won't. "We need to keep up our standards" is all I get when I suggest it so I've

126

learned to keep my mouth shut now. Mind you, she does have a lot of good points,' she added hastily. 'She's generous to a fault, is Ruby, I can't deny that. But anyway, that's not for you to concern yourself over. Now I'm off upstairs to see if she needs a hand with dressing. Enjoy your breakfast, dear, and there's some magazines over there.'

Kitty let out a long sigh after she had finished and left the room. It looked like she had a whole morning ahead of her with nothing to do, but then she remembered that she had decided to go outside and explore the garden. She hated to be cooped up on such a beautiful day even in a house as luxurious as this.

Once outside in the hallway she paused, trying to remember which way to go. There were so many doors but then seeing the one that she thought led down to the kitchen she headed for that. Her hunch proved to be correct and seconds later she emerged into the kitchen, much to the horror of the cook who looked at her as if she had committed a cardinal sin. She was at the table rolling pastry and on spotting Kitty she gasped, 'Oh my goodness, whatever are you doing in here, miss?'

'I was trying to find a way into the garden,' Kitty answered, painfully aware that all the staff present had their eyes focused on her.

'Well, just this once you can go out this way, but in future you should go through the French doors in the dining room,' the cook told her. 'They lead directly into the part of the garden you'll want. This way you'll have to go through the vegetable garden.'

'That won't trouble me,' Kitty told her with a smile. 'I used to work in the vegetable garden often when I lived at home.'

The cook and the mousy-haired little girl who was tackling a pile of dirty dishes at the sink looked shocked but they didn't comment as Kitty sidled past them. After slipping out of the back door she found herself in a walled garden where rows of vegetables peeped from the earth in neat straight rows. They reminded her of th vegetable garden at Treetops and she suddenly experienced a painful bout of homesickness as she wondered what Sunday, Tom and Ben would be doing now.

Hurrying past the rows of carrots, cabbages and onions she headed for a door set in one of the walls and after pushing it open she emerged into another garden. But this was nothing like the other; this had paths that curved through a lush green lawn and to either side of it the borders were full of shrubs and rose bushes. She had gone no more than a few steps when she spotted what appeared to be the rear end of a child protruding from one of the borders, and as she approached, a young boy who looked to be in his early teens suddenly sat back on his heels to stare at her with a startled expression on his face.

'Hello there.' Kitty smiled at him, hoping to put him at ease. 'I'm Kitty, do you work here?'

The boy nodded after glancing towards the door she had just come through to make sure that she was alone.

'Yes, I do. Me name's Arthur Partridge, an' you must be the missus's niece what's come to live wiv her.'

'That's right.'

They eyed each other for a second and then suddenly Arthur burst out, 'I heard 'em say in the kitchen that you were pretty, an' they were right.' He then blushed to the roots of his hair and bowed his head, wishing with all his heart that he had kept his mouth shut. From that second on, young Arthur's heart belonged to Kitty.

'Why, thank you,' Kitty replied, bending to smell one of the roses. 'Are you the gardener here?' It seemed like an awfully large garden for one small boy to maintain but he nodded proudly.

'I am that, miss. I do all the weedin' an' prunin', an' I tends to the veggies.'

'You do a very good job.' She glanced around approvingly as his small chest swelled with pleasure.

'That shrub there is a rhodo . . . rhododen . . . Well, it's real

128

pretty when it's in flower, an' this one 'ere is a . . . Oh 'eck, I forget the name but it's one of me favourites.'

She nodded as she studied him. He was stick-thin and his hair looked as if it hadn't been washed for months; neither did th of him, if it came to that.

'How old are you, Arthur?' she asked pleasantl was shocked when he answered.

'I'm fourteen, miss. I live in Pimlico wiv me ma an' me dad an' bruvvers an' sisters.'

'I see. Is that far from here?' Kitty didn't really know anywhere in London as yet.

'It's a couple of miles or so,' he replied – and she was shocked.

'And you walk all that way to work here? But it must take you ages.'

'Nah!' He pointed proudly towards a rusty old bicycle that was propped against the wall as if it was a Rolls-Royce. 'Hardly takes me any time at all on me bike an' I like workin' 'ere. The missus is good to me, an' every day the cook gives me some leftover grub to take 'ome fer the kids.'

'How many of you are there?' Kitty was curious now.

He swiped a dribble of snot from his nose with the sleeve of his shirt and began to count on his fingers, his mouth working silently. 'There's ten of us nippers,' he said eventually.

'Crikey, that must keep your parents busy. You must live in a very big house,' Kitty chuckled.

The youngster shook his head. 'We live in a two-up two-down, an' we don't see so much of me dad. He spends half his life in the pub if he's got money in his pocket so it's up to me an' me older bruvver to make sure our mum 'as food to put on the table.'

Kitty's heart went out to him as she realised how lucky she had been. She had never been hungry in the whole of her life, thanks to Sunday and Tom.

It was then that the cook appeared in the doorway and called to him, 'There's some breakfast in the kitchen for you, lad.' Then spotting Kitty who was standing the other side of him she blushed.

'... yer pardon, miss. It's only a few leftovers.'

Arthur, ...miled at her reassuringly. 'I'm sure he'll enjoy it.' Then to other again.' ... go while it's nice and hot. I'm sure we'll see each

'I hope so,' he said ... ckly and with a wide grin he scooted off after the cook, his mouth al... dy watering at the thought of the forthcoming meal.

At lunchtime Kitty sat down to dine with Miss Fox and Ruby, who had finally put in an appearance.

Kitty made a valiant attempt to start a conversation beginning, 'I've been out in the garden today and I met Arthur. He's a lovely lad, isn't he?'

'Yes, I suppose he is,' Ruby answered absently as she began her meal.

'He comes from quite a large family, apparently,' Kitty went on but her mother was keen to get off to the shops now and barely responded so they ate lightly and soon after they were ready to go.

'Now you watch what you're spending, Ruby,' Miss Fox warned after stepping into the road to hail them a cab. 'You know there's bills waiting to be paid.'

'Oh, don't be such a grump, Foxy,' Ruby replied airily, seemingly with not a care in the world. 'There are no pockets in shrouds, you know. And life is for living and enjoying.'

A cab drew into the side of the road then, and after helping Ruby to climb into it, Miss Fox stood and waved them off.

'She means well but she can be such a worrier,' Ruby told her daughter, taking a long hard look at her, then suddenly she said, 'Foxy tells me you like to sing. Are you any good?'

'My teacher Miss Lark seemed to think I was,' Kitty answered as the horse gathered speed and they began to clip-clop along at a good old rate.

'Hmm.' Ruby continued to scrutinise her closely. 'Have you ever sung on a stage?'

'Oh no – I mean, I've always just sung because I enjoy it,' Kitty replied red-faced.

'Perhaps you should try it,' Ruby suggested. 'There's a lot of money to be made in the music halls. If your voice matches your looks you could go far. And I have all the right contacts. How about when we get home, you can sing for me while I accompany you, and I'll give you my honest opinion.'

Kitty's heart raced with excitement but for now they had to concentrate on their shopping trip so she merely nodded and said politely, 'That would be lovely. Thank you, Aunt.'

'And you must tell me about Treetops and the people who brought you up,' Ruby went on, showing an interest in her daughter's past for the first time. 'Then tomorrow we could go sightseeing. There is so much to do in London. I'm sure you'll love it when you get used to living here, and when you've made a few friends. I don't doubt the young men will be queuing up to meet you, but first we really must get you some decent clothes. We can't have you walking about like a country bumpkin!'

Kitty looked down at her skirt and blouse. They looked perfectly all right to her, but then compared to the flamboyant outfit and hat that her mother was wearing, she supposed they were a little drab. She watched with interest from the window as the cab went along and soon they were in what Ruby told her was Oxford Street.

'We'll go to Marshall and Snelgrove's first,' Ruby said. There was nothing she loved more than spending money and she could hardly wait to get into the shop.

Once inside, Kitty stared around in amazement. Compared to the shops in her home town this one was huge and she didn't know where to look first. There were counters displaying all manner of things in every direction, with smart young assistants standing behind them.

Ruby stopped at most of them, fingering gloves and scarves before dismissing them and moving on again, and soon Kitty's head was buzzing. There was so much to take in and now amongst the finely dressed ladies who were milling around she understood what her mother meant. Her outfit really did look plain compared to theirs.

'I think we'll walk along to Selfridges,' her mother said after a time. 'They have a much better selection of everything there and on the way, we'll stop in a tea shop for a pastry and some tea.'

Kitty found herself smiling, her mother really did love her food. It didn't feel like any time at all since they'd had lunch. The tea shop she chose was very quaint with waitresses flitting about in pretty lace aprons and black dresses. Ruby ordered them a pot of tea and a selection of pastries, and when they were delivered on a fancy three-tier cake-stand, Kitty gaped at it. There must have been at least a dozen small fancies on there. Ruby wasn't fazed though and three had disappeared in seconds while Kitty was still nibbling away at her first.

'Mm, you really must try these jam and cream scones. They're quite delightful,' Ruby enthused with a blob of jam on the end of her nose. Kitty giggled. Already she had formed the opinion that her mother was used to having her own way and was rather spoiled – and yet she was also very likeable.

Eventually they arrived at Selfridges and if she had been surprised in Marshall & Snelgrove's Kitty was positively shocked in there and didn't quite know where to look first.

'We must visit the perfume counters,' Ruby said, her eyes spark-ling, and before Kitty had a chance to answer, Ruby was off. She then proceeded to dab and spray all kinds of perfume on her wrists until Kitty felt as if she was going to choke, the combined scents were so overpowering.

'Oh, I'll take a bottle of this French one, I think – charge it to my account,' Ruby told the young assistant eventually as she sniffed at her wrist with an expression of ecstasy on her face. 'And we'll also have a bottle of that one for my niece. It's lighter and more suited to a younger person, I think.'

'Large or small bottles, madam?' the girl asked and Ruby laughed.

'Why, large of course. When have you ever known me take less?' Ruby was clearly well known here and the girl nodded.

'And would you like them delivered to the usual address?' she asked.

'Perfect!' Ruby was off like a greyhound again. Kitty wondered why they couldn't have taken the bottles with them. After all, she was more than capable of carrying them but it was already becoming apparent that Ruby did nothing for herself if there was someone else to do it for her, and furthermore, she almost seemed to have forgotten that Kitty was with her. Suddenly Kitty couldn't help but compare this new-found mother with Sunday, who was always dashing about after one or another of them, loving them and putting herself last. In that moment, she realised what a momentous step she had taken and another great wave of homesickness swept through her. She was in one of the busiest department stores in the whole of London, surrounded by people – but she felt more alone than she had ever felt in her life.

Chapter Sixteen

'Ah, so here you are at last,' Miss Fox said disapprovingly when they finally returned home late that afternoon. 'What's all this lot? It's been arriving at regular intervals all afternoon.' She gestured to a number of bags and boxes piled up at the side of the door. 'You must have spent a king's ransom.'

Kitty bowed her head guiltily. Most of the bags and boxes contained things that her mother had insisted she must have, but Ruby only said carelessly, 'Oh, now don't be a grump and start on that again, Foxy. It's almost all things that Kitty needed, although there are a few bits in there that I couldn't resist for myself.'

'Huh! As if you hadn't got enough clothes already,' Miss Fox grumbled. Then turning to the maids she asked, 'Fetch us a good pot of tea into the drawing room, would you? Kitty here looks ready to drop.'

'Oh, I'm all right really,' Kitty protested. 'And I'm sure some of the things could be returned. I did say I really didn't need so many new clothes.'

'They will *not* be returned, young lady,' Ruby said indignantly. 'You're going to need smart clothes if you want to meet people in the business and to go on stage.'

'What are you talking about?' Miss Fox frowned.

'Come into the drawing room and I'll explain over our tea.' Ruby tripped away as the other two followed close behind her.

'Now what's all this then?' Miss Fox demanded as Ruby gracefully sank into a chair and straightened her skirts across her knees.

'Well, Kitty was saying earlier that she had taken singing lessons so I thought I might introduce her to Max. He's my agent,' she informed Kitty. 'If she's half as good as me, he could get her some bookings and I shall be her manager.'

'I think we'll have this conversation later on when we're alone.' Kitty noticed that Miss Fox's lips had set in a grim line and wondered why. She found the idea of singing on stage quite exciting. Of course, as her mother had pointed out, she would have to listen to her first to ensure that Kitty was good enough, and she planned to do so that very same evening, immediately after dinner.

There was a distinct atmosphere now so as soon as Kitty had hastily swallowed a cup of tea, almost burning her throat in the process, she excused herself and hurried away to her room. She found her bed piled high with bags and boxes and Mabel there beginning to unpack them.

'There's no need to do that, honestly,' Kitty told her but Mabel merely smiled.

'I'm quite enjoyin' it, as it happens, miss.' The girl sighed enviously as she lifted a beautiful rose-pink gown from one particular box, wrapped in tissue paper.

'It is lovely, isn't it?' Kitty admitted, stroking the silken material. 'But it was ridiculously expensive. I did tell my . . . aunt that it was too much.'

'Oh, she spends money like water, that one does,' Mabel replied, then flushed a dull brick-red. 'Sorry, miss, it ain't fer me to comment.'

'It's all right,' Kitty told her. 'I rather got that impression myself.' She then set to and began to help and soon the entire bed was covered in lovely new clothes and shoes. It was then as the two girls stood back to admire them that Kitty suddenly asked, 'Do you know the lad who works in the garden? Arthur, he said his name was. I met him earlier when I went out for a bit of fresh air.'

'Yes, that's Arthur, God bless him. Poor little bugger . . . Oops, beggin' yer pardon again. We all know Arthur. Cook's got a soft spot for him, an' between you an' me she often sends leftovers back with him for his mum an' his brothers an' sisters. I don't reckon they'd eat half the time if she didn't. His dad enjoys a drink, see.' She bit her lip then. It wasn't her place to be so familiar with the mistress's niece but Kitty was so easy to talk to and had no airs and graces whatsoever. 'You won't let on to the mistress about what Cook does, will you?' she pleaded. 'I wouldn't want to get her into trouble.'

'Of course I won't. I'd do exactly the same if I was her,' Kitty said stoutly. The next time she saw Arthur she would slip a little money to him, she decided. That should help a bit. Then changing the subject, she asked, 'Have you worked for my aunt for long?'

'About two years or so now,' Mabel answered as she hung one of the dresses on a hanger and carried it to the armoire. 'An' in fairness she's a good mistress. I live in an' get plenty to eat plus some wages to take home to me mum once a month, so I mustn't grumble.'

'Good.' The two girls put the rest of the clothes away and then Mabel headed off to the kitchen to see what needed to be done.

That evening after dinner, which was just as substantial as it had been the night before, Ruby led Kitty into the day room, where there was a beautiful baby grand piano. She sat down in front of it and surprised Kitty when her fingers flew gracefully across the keys. Her mother was clearly a gifted pianist as well as a renowned singer.

'Do you know "Little Vagabond Boy"?'

Kitty nodded.

'Good, then you sing it to me while I play for you. What key do you prefer?'

Kitty told her, gulping nervously, but as the music flooded the room she began to sing, hesitantly at first and then as her confidence grew, in a clear ringing voice. She accompanied the words with gestures.

When the music died away, Kitty watched her mother anxiously for her reaction.

'That was excellent. Your singing teacher taught you well,' Ruby told her with an approving smile. 'There is still a little work to do on your posture and your breathing, but I'm sure you would be a hit in the music halls.'

'Do you *really* think so?' Kitty was delighted.

'Yes, but we also need to do something with your hair and you'll have to learn how to apply stage make-up. Have you ever worn make-up before?'

'No.' As yet, Kitty thought, she hadn't seen her mother without it.

'No matter,' Ruby told her. 'The trick is not to overdo it, and with your skin you won't need too much. But now you must excuse me. I have a visitor due in less than an hour and I need to get changed.'

Kitty's spirits sank. Yet another evening on her own! But she held her tongue. Life here was clearly going to be very different to the one she had lived at Treetops, but no doubt she would get used to it. When her mother left the room, Kitty slipped through the French doors into the garden – just in time to see young Arthur heading towards his bicycle. His face lit up at the sight of her approaching him and she beamed back at him.

'Here.' Dipping her hand into the pocket of her skirt, she withdrew half a crown. 'Treat your brothers and sisters to some sweets from me on the way home.'

He stared at the big silver coin as if he could hardly believe his luck. 'It's an 'eck of a lot. Are yer quite sure, miss?'

'Of course.' Kitty pressed it into his hand as he blushed furiously. 'And please, don't call me miss. My name is Kitty.'

137

'Right you are, mi . . . Kitty. See you tomorrow.' He then wheeled his bicycle towards the back gate and with a last smile and a wave Kitty went back indoors. She ran upstairs to admire all her new clothes and to write a letter to Sunday and Tom as she had promised.

She sat pondering on what she should write for a long time as she anxiously chewed the end of the pen but eventually she began,

Dear Sunday and Tom,

I hope this finds you both and everyone at Treetops well. I'm sorry I haven't written before but things have been so hectic here.

She paused then as she wondered what else to write. She desperately wanted to tell them how lonely she was and how much she missed them, but pride wouldn't allow her to do that so she went on, choosing her words carefully:

My mother and I are getting along famously and I'm very much enjoying living in London. It's so different to Nuneaton and there's always so much to do, shopping, sightseeing, my feet have barely touched the ground! We have staff here who see to my every need and Mother has bought me some lovely new clothes, all the very latest fashion. My room is very beautiful too, very luxurious.

She paused again then to read what she had written and even to her it sounded shallow in the extreme, but better that than admit what a disappointment her mother had been to her so far. The letter continued for a while longer in the same vein, before she added her address and urged them to write to her when they had time. She then finished it and signed it, *With much love, Kitty* xxx

All she had to do now was ask Ruby where she might post it, and then hopefully she would hear from them before too long.

It was two days later, in the evening after dinner when Mabel tapped at Kitty's bedroom door to tell her, 'The mistress says will you come down to the drawing room, please, miss? There's someone she would like you to meet.'

'Oh.' It was the first time her mother had ever asked to see her in the evening and Kitty wondered who it was she wanted her to meet. 'Thank you, Mabel. Would you tell her I'll be down in five minutes?'

As soon as Mabel had gone Kitty laid down the book she had been reading and dashed over to the dressing table, where she snatched up her hairbrush and tidied her hair. She then smoothed the creases as best she could from one of her smart new skirts, and satisfied that she was as tidy as she could make herself for now, she went downstairs.

She tapped tentatively at the drawing-room door and when her mother bade her come in, she entered. The first thing she saw was a very good-looking gentleman reclining on the chaise longue as if he owned the place, blowing smoke rings into the air from a very fat cigar and looking incredibly bored. He was very smartly dressed in a navy-blue pinstriped sack suit and a crisp white shirt, and he had fair hair and a moustache. He looked to be in his mid-thirties and was easily one of the most handsome men Kitty had ever seen, even if she did consider him to be rather old. The second he clapped eyes on Kitty, however, his bored look disappeared and he sat up straighter with a spark of interest flaring in his eyes.

'So *you* are Kitty, Ruby's little niece.' He stubbed his cigar out in a nearby ashtray and advanced on Kitty with his hand extended. She shook his hand solemnly, embarrassed when he held on to hers for a fraction longer than was necessary, then he walked a full circle all around her, eyeing her critically up and down as she cringed beneath his scrutiny.

'Quite enchanting,' he commented to Ruby. 'I can see you are related. She's your sister's daughter, did you say? And you reckon she can sing as well?'

This must be how the poor beasts in the cattle market feel when the farmers are walking around them considering which one to buy, Kitty thought.

'She has the voice of a little angel,' Ruby assured him, then smiling at her daughter she told her, 'Kitty, this is Max Thomas, my agent, the one I told you about.'

'How do you do, Mr Thomas,' Kitty said politely and he threw back his head and roared with laughter.

'I do very much better for meeting you, dear girl,' he chuckled, then to Ruby: 'I see what you mean about her being unspoiled. The public would love her.'

Kitty flushed, wishing they wouldn't keep talking about her as if she wasn't in the room.

At last he directed a comment to Kitty when he told her, 'I think it would be a good idea if you came along to see your aunt perform at the Prince of Wales Theatre in a couple of days' time. You can decide then if a life on stage is really what you want.'

'And do you have any more bookings lined up for *me* yet, darling?' Ruby purred, feeling slightly jealous of all the attention he was bestowing on Kitty.

He shook his head. 'Not yet, I'm afraid. But let's wait and see how this next booking goes, eh?'

She pouted her pretty red lips and he grinned and was putty in her hands again. It was almost as if he had forgotten that Kitty was there.

'Did you need me for anything else, Aunt?' Kitty was beginning to feel decidedly in the way.

Max was seated at the side of Ruby now, stroking the soft skin on her inner arm.

'No, dear. I just wanted to introduce you. Do go back to whatever it was you were doing,' Ruby murmured, fluttering her eyelashes becomingly.

Kitty hastily left the room. It was looking rather as if Max Thomas was a little more than just her mother's agent and she was only too glad to leave them to it. *But at least I've got the theatre trip to look forward to now*, she thought, and humming merrily she wandered back upstairs to her room and her book. There wasn't much else to do. She now had someone to cook, clean and wait on her hand and foot, and if truth be told it wasn't turning out to be as nice as she'd imagined it would be. In fact, half the time she was bored almost to tears and thought back fondly to the full and busy life she had led at Treetops. But she had made the choice to come here and now, the way she saw it, she had to become accustomed to it. It didn't stop her missing everyone though and some nights her silk and lace pillows were damp with tears from where she had cried herself to sleep. *I'll ask Ruby where I might post my letter tomorrow*, she promised herself as she was drifting off to sleep. She still hadn't got round to sending it, and until she did it was unlikely she would hear from them as they didn't have her address.

Chapter Seventeen

'I was wondering if you could tell me which way it is to the post office?' Kitty asked her mother late the following morning. 'I've written to Sunday and Tom and my friend, Ben, and I need some stamps.'

'Oh, you don't need to trouble yourself with things like that. That's what we have servants for,' Ruby told her as she daintily stifled a yawn with her hand. 'Just pop them on the tray over there with my mail and one of the maids will post them later.' It was almost twelve o'clock, but Ruby had only just got up and was still clad in her peignoir. Kitty had rarely seen her up and about before lunchtime.

Crossing to the tray, she laid her letters on it.

'Don't worry,' Ruby told her as she helped herself to a cup of coffee. 'I have written to Mr and Mrs Branning and given them our full address so no doubt they'll be writing to you very soon. If they've forgiven you for leaving them so abruptly, that is.'

Kitty blinked. Her mother might have a point. She *had* left Treetops in rather a rush, despite being fully aware of how upset Sunday was about her sudden departure. But surely Sunday wouldn't have expected her to miss the chance of meeting her birth mother? The girl tapped her lip with her forefinger. Never mind. In her letter she had told them truthfully how very much she missed them all, so Sunday and Tom were bound to respond when they received it. Feeling slightly happier, she then asked, 'Did you have anything planned for this afternoon?'

'What?' Ruby already had her head buried in the latest copy of the *Ladies Home Journal* magazine. She was a great fan of the fashion section inside it. 'What did you say, dear?'

'I said, have you got anything planned for this afternoon – for us, I mean?'

'Oh . . . no, no, I'm afraid not. I have a performance tomorrow evening and I always like to rehearse then rest the day before so that I look and perform at my best.'

'Oh, I see.' Kitty couldn't help but feel let down. But then she brightened a little when she asked, 'In that case would you mind if I went out for a while? I could take myself off and do a bit of sightseeing.'

Ruby raised an eyebrow. 'On your own? What if you get lost?'

'I shall be fine,' Kitty said as Miss Fox joined them. 'I can always hop in a cab and give them this address if I do get lost, and they'll bring me home.'

'Hmm!' Miss Fox didn't look any too pleased with the idea. 'I'm not so sure it's safe for a young lady like you to be out and about by herself. There's pickpockets and all manner of rogues just waiting to rob you blind.'

'Oh, Foxy, stop fussing,' Ruby scolded with a giggle. 'She's not a child.' Then to Kitty: 'Just be sure to stay in the places where there are lots of people and don't venture into the back streets.'

'D'you know what? I think I might just come with you,' Miss Fox suddenly declared. She didn't like the thought of Kitty going out alone at all, not until she knew her way about a little at least. She was also annoyed with Ruby, who didn't seem to be making any effort whatsoever to spend time with her daughter. Phyllis Fox sometimes wondered why she had even bothered sending for the poor girl, but at least she could make what was left of the day enjoyable for her.

143

'Go and get yourself ready,' she told Kitty kindly and when the girl had skipped away she rounded on Ruby. 'Would it hurt you to pay a little more attention to the girl?' she demanded.

Ruby instantly went into a sulk and blinked rapidly. 'Oh, please don't be horrible to me, Foxy,' she said in a small voice. 'You know how upset it makes me when you get cross with me. I'm sure Kitty is more than capable of taking care of herself. And you know how I need to rest before a performance. It takes so much out of me.'

'No wonder. You're no spring chicken any more, are you?' Miss Fox retorted bluntly, and now real tears appeared in Ruby's eyes.

'How *could* you be so cruel?' she whimpered.

Miss Fox sniffed as she made for the door. 'I'm not being cruel, I'm just stating a fact.' And with that she left the room, slamming the door resoundingly behind her, leaving Ruby to jump up and closely examine her face in the mirror above the fireplace.

As it turned out, Kitty enjoyed herself enormously that afternoon. Miss Fox proved to be surprisingly good company. She took her to see Buckingham Palace and Westminster Abbey, followed by Nelson's Column and the Tower of London and finally, late in the afternoon, they stopped for refreshments in a very pretty tea room near Tower Bridge.

'Thank you for coming with me,' Kitty told her as she sipped at her delicious cup of hot chocolate. 'I wouldn't have got to see nearly as much if I'd come on my own.' Then becoming serious, she asked quietly, 'Do you think I'm a disappointment to my mother, Miss Fox? She doesn't seem overly fond of spending any time with me.'

The older woman's heart went out to the girl. How disappointing it must be for her to finally have her birth mother claim her, only to then be told she must address her as Aunt and be left to her own devices. She still worried deep down that Ruby might have something in mind for the girl – although as yet she hadn't worked out what it might be.

She chose her words carefully as she answered, 'What you have

144

to understand is that your mother is used to being the centre of attention. She's never had to put anyone else before herself, and much as I care about her and hate to say it, I have to confess she can be very selfish. But I'm sure things will come right in the end. You just have to give her time because, my dear, I fail to see how you could be a disappointment to anyone.'

Kitty blinked rapidly to stop the tears that the woman's kind words had caused to spring to her eyes. Perhaps it was she herself who was being selfish? After all, she had a wardrobe full of new clothes and was living a life of luxury now. Ruby had also told her that she would have a small allowance each week from now on, so all in all she had nothing to complain about. So why, then, was she missing Sunday and Tom so much? she wondered.

'Now come on,' Miss Fox said cheerily, hoping to jog the girl back into her former happy mood. 'I reckon I can just about squeeze another cuppa out of this pot then we'll take a stroll down past the river and see how far we get. How does that sound?'

'Wonderful,' Kitty said, and settled back to finish her scone.

It was quite late when they arrived home to find Ruby already entertaining her agent, Max, in the day room.

'Had a nice time, have you?' he enquired as Kitty and Miss Fox walked past.

Then Ruby surprised Kitty when she said, 'Come in, darling. Max has decided that he'd love to hear you sing. He's a very gifted pianist as it happens, so will you oblige him?'

'Well, I err . . . I suppose so,' Kitty mumbled, blushing.

'Wonderful.' Ruby clapped her hands together in that girlish way she had. 'Well, there's no time like the present, is there? And after that, Cook has kept some dinner hot for you and Foxy.'

Tight-lipped, Miss Fox frowned and went on her way as Max

rose and made for the piano. Kitty slowly went to stand beside it, feeling thoroughly self-conscious and very aware of his eyes watching her closely. Could she have known it, his heart was beating fast and he was praying that this girl would sing half as well as she looked. It was getting more and more difficult now to get bookings for Ruby, much to her chagrin, but if this girl had talent, he had no doubt whatsoever that he would be able to make her into a star.

'Right – do you know "The Boy I Love is Up in the Gallery"?'

It was one of her favourite songs. She swallowed and nodded solemnly as he took a seat on the piano stool and flexed his fingers. She then tried to relax and took some deep breaths as she remembered all that Miss Lark had taught her.

When she was ready, he began to play – and as she sang the poignant lyrics she became lost in the song, and even forgot that Max and her mother were in the room.

When it was done, she stood with her hands joined neatly in front of her and there was utter silence . . . until Max exclaimed, 'Bravo! My dear girl, that was wonderful!'

Kitty flushed prettily. Max was quite old, she considered, but he was still a very handsome man and she preened at his praise.

'Yes, well done,' Ruby said somewhat begrudgingly as she saw the appreciative way Max was watching the girl. 'Why don't you pop along to the dining room now and tell the maid you're ready for your meal.' The moment the door closed behind her, Ruby asked him, 'So what did you think?' Although she supposed it was a rather unnecessary question as he was almost drooling. She could remember a time in the not too distant past when she herself had had that effect on him.

'I think with a little training and the right clothes she'd go down a storm with audiences everywhere. And we would have to think of a new name for her, of course. Kitty Smith doesn't sound quite right, does it? We need something a little more romantic.'

'Hmm.' Ruby frowned. 'But only if you don't get further bookings for me,' she responded somewhat sulkily. Although she could see the possibility of Kitty bringing in a lot of money for her, she didn't want it to be at the expense of her own career.

'The thing is, Ruby darling,' Max said smoothly, 'you and I both know that this business is very fickle. The public like young, fresh entertainers and while you still sing beautifully . . .'

When his voice trailed off she stuck her bottom lip out. 'Are you trying to say that I am past my prime?'

'I wouldn't say that exactly.' He had no wish to hurt her feelings but felt it was time to be honest. 'But you and I both know that, managed properly, Kitty could become a highly paid artiste. That's assuming you would wish to be her manager, with me as her agent?' Max knew he really had no need to ask. He could see exactly the way Ruby's mind was working.

'Of course I would be her manager,' she said immediately. 'My niece is very young and green so would need someone to look out for her.'

'That's what I thought.' Max tried to hide his amusement. Ruby was no fool; she knew what kind of fees Kitty might command, and he had no doubt that as her manager Ruby would take the lion's share.

'Well, let's get your performance tomorrow night over with and then we'll talk some more about it,' he suggested, only too aware that, as yet, he hadn't managed to procure any further bookings for her. Ruby was no longer in demand and despite his best efforts he'd had no success at all. Things weren't helped by the state of unrest in the country. The possibility of war was becoming more likely and if that happened then the entertainment world would be badly affected.

'Very well.' Ruby sighed as Max poured them both a glass of whisky from the cut-glass decanter on the sideboard.

Chapter Eighteen

The following evening, Kitty expectantly took her seat in one of the balconies next to Miss Fox at the Prince of Wales Theatre. The atmosphere was alive with chatter and laughter as the audience waited for the curtain to go up and the first act to appear, and the girl stared about in awe, thinking she had never seen so many people gathered together in one place before in her whole life.

Miss Fox watched her with an indulgent smile on her face. She had lost count of the times she had gone along to Ruby's performances and it was all old hat to her now, but for the young girl at her side she realised that it was all new and no doubt very exciting. Kitty was looking very pretty in one of the new outfits her mother had bought for her, and with her fresh complexion and sparkling eyes, Phyllis Fox saw that she was attracting more than a few admiring glances from certain gentlemen in the audience.

And then suddenly the lights dimmed and the enormous red curtains on the stage swished aside to reveal the compère, Billy Ball, who was almost as well known as the acts he was presenting.

Silence settled as he announced, 'Good evening and welcome, ladies and gentlemen. We have some wonderful acts for you tonight, so with no more ado, I am thrilled to introduce Ted West, the Ukulele Man! Let's give him a big hand!'

There was loud applause as the musician came running on to the stage and immediately began to play a selection of rousing popular tunes. Kitty beamed as she tapped her foot in time to the music. The show went on and they were entertained by a male singer, a comedian and a ventriloquist. And then the compère returned to the stage to announce that there would be a twenty-minute interval, so plenty of time to visit the bar. It was then that Max joined them and took a seat at the side of Kitty.

'I've taken the liberty of ordering some champagne for us all as I didn't know your preference, my dear,' he informed Kitty, who was all but glowing.

'Thank you,' she said shyly. Max was looking very handsome and she suddenly felt very grown up. The champagne duly arrived, delivered on a tray by a slightly harassed-looking attendant, and Kitty giggled as she sipped at it and the bubbles went up her nose. 'Oh, it's quite lovely,' she informed him, very aware that Miss Fox was watching them like a hawk.

Almost before they knew it the lights were dimmed and the curtains swished aside again as the compère strode onto the stage to announce the second half of the show.

'Your aunt will be on after the next act,' Max whispered to Kitty as he leaned towards her. 'At one point in her career she commanded star billing and would be the grand finale.'

Kitty nodded and waited impatiently. Eventually Ruby was announced by her stage name, and she glided onto the stage in the most beautiful gown Kitty had ever seen. It was in a deep lilac colour, heavily trimmed with guipure lace, and very low cut. It was also extremely flattering. Her hair had been curled and piled high on her head, and about her throat she wore an amethyst and diamond necklace and matching earrings that dangled from her ears and sparked fire in the stage lights. From the balcony, she looked surprisingly youthful.

Kitty leaned forward eagerly in her seat and hung on her mother's every note, thinking how beautifully she sang as Ruby warbled her way through three songs. She could only imagine how exciting it must be, to be up there on the stage, the centre of everyone's attention, and sighed dreamily at the thought of it. When she had done, Ruby curtsied and blew kisses as the audience applauded and Kitty leaped to her feet, clapping as loudly as she could. Then she watched in awe as her mother ran gracefully from the stage.

'Oh, she was just *wonderful*!' Kitty declared and Miss Fox sniffed. She was never one to give compliments lightly.

'If you think that was good you should have seen her in her day,' she remarked, then they all settled back in their seats to enjoy the rest of the show.

When it had ended, Max took them backstage and paused at a door with Kitty's mother's name on it. 'This is your aunt's dressing room,' he told Kitty as performers bustled up and down the corridor. 'Let's see how she's doing.'

He tapped at the door and entered with the two women behind him to find Ruby still in her stage outfit and full stage make-up, sitting with an elderly gentleman sipping champagne. A large bouquet of flowers addressed to 'Miss Ruby Darling' stood on her dressing table and she smiled as they entered.

'Ah, here you are,' she trilled. Then to the gentleman, 'Do allow me to introduce you. This is my agent, Mr Max Thomas, my niece, Kitty, and my maid, Miss Fox.'

He stood and gave a gallant little bow. 'How do you do. I am Mr Hector Smethwick.'

Max inclined his head and stifled a grin. It appeared that Ruby could still attract admirers even if they were rather elderly. Not that she'd mind that, so long as they had nice fat wallets. The man then bowed to Ruby, saying, 'I shall take my leave now then, dear lady. I do hope you enjoy the flowers and I shall look forward to our dinner date. I shall collect you from your home promptly at seven o'clock on Wednesday evening. Goodbye for now.' He nodded at them all.

When he had left the room, Miss Fox dropped onto a chair and snorted, 'Crikey, you're scraping the bottom of the barrel with that one, aren't you? He must be sixty if he's a day!'

Ruby shrugged carelessly as she sat at her dressing table and began to wipe the thick greasepaint from her face. Kitty was surprised to see that it didn't look very nice at all close to, more like it had been plastered on with a trowel.

'It has to be applied thickly because of the stage lights,' Ruby informed her as if she had read her thoughts, and once it was all removed Kitty thought how tired she looked. Nothing at all like the glamorous vision who had appeared on the stage.

Then addressing Miss Fox, Ruby told her shortly, 'As for Mr Smethwick, he's very pleasant and ridiculously wealthy. He's recently become a widower – so why shouldn't I go out to dinner with him? I feel sorry for him as it happens.'

'I bet you do,' Miss Fox said sarcastically, but Ruby ignored her comment.

'Wait for me outside, would you? The dresser will be coming in to help me get changed now.'

The three of them made their way outside to wait in Max's motor car, and sometime later Ruby slipped through the stage door and came to join them.

Max drove them home and followed them inside, and as usual Ruby asked him, 'I dare say you'd like a drink before you go?'

'I'd love one,' he answered. 'And of course the lovely Miss Kitty must join us.'

Ruby flushed with jealousy as she saw the way he was smiling at the girl, but not wishing to appear childish, she shrugged. 'As you wish.'

'Actually I'm rather tired,' Kitty responded quickly, 'so if you don't mind I'll just turn in. But thank you so much for a wonderful evening, one I shall never forget.'

Just for a second Max looked annoyed but then taking her hand he kissed it gallantly. 'I don't mind at all, my dear. A young girl like you needs her beauty sleep and it was a pleasure to be in your company. Perhaps tomorrow I shall start to look around for some bookings for you. It would be a crime to let such a lovely voice go to waste. Then we must take you shopping for some suitable stage outfits and look at getting you a maid.'

Kitty looked shocked. 'But I don't need a maid,' she said.

'Perhaps not now, but you will when you are in the theatre. You'll need someone to help you get changed and dress your hair. Your aunt has always had Miss Fox to help her if there was no dresser, but I was thinking someone nearer to your own age might be more suitable.'

'Oh!' Kitty didn't argue. It would be a shame to spoil such a very special evening so she simply wished them all goodnight and ran up to her room, where she thought of all she had seen that evening and relived every second. But it didn't stop her missing Sunday or stop her wondering what she would have thought of her new way of life!

Once they were alone in the living room, Ruby rounded on Max. 'I hope you are not getting any romantic inclinations towards my niece!' she spat. 'She is too young to be seduced, so keep your hands off her.'

Max snipped the end off a cigar and slowly lit it before blowing a plume of blue smoke into the air.

'Don't be so ridiculous, darling. Kitty is young enough to be my daughter, but if handled properly she could become a success and make us both rich. And I'm sure you wouldn't turn your pretty nose up at *that*.'

'Well, no, I wouldn't,' Ruby admitted grudgingly, 'but if I am to be her manager I would want her fees paid directly to me and then I would pay her her share.'

And a pitiful share it will be, no doubt, Max thought, although he didn't say it aloud. He had handled some of the biggest stars on stage and was well aware of the sums they were capable of earning, but he doubted that Kitty would ever become wealthy with Ruby as her manager. Even so, he knew that he must placate her, so he smiled at her disarmingly as he said, 'I doubt Kitty is aware of just how lucky she is to have you as her aunt, my dear. With you to teach her all you know, she could well go to the top, which would be to all our advantages.'

At the compliment, Ruby's good mood was restored and she simpered at him as she fluttered her eyelashes and tripped away to pour them both a drink.

Max had no illusions about Ruby. She was very spoiled and ridiculously vain. Over the years she had earned him a vast amount of money, but he had a funny idea that that might be as nothing compared to what Kitty might be capable of bringing in. He had no doubt that she could become a star, and he was genuinely excited about launching her onto the stage. But to achieve that, he would have to play his cards right – and above all, keep Ruby sweet.

The following morning at Treetops Children's Home, Tom found Sunday hovering in the hallway. She started when she saw him and said guiltily, 'I was just arranging these flowers.' She then began to fuss with the blooms standing in a tall cut-glass vase on the hall table.

'And very nice they look too,' he said, sadly aware that in reality she was hovering, waiting for a sign of the postman, just as she had done each morning since Kitty had left.

'Has the post come yet?' he casually asked then, as he headed for his study.

'Err . . . no.' She lowered her eyes and added, 'Perhaps we'll have some word from Kitty today.'

'Perhaps we will, pet. But don't get worrying. She's barely had time to settle in yet. I'm sure she'll write as soon as she finds time.'

His wife nodded and Tom continued on his way with a frown on his face. He was beginning to wonder if Kitty would write, if truth be told. After all, she had been whisked off to a new way of life in London and she'd probably be enjoying herself. And, much as he hated to admit it, she certainly hadn't taken much persuading when her mother's maid had come for her. She'd been off to the bright lights like a shot from a gun! He supposed he couldn't blame her really. Kitty had the world at her feet and looking back, he wondered if he and Sunday hadn't kept too tight a rein on her when she'd lived with them. Perhaps they should have allowed her a little more freedom to go out and meet young people of her own age? The trouble was, because of her beauty Kitty had attracted attention wherever she went and Sunday had barely let her out of her sight for fear that some young rip might take advantage of her.

Well, it was all out of their hands now but he hoped that at some stage the girl would write to them. At least then they would know that she was all right and being well taken care of. He had suffered all manner of guilt since she had left because he hadn't insisted on having her mother's address, but it had all happened so quickly and Miss Fox had – quite rightly – made it clear that it was Kitty's decision to make. She had been there one day and gone for good the next, and Sunday hadn't been the same since. He'd always known that Kitty was special to his wife and because things were still somewhat strained between them, the loss of Kitty seemed to have driven them even further apart.

With a sigh, he entered his office and tried his best to concentrate on the open ledger on his desk, but for some reason the figures kept blurring into one another and in the end he gave up and wandered out to the stables as he too kept an eye on the drive for the postman. He was feeling desperately unhappy because with each day that passed, the rift between him and his wife seemed to get wider.

Chapter Nineteen

Could Tom have known it, in London, Kitty was also looking out for the postman each morning and with every day that passed, her spirits sank a little lower. There had still been no reply to the letter that she had written to Sunday and Tom, and now she was beginning to think they might not bother writing to her at all. After all, she had been just one of a number of children and young people they had cared for, so perhaps their time and attention was centred on the ones who were still at Treetops?

Kitty had taken to going for little walks alone out of sheer boredom and was now getting to know the streets surrounding her mother's house fairly well. She had also ventured into the West End a few times and never tired of all the hustle and bustle, now that she was becoming used to it. She particularly loved the old flower-sellers who stood on street corners with their colourful baskets of blooms, and would often take a small posy home to her mother – not that Ruby ever seemed particularly thrilled with them. The house was always full of expensive hot-house flowers, which no doubt made the ones she offered look rather dull in comparison. But she wouldn't be going out today, not alone anyway. Max had informed her that after lunch he would be taking her to buy something special to wear for her debut performance at a club in Soho the following weekend. Kitty had expected to be launched somewhere like the Prince of Wales Theatre where her mother had sung recently, but as Max had explained, she had to start small and work her way up.

'I'm bringing along an acquaintance to see you,' Max told her. 'He is a very well-respected theatre critic who is always looking out for new talent. If you can impress him enough to get your name into the newspaper he works for, the managers of the music halls will be clamouring to book you, trust me.'

Kitty did trust him – completely – and now she was looking forward to the outing, although there was another aimless morning to get through first. She found the mornings the worst time, which was why she'd taken to going out exploring the neighbourhood. She rarely saw Ruby until early afternoon and often wondered how the woman could bear to spend so long in bed. The day was usually more than half over before she put in an appearance.

Kitty was sitting in the window strumming her fingers on the sill, watching the traffic in the street below as she tried to think what she could do to pass the time. And then it occurred to her. She could write to Sunday and Tom again. Perhaps her last letter hadn't reached them. After all, letters did sometimes get lost in the post! Rising, she gathered together some paper and a pen and for the next half an hour she wrote, telling them all about her new life, but this time she was a little more honest than she had been in the first letter.

Dear Sunday and Tom,

I hope this letter finds you all well there at Treetops. As I write this I can picture you all rushing about doing everything that needs to be done, and in my mind I can see the children playing along the hallway. I am settling in here reasonably well although I do get a little homesick from time to time. My mother, who has asked if I would call her 'Aunt', is a very busy lady, so I tend to be on my own for much of the time and the house here

157

is so quiet inside compared to Treetops, although the same cannot be said for the outside. I am still getting used to all the noise and the traffic, although I'm sure Tom would love seeing all the automobiles that are so much more common here than they are there up in Nuneaton.

On a happier note, my mother's agent is taking me shopping for a new outfit for my debut performance at a club in Soho where I will be singing next week! He assures me that if all goes well I might soon be appearing in the music halls and earning my own living. I'm very excited at the prospect. Perhaps I will be good enough to follow in my mother's footsteps? I am a little disappointed that you haven't replied to my first letter as yet, but I do understand how very busy you all are. It would be lovely to hear about all that's going on at home, though, if you could perhaps spare the time? I often think of you all but now I should be thinking of getting ready to go shopping so I will end my letter and hope to hear from you very soon,

My deepest love to all of you,

Your Kitty xxxxxxxx

She then quickly wrote a little note to Ben too, saying much the same as she had to Sunday and Tom, and enclosed it with theirs in the envelope before sealing it and carrying it downstairs to place it on the tray with Ruby's outgoing mail. Now all she could do was wait – but *surely* they would write soon?

That afternoon, Max arrived punctually and drove Kitty and Ruby into the West End, where he parked his car. Kitty's face was flushed with excitement and as he peeped at her from the corner of his eye, Ruby noticed and clung possessively to his arm. From the way

Kitty fluttered her eyelashes becomingly at any young man who dared to look admiringly at her, Max sensed that she had already discovered the power she could wield over men. But for all that she was still naively innocent and he was sure that she had never gone further than mildly flirting with anyone. He smirked. Handled properly, she would be putty in his hands – although he would have to tread carefully so as not to upset Ruby. But who knew what the future might hold?

Once again they visited Selfridges where they were escorted to the department that sold ballgowns. An assistant brought out a selection for her to look at and Kitty almost drooled over each one – although when she dared to look at the prices her eyes opened wide.

'Don't get worrying about the expense.' Max waved his hand airily. 'Just consider it an investment. We must have you looking your absolute best for your debut.' Then when he saw Kitty stroking a gown in deep purple he advised her, 'No, I think we should stick to a pastel colour to play on your youth and your innocence. What about this pale blue one here?'

Kitty thought it rather plain, but she supposed it wouldn't hurt to humour him and try it on so she obligingly followed the assistant to the fitting room while Ruby and Max took a seat to wait for her.

'I think this will show your colouring off to perfection,' the shop assistant told her as she did up the row of tiny buttons at the back. She then turned Kitty to the mirror and as she glimpsed herself, the girl gasped.

The dress was daringly low cut and off the shoulder, emphasising her smooth skin. It was then drawn to one side beneath the bust before falling away into a long skirt that rustled delightfully with every movement.

'You look exquisite,' the assistant breathed as Kitty turned this way and that, admiring herself in the tall cheval mirror. There was no decoration of any sort anywhere on it and yet the superb cut of the gown and the sheer simplicity of it against her dark hair was quite stunning.

'Shall we go out and see what your parents think about it?'

Kitty giggled but didn't say anything as she followed the assistant from the room.

Ruby blinked with surprise when she emerged while Max stared at her, openly admiring.

'It's perfect,' he decided. 'But now she will need some long evening gloves and satin slippers to go with it.'

'Of course, sir.' The assistant hurried away as Kitty did a twirl for them.

'I wasn't that keen when you chose this one,' she admitted then. 'But now I have to say I love it.'

Ruby was feeling more than a little miffed. She could well remember the time when she would have fitted into that gown, but those days were long gone and suddenly she felt old and frumpy.

The assistant arrived back then and Kitty lifted the hem of the gown and slipped her foot into the dainty satin slipper. 'I feel like Cinderella,' she joked, and Max laughed with her. The long gloves completed the look and Kitty felt sad when she was led back to the changing room to have her new finery taken off. While the assistant gave orders to have everything wrapped in tissue paper and boxed, Kitty got dressed and rejoined Ruby and Max.

'The next thing we need to do is get some photographs of you taken,' Max told her as they stepped out of the shop.

'Photographs?' Kitty was puzzled. 'What do we need them for?'

'Publicity, of course.' Max smiled at her broadly, revealing a set of straight white teeth. For a split second, the image of a wolf flashed through the girl's mind. 'We shall need one for a poster advertising your appearance at the club, and then my journalist friend will want one for his newspaper if he likes you.' Personally, he failed to see how anyone could *not* like Kitty, although he wisely didn't say that in front of Ruby. He had an idea that she was feeling a little put out and for now was keen to stay on the right side of her. 'Luckily,' he went on, 'I know just the chappie. He has his own little studio in Mayfair and he's photographed quite a few of my clients for me. We'll go there now, I think. There's no time like the present.'

'But I'm feeling rather tired,' Ruby objected peevishly. Max had informed her when he'd arrived at the house earlier that he'd not managed to secure any further bookings for her as yet and she was still stinging about that.

'Not a problem, my pet.' He patted her hand and she smiled sweetly at him until he went on, 'We'll just hail you a cab to get you safely home and then I shall take Kitty myself.'

'No, no.' The smile slid from her face. 'I wouldn't dream of allowing poor Kitty to go without me.' Inside, she was seething. There had been a time when Max had danced attendance on her, and her wish had been his command . . . but lately she had been seeing less of him. She'd also noticed the way he looked at Kitty and didn't like it one little bit! But then she also knew that she must be sensible. She wasn't getting any younger and needed to think of the future. Kitty was capable of earning her a lot of money, so for now she would remain all sweetness and light, but it would be woe betide him if Max tried to push her too far.

Soon they were back in the automobile and heading for Mayfair. Ruby insisted on sitting in the front while Kitty sat in the back, and on the way she was ominously quiet although when eventually arrived she plastered a smile on her face and told Kitty, 'There's no need to look so nervous, dear. Just relax and do what the photographer tells you.'

Kitty glanced around at the houses. It looked to be a very nice neighbourhood, but she could see no sign of a studio. She was somewhat surprised when Max led them to the door of a tall terraced house surrounded by low white wrought-iron railings.

'Richard has his studio at the back of the house,' he explained.

'He's such a good photographer he doesn't need to advertise. Richard has photographed royalty, so you needn't be worried.'

Kitty nodded as she clutched the large flat boxes containing her new outfit and accessories. Max had told her she would need to wear them and she hoped there would be somewhere private where she could put them on.

A young maid opened the door and ushered them inside.

'Could you tell Mr Fitzherbert that Max Thomas is here?' Max said pleasantly and bobbing her knee the young maid hurried away to do as she was told.

She returned almost immediately to inform him, 'Mr Fitzherbert is expecting you, sir, and said for you to come straight through.'

They began to follow her along a hallway and as they went Kitty stared admiringly at the opulent surroundings. It was more than obvious that this Richard Fitzherbert wasn't short of a bob or two if his home was anything to go by. The wallpaper alone looked as if it had cost a king's ransom and Kitty wondered if it was silk. It certainly looked as if it was. Photography must be a lucrative business, she thought.

They passed a number of closed doors before the maid stopped in front of one right at the back of the house and threw it open. She ushered them inside – and instantly the most handsome man Kitty had ever seen came towards them with his hand outstretched, and Kitty's heart began to thump wildly. He had thick blond hair and eyes the colour of bluebells, and he was so tall that she found herself having to look up at him. His white shirtsleeves were rolled up to just above the elbows and she found herself unable to look away from his bare muscled arms. She knew that she should say something in reply even if it was only 'hello', but to her dismay she found that she was speechless, and so he turned his attention back to Max with a broad grin on his face, making her blush an even darker shade of red. She silently cursed herself. What a naïve little country bumpkin he must think she was!

'Why, Max, old chap, how lovely to see you.' He shook Max's hand warmly. 'And our Ruby too, looking as lovely as ever.' He raised Ruby's hand and kissed it gently as she giggled girlishly, then he turned his attention to Kitty and suddenly her legs went all wobbly and for the first time in her young life she was well and truly smitten. She thought he must be about thirty years old and as he then kissed her hand she started to tremble. 'And this must be Ruby's niece, Kitty, the new star in the making.' His look was openly admiring. 'It seems that good looks and talent run in the family.' As Ruby preened herself at the compliment, he went on: 'Why, it's going to be an absolute pleasure to photograph you, my dear.'

Kitty blushed to the very roots of her hair but then she began to look around and was astounded at the room in which she found herself. It was absolutely enormous. Various cameras stood about on tripods, and there was a selection of different backdrops pinned all around the walls. On one wall was what appeared to be a Roman temple with marble pillars that reached up to the ceiling, and another wall made her feel as if she was back at Treetops in the bluebell wood. She had a sudden yearning to be there and quickly looked away from it. If she was going to be a star it wouldn't do to burst into tears at the drop of a hat.

The third wall was covered in photographs and she moved closer to examine them. Many of them were what she would have expected to find in a photographer's studio, such as family portraits, but these were nothing like the stiff formal poses she had seen many times before: these were of happy relaxed family groups, and others of children in natural laughing poses. Another series showed London's famous landmarks. There was a beautiful one of the sun setting above Westminster Abbey, another of the River Thames at sunset that she could barely drag her eyes away from. And then the breath caught in her throat. She had spotted framed photographs of young women draped in voile, in various stages of undress, and she quickly averted her eyes.

163

Two large glass doors took up most of the fourth wall and through them she glimpsed a garden, which again reminded her of Treetops. The wide-open spaces she had been surrounded by as she was growing up were yet another thing that she missed about home.

'Now why don't you go behind that screen there and get changed while Max and I have a whisky and a little chat. I assume you have brought a more suitable gown to be photographed in?' Richard's voice brought her thoughts sharply back to the present and she nodded numbly.

'I'll come and help you,' Ruby volunteered. When ~~Ruby~~ Kitty was in her new gown, her mother said: 'We shall have to leave your hair loose about your shoulders for today, but on the night of your performance I think we might pile it on top of your head and tease it into gentle curls.' Then she changed her mind. 'Though saying that, wearing it loose makes you look young and vulnerable, which is what the public likes so we'll have to decide.'

When Kitty was ready, Ruby arranged her hair and hitched the low neckline of the dress down a fraction, revealing yet more cleavage, which made Kitty feel very uncomfortable. But then her mother clearly knew what she was doing so she didn't dare to protest.

When she stepped from behind the screen in the beautiful new gown, Richard said, 'I say!' and began to look excited. 'Beautiful!' He quickly took his place behind a camera and waved Kitty over to the backdrop of the bluebell wood. 'A nice natural setting for you, I think,' he said, his voice preoccupied. 'Now turn slightly away from me and glance back across your shoulder, and be sure to stand still until I tell you to move.'

Kitty self-consciously did as she was told.

'Wonderful!' he exclaimed as the camera eventually clicked. 'Now lean towards me and let your hair drape down across your neckline – that's it, lovely! Now hold your arms out to me and give a little pout. Well done, Kitty.'

He was so complimentary and excited that it was infectious and soon Kitty's confidence grew and there might have only been the two of them in the room as she did everything he asked her to. She suddenly wondered what Sunday would think if she could see her now, and just for a moment wished that she was there with her so that she could ask her for guidance. But then she pushed the thought aside and gave herself up to the pure joy of being in Richard's presence.

Chapter Twenty

'You did really well, my dear,' Max praised her as he drove them back to Chelsea sometime later. 'I'm sure Richard will have some wonderful shots from this afternoon's session and we should be able to see them before long. He has his own dark room and develops his photographs himself.'

Kitty smiled in the back seat as she basked in his praise.

'I've also been giving your name some thought. How about Kitty Nightingale? It has a nice ring to it, don't you think, Ruby, my love? And it's perfect for a singer.'

'Yes, I quite like that.' Ruby was keen to turn the subject back to herself now. Kitty had had far more than her share of attention for the afternoon, the way she saw it, so she began to chat of other things as Kitty sat silently staring from the window and dreamily thinking of Richard's handsome face.

Once back at the house Ruby dismissed her, saying, 'You'd best go and get Mabel to hang your new gown up for you. It was ridiculously expensive and we don't want it all creased on the big night, do we?' She then took Max's arm possessively and marched him off towards the drawing room as Kitty tripped lightly away up the stairs.

As it happened Mabel was already in her room when she got there, putting away her freshly laundered clothes. This was another thing that Kitty was finding strange. Back at Treetops, Sunday had taught the older girls to wash and iron their own clothes as part of her plan for their independence, but here everything was done for her. Mabel even came to her room to turn the bedclothes back for her each night and it was taking some getting used to.

'Oh, hello, miss,' the friendly maid greeted her as she eyed the box in Kitty's hands curiously. 'I shan't be a jiffy. Just need to finish this and I'll be out of your way.'

'Oh, it's quite all right, Mabel,' Kitty assured her, and as she gently lifted the gown from its box, Mabel couldn't stifle an exclamation.

'Blimey!' She came to stand beside Kitty and stroked the material reverently. 'Why, that is just *so* beautiful! I can't imagine ever wearing summink like that, let alone owning it.'

'I'm going to wear it for my first stage performance,' Kitty explained excitedly. 'And that's not all. I've been and had lots of photographs taken today for publicity.' Kitty found Mabel very easy to talk to, probably because they were of a very similar age.

'Really? Where did you have them took?'

'Mr Thomas took me to a photographer in Mayfair. He's very well known, apparently. His name is Richard Fitzherbert.'

Mabel snorted. 'Oh, he's well known, all right, miss. Always in the newspapers he is, with some pretty girl hanging off his arm. And he's rich too – has no need to work from what I've heard. His father is an earl, I believe. Cor, it must be nice to be born with a silver spoon in your mouth, mustn't it?' Then, suddenly remembering who she was talking to, she bit her lip. Ruby liked the servants to stay firmly in their place and wouldn't approve at all of her talking to her niece like this. And Mabel couldn't afford to lose this job, as her family in Vauxhall relied on her wages. 'Begging your pardon, miss. I didn't mean to talk out of turn.'

'It's quite all right.' Kitty smiled at her as she fetched a hanger from the wardrobe and hung the gown on it. Mabel quickly whisked it off her and placed it in the armoire. 'Now what's for dinner this evening? I'm actually quite hungry for a change.'

'I reckon Cook's done a leg of lamb,' Mabel answered as she made for the door, leaving Kitty to think about the handsome photographer and to remember the way he'd looked at her.

When she went down to dinner later on, she found Ruby in a dark mood. Max had left – to have dinner with another client, he had said – and she was none too happy at the prospect of spending an evening without a male companion.

Kitty, however, was still excited about the afternoon they had just spent and chattered away to Miss Fox about it. When she came to the part about the photographs the older woman scowled at Ruby.

'You took her to Fitzherbert's?'

'Yes, why shouldn't I?' Ruby snapped, ready for a row. 'Everyone knows he's a wonderful photographer and Max needed some photos to use for publicity.'

Miss Fox clamped her lips together and Kitty noticed that from then on the atmosphere became strained. When the meal was over she was glad to escape to her room. The second she had gone Miss Fox turned on Ruby furiously.

'Whatever made you take that young girl to the likes of Richard Fitzherbert?'

'Oh, Foxy, don't start, I can feel a headache coming on,' Ruby groaned, stroking her forehead dramatically.

Miss Fox glared at her. 'Don't come that with me, my girl,' she scolded. 'You can develop a headache at the drop of a hat, usually when you're hearing something you don't want to hear. But it's Kitty I'm concerned about. I thought it was strange when you agreed to have her after all these years of never giving her a second thought – but now I'm beginning to see the light. You want to exploit her, don't you? I'm not daft, you know! Your income is drying up, along with your admirers, because of your fondness for chocolates and gin, so could it be you want your own flesh and blood to go out and earn for you now?'

168

'Of course not,' Ruby denied, a little too quickly for the older woman's liking. 'You've heard Kitty sing. She has the voice of an angel and she wants to be on stage – so who am I to hold her back?'

'Hmm!' Phyllis Fox still wasn't convinced and decided there and then that from now on, she would be keeping a very careful eye on things.

The next morning Kitty was down in the hall waiting for the postman as usual, but once again there was no letter from Sunday and after the postman had gone she trooped into the drawing room with a miserable expression on her face. Mabel found her there when she went in with a feather duster.

'Are you all right, miss?' Kitty had a face as long as a fiddle.

'Yes, I'm fine thanks, Mabel. I'm just disappointed that I haven't received a letter from home as yet, that's all. I'm beginning to think they have forgotten me.'

'I'm sure they haven't, miss. But *this* is your home now.'

'I suppose you're right,' Kitty sighed.

'Look, I have to go out in a while to do some shopping for Cook. Why don't you come along an' keep me company?' Mabel suggested kindly. 'It won't be very exciting but at least it will get you out of the house.'

Kitty brightened instantly. 'I'd like that. Thank you, Mabel, but can't you please call me Kitty? "Miss" is so formal.'

Mabel glanced towards the door. 'Well, all right then . . . but only when we're on our own. Miss Ruby wouldn't like it if she heard me being over-familiar.'

The two girls set off with a basket and a list of things Cook needed, and when they reached the local market in Fulham, the sights and smells reminded Kitty of the market back in Nuneaton and she pattered happily after Mabel, eyeing the goods on the

169

various stalls. The first part of the market consisted of stalls selling food: fruit and vegetables, fish, meat and one selling freshly baked bread and cakes. Mabel went from one to another efficiently purchasing and ticking off the list of things Cook had asked her to get, and then the girls went on to the second part of the market where the stalls stocked everything from brooms and buckets to ribbons and bows. Kitty was relieved to leave the food market behind. The sight of hungry-looking children scavenging beneath the stalls for bruised fruit or anything edible they could find was very disturbing. She herself had never known what it was to go hungry, and she could only imagine how hard life must be for the poor little waifs.

'Would you just look at that colour,' Mabel said dreamily as she fingered a length of sea-blue ribbon. 'Wouldn't you feel grand with that in your hair.'

'Why don't you treat yourself to it?' Kitty suggested.

Mabel snorted. 'I can't be wasting money on fripperies. My wages go straight to my mum when I get paid. At least that way I know my brothers and sisters will eat, unless our dad finds the money first, that is, then it just goes straight over the bar of the Skinners Arms.'

Like Arthur Patridge, it seemed that Mabel too, came from a family where a drinking man ruled the roost.

Kitty felt sorry for her, and when Mabel moved on to the second-hand clothes stall to have a poke about, she quickly purchased the length of ribbon for her and popped it in her pocket. She knew that she was attracting more than a few curious glances. The other shoppers were clearly working-class people but in the fine skirt and blouse which Ruby had bought for her, Kitty felt as if she stuck out like a sore thumb. Quickly moving on, she caught up with Mabel and with their purchases complete, they set off for home, taking it in turns to carry the basket. On the way, Kitty gave Mabel the little gift she had bought for her, and the girl was so touched that there were tears in her eyes as she said, 'Oh, miss, you shouldn't have done that, but I'm glad you did and I'll keep it for special occasions. Thank you.'

When they arrived home, Mabel entered the house by the back door as was expected of the staff while Kitty entered through the front to find Ruby in the hall fussing over an enormous basket of flowers that had just been delivered.

'They're from dear Hector,' Ruby informed her gleefully. 'Do you remember him? You met him in my dressing room after my performance at the Prince of Wales. He's such a *sweet* man! And he's taking me out to dinner again this evening. You won't mind dining alone, will you, darling? Foxy will keep you company.'

'Of course not,' Kitty answered her just as a knock sounded on the door. The housemaid answered it to admit Max and Richard Fitzherbert – and the second she set eyes on the photographer Kitty felt hot colour flood into her cheeks.

'Ah, I'm glad we've caught you both in.' Max slung his hat onto the hall chair as if he owned the place. 'I've brought Richard along to show you the photographs. They are really outstanding. I'm sure you're going to be pleased with them.' His eyes settled on the basket of flowers then and he grinned. 'New admirer, Ruby? Good for you. Now shall we go and look at these pictures?'

Without waiting for an answer, he strode towards the day room, and incensed that he hadn't appeared to be the least bit jealous about her new beau, Ruby followed with a face like a dark raincloud.

Once inside, Richard took the photographs from a large envelope and proudly spread them out on a table that stood in the window. Kitty stared at them, hardly able to believe that they were of her. The one of her leaning slightly forward showed an awful lot of cleavage to her mind and was quite risqué, although no one else seemed to be anything but thrilled with them.

'Oh, definitely that one.' Ruby poked a plump finger at the one Kitty had been eyeing uncertainly.

'I agree,' Max said. 'That one will be perfect to put up outside the club. I shall take it to the printers this very afternoon and have it blown up into a poster advertising Miss Kitty Nightingale's debut performance. It'll have the clients flocking in. But now we really should do something about getting her a lady's maid.'

Kitty felt as if she wasn't even present in the room, the way they were discussing her. But then she supposed they all knew what they were doing so she remained silent and let them get on with it. And then for the first time she began to feel nervous as she thought of her opening night. What if she made a total mess of it? What if she forgot the words to the songs she was to sing . . . She suddenly realised they hadn't even been decided on yet! And what about rehearsals? Far more than a lady's maid, she needed a new teacher – for rehearsals and for expanding her repertoire.

And then her former teacher Miss Lark's words came back to her. 'Breathe in and out, relax and sing as if you are completely alone.' *Yes, that's what I'll do*, Kitty told herself. *I won't even look at anyone in the audience, I'll just focus on something above their heads.* But the big night was getting ever closer now and she couldn't prevent the butterflies in her stomach fluttering to life every time she thought about it.

Chapter Twenty-One

'Here, you'll never believe what I've just heard,' Ben told Sunday as he burst into the hallway at Treetops the next morning. 'I bumped into one of the Daweses' maids out in the lane on my way back from town and apparently, Mr Dawes had a massive heart attack last night. They reckon it's touch and go whether he'll survive. And that's not all – it was brought about when he and Maggie had a terrible row. She's run away from home!'

'No!' Sunday was shocked. Despite all her best efforts, they had seen little of Maggie since she had left them to live with Stella and Victor all those years ago, but she was still fond of her. 'I always thought it was Mrs Dawes who was unnecessarily strict with her,' she muttered, speaking her thoughts aloud.

Tom came out of his office then and Ben immediately repeated what he had heard.

'Oh dear.' Tom scratched his chin. 'Do they have no idea where she might have gone?'

'None whatsoever, according to the maid,' Ben said. 'Maggie just took off late last night without packing a thing, so she won't get far surely?'

'Do you think she might come here?' Sunday asked but Tom shook his head.

'I shouldn't think so. I think she'd already have arrived if she was going to do that.'

'Then what should we do?'

Tom could see that his wife was distressed, more about Maggie's disappearance than Mr Dawes's heart attack. 'I don't see that there's anything we can do without looking as if we're interfering. And no doubt she'll return when she's calmed down and hears what's happened to her father.'

'I suppose you're right.' But Sunday was far from satisfied. Now she would have Maggie to worry about as well as Kitty!

An awkward silence settled between them then and Ben turned to leave and make his way round to the stables. Things had got no better between him and Sunday, and although she was always polite to him, the young man felt that she was holding him at arm's length. *Perhaps it would be better if I were to clear off an' all*, he thought. At least then Sunday and Tom might stand a chance of regaining their old closeness without him being there as a constant reminder of Tom's brief affair. It was something to think about.

'Now eat lightly,' Ruby advised Kitty on the night of her debut. 'It doesn't do to try and sing on a full stomach. Max and I will take you out for supper when it's all over if everything goes well.'

Kitty couldn't have eaten much even had she wanted to because her stomach was in knots. Miss Fox watching her so closely didn't improve her nerves either.

'You know you don't have to go through with this if you don't want to, dear,' she said, earning a glare from Ruby.

'Why of course she does, Foxy. Do you have any idea at all how much time and money Max has put into setting this evening up? He'd be devastated if she backed out now.'

'It's quite all right – I have no intention of backing out,' Kitty told them both and Ruby seemed to relax a little as she loaded her plate with crispy roast pork and vegetables.

Kitty was glad when the meal was over and scurried away to her room to steal a few quiet minutes before Max arrived to drive them to the club.

He arrived promptly at seven o'clock and chucked her under the chin. 'All ready are you, my dear? I'm sure you're going to knock them dead!'

Kitty managed a weak smile as she and Ruby followed him outside. Max skilfully manoeuvred the car through the London streets, and as they entered Soho, Kitty frowned. It didn't appear to be too nice an area but then the club would probably be all right. Groups of heavily made-up women were standing on street corners and they all smiled at Max as he drove past them, much to Ruby's disgust. Eventually he pulled up in front of a small club. The poster he'd had made was pinned up on a noticeboard outside beneath a sheet of glass, and above the doors was a sign which was drunkenly leaning to one side with THE PALM BEACH CLUB written upon it, but the place to Kitty's dismay looked rather run down. She followed Max and Ruby inside, clutching the huge bag with her new gown inside and found that the interior didn't look any better than the outside. The glass in the windows was grimy and the wallpaper was peeling in places.

The manager met them and after introducing himself as Mr Ricardo he led them into a large room with tables dotted around a small stage and a bar along one wall. Dusty palm trees in huge pots, all looking in desperate need of a drink, were dotted here and there, and Kitty supposed this was where the club had got its name from. A band was tuning up at the side of the stage and the musicians welcomed her, making her feel a little easier. Max had already told them what songs she would be singing, and in what key, so there should be no problem there; Kitty would have liked to do a rehearsal with them, but there was no time for that now. The club would be opening shortly, but she wouldn't be appearing until later in the evening.

'Are you quite sure she's ready for this? She looks awfully young.' Mr Ricardo wore a worried expression on his face as he eyed Kitty dubiously up and down.

'I haven't got to be one of the best theatrical agents in the business by chance,' Max told him coldly and the manager shrugged. What would be, would be. If the girl did turn out to be a flop at least he wouldn't have to book her again. Clicking his fingers, he instructed a young waitress, 'Show Miss Nightingale to her dressing room.'

'Yes, sir, right away.' The girl smiled at Kitty in a friendly fashion and Kitty began to weave her way in and out of the tables as she followed her to a door in the back room.

'I shall join you shortly to help you get changed,' Ruby shouted after her and Kitty nodded. After passing through the door she found herself in a long corridor with other doors leading off it. There were also steps leading up to the stage behind the curtains that were presently drawn across it.

'Your first time here, is it?' the girl asked conversationally as Kitty kept close to her heels, dodging the other performers who were milling about.

'It's my first time anywhere,' Kitty admitted with a rueful grin. 'And I have to admit I'm a bag of nerves.'

'Don't be,' the girl told her. 'By the time you come on, the clientèle we get in here will probably be so drunk they won't even listen to you. Half the time they just carry on talking through the acts.'

It wasn't exactly what Kitty had wanted to hear but she was determined to make the best of it for Max. He had gone to so much trouble that she was terrified of letting him down now – and Ruby, for that matter.

The girl stopped in front of a door with paint peeling from it. Kitty's name was written on a piece of paper that had been tacked to it and the girl told her, 'This is your room then, such as it is. Good luck, dearie. I'll perhaps see you later.' With that she was gone and Kitty pushed the door open and stepped inside.

She found herself in a tiny box-like room that smelled of smoke, greasepaint, stale sweat and cheap perfume. A dressing table with a cracked mirror and a small stool in front of it stood against one wall, and a selection of paint and powder was set out on it, along with an overflowing ashtray. There was a screen in one corner for getting changed behind and a chair – but she saw at a glance that the only place where she could hang her precious gown was on a nail that had been hammered into the wall. With a sigh, she supposed it would have to do.

Once the dress was hung up she straightened her back and began to practise her scales as Miss Lark had taught her. Max had decided to go for tried and trusted numbers that were popular with the public. As the minutes passed Kitty began to grow ever more nervous. She had no idea what the time was as there wasn't a clock in the room, but at last the door opened and Ruby appeared.

'Right, let's get you changed. It's almost time for you to go on and there's a full house tonight,' she told her cheerily.

By then Kitty just wanted to get it over with so she stood still as Ruby helped her into her dress and fastened it. She then slid her feet into the pretty satin slippers and pulled her gloves on before sitting down at the dressing table for Ruby to brush her hair. They had decided to leave it loose as Ruby thought it made her look innocent. They had also discussed whether or not she should wear any jewellery but again Ruby had insisted that the simplicity of her gown was what made it so stunning.

'There then,' Ruby said with satisfaction after she had brushed Kitty's hair until it gleamed in the dim lights. 'You go out there and break a leg, my girl!'

When Kitty looked horrified she giggled. 'Don't worry, I don't mean it literally. It's just a showbusiness expression that's used meaning "go out there and make them sit up!"'

'That's a relief then.' Kitty managed a faltering smile as Ruby made for the door. This was all so new to her. 'What do I do now?'

'Just sit there and when it's time for you to go on, someone will come and take you into the wings. It should only be a few minutes now. There's a comedian on at the moment. He's awful and the audience are giving him a terrible time so you're going to have to work hard to get their attention back, but I'm sure you can do it. Good luck.'

Kitty gulped as she stared at herself in the mirror, wishing she was safely back at Treetops, or anywhere rather than here. But there was no going back now. All she could do was her best and hope that it was good enough. When the tap came to the door she almost jumped out of her skin as a voice called, 'Miss Nightingale. Into the wings, please. You're due on in five minutes.'

Kitty took a deep breath then followed the stagehand out into the corridor and up onto the side of the stage.

The poor comedian was indeed having a hard time of it. The audience were booing and as he made a hasty exit and hurried past her she felt sorry for him. But then the compère was announcing, 'And now, ladies and gentlemen, what you've all been waiting for, the star of the show, *Miss Kitty Nightingale.*'

He turned towards her, and forcing herself to put one foot in front of the other, Kitty walked onto the stage. The conductor of the band was watching her and when she gave him an imperceptible nod the band began to play. Focusing on the wall beyond the top of the audience's heads she hesitantly began to sing but she could barely hear herself above the noise as people laughed and chatted. There was a fug of cigar smoke hanging like mist about the audience but as she gradually relaxed, her voice grew stronger as she sang 'You Are My Honey . . . Honeysuckle', one of the tried and trusted songs Max had chosen for her. She was almost halfway through when she became aware that the place was growing quieter, and as she dared to glance at the audience she noted that she was beginning to get their attention – which spurred her on to try even harder.

When the song ended, there was a short burst of clapping before she started to sing the next number, 'Let Me Call You Sweetheart'. It was a song that Sunday used to sing around the house, and Kitty's voice rang out clear and true with emotion as she thought of her loved ones back at Treetops. By the time she was halfway through, everyone in the room was watching and listening, and you could have heard a pin drop. And then suddenly it was over and there was enthusiastic applause as people got to their feet, clapping wildly. Feeling overwhelmed, Kitty sought in the crowd for Ruby and Max. They, too, were on their feet and she was shocked to see that Richard was there too, as well the newspaper reporter that Max had told her about.

'Bravo! Bravo!' The crowd called out as she curtsied prettily and left the stage. The manager was waiting for her in the wings and he grabbed her hand and shook it up and down.

'Well done, Miss Nightingale,' he congratulated her with a beaming smile. 'I've never known the audience to be so quiet or so enthusiastic apart from when Marie Lloyd once performed here. I think I should like to book you to appear here again.'

'Hold on, old chap.' Max had come to join them by then. 'Not so fast. I have an idea Miss Nightingale is going to be in demand after this evening. Even if she does come back I think the fee will have to be negotiated. But now if you will excuse us, I'm sure our little star must be ready for a drink.'

With that he bustled Kitty back to her dressing room where they all squeezed in. Max produced a bottle of champagne and after sending for glasses they all drank a toast to her successful debut.

'Well done, Kitty,' Ruby praised her and Kitty flushed with pleasure. It was the first time that her mother had ever appeared to be proud of her, and it momentarily filled her with joy and hope for the future. The young reporter that Max had invited along was clearly smitten with her and scribbled furiously on a small pad as he asked her questions. She giggled as she sipped the champagne and answered them as best she could.

'I'm sure you have a wonderful career ahead of you,' he told her and she blushed prettily, feeling heady with success. It was a glorious feeling and she didn't want it to end.

'Now then – out, you gentlemen,' Ruby ordered bossily when the champagne bottle was empty. 'I need to help Kitty get changed now, if you please.'

'And then, if I may, I would love to drive you home,' Richard told her.

Kitty looked at Ruby for permission. The evening was just getting better and better.

'I don't see why you shouldn't.' Ruby nodded. Suddenly she was glad that she had left it too late to have an abortion all those years ago. Kitty could well turn out to be an asset.

Once they were alone, Ruby smiled at her daughter. 'You did really well. That audience was in the palm of your hand by the time you'd finished – and that's no easy task in this place, believe me. How did you enjoy it?'

'I loved it!' Kitty smiled back at her through the cracked mirror as Ruby undid her gown at the back.

'I can understand that. Success gives you a heady feeling. But this is only the beginning. Everyone has to start somewhere but there are better places in store for you, I'm sure of it, if you listen to me and Max.'

'Oh, I will,' Kitty assured her ardently and soon they were ready to leave.

Richard was waiting for her in the corridor with the prettiest bunch of flowers she had ever seen, tied up with pink ribbon, and as he led her outside with her arms full of the lovely blooms she saw Max and Ruby talking to the manager. He appeared to be paying them, but money was the last thing on her mind at that moment. Having Richard take her home would be the perfect end to the night and she followed him willingly.

Chapter Twenty-Two

As Mabel flicked aside the bedroom curtains the following morning, the spring sunshine streamed into the room and Kitty woke and stretched lazily. Then as she remembered the night before she purred like a little cat and pulled herself up onto the pillows.

'Morning, Miss Kitty.' Mabel carried a laden tray over to the bed and plonked it across her lap. 'I thought you might like a cuppa in bed, seeing as you had such a late night. Miss Ruby is already up and about, can you believe it? And Mr Thomas is here too, with the newspaper. There's a write-up about you in the *Daily Express*. Apparently, you went down a treat. Well done, miss.'

'Thank you, Mabel.' Kitty couldn't stop smiling. Last night after the show, Richard had taken her for supper to a very swish restaurant before driving her home, and when they said goodnight he had kissed her lightly on the lips, making her tingle all over.

Mabel had poured her a cup of tea but now Kitty was keen to see the report in the newspaper so she merely gulped at it then flung her legs over the side of the bed and reached for her robe.

'I haven't got time to get dressed just yet,' she told Mabel with a radiant smile and before the girl could say a word she had disappeared off through the door faster than a rabbit down a rabbit-hole.

Ruby raised an eyebrow at her state of undress when she erupted into the day room, but Max smiled indulgently as he passed her the newspaper. And there it was on page three, in big bold letters:

The Nightingale Enchants Her Audience

Miss Kitty Nightingale wooed the audience with her debut performance at the Palm Beach Club in Soho last night. Great things are forecast for the young singer. Her agent Max Thomas has said that she is a star in the making, and after her performance last night no one is doubting it.

Kitty gasped and by the time she had finished reading she was beaming from ear to ear.

'That's all well and good, young lady, so long as you don't let it go to your head,' Miss Fox commented sourly.

'Now then,' Max chided. 'Don't go spoiling it for her. Success is sweet, let her savour every minute. I've already been approached by one of the managers from a theatre in Drury Lane this morning and I've no doubt he'll be the first of many. You'll go far if you follow my advice, Kitty.'

'Oh I shall, Mr Thomas,' she said excitedly.

It was at that moment that the maid tapped on the door to bring Ruby her mail. The postman had just called by, and for the first time, Kitty didn't even think of checking through it to see if there was a letter for her. She had more important things on her mind now, like becoming famous!

'So what will happen now?'

'Well, I shall wait to see what offers we have, then choose the one I think best,' he said. 'But this means you will need another stage gown. It doesn't do to be seen in the same one too many times. It's a pity you and your aunt aren't the same size as there are any number she could have lent you, but I'm afraid they would all be far too big for you.'

182

Ruby struggled to keep her smile in place at the reference to her weight. It was a touchy subject just lately. But then, as she kept insisting, 'I am not fat, I am merely rounded, and men prefer women with curves!'

'What I can say is I'm fairly confident you will have bookings coming out of your ears from now on,' Max went on. 'It's just a matter of setting them all up now, so bear with me. I want your next performance to be well publicised in order to pull the audiences in, and I'm sure our reporter friend Guy will help us with that. He was quite smitten with you – but then so were half of the men there, from what I could see.'

Kitty preened then tried to suppress her glee as she noticed Miss Fox looking at her disapprovingly. Max stayed only long enough to arrange another shopping trip for the following day and as soon as he had gone Kitty went up to her room to get dressed while Ruby went back to bed. It was far too early in the day for her to be up and about, she declared, and she needed her beauty sleep.

Kitty was too keyed-up to be bothered with any breakfast so after coming back downstairs she wandered out into the garden as she did most days, and found young Arthur setting a row of spring cabbages in the garden patch.

'Cook was sayin' when I went in for me breakfast that you're a star now,' he said, staring at her adoringly.

She giggled. 'Not a star yet, Arthur. But hopefully I'm on my way.'

Arthur looked down and she suspected she saw nits run across the parting in his hair, poor little chap. He was so small and under-sized through poor nourishment it was hard to believe that he was almost fifteen years old. She asked him to hold out his hand then gave him the sixpence she found in her pocket. The coin would go a long way towards feeding his family tonight. Even so, the boy had his pride and he told her, 'Yer don't have to keep giving me money, miss.'

Kitty shrugged. 'My aunt gives me a small allowance each week,

183

which I never spend, so why shouldn't I? I'm sure you can find something to spend it on, eh?'

He nodded solemnly. In actual fact that sixpence would go on basic food such as potatoes and flour to feed his family, but he didn't admit that. They spent a little more time chatting until Kitty went back inside feeling rather restless. Now that her first perform-ance was over she was experiencing something of an anticlimax. *I'll go for a walk,* she decided. She wondered if she could find the way back to the market she had visited with Mabel. It was a fair way to Fulham but she had tried to remember some of the land-marks in various places and she supposed that if she did get lost she could always hop in a cab and get that to bring her home. She doubted she would see Ruby again before early afternoon and she had nothing else to do.

Kitty set off and was soon at the gates of the nearby park, which she visited regularly now. It was the only place where she didn't feel hemmed in by buildings, and it always reminded her of home. Moving briskly on, she followed her nose and after a couple of false turns she finally saw the market ahead. It was a beautiful day and she strolled amongst the stalls enjoying her freedom.

Eventually she stopped at a cart that was selling lemonade and bought herself a cup. It was as she was enjoying it that she noticed a young woman huddled in the doorway of an empty shop. The girl's head was bowed so Kitty couldn't see her face clearly but still there was something about her that seemed familiar . . . And then suddenly the young woman stood up. Her dress appeared to be of a fine quality although it was creased and grubby. She was very tall for a woman and big-boned, and her light brown hair had come loose from its pins and straggled around her face. And then it hit Kitty like a thunderbolt. She would know those soft grey eyes anywhere, even after all these years. It was Maggie, the girl that the Daweses had taken to live with them while she and Kitty were still small.

Maggie obviously recognised Kitty in the same instant and stood quite still as if she had been turned to stone.

'Maggie.' Kitty was breathless. 'I thought it was you. What are you doing here?'

Maggie shrugged as she scraped the toe of her boot along the cobblestones. It was then that Kitty saw how red and puffy her eyes were and realised that she'd been crying.

'Is anything wrong?' she asked, then berated herself for being a fool. Of course there was something wrong! A blind man on a galloping horse could see that. She glanced around for a sign of Mr and Mrs Dawes before going on, 'Are you alone?'

Maggie remained stubbornly silent but even standing away from her Kitty could hear her stomach rumbling. 'Have you eaten today?' she asked warily as she placed her hand on Maggie's arm.

The girl sprang away from her as if she had been scalded and pressed herself against the wall of the warehouse they were standing beside.

'What's it to you?' she cried hoarsely, suddenly wondering if this had been such a good idea. 'Go away and leave me alone.'

'No, I won't.' Kitty could be stubborn too. 'Not till you tell me what's going on.'

Maggie looked at her suspiciously for a moment before muttering, 'I've run away, if you must know! And don't try to persuade me to go back because I won't. I'd rather die than go back there.' She shuddered. 'I . . . I came here because I didn't know where else to go, although I doubted that I would find you.'

'All right, all right,' Kitty soothed. 'But just tell me . . . have you somewhere to stay?'

For a moment, she thought Maggie was going to ignore her but then the other girl slowly shook her head as tears trickled down her cheeks.

'N-not yet.'

'And have you any money?'

185

Another shake of the head was her answer.

'Right then. First off, let's get you something to eat,' Kitty said in a voice that brooked no argument, and taking Maggie's arm firmly she led her over to the stall that sold jacket potatoes. When she had purchased the largest they had, filled with cheese, she handed it to Maggie and the girl gobbled it down greedily. Kitty then bought her a mug of steaming tea and when Maggie had drunk that too she looked slightly better.

'Right, now we need to find you somewhere to stay,' Kitty said thoughtfully and Maggie started to cry again.

'Why would you do that for me? I was horrible to you when we lived at Treetops together.'

Kitty smiled. 'We were just little children back then,' she reminded her. 'And until you went to live with the Dawes family we had been brought up together as sisters. I missed you terribly for a time when you left, so did Ben.'

Maggie looked amazed and seemed to relax a little. 'Believe it or not, I missed you too,' she said. 'We heard that you'd come to live in Chelsea with your real mother. It must be nice for you.'

Kitty grinned ruefully. 'It is, but I have to call her Ruby or Aunt.' When Maggie raised a puzzled eyebrow, she went on, 'It's a long story. I'll tell you all about it one of these days.' It was then that she had an idea, and grabbing Maggie's hand she began to haul her along, saying, 'I know who might be able to put you up for a while. Come with me.'

They walked back to the house in silence. Kitty noticed that Maggie seemed tired and dispirited, but then that was to be expected after what the girl had been through. She entered the kitchen garden from the gate at the back of the house and just as she had hoped there was young Arthur hoeing amongst the vegetables.

'Psst! Arthur – over here!'

He glanced up, somewhat surprised to see Kitty standing over by the shed where he stored his tools and beckoning to him. They couldn't be seen from the kitchen window from there so he laid down his hoe and hurried across, noting that another young woman was with her.

'Do you think your mother might be interested in taking in a lodger – just for a few days?' she asked, getting straight to the point.

Arthur scratched his head. 'Well, we ain't really got the room,' he answered truthfully. But Kitty wasn't going to give in that easily.

'I just need somewhere for my friend here to stay,' she went on. 'And I'd pay well. Five shillings for two nights for a start-off. How does that sound?'

Arthur's eyes almost popped out of his head at the promise of such an amount. He already had the sixpence from this morning. With eggs at a penny a dozen and a loaf at the same price it would mean he and the family could eat like royalty for weeks. His mum might even be able to pay off a bit of the rent arrears.

'She'd have to kip down wiv me sisters in their room,' he said cautiously. 'An' we ain't very posh.'

'Oh, I wouldn't mind that at all,' Maggie piped up. She liked the look of Arthur, and anything was better than the prospect of another night in a shop doorway. London absolutely terrified her.

'All right then. But you'll have to wait here till I'm finished work. And it's a rare old walk to my house, I warn you.'

'Good, that's settled then.' Kitty beamed her thanks at him. 'Now I'll go and get you the money and coax Cook into giving me and Maggie something to eat.' The baked potato had, she knew, barely touched the sides, and she was sure that Maggie was still ravenous.

Maggie followed her down the path and as they entered the kitchen the cook raised her eyes.

'Ah, Cook,' Kitty said breezily, pulling out a chair for Maggie at the kitchen table. 'This is my friend, Maggie. We used to live together and we just bumped into each other. Is there any chance of you rustling up a meal for her?'

187

'I dare say I could manage that, if she doesn't mind a slice or two of cold pork and some of my home-made pickle,' the woman agreed. She liked Miss Kitty, there were no airs and graces about her, unlike her aunt who insisted on being waited on hand and foot like royalty.

Within minutes of the woman placing a meal in front of Maggie, she had cleared the plate. She looked very tired, so Kitty then suggested, 'Come up to my room for a while.' She didn't think that her mother would object to her entertaining a friend and she was hoping that Maggie would be able to have a rest before moving to Arthur's for the night. Then once she was gone it would be time to speak to Ruby and put the second part of her plan into operation. She just hoped that Ruby would agree to it, but only time would tell now. If her mother turned her down, then Kitty wasn't sure what she would do.

Maggie trudged up to her room but made no comment as she looked around at the luxurious surroundings. Her eyes were dull and lacklustre, and Kitty sensed that it must be something really bad that had made her run away from Witherley. But she didn't question her. Maggie clearly wasn't ready to talk about it yet but perhaps she would confide in her, given time.

'Why don't you pop onto the bed and have a rest for a while?' she suggested and Maggie kicked off her shoes and gladly did as she was told, feeling safe for the first time since she had left The Gables after that awful confrontation with her so-called father. Kitty pottered about quietly and when she looked towards the bed minutes later, she saw that Maggie was fast asleep so she tiptoed from the room.

Chapter Twenty-Three

'Maggie, wake up. Arthur is about to leave now.' As Kitty gently shook Maggie's arm, the girl started awake and flinched away from her. Then as she saw who it was, she let out a deep sigh of relief.

'Sorry. I . . . I'll come straight away.' She slithered off the bed and put on her shoes before following Kitty downstairs and out into the garden. Arthur was there waiting for them, holding the handlebars of his rusty bicycle.

'I'm afraid it's a couple of miles to where I live,' he warned them again, but Maggie told him that didn't matter.

'Here's the money I promised.' As Kitty slipped the coins into Arthur's hand his eyes lit up. 'And here's a little more for you and Maggie to get the omnibus home. I don't think she's up to walking too much further today. My friend needs a good night's sleep.'

Maggie smiled at her falteringly, wondering why Kitty was being so kind to her and wishing she herself had been nicer to the girl all those years ago.

'Ta, Miss Kitty.' Arthur felt like the cat who had got the cream as he thought of his mother's face when he gave her such a goodly sum of money – behind his father's back, of course. He was quite sure that she wouldn't mind having an extra person in the house for a while, for despite being as poor as a church mouse, Clemency Patridge had a heart as big as a bucket.

Kitty squeezed Maggie's hand encouragingly then and promised, 'I shall be in touch very soon, hopefully with a long-term solution to your problems, but in the meantime, I'm sure Arthur's mother will look after you.'

'Thank you,' Maggie replied in a choky voice then she marched purposefully towards the gate before she burst into tears at this unexpected kindness.

Once they were gone, Kitty turned and went to get tidied up before dinner.

The three women were enjoying dessert – a delicious apple turnover served with thick cream – when Kitty asked casually, 'Do you still think I may need a maid, Aunt?'

Ruby looked mildly surprised. Kitty had always seemed so averse to the idea whenever it had been mentioned before.

'I do, as it happens,' she answered as she served herself with second helpings, making Miss Fox sniff with disapproval. 'Why do you ask?'

'Well . . .' Kitty chose her words carefully. 'I just happened to bump into an old friend of mine earlier today when I was out walking. She's recently moved to London and is looking for a job – and I think she'd be perfect for me.'

'Has she had experience of being a lady's maid?'

'Not exactly,' Kitty answered cautiously. 'But we get on famously and she's a very quick learner. I think I would feel more comfortable with someone I know rather than a stranger.'

'Hmm . . . I dare say that's a point,' Ruby conceded. After Kitty's success the night before, pound signs were flashing in front of her eyes, and she was keen to keep the girl happy.

'Would this friend of yours want to live in? It would be preferable.'

'I think she'd agree to that – if there's a spare room for her, that is,' Kitty answered, trying to conceal her delight. This was turning out to be a lot easier than she had anticipated.

'There is one empty room as it happens, up in the servants' quarters, so why don't you bring her along to meet me?' Ruby suggested. 'We can discuss her wages and time off, et cetera, then.'

Kitty beamed. 'When would be best for you?'

'Not tomorrow because we're going shopping with Max to get you another new outfit,' Ruby reminded her. 'But I could see her the day after. Not too early though. Shall we say at three o'clock in the afternoon?' Then suddenly remembering something, she reached into the pocket of her gown and pushed a one-pound note across the table to Kitty. 'Your fee for last night,' she told her.

Kitty was silent with amazement, although Miss Fox grimaced. 'Is that all she earned? One pound?'

Ruby pouted. 'Now, Foxy, don't get interfering in that side of things. Max, as her agent, has to take his share – and then there are expenses, not to mention the money we need to spend on clothes for her until she has a decent selection of stage outfits in her wardrobe. They don't come cheap, as you well know.'

Miss Fox did know, but she also knew that Kitty would have earned at least ten times that amount the evening before.

'I'm more than happy with this,' Kitty said, hoping to prevent an argument between the two women. She had taken the five shillings for Arthur's mother from the money that Sunday had given her when she left Treetops, but now she would be able to put it back. Sunday had asked her to keep that as an emergency fund and that was exactly what she intended to do.

Sometimes she wondered again at the relationship between Miss Fox and her mother. Miss Fox didn't talk to Ruby as one would expect a maid to speak to her mistress, but then as Cook had told her one day when she had commented on it, the woman had been with Ruby for years.

Scraping her chair back from the table, she yawned then excused herself and went up to her room. It had been a very long day, one

191

way or another, after a very long night and all she wanted to do now was sleep.

Over in Arthur's house in Pimlico, Maggie was preparing to sleep in a room very different to Kitty's. Arthur's mother, Clemency, had welcomed Maggie when her son explained the situation, even before he had given her the money for Maggie's keep. Mrs Patridge might not have much herself but she was always willing to help those worse off, and from the moment she set eyes on Maggie she sensed that here was a very troubled young woman.

'You'll 'ave to share a bed wiv my girls, an' I've no doubt it won't be as posh as what yer used to, but yer welcome, luvvie,' she told her, and Maggie was grateful for her kindness. She had shared the family's meal with them – a thin stew of some sort with lumps of meat which were rather gristly – and then she had shared their fireside as they all chatted about what they'd done that day. The house was a tiny terraced two-up two-down in a grimy little court-yard that was bulging at the seams with bodies, and yet within minutes of being there Maggie felt herself beginning to relax. There was no standing on ceremony here, no strict regimes to follow as there had been at The Gables. Thank God she had bumped into Kitty when she had, or goodness knows what might have happened to her. She'd been at the end of her tether. Arthur's brothers and sisters ranged in age from a toddler to some older children but the banter between them was pleasant to behold.

After the meal, Maggie helped Mrs Partridge clear the table and wash up in the deep stone sink.

'I know this ain't what yer used to,' the woman apologised, for she sensed that Maggie had come from good stock and was upper class. 'And it ain't as clean as it could be neither, but it's hard with so many of us in the 'ouse to keep on top of it all. I take in washin' an' ironin' to 'elp make ends meet, so there never seems to be enough hours in the day. My Bert works as a wherryman – when he ain't in the pub, that is!' She snorted with laughter. 'But he ain't got a bad 'eart, not really.'

Maggie was amazed that anyone who clearly had so little could be so cheery, and yet the woman was obviously happy with her lot, and the love she felt for her family shone out for all to see. Clemency was a tiny little thing, as thin as a rake, in fact, with greying hair, but her blue eyes brimmed with laughter and Maggie guessed that she must have been a beauty in her time. Sadly, hard work and the births of numerous children had made her old before her time.

Maggie did what she could to help and eventually Mrs Partridge told one of the younger girls, 'Nellie, take Miss Maggie up to your room. She'll be sleepin' in wiv you lot tonight, so don't get chatterin' and gigglin' an' keepin' her awake 'alf the night now, do yer hear me?'

'Yes, Mum.' Nellie led Maggie upstairs, and when she showed her where they were to sleep Maggie's eyes widened with shock. There were two iron-framed double beds side by side, with hardly an inch between them.

'You can sleep in whichever yer choose,' Nellie told her generously. 'An' if yer get in now, yer can sleep on the edge before the others all come up. It's worse if yer squashed in the middle, though it ain't so bad in the winter 'cos the middle bit is the warmest then, see?'

Maggie gulped then managed a smile as Nellie skipped out of the room. She had no nightclothes so she quickly removed her dress, deciding that she would just have to sleep in her petticoat. She then looked around for somewhere to put it but every inch of space was taken up with the beds so eventually she just laid the dress on the floor, then she hastily used the chamber pot and got into bed. Tears leaked out of her eyes and slid down her cheeks as she thought of her predicament. But at least there would be no chance of the Daweses finding her here. Even so, she was sure that she would never be able to sleep. The flock mattress was lumpy, the springs dug in, and the blankets were scratchy, but surprisingly swiftly, exhaustion claimed her and her eyes closed.

'Sorry to disturb you so early, miss, but these were just delivered an' the lad who brought 'em is at the door askin' if there's a reply.'

Kitty blinked awake and was shocked to see Mabel standing there clutching a beautiful bouquet of pink tulips, wrapped in a pink satin bow. A little card was tucked in amongst the blooms and after plucking it out Kitty quickly read it.

Dearest Kitty, could you bring yourself to dine with me this evening? If the answer is yes I'll pick you up at seven, Yours, Richard xxx

Kitty was suddenly wide awake. 'Tell the boy to wait while I just scribble a quick reply, would you, Mabel? Oh, and do you think you could put those in water for me, please?'

Mabel chuckled as she went to do as she was asked. No wonder Miss Kitty was in such a good mood. So would she be an' all if she were to be woken with a bunch of flowers such as these. She wondered who they might be from as she went to find a vase big enough to accommodate them all.

Kitty's mood improved further when Max arrived while she and Miss Fox were breakfasting to tell her triumphantly, 'I have you a booking for next week at the Gaiety Theatre in Westminster.'

'Really?' Kitty leaped out of her chair and did a little twirl. After the success of her first performance she could hardly wait. Miss Fox merely looked on, saying nothing, and sensing her disapproval,

Max left soon afterwards, promising to return that afternoon to take Kitty and Ruby shopping.

'You know, you mustn't get carried away by all this,' Miss Fox said stiffly when Max had gone.

'What do you mean?' Kitty dared to ask.

'The adulation soon passes,' the older woman warned like a prophet of doom. 'And then you could find yourself alone, like your mother. She should have married a decent man while she was younger and had the opportunity, but she was too busy having her head turned.'

'But singing is so enjoyable!'

'It may well be, but there's more to it than that. It's the whole way of life. The late nights, the sound of the applause, the men who queue up to pay court to you – most of them married, by the way – it can become addictive.'

Kitty thought for a moment before asking tentatively, 'Did you know my father well?' All she had been told about him so far was that he had been a well-known politician and married into the bargain, but she was curious to know more.

As always when the girl asked any questions about her father, Miss Fox closed up like a clam. 'The least said about that the better,' she muttered and without another word on the subject she left the room.

Kitty felt a little annoyed. She had only been trying to find out a little more about her father, after all. She didn't even know his name – and if it was left up to Miss Fox, no doubt she never would! Still, she had all the time in the world to discover who he was, she consoled herself, and humming merrily she tripped away to find Arthur and ask how Maggie was before getting ready for the next shopping expedition.

She found him in the shed cleaning his tools.

'Your mate is right as rain,' he told her, before Kitty could even ask. 'When I left this morning, Mum was just doing her a bit of breakfast. She's been very quiet though. Mum reckons there's something on her mind that's troubling her.'

'I think your mother is right, but I'm hoping there will be a position here for her. My aunt has promised to meet her tomorrow afternoon, after which Maggie may be set on as my lady's maid. Will your mother mind her staying another night?'

He shook his head. 'Not at all.' He glanced up to see the housekeeper watching him from the landing window then and told her, 'I'd best get on, miss.'

'Yes, of course. Goodbye for now, Arthur, and thank you.' At least she could enjoy the rest of the day knowing that Maggie was being taken care of. But she couldn't stop herself from wondering what it was that had made her friend run away from home. It must have been something very bad indeed, she decided.

Chapter Twenty-Four

Once again that afternoon, Kitty found herself being dragged from one large emporium to another in search of a suitable gown for her next performance. Ruby was just declaring that it might be best to use the services of a dressmaker who was used to designing for the stage, when they found it. The dress was a beautiful sea-green shot silk, which clung to show off her slender figure, but again, it was very simple. Kitty fell in love with it on sight and when she tried it on, it fitted as if it had been made for her.

'Perfect!' Ruby declared. 'And the gloves and the satin slippers you already have will complement it.' Turning to the assistant who was hovering nearby she told her imperiously, 'We'll take it. See that it's wrapped for us, please.'

The girl was only too delighted to do as requested. The gown was very expensive and the shop-floor manager would be pleased with the sale. Ruby then treated herself to a gown in a striking royal blue, but this one had so many frills and flounces on it that Kitty barely knew what to look at first when Ruby tried it on. But then as she was discovering, Ruby was very flamboyant and loved to stand out.

By then Kitty was impatient to get home. She wanted to get ready for her evening out with Richard to ensure that she looked her best, and she could hardly wait to see him. Just the thought of his handsome face was enough to make her heart flutter. Luckily, Max had an appointment with a client, and he drove them home soon afterwards. Ruby looked none too pleased at having the trip curtailed. Kitty was sure she would have shopped all day every day if she could.

The moment they arrived back at Brunswick Villa, Kitty shot off to her room. Mabel ran a bath for her and after slipping into the sweet-scented water Kitty scrubbed herself from head to toe and washed her hair. When she was done, she went to sit by the open window to let her hair dry in the breeze as she looked out across the streets of Chelsea. She still missed the wide-open spaces that surrounded Treetops. There was nothing to be heard there but the sounds of birds and the wind in the trees, whereas here there was a constant hurly-burly. But even so she was beginning to enjoy her new life and felt more than a tiny bit peeved that none of her former family had taken the trouble to write to her. *Perhaps it's a case of out of sight out of mind*, she mused and tossed her head defiantly. She certainly didn't intend to write to them again until they wrote back to her.

'So what would you like me to lay out for you to wear, miss?'

Mabel's voice brought her thoughts firmly back to the present and she started. 'Oh, I err . . . I'm not sure. What do you think, Mabel? Mr Fitzherbert is taking me out for a meal so nothing too fussy, I think.'

'What about this one?' Mabel held up one of the new gowns Ruby had bought for her in a soft blue colour. 'This one would look lovely with the new coat you bought the other day, and it's smart rather than dressy.'

Kitty nodded in agreement. The dress was pretty but not overly fussy so Mabel carefully laid it out on the bed without a word although Kitty sensed that there was something she wanted to say. When she caught her eye, Mabel flushed and Kitty asked, 'Is there anything bothering you, Mabel?'

'Well, it's just . . . be careful, miss. Mr Fitzherbert has a reputation with the ladies, and I wouldn't like to see you get hurt. I mean, you're only seventeen, miss, and well, he's all of thirty. Oh dear. I hope I haven't spoken out of turn, miss.' Mabel looked mortified.

Kitty sniffed. As far she was concerned it was nothing to do with Mabel who she chose to go out with, and yet deep down she knew that the girl was only trying to look out for her so she forced a smile.

'I'm only going out for a meal with him,' she said quietly. 'It's not as if I'm going to marry him.'

'Huh! From what I've heard of him, no one will ever get him to put a ring on their finger. Mr Fitzherbert is the love 'em an' leave 'em type o' chap,' Mabel snorted, then remembering who she was talking to again she blushed an even deeper shade of red and said quickly, 'Looks like your hair is dry now, miss. Shall I dress it for you?'

The atmosphere was somewhat strained between them as Mabel helped her to get ready and Kitty found herself thinking what a good idea it might be to have Maggie as her maid, after all. She was sure that Maggie wouldn't go poking her nose in where it wasn't wanted, but it would all depend on the outcome of her interview with Ruby the following day. She could only cross her fingers that all would go well.

As soon as Kitty was ready she made her way downstairs where she found Miss Fox waiting for her in the hall ready to put in her two penn'orth.

'Now don't get staying out too late.'

Kitty eyed her coldly. Here was yet another servant trying to tell her what she could or couldn't do.

'Please don't concern yourself, Miss Fox. We're only going for a meal, not planning to elope.' She couldn't keep the sarcasm from her voice but Miss Fox appeared unfazed.

'That's as may be, but Richard Fitzherbert eats little girls like you for dinner and spits them out afterwards – so just be mindful of that.'

Ruby swept out of the drawing room then. She too was going out for dinner with her gentleman admirer that evening and was surrounded by a cloud of expensive perfume. Sensing immediately what was going on, she wagged her finger at Miss Fox.

'I hope you're not giving our girl a hard time, Foxy,' she scolded. 'She is entitled to enjoy herself, you know. Kitty is a very beautiful young woman and she's bound to attract admirers.'

'I know that well enough.' Miss Fox glared right back at her. 'And you shouldn't scowl. It gives you wrinkles.'

Ruby instantly composed herself and gave a charming smile as a knock sounded on the front door.

'Ah, that will be dear Hector. He's always so punctual.' Then glancing at Kitty, she giggled. 'Do have a good evening, my dear, but don't do anything that I wouldn't do.'

'Well, that gives her plenty of scope,' Miss Fox muttered.

Ruby glided towards the door just as the maid answered it – and sure enough, Hector Smethwick was standing there clutching an enormous box of expensive chocolates.

'Oh, Hector, you really shouldn't have,' Ruby simpered as she took them off him and handed them to the maid. 'A girl must watch her figure, you know.'

'Your figure is perfect, my dear.' He smiled at her adoringly and proffered his arm, and as the door closed behind them, Miss Fox rolled her eyes towards the heavens.

'She never learns,' she sighed, but Kitty had no time to answer before another knock sounded. Once again the little maid tripped away to answer it, and this time Kitty's heart skipped a beat as she saw Richard Fitzherbert on the step, looking so handsome that he almost took her breath away.

'I don't want her late back – do you hear me?' Miss Fox said rudely and Kitty wished the ground would just open up and swallow her. Richard, however, took it in his stride as he doffed his hat in her direction.

200

'I wouldn't dream of keeping her out too late,' he said smoothly, and then he and Kitty left too, and Miss Fox watched them go with her hands on her hips, looking none too pleased.

'I apologise for that. I think Miss Fox must be in a bad mood this evening,' Kitty said as Richard chivalrously helped her into his motor car. This was her first proper date with a gentleman – or with anyone, if it came to that – and Kitty suddenly felt shy.

Richard came around to the driver's side and hopped in beside her, before taking her hand and kissing it.

'Your Miss Fox need not worry. I shall take the greatest care of you,' he told her, and Kitty's young heart began to race again as he started the car and drove them towards the West End. Kitty was so excited that she paid no attention to where they were going and she kept peeping at him from the corner of her eye.

'I know of a very good restaurant in Dean Street in Soho. It's called The French House and the food is quite superb – unless there is somewhere else you would prefer to go, that is?'

'Oh no, that sounds lovely,' she said shyly, and they were soon negotiating the narrow streets of Soho, quite close to the Palm Beach Club.

'You look quite delightful this evening,' Richard whispered as he took her arm possessively and led her up a flight of stairs to the restaurant. 'Every man we meet will be green with envy when they see you on my arm, and every woman will be jealous of your beauty.'

Kitty felt as if she was floating on a cloud as she tripped along at the side of him. They were shown to a table set in a small alcove and from the waiter's greeting it was clear that Richard was a well-known client there. The table was laid with a crisp white cloth and gleaming silver cutlery; crystal glasses winked in the candlelight.

Richard ordered for both of them with Kitty's consent but truthfully afterwards she couldn't even recall what they had eaten, she was far too busy basking in the admiring glances she was receiving from Richard and the other diners.

When the meal was over he led her back to the car and told her regretfully, 'There is nothing more I would like than to take you dancing now, but I don't want to upset your aunt and deliver you home at an ungodly hour. Perhaps next time?'

Kitty doubted whether Ruby would even be in when they got back and she would have loved the night to continue. Even so, she did not wish to appear forward so she remained silent as he drove her home through the busy night-time streets of London. Once they were parked outside Brunswick Villa he slid his arm along the back of her seat and took her hand, making little shocks of pleasure ripple all the way up her arm.

'I've really enjoyed this evening. Perhaps we should do it again soon? And I'd like you to come to the studio to have some more photographs taken too, if you could spare the time, darling Kitty. There would be no charge, of course.'

Richard leaned over then and brushed her lips with his, and Kitty was disappointed when he moved away. He had awakened sensations in her that she had never known before – but he was walking around to her side of the car now, and once he had helped her out he escorted her to the front door, saying, 'I shall be in touch again very soon. Goodnight.'

'Goodnight.' Her voice came out as a squeak and she stood there as if she was glued to the ground, watching until his car turned the corner and disappeared from sight.

Her happy mood vanished instantly when the door was flung open by a stony-faced Miss Fox, who caught her by the arm and almost hauled her over the doorstep.

'Ah, so you're back then. I couldn't rest until I knew you were in safe.' The woman looked rather comical. She was covered from head to foot in a long nightgown covered by a thick robe, and her grey hair was twisted into a plait that hung across her shoulder like a snake.

'I'm not all that late,' Kitty protested. Surely if anyone should be checking her time in, it should be her mother – who was no doubt still out and about with Mr Smethwick somewhere – and not her mother's maid?

'It's late enough for an innocent young lady like you.' Miss Fox's disapproval was etched across her face. 'London is no place to be out and about at this time of night.'

'But I wasn't on my own,' Kitty pointed out.

'Precisely. Anyway, I suggest you get yourself off to bed now. I asked Mabel to wait up for you, to help you undress.'

Kitty obediently headed for the stairs after wishing Miss Fox goodnight. She couldn't see what all the fuss and palaver was about, but she didn't want the wonderful evening to end with a row, so she took herself off without another word. She'd be having plenty of words with her mother in the morning though, she decided.

Chapter Twenty-Five

Miss Fox seemed to have mellowed the following morning and over breakfast she asked, 'So what time is this friend of yours coming for her interview?'

'At three o' clock, after I've had my rehearsal with the band at the Gaiety Theatre.' She and the musicians had been working hard under the keen eye of their conductor, Boris. Kitty loved the band, and they loved her.

'Well, I just hope she's punctual and a respectable young lady. We don't want some flibbertigibbet leading you astray.'

'Maggie is *very* respectable,' Kitty replied. 'In fact, she had a very strict upbringing indeed.'

'Hmm, that's all right then – though I like to form my own opinions. I shall be sitting with your mother when she arrives.'

Kitty's heart sank. Miss Fox was so protective of her that she feared she might not give Maggie a fair chance, but the matter was out of her hands now and she would just have to wait and see how it went.

As soon as breakfast was over she escaped to the garden to find Arthur. He was pruning the rose bushes and gave her a dazzling smile.

'Mornin', Miss Kitty. An' what a grand mornin' it is, eh?'

'It is indeed, Arthur.' She returned his smile. 'And how is Maggie today? Is she all ready for her interview?'

'She is, although I reckon me mum will fair miss her if she gets the post. She's been a good help with the little 'uns and not a spot of bother. She's using the rest of the money you gave her to get an omnibus here so she don't get lost.'

Kitty nodded her approval as Arthur cut a beautiful red and gold wallflower and shyly handed it to her.

'Why, thank you. It's lovely.' Kitty sniffed the wonderful rich scent, then with a last smile she turned and hastened back to the house leaving Arthur to stare dreamily after her.

The rest of the morning was spent preparing for the show, and Kitty had no appetite at lunchtime. Just before three o'clock she positioned herself in the hallway and promptly on time there came a knock at the door.

'I'll get it,' Kitty told Mabel and hurried to answer it to find Maggie standing on the doorstep looking very nervous indeed. She had clearly made a great effort to tidy herself up as best she could. No mean feat at Mrs Partridge's, Kitty imagined. She had sponged the worst of the stains from her dress and pressed it with Mrs Partridge's flat-iron, and her face and hands were clean and her hair was neat and tidy. More than that she had been unable to do, seeing as she had fled from her home with nothing.

'You look very nice,' Kitty told her, hoping to build her confidence a little. 'They're all ready to see you, so come along and I'll take you in to them.' Then in a whisper, 'Don't look so worried. Just be yourself and everything will be fine.'

Maggie nodded and straightened her back as Kitty led her into the drawing room.

Ruby was reclining on the chaise longue as usual with the box of chocolates Hector had given her on a small table at the side of her, and Miss Fox had her nose buried in the newspaper. She liked to keep up with world events and read *The Times* from cover to cover every day. However, when Kitty and Maggie entered she folded it and laid it aside.

'Ah, Kitty, darling, here you are.' Ruby beamed. 'And this must be Maggie.'

Maggie gravely inclined her head. 'How do you do.'

Ruby frowned for an instant. The girl wasn't at all what she had expected. In fact, she was rather plain and solidly built. Kitty looked positively fragile beside her.

'Come and sit down, dear,' she invited and Maggie perched nervously on the edge of the seat Ruby pointed to and folded her hands primly in her lap.

'So, I believe you have never had any experience of being a lady's maid before?'

'No, ma'am. But I learn very quickly,' Maggie answered.

Ruby then went on to tell her of some of the things that being a lady's maid entailed and was gratified to see that Maggie was listening closely. Perhaps her being a rather dull girl wouldn't be such a bad thing, after all? At least Kitty would shine beside her.

Kitty stood back and said nothing, grateful to see that Miss Fox did the same, and eventually Ruby reached over and rang the bell. When Mabel appeared she ordered a tray of tea and cake for all of them and then when the maid had gone again she asked Maggie, 'So do you think the role would suit you? As I explained, it would involve a number of very late nights when Kitty has a performance.'

'Oh, I wouldn't mind that at all,' Maggie assured her. 'And I think the role of lady's maid to Kitty would suit me very well.'

'In that case why don't we give it a trial? Shall we say for one month?'

'I'd be very grateful of that,' Maggie said fervently and Ruby nodded before going on to tell her what time off she could expect and what wages she would earn.

'So when would you like to start then?' Ruby asked finally as Mabel struggled in with their afternoon tea on a huge tray.

'Today?'

Ruby looked a little surprised but nodded. 'Very well. I think

Miss Fox here already has a room in mind for you up in the servants' quarters, don't you, Foxy dear?'

The woman watched as the maid handed Maggie a cup of tea. She noted the way the girl held it and sipped at it, and saw at a glance that she had remarkably good manners. That was something at least.

'I do,' she agreed. 'So if you'd like to go and fetch your things I'm sure the housekeeper can have it ready for you in no time.'

'I err . . . don't have anything to fetch,' Maggie admitted, lowering her eyes and Kitty saw Ruby and Miss Fox exchange a glance. But neither enquired further. Both knew that life could throw up some surprises.

'I see. Then we must get you kitted out with some suitable clothes immediately. You could perhaps take her shopping for them, Kitty?' Usually Ruby loved shopping but not for the sort of clothes that Maggie would need.

The girl nodded eagerly, delighted with the outcome of the interview. 'I certainly can, and meantime Maggie can come up to my room while the housekeeper gets her room ready.'

And so it was decided. Maggie thanked Ruby profusely, feeling very relieved to think that she wouldn't have to spend any more nights in shop doorways. She wondered what might have happened to her if she hadn't had the good luck to run into Kitty as she had.

'Let's go and tell Arthur the good news. He'll be in the garden and can let his mother know that you won't need to stay at their place any more,' Kitty said, and taking Maggie's hand she tugged her through the house.

Arthur was genuinely pleased when he heard the good news.

'Please do thank your mother for me,' Maggie told him. 'Clemency has been so kind to me.' The Partridge family had very little in the way of material things, Maggie thought, but they all seemed content and happy, whereas she herself had never known a happy moment since the day she had left Treetops as a child. Oh, she was aware

207

that to the outside world she must have appeared privileged, but no one knew what went on behind closed doors and she hoped that she would never have to set eyes on her adoptive parents again for as long as she lived. The girl still had no idea that her chief tormentor, Victor Dawes, was now lying in St Peter's churchyard, in Witherley, no longer able to make her life a misery.

'Let's go and see how the housekeeper is getting on with your room now,' Kitty suggested and Maggie shook off her gloomy thoughts and after a final weak smile at Arthur, followed her friend inside.

The room, she discovered, was very basic but clean and comfortable and Maggie was happy enough with it. After pointing out where the servants' bathroom was situated, the housekeeper took her leave. A large sash-cord window overlooked the surrounding streets, and Kitty couldn't help but think what a long way down it was to the ground below when she peeped through it.

'I shall let you have some of my toilette things and a nightgown until we can go shopping.' Kitty turned her attention back to Maggie and again the girl was grateful, although she looked as if she might burst into tears at any second. 'Come on, let's go down to my room and collect a few things now, although I don't think my day clothes will fit you.' Kitty eyed her doubtfully up and down. Maggie was considerably taller than her. Very tall for a woman, in fact, and she was also a much bigger build. 'But never mind, we'll set off and go shopping for whatever you need first thing in the morning.' She was trying desperately hard to cheer Maggie up but the girl stood rigidly and was very pale.

Without thinking, Kitty held her hand out to her and asked, 'Are you missing your family?'

A quick shake of Maggie's head was her answer as she ignored Kitty's outstretched hand and again Kitty wished that the girl would confide in her. She was sure that Maggie would feel so much better if she did, but she didn't want to try and force her.

'I'm so happy we bumped into each other, we're going to have so much fun together. I feel as if you've brought a little bit of home with you,' Kitty said brightly, dropping her hand and turning towards the door. 'Come on, let's go and fetch the things you're going to need and get you settled in, then I'll introduce you to the cook and the rest of the staff. You'll soon get to know them all if you're eating with them in the kitchen.' She would have preferred for Maggie to dine with her mother and herself in the dining room as Miss Fox did, but hadn't liked to suggest it just yet. But she would when the time was right.

Maggie quietly followed her down to the next landing where Kitty's room was situated and Kitty began to toss things she thought her friend might need onto the bed.

First was a very pretty linen nightgown trimmed with lace that Maggie was reluctant to accept.

'Ruby bought me three so I won't miss it,' Kitty assured her as she saw Maggie's puzzled expression.

'If she is your mother, why do you always address her as Ruby or Aunt?' Maggie dared to ask. It had been puzzling her.

Kitty shrugged. 'Because that's what she wishes me to call her,' she said. 'To be honest, I think she is rather vain. Perhaps she just doesn't want people to know that she has a daughter my age?'

'How very odd.' Maggie perched on the end of the bed as Kitty added underwear, and soap, eau de cologne and rose-scented creams to the nightdress.

'Oh, and you'll need a hairbrush,' Kitty said. 'Luckily I have two, so one can be for you.'

That final kindness was Maggie's undoing and suddenly tears began to course down her cheeks.

'Ah, you poor thing!' Kitty was beside her in a second and put her arm about her. 'Do you want to talk about whatever is troubling you?'

She felt Maggie stiffen; she clearly wasn't used to being shown affection and for a moment Kitty thought that she wasn't going to answer her, but then she choked out, 'I don't think I *can* talk about it. It's too horrible and if you knew what had happened, you might not want to know me.'

Kitty said gently, 'I think I might already know. Sunday worried about you dreadfully when you left us, and I believe she always regretted letting you go. Mrs Dawes was very strict with you, wasn't she? You never seemed to be happy whenever we bumped into you. Sunday and Tom always felt that she was keeping you away from us deliberately. It was almost as if she didn't want you to have any friends. But whatever has happened, I would never turn my back on you.'

Maggie blinked through her tears. 'You wouldn't?'

'Never!' Kitty said vehemently, and felt the girl relax slightly.

Maggie was battling with her conscience but the secret she had been forced to keep was eating away at her and she longed to speak to someone about it. Until now there had been no one she could trust. Would Kitty be different?

For some moments, she sat lost in thought before stammering, 'It – it wasn't actually Mother that was the problem. It was Father.' She gulped, then said in a tiny voice: 'You see, he took my virginity.'

Chapter Twenty-Six

Kitty was so shocked and horrified that she was rendered temporarily speechless as she tried to digest what Maggie had just confided to her.

'You see?' Maggie sobbed even harder. 'I told you it was horrible and that you wouldn't want to know me. I'm dirty – *soiled* – nobody will ever want me now!'

'No, no, you're not!' Kitty told her hotly. 'It's not *you* that's dirty, it's *him*. I can hardly believe it. He always seemed to be such a nice man. But when did this happen? Is this why you ran away?'

Maggie nodded. Strangely, now that she had confided in someone, she felt as if a great weight had been lifted from her shoulders.

'It began when I was just a little girl,' she said tremulously. 'Father started to come to my room to read me a story on my nanny's day off. Then after a while he started to . . . to . . . touch me.' Colour flamed into her cheeks but she forced herself to go on. 'He said that all daddies did that to their little girls, but that I mustn't tell Mother or Nanny. After a time, I told him I didn't like it and he got angry. He said that if I didn't do as he said, the devil would come out of the mirror and get me in the night, and that it must always be our little secret. I believed him, and after that I used to hide under the covers when he left the room until it got light. Then when I was about ten years old he made *me* touch *him* . . .' She shuddered at the memory.

'But didn't Mrs Dawes realise that something was going on?' Kitty asked, appalled.

Maggie shrugged. 'I'm not sure. When I was about twelve I heard them having an argument one day and she told him that she didn't think he should go into my bedroom alone any more because I was getting older and the servants might think it was unseemly. By then my nanny had left and I had a governess and a tutor who only came during the day. I was so relieved because I thought he'd stop then and do as she said, but after that he used to wait until she went out. She was involved with lots of different charities, as you know, and often went out at night – so he would sneak into my room then. And then on my thirteenth birthday he came and said that I was a young lady now and it was time to learn how to please a man, and he—'

'It's all right,' Kitty said hastily. 'You don't have to go on.' Kitty herself was very naïve – in fact, Richard was the first man who had ever kissed her – but she had heard enough from the other girls at Treetops and the odd snatches of conversation between the staff to know vaguely what went on between a man and a woman.

'And you've had to endure this all that time?'

Maggie loudly blew her nose. 'Yes – but then suddenly I couldn't stand it any more, and a few days ago when he sneaked out of my room after he'd . . . Well, the next day, after a blazing row, I just snatched what money was at hand and left. I walked and ran all the way into town and thankfully I found I had just enough for the train fare to London. I'd thought that once I was here I would be able to somehow find you in Chelsea and get a job and somewhere to live, but I soon discovered it wasn't going to be as easy as I thought and I ended up sleeping in shop doorways. I don't regret running away though,' she said fiercely. 'I'd do the same again if they ever tried to make me go back. Or I'd kill myself.'

'You should have told someone what he was doing to you!' Kitty's shock had been replaced with fury now. How could a man who had forced Maggie to call him Father do such a dreadful thing to her? He was worse than an animal.

Maggie laughed, a brittle laugh that held no humour. 'What would have been the point? Mr Dawes was a well-respected member of the community while I was just a stray that had been lucky enough to be taken in by him and his wife. No one would have believed me.'

'But it's so unfair!' Kitty stood up and began to pace the floor, her hands clenched into fists. 'He should be punished and people should know what he really is.'

'No,' Maggie said softly. 'It's all behind me now and I hope I shall never have to set eyes on either of them again.'

'Was Mrs Dawes cruel to you too?' Kitty asked then.

'Not cruel exactly but I always felt that she was trying to replace the little girl she had lost with me and I could never live up to her. I was too fat; I was too cheeky. From the day I left Treetops I never had a decent meal again. Mrs Dawes instructed the cook that I must only eat healthy food and she tried to dress me like a little doll. The trouble was, I wasn't pretty enough to do justice to the clothes she bought for me. I was always too tall and big-boned whereas I was told her own daughter was dainty and petite like you. She was always more concerned about teaching me good manners than showing me any affection, and I learned very quickly that if I didn't do as I was told I would be banished to my room until I apologised. As you may remember, I'm a stubborn so-and-so, so I seemed to spend half my young life locked away upstairs. Believe me, within weeks of moving in with them I would have given anything to be able to return to Treetops, but it was too late by then.'

'Oh, Maggie.' Kitty was crying herself now at the thought of all the poor girl had gone through. But then, straightening up, she told her, 'You're quite right. You must put all this behind you and go on with your life now. None of what happened was your fault so you certainly have nothing to be ashamed of, so try not to think about it any more. You'll be perfectly safe here with me – and think what fun we're going to have! You'll see me perform at the Gaiety Theatre in Westminster soon and Max, that is Ruby's agent, says that after that I'll be in great demand.'

'I'm not really surprised,' Maggie told her. 'You always were pretty and even as a little girl you were always singing. It must be very exciting.'

'It is!' Kitty's eyes were glowing again now. 'And better still is a gentleman I've met. He's a photographer and he did the photos to advertise me outside of the club I performed at last week. He's said that he wants to take some more of me and he took me out to dinner last night.'

'What – just you and him? Didn't your moth— I mean Ruby, mind?'

'Not at all.' Kitty giggled, pleased to see that she had taken Maggie's mind off her own problems. 'She seems to have quite a large following of gentlemen admirers of her own so she isn't going to mind me having some, is she?'

'I suppose not,' Maggie agreed doubtfully, for she couldn't imagine that Sunday or Tom would have allowed Kitty to go out with a gentleman unescorted.

Kitty helped Maggie to carry all the things she had sorted out for her up to her room, and once they had put them away she led her downstairs to introduce her to the cook and the rest of the staff. Shortly after, Maggie dined with them in the kitchen and they all made her feel so welcome that she began to feel a little better.

'It'll be a great help having you to assist Miss Kitty,' Mabel told her cheerily as she speared a second lamb chop onto her plate. 'Miss Ruby takes forever to get ready, and I've been running between the two of 'em like a blue-arsed fly, not knowing if I was on me arse or me elbow.'

214

'That'll be enough of that kind of language at my table, if you don't mind, miss,' Cook scolded and Mabel winked at Maggie, who tried hard not to laugh.

Maggie stared down at her plate thinking how very different the atmosphere was in this house compared to that in The Gables, where she'd had to watch her ps and qs every second of the day. Perhaps things really would start to improve from now on, after all.

She looked slightly brighter when she met Kitty later that evening and asked, 'So what do I have to do in the morning and what time would you like me to come to your room?'

'I think the staff have their breakfast in the kitchen at about seven o'clock then perhaps about nine o'clock you could come to my room and run my bath and we'll decide what I'm going to wear,' Kitty suggested. 'Then after I've had breakfast we'll go shopping for some clothes for you.'

She was pleased to see Maggie looking slightly better although her red eyes betrayed the fact that she had been crying. Inside, Kitty was still seething. The way she saw it, Mr Dawes should be punished for the despicable things he'd done, but she was aware that she must respect Maggie's wishes and even if she had wanted to expose him for the pervert that he was, how would she go about it? Sunday and Tom still hadn't replied to any of her letters so she was becoming resigned now to the fact that she never would. Oh well. She had Maggie now, and Richard of course, and the future looked rosy. Even so, deep inside she knew that she was only putting on a brave face. She felt betrayed and abandoned, and wondered how her dear family at Treetops could have forgotten her so very quickly because she still missed them every single day.

The next morning, Maggie and Kitty set off for the shops bright and early. Ruby, as usual, was still in bed but she had left what the girls considered to be a very generous amount of money with Miss Fox to cover the cost of anything Maggie might need.

'Spend it wisely now,' Miss Fox warned and with a cheeky grin, Kitty promised her that they would.

They took the omnibus to High Street Kensington and were soon browsing around the store called Derry & Toms, which had been opened in 1860 by Joseph Toms and his brother-in-law, Charles Derry.

'I really don't want anything fussy, I'm not a frilly sort of person,' Maggie said stubbornly, turning her nose up at the dress Kitty was holding up for her to see.

Eventually she chose two day dresses. To Kitty's mind they were far too plain but Maggie seemed happy with them. One was a dark navy blue and the other was an unobtrusive pale silver grey.

'The grey one will be ideal for about the house and the navy one will be nice when I have to accompany you to rehearsals,' Maggie stated. They went on to find her a pair of sensible black shoes, the only sort she would look at, a good quality navy coat and hat, and a selection of underwear and nightwear.

'We still have a considerable amount of money left,' Kitty said, counting out the cash in her bag. 'More than enough to get you a fancier dress for going out in.'

'And where am I supposed to go, to wear a fancy dress?' Maggie raised an eyebrow. 'I only know you in London and I am a servant now, remember.'

'That's not strictly true. You know Arthur and his family, and Mrs Partridge has already said she'd love you to visit her on your days off. And as far as I'm concerned, you're my companion – that sounds much better and you could wear a pretty dress when you accompany me to the theatres on my performance nights.'

'I think all eyes will be on you while you're onstage; I'll be hidden away in your dressing room,' Maggie pointed out and Kitty didn't really have an argument for that. 'Besides,' her friend went on, 'we've spent quite enough money already and I intend to pay back every penny from my wages.'

'Well, at least we can go somewhere nice for lunch before we head for home.'

Maggie sighed but gave in gracefully as Kitty led the way to a very expensive little eating-house that Ruby had taken her to.

They arrived home mid-afternoon laden down with boxes and bags to find Ruby entertaining Richard and Max in the drawing room.

'Ah, here you are, sweetheart,' Ruby cried girlishly. She was wearing a gown that displayed so much cleavage, Kitty was in fear of her breasts spilling out of it, but she went in to join them as Maggie carried all her new things up to her room in several journeys. Kitty was still inwardly reeling from the terrible secret that Maggie had confided to her. Now she knew why the other girl had always looked so sad and haunted. But as ever, her heart began to beat faster at the sight of Richard and when he patted the sofa at the side of him she went to join him willingly.

'Are you all ready for your big night tomorrow?' Max enquired through a blue haze of cigar smoke and Kitty nodded.

'Yes. I have a class tomorrow morning here, to run through my songs and to practise two new ones.'

Kitty knew she still had a lot of stagecraft to learn, along with extending her repertoire, and her new teacher, Madame Sophie, was well known for bringing singers on. She had taught Ruby too, back in the day.

'Excellent, that's the ticket. And I have some more good news for you as well.'

'Really?' When Kitty gazed at him quizzically, he chuckled.

'Richard here has been showing some of the photos he took of you around and there's been keen interest from a modelling agency.'

Kitty frowned. 'What sort of a modelling agency?'

'Why, clothes modelling, of course. You must have seen the models in magazines wearing the latest fashions?'

She nodded. 'Well, yes . . . but I thought I was going to be a singer?'

'You are, my dear,' he assured her. 'But there's no reason why the two careers can't run side by side. There's a lot of money to be made from modelling. What do you think of the idea?'

Kitty noticed that Ruby was watching her avidly and she shrugged.

'It would be me taking the photographs, of course,' Richard piped up and suddenly the idea was more appealing.

'Then in that case I don't see why not,' she said quickly. It would mean she got to spend a lot more time with him at least. The money would be secondary, although she knew that lessons with Madame Sophie did not come cheap.

'Good, then go and take your coat off and we'll talk about it more tomorrow evening after your performance,' Max told her with a charming smile.

Kitty thanked him, then dashed upstairs to tell Maggie the good news. The girl was already in her room waiting for her but when Kitty told her about the modelling idea, she immediately asked suspiciously: 'Have they told you how much you'll be earning?'

Kitty merely giggled as she took her hat off and tossed it onto the bed. Maggie instantly picked it up to put it away.

'I don't have to worry about all that,' she said, ignoring a momentary flicker of disquiet. 'My aunt is looking after that side of things for me. She is my manager, you see.'

'Is she now?'

Kitty laughed again as she rang the bell for afternoon tea. She was as dry as a bone after all that shopping even after their stop for refreshment, but things just seemed to be getting better and better.

Chapter Twenty-Seven

Later that afternoon, after she had had a short rest, Kitty left her room to find Maggie speaking to Miss Fox on the landing.

'I think your friend has been very sensible in her choice of clothes,' Miss Fox said approvingly. 'But now I really must get on.'

With that she left them, and taking Maggie's hand Kitty dragged her into her bedroom. She was still stinging slightly about Maggie's muted response to her possible modelling prospects, but then Maggie was so cautious it was sometimes hard to believe that they were of a similar age. But then Kitty supposed that after what Maggie had been through she was bound to be wary of men, so she made allowances for her.

She was becoming accustomed to being waited on now though, and was actually beginning to quite enjoy it.

'So what sort of clothes did this Richard say you might be modelling then?' Maggie asked once they were alone. It was clearly preying on her mind.

'I'm not sure yet,' Kitty replied patiently. 'Dresses and such, I should imagine. Oh, it'll be lovely to be decked out in the very latest fashions and Richard says—'

'You seem to be very in awe of this Richard. How old is he?' Maggie interrupted as she hung Kitty's coat neatly away in the wardrobe.

Kitty was exasperated. 'Well, I don't know! I haven't asked him. About thirtyish, I should imagine.'

'Good. He's too old to be romantically interested in you then.'

Kitty flushed as she sat at her dressing table and tidied her hair in the mirror. 'He's not *that* much older than me,' she muttered sullenly and alarm bells went off in Maggie's head. 'In London you often see younger women on the arms of older men.'

'Well, if you ask me that's rather dangerous.'

'What do you mean?'

Maggie shrugged. 'Older men prey on younger women and I'd hate him to take advantage of you.'

'Oh, Maggie, you sound just like Miss Fox,' Kitty sighed. 'On a different subject, I think I might get changed for dinner. Why don't you go do the same? You could wear one of your new dresses.'

But the other girl shook her head, saying, 'If you don't need me for anything, I think I'll pop down to the kitchen and see if Cook needs any help.'

'But you're not paid to do that sort of work, you're paid to be my companion,' Kitty argued.

'Even so, you know what they say, idle hands make work for the devil and I'd rather keep busy.' And with that Maggie left, leaving Kitty to gaze after her.

The following morning, after Madame Sophie had gone, Kitty ran upstairs. Maggie was laying her clothes out ready for the evening's performance – although Kitty wouldn't change into them until she was in her dressing room at the theatre. Max had promised to take them there in his car and Kitty was starry-eyed.

'You'll have to help me with my stage make-up. Have you ever done anything like that before?' she asked Maggie.

Maggie snorted. 'When would I have needed anything like that back in Witherley? The furthest we ever ventured was to church or into town occasionally. It shouldn't be a problem though. How hard can it be to put a bit of make-up on?'

'But it's not ordinary make-up. It's very thick and looks quite horrible close to, although it looks good to the audience under the stage lights.'

'I'm sure we'll manage.' Maggie folded Kitty's new gown carefully into a long clothes bag then told her, 'That's about it then. We're all ready for later, but what do you want to do until then?'

'I know – let's go on a river cruise. We've got a few hours. I can point out some places of interest to you from the boat.'

Maggie seemed quite taken with that idea and shortly after, the two girls set out for Wandsworth Bridge, with Maggie looking very prim and proper in her new grey dress and Kitty in a much more stylish plum-coloured two-piece outfit. They joined the queue for a tour boat and were soon installed in seats on the deck of the *Chelsea Belle*. The hours slipped away and for the first time since they had been reunited, Kitty was pleased to see that Maggie seemed to be a little more light-hearted. As they cruised along the Thames, the guide pointed out the Tower of London and the girls discussed how terrifying it must have been for all the poor prisoners who had been incarcerated there in days gone by.

Once the cruise was over they took the Underground back to Chelsea. It was the first time either of them had dared to try it out, and each was so glad at the reassuring company of the other. However, it was mid-afternoon now, and Maggie pointed out that Kitty should have a nice hot bath and rest before her performance that evening.

They were still chatting animatedly about their outing and the places they had seen when they arrived back at Brunswick Villa, but their happy mood was interrupted when Ruby stormed out of the drawing room and said in a voice shaking with rage: 'Just where

221

the hell have you been all day? I was beginning to think you'd forgotten all about your performance this evening!'

Kitty had never seen her angry before and her smile vanished. 'We – I wanted to show Maggie around. And of course I haven't forgotten about this evening. We're back in good time, aren't we?'

Ruby swallowed and visibly brought herself under control. Fixing a smile on her face, she was suddenly all sweetness and light again. 'Of course you haven't. Forgive me, darling. It's just that I get worried when I don't know where you are.'

The sudden change of mood completely bewildered Kitty but she smiled back nervously then ran upstairs with Maggie close on her heels.

'Have a nice rest, sweetheart,' Ruby's sugary voice floated up behind them and Maggie shivered.

'Crikey, I thought we were in for it then,' she whispered once they'd gained the safety of Kitty's room.

'So did I,' Kitty whispered back. 'That's the first time I've ever seen her so irate.' Even so, she was determined that she wouldn't let it spoil her day. The best bit was still to come and she intended to enjoy every single second of it. Maggie ran her a nice hot bath and after washing her hair until it was squeaky clean Kitty lay back in the sweet-smelling bubbles for a nice soak.

It wasn't until shortly before Max was due to collect them that Kitty's nerves kicked in and suddenly she was a wreck.

'What shall I do if I forget the words?' she squeaked in a panic. 'I can't even remember what songs I'm supposed to sing!'

'You'll be absolutely fine,' Maggie told her calmly as she pinned Kitty's hair up. Just as she finished, they heard the doorbell ring and told her, 'This is it then. Come along. You won't want to keep your audience waiting.'

On legs that felt as if they had turned to jelly, Kitty followed her downstairs. Max and Ruby were waiting for them in the hallway and after taking Kitty's dress from Maggie, Max bowed theatrically and motioned towards the door.

'Your carriage awaits you, ladies,' he told them with a cheeky grin and they all trooped out to his car. Ruby sat next to Max in the front while Maggie and Kitty piled into the back.

'I think you'll enjoy this evening,' Max told Kitty as he started the car. 'And you'll find it's a very far cry from the Palm Beach Club.'

Kitty nodded as she twisted her fingers together nervously, but as they approached the theatre her mouth gaped open. Outside the doors was a large poster of her, and queues of people were waiting to go inside.

'We're going around to the back of the theatre to the stage entrance,' Max said, as he turned into a dark alley and pulled up outside a set of double wooden doors. 'Here we are.' And he leaped from the car and tapped at the doors. They were opened almost immediately by a small harassed-looking gentleman with a huge moustache.

'Ah, Mr Thomas, you've brought Miss Nightingale, have you?' The stage door keeper recognised Max instantly. 'Follow me, sir, and I'll show you to her dressing room.' And then they all stepped inside to what Kitty could only describe as absolute chaos. The corridors were full of people – stagehands, musicians, and the other artistes – hurrying to and fro, and somewhere in the distance she could hear the band tuning up and the murmur of the audience taking their seats while chatting animatedly.

The man stopped outside a door and Kitty flushed with pleasure as she saw her name on it alongside a big gold star.

'Here you are then, Miss Nightingale, break a leg,' he said jovially as he set off back to his post.

Maggie looked horrified. 'Whatever did he mean? Break a leg!'

Kitty chuckled. It was her turn to explain: 'It's a theatrical term meaning good luck.'

As they all walked into the dressing room, Kitty gasped with delight. There were flowers everywhere she looked and their perfume hung on the air. A bottle of champagne stood cooling in a silver bucket and boxes of brandied cherries, marrons glacés and other treats were scattered about every available surface.

'It appears that after your last performance you've already attracted some admirers,' Max told her. 'But now Ruby and I will go and take our seats and leave you to get ready. Just do your best, my little angel, and you'll be wonderful.'

But Ruby didn't appear to have heard him. She was busy reading the cards on the flowers with a peeved expression on her face. It didn't seem so very long ago that she had warranted this same adoration herself, but those days, it now seemed, were over. Still, she consoled herself, Kitty could earn them a lot of money, and that wasn't to be sniffed at so she wished her daughter good luck and floated away on Max's arm.

Maggie was clearly flabbergasted. This was her first glimpse of the theatrical world and life behind the scenes, and now she understood why Kitty's head had been slightly turned. Even so, she was there to do a job so she ordered bossily, 'Come along, you can read all these cards later. Right now, we have to get you ready.'

After completing Kitty's stage make-up, Maggie helped Kitty into her fine new gown, careful not to disturb her hair, which Maggie was rather proud of, seeing as it was her first real attempt at hairdressing for a stage appearance. The stage make-up hadn't been quite so easy to master, however. After her first attempt to make Kitty's face up, the poor girl had resembled a clown.

'Perhaps if we wipe off some of the rouge and tone down the lip colour, it won't look so bad,' Kitty suggested patiently.

Three attempts later they both agreed it looked much better – and even if it hadn't time was passing, so it would just have to do.

'I'm sure I'll get better at it with time,' Maggie apologised, wringing her hands. 'Perhaps we should have asked Ruby to stay and show us how to do it properly. That panstick stuff is so thick I reckon it would go on easier with a trowel.'

'It's fine,' Kitty said. And soon enough, someone tapped at the door and called out: 'Miss Nightingale, five minutes,' and she went to stand in the wings of the stage as the compère introduced her.

'And now, ladies and gentlemen, what you've all been waiting for, the little songbird who has taken London by storm, our own, our *very* own, *Miss Kitty Nightingale*!'

Tonight, Kitty sang three ballads to a packed audience, letting her rich, poignant voice flow above their heads, and at the end of the last one she curtsied to heartfelt applause. The girl felt a thrill of power run through her. She knew that she had the audience in the palm of her hand and it was the best feeling in the world.

Max and Ruby were waiting for her in the wings and the audience were shouting, 'Encore! Encore!' Kitty would have been more than happy to go back onstage and sing another number, but Max caught her arm and shook his head.

'You did very well, Kitty dear, but it's best to leave them wanting. Come on, I think we ought to go and open that champagne.'

When they arrived back at her dressing room they found Maggie frantically trying to find room for yet more baskets of flowers that had been delivered.

'It's like a florist's shop,' Kitty giggled as Max jubilantly popped the cork on the champagne.

'To our little nightingale,' he toasted when all their glasses were full and Kitty sipped at hers and basked in the glory.

Chapter Twenty-Eight

'Still in bed, is she?' Miss Fox asked the next morning as Maggie descended the stairs with the dress Kitty had worn the night before folded over her arm. Miss Fox had taken a real shine to Maggie; she was a down-to-earth kind of girl who would help to keep Kitty's feet firmly planted on the ground.

'Yes, Miss Fox, I was just taking this to sponge it and press it before hanging it away.'

'Hmm, that's her and Ruby lying in bed till all hours now,' Miss Fox grumbled, but she had no time to say more before a knock sounded on the door. It was Max and he was waving a newspaper at them with a grin all over his face.

'She's done it again,' he told anyone who cared to listen. 'There's a whole half page on how our Kitty stole the show.'

'That's all well and good, but she's still very young and we don't want it going to her head, do we?' Miss Fox retorted.

'Nonsense. Kitty is a sensible girl and she has me and Ruby to look out for her. Is Ruby up yet?'

Miss Fox tutted. 'Silly question. When is she ever out of bed before lunchtime?'

'Then kindly send someone to go and tell her that I need to see her,' Max said firmly.

Miss Fox hesitated for a second, but then with a shrug she asked Mabel to go and do as she was asked and the maid scuttled away.

Before too long, Ruby appeared at the top of the stairs, her eyes bleary and her hair all over the place.

'What is it that's so important, Max, that you should wake me at this ungodly hour,' she yawned as she came down the stairs.

He chuckled. 'Ungodly hour? Why, it's past eleven o' clock! Half the day is almost gone already. But come and read this. It's worth losing a bit of beauty sleep for.' He secretly thought Ruby could do with all the beauty sleep she could get, seeing her without her paint and powder, but he wisely didn't comment.

Once they were in the drawing room he handed her the paper and she scanned the piece about Kitty.

'I've already taken four more bookings for her this morning,' he crowed. 'And the fees they're offering are substantial.'

'Yes, well, there's no need to discuss that side of it with Kitty,' Ruby told him just as Kitty herself appeared at the door.

'No need to discuss what with me?' She rubbed at her forehead to try and ease the pain that was throbbing behind her eyes. 'I think I might have had a bit too much champagne last night.'

'Never mind about that, darling, you were entitled to celebrate your success. Come and read this, it's a wonderful piece, and Max and I were just saying that although you will be in great demand now, we don't want you to overdo it and tire yourself out.'

Her mother was suddenly all dishevelled sweetness and light again and Kitty accepted what she was telling her without question as she took the newspaper from her and quickly read the write-up.

'That's excellent!' she exclaimed when she'd done.

'It certainly is,' Max agreed. 'And I was just telling your aunt that I've already secured you four more bookings all over London.'

'Really?' Kitty hugged herself with delight. 'When is the first one?'

'At the beginning of next week, which will give us time to order another new stage costume. You're going to need quite an extensive wardrobe at this rate. Oh, and Richard is very keen to take some

227

photographs too. I was wondering if you could visit his studio again tomorrow afternoon?'

'Of course,' Kitty willingly agreed. 'Maggie can come with me.'

Max intervened with: 'Actually, I think Richard would prefer you to go alone. He doesn't like an audience when he's working and I think you would be more relaxed with no one else there.'

'Very well.' Kitty was feeling too happy to object although she couldn't help but grin as she thought of what Sunday's reaction would have been at the thought of her spending time alone with a gentleman. At Treetops, Sunday had tended to be very protective of her, and now Kitty was beginning to spread her wings and enjoy a whole new way of life. Just the thought of being alone with the handsome photographer made her heart beat faster. After agreeing a time with Max she raced off to share the good news with Maggie, but once again her friend was far less thrilled than Kitty had thought she would be.

'Are you quite sure that all this is what you want?' she asked, and Kitty tossed her head, suddenly annoyed with her.

'Why wouldn't it be? Doesn't every young woman dream of seeing her name in lights and being a star?' Then remembering what Maggie had been through she instantly felt guilty. Of course she was bound to worry about what every gentlemen's intentions were! Her voice was soft when she added, 'This is like a dream come true for me, Maggie. I hope you will try to understand.'

Maggie nodded, but inside she was extremely concerned. Kitty looked every inch the young lady-about-town in her smart new outfits, but she had had such a sheltered upbringing at Treetops and was surely still very naïve and vulnerable. *Still*, Maggie consoled herself with a touch of bitterness, *at least I'm here now to keep my eye out for her – and I've got no illusions*, and she then got on with putting Kitty's clean laundry away.

'Are you all right?' The words made Sunday start and hastily wiping her eyes on her sleeve she turned to see that Tom had just entered the room.

'Fine!' She silently berated herself for being so short with him, but she couldn't seem to help it. She was consumed with jealousy every time she thought of him lying with Ben's mother, even though she knew she was being unreasonable.

'Are you worrying about Kitty again?' Tom's voice was gentle as she began to straighten the fashion magazines on the small table in the middle of the room. When Sunday had read them she always brought them into this room for the other women and the older girls to enjoy. They were one of her very few indulgences.

'I'm naturally concerned that we still haven't heard from her.' Her voice was stiff, almost as if she were answering a stranger, and it wasn't lost on Tom who was almost at the end of his tether. Sometimes it was hard to remember now how happy they had once been. In truth, he was desperately worried about the girl as well. It wasn't like Kitty to just ignore them for all these weeks, but he had kept his thoughts to himself rather than worry Sunday any more than she already was.

'Your mother has just left with Mr Dewhurst to see Reverend Lockett and arrange a date for the wedding,' he informed her, hoping to turn the conversation, if it could be termed as that, to happier things.

'About time too – those two were made for each other,' Sunday replied. *Just as we were*, she wanted to tell him, but couldn't.

'They're talking about sometime in August.' Tom fiddled with the petals of one of the tall golden chrysanthemums that stood in a large vase in the window. George had grown them in the garden and they were quite stunning. 'She says that now they've finally got around to it, there's no point in delaying at their age.'

Sunday merely nodded and realising that she wasn't going to say any more he turned to the door – but then suddenly turned back

229

again. He felt as if he was walking on eggshells and had had quite enough of it.

'How much longer is this going to go on?'

Sunday looked at him and noted his cheeks were flushed. 'I don't know what you're talking about,' she lied.

'Oh, but I think you do.' It was the first time that Tom had addressed their situation this strongly. 'It's as if you can't bear me to be near you. Is that how you feel?'

Sunday shrugged and something in Tom seemed to shrivel and die as he was forced to accept that their relationship might truly be over. 'I see.' His voice was heavy with unshed tears. 'In that case, it might be better if I were to move into one of the spare bedrooms?' He prayed that she would argue with him and beg him not to do that but instead she merely shrugged again. Sunday wanted so desperately to try to explain to him how bereft she felt. She had loved Kitty as if she were her own child and now the girl was gone, and the sense of despair she felt at her loss had been heightened by discovering that Tom already had a child with someone else while she herself was barren. But the words stuck in her throat.

His shoulders visibly sagged but his voice was icy when he told her, 'Very well. I shall move my things out of our room straight away.' He left the room without another word.

Once he had gone, Sunday's face crumpled and she chewed on her knuckles as tears blinded her. To think that it had come to this, and worse still, to know that it was all her own stupid fault. *If only we could have had a child of our very own, things might have been so different*, she thought – and the resentment was back that another woman had given Tom what she could not. And why, oh why, had he never told her about the relationship with Cecile Randle?

It was much later that evening as Sunday was reading the newspaper after finishing her chores and seeing the children safely to bed that an article caught her eye.

Sunday read on and her heart began to beat faster. The article went on to say that Miss Kitty Nightingale, who had recently made her debut at the famous Palm Beach Club, was fast becoming a favourite on the music-hall stage, and although there was no photograph, the description they gave fitted Kitty to a T. Miss Fox had said that Kitty's mother was a well-known music-hall performer – so could it be that this was their very own Kitty, following in her footsteps? It just seemed to be too much of a coincidence. Kitty had always loved singing and had the voice of an angel, so if this Miss Nightingale *was* her, surely it would make it easier for them to find her? As yet, the girl hadn't written to them once, but perhaps now it would be worthwhile for Sunday and Tom to go London to track this singing star down. If it was their Kitty, it would be worth the trip. And at least it seemed as if their darling girl was safe and sound, and making quite a name for herself! Suddenly, she could hardly wait to talk to Tom.

'So, what would you like to wear today?' Maggie asked as she entered Kitty's bedroom the following morning and placed her breakfast tray down on the table at the side of the bed.

Kitty blinked as Maggie swished the curtains aside, letting the morning sunshine flood into the room.

'What time is it?' she asked grumpily.

'It's gone nine o'clock and time you were up and dressed. Now as I asked before – what do you want to wear?'

Kitty perked up as she remembered that she would be spending the afternoon with Richard. 'Well, seeing as I shall be modelling clothes today I don't suppose it really matters what I arrive in. Just choose something you think will be suitable.'

Maggie crossed to the armoire and began to sort through the outfits hanging there, eventually picking out a smart blouse and skirt. She laid them across the back of a chair then went to pour Kitty a cup of tea.

'I was thinking last night how strange it is that Sunday and Tom haven't been in touch with you,' she commented and Kitty nodded in agreement.

'I dare say they're too busy looking after the rest of the children in their care,' she answered airily but deep down she still felt hurt. Admittedly she had known that they didn't want her to leave them, but she had never dreamed that they would ignore her once she had gone. It was like a punishment.

Sometimes Kitty questioned why Ruby had bothered after all that time. She didn't even want her daughter to address her as 'Mother' and certainly didn't go out of her way to spend any time with her and get to know her, but then perhaps her conscience had finally pricked her now that she was getting older. On a couple of occasions, Kitty had tentatively asked about her father, but each time Ruby had changed the subject or closed up like a clam. Miss Fox had done the same. It was very frustrating but then Kitty was aware that a whole new world was opening up for her now, so she should be grateful to her mother for that, at least. Kitty was beginning to enjoy life in London. It was so different to the one she had led back in the Midlands where the highlight of the week had been a trip into the little market town where they lived. And of course, there was the undreamed of career that was opening up to her.

Sighing like a cat that had got the cream she settled back against the pillows and nibbled at the toast that Maggie had brought up for her. It wouldn't do to go putting too much weight on now that she was in the public eye, so she would have to watch her diet. Maggie frowned when she returned the half-eaten slice to the tray but Kitty ignored her as she swung her legs out of bed and stretched. Maggie was kind, and Kitty was pleased that she had been able to help her, but she was so . . . Kitty sought in her mind to find a way to describe the girl. Plain as a pikestaff and boring. Yes, that was an apt description, whereas she herself was beautiful. Richard and Max had told her so and it appeared that the public were in agreement with them, so from now on she intended to make the most of it!

Chapter Twenty-Nine

'Ah, here you are at last, my darling girl. Come in, come in,' Richard greeted her when Kitty arrived at his studio early that afternoon. 'And looking as beautiful as ever.' He took her hand and gently kissed each of her fingers in turn, sending tingles all up her arm and hot colour rushing into her already rosy cheeks.

He was dressed very casually in a shirt that was partially unbuttoned, showing off his hairy chest, and Kitty found it hard not to keep looking at him. The doors into the garden were open and she could hear the birds singing. It was hard to believe that they were in a busy part of London.

'I saw the other piece about you in the newspaper this morning.' He pointed to the paper lying on a table to one side of the studio as he began to set his camera up on a tripod facing a chaise longue. 'You will be so famous soon that I fear I shall have to make an appointment to see you.'

She dimpled prettily. It was nice to be admired as she was discovering more and more, particularly by someone as handsome as Richard. But then glancing around she asked, 'But where are the clothes I am to model?'

'Ah, I thought we would use today as a trial run,' he explained. 'And it will give us more time to get to know one another properly. It always helps when the model is fully at ease with the photographer.'

'Oh, I see. So . . . what do you want me to do?'

'You'll find a dress behind the screen. Pop that on while I finish setting the camera up, would you?'

Kitty obligingly disappeared behind the screen but when she saw the dress that Richard expected her to wear she sucked in her breath. It was the sort of thing she had become accustomed to seeing Ruby in, so low cut that it was almost indecent. Even so, she shrugged out of her sensible blouse and skirt and slipped it on, hoping to be able to adjust the bodice a little when it was in place. However, the many tiny buttons that ran all the way up the back of it proved impossible to manage by herself so after struggling with them for a few minutes she asked timidly, 'Could you help me with the buttons on this dress, please, Richard? I'm afraid I can't do them up by myself.'

He appeared so quickly that she jumped, and clutching the dress to her breasts she turned her back on him, blushing furiously. She blushed even more when she felt him trail his finger gently up her bare back.

'Your skin is just perfect,' he breathed huskily and she flinched. He was awakening very delicious but also very frightening feelings within her. She'd never been in a state of partial undress with a man before and while it was exciting she was also terrified and feeling torn in two. Half of her wanted to turn towards him and fling herself into his arms, the other half wanted to run for home and safety. Thankfully he must have sensed her unease for he then gently did up the buttons and after turning her to face him he kissed the end of her nose and led her to the chaise longue.

'Just lie back against that and try to look relaxed,' he instructed.

She tried to do as she was asked but his close proximity was making it very difficult. The fact that she kept trying to yank up the bodice of the pale blue silk dress didn't help either. She was afraid that he'd grow impatient with her but to her surprise after a few minutes of her fidgeting he began to laugh.

'I think we need to get you in a more relaxed mood. Let's have a little drink,' he said, crossing to a cut-glass decanter. He poured out two glasses and handed her one. 'I think you'll enjoy this. It's a very nice wine, not too strong.'

Kitty eyed it suspiciously. 'Isn't it a little early in the day to be drinking wine?' She could still clearly remember the raging hangover after her performance at the theatre the evening before.

Richard chuckled. 'It's never too early in the day to drink fine wine and this one is particularly pleasant. Go on – just try it.'

Cautiously she did as she was asked and was surprised to find that it was indeed very nice.

'That's better,' he told her approvingly when she'd drained the glass. 'I can see you beginning to loosen up already. Now lean back and throw your arm behind your head as if you're just about to take a nice little nap.'

After the wine, it was surprisingly easy to do. In fact, she felt so mellow she was sure she was in danger of taking the nap properly.

'That's it, lovely. Now turn a little towards me and move your chin up . . . that's it. Capital!' She could hear the camera clicking every so often and after a time she began to enjoy herself. After all, there was no one there but Richard to see her so she reasoned there was no need to feel self-conscious. A few times he came over to tease her hair or adjust the bodice of her gown, and she let him do so without demur. He was the photographer and he obviously knew what he was doing. At last he straightened and smiled, then poured them another drink.

'Excellent!' he told her. 'I'm sure there will be some beauties in amongst that lot.'

'Do you think we might start modelling the clothes properly now we've had a rehearsal?' she asked innocently and he roared with laughter as he sat beside her and draped his arm across her shoulders.

'Oh, my *dear* little Kitty Nightingale. You are so very refreshing,' he told her, then, 'Yes, I think we can start modelling the clothes properly very soon now, but perhaps one more rehearsal, do you think?'

She nodded as she started on the second of glass of wine he handed her. It tasted very fruity so she was sure that it couldn't be very strong. And what if it was? *I'm almost grown up now, aren't I?* she asked herself as she snuggled into his broad chest. She could feel his heart beating and hers seemed to be beating in tune with it. And then he gently took her glass from her and began to kiss her. She kissed him back eagerly and eventually she felt his strong hand close over the bodice of her gown and a little moment of panic made her stiffen.

'It's all right, sweetheart, I would never do anything to hurt you,' he told her throatily, barely moving his lips from hers and so she relaxed again and gave herself up to the moment. It was only when she felt his hands fiddling with the buttons on the back of her dress that she breathlessly pulled away. She longed to give herself to him completely but Sunday's warnings were echoing in the back of her head. *A man and woman should not lie together until they are wed otherwise an illegitimate child might be the result.*

'I'm so sorry,' Richard said instantly. 'But I'm afraid you're so lovely it's easy to forget myself.'

'It's all right.' Kitty got up and scuttled away behind the screen to get changed before he touched her again. She didn't know if she would be strong enough to stop him from going any further a second time. She struggled terribly with the buttons on the back of the dress but eventually she was in her own clothes again, and when she came from around the screen she found Richard adjusting his camera as if nothing untoward had happened at all.

'Would you like me to run you home?' he offered but she shook her head. At that moment, all she wanted to do was have a little time to herself to put her thoughts into some sort of order. Did the way that Richard had behaved mean that he had feelings for her?

She could only assume that it did, and if that was the case then she was thrilled. Oh, she knew that he was somewhat older than her, and with a reputation for being a bit of a ladies' man. Had Sunday been there she would have had something to say about her being alone with him. But Sunday *wasn't* there, she told herself smugly. She was living with Ruby now who was far more lenient and gave her far more freedom than she had ever known back at Treetops.

'I shall hop in a cab and be home in no time,' she assured him as she collected her bag. She was becoming quite adept at flagging the cabs down now so with a nod he saw her to the door.

'Come again about the same time the day after tomorrow,' he told her as he gently kissed her lips. Then patting her bottom familiarly, he sent her off down the steps to the pavement. When she turned back to say a final farewell he had already gone and she felt quite bereft. *I think I may be in love*, she thought and tripped away with a smile on her face.

Maggie was waiting for her when she got home but there was no sign of Ruby.

'She went out with a gentleman who called for her,' Maggie informed her. 'And it *wasn't* Mr Smethwick.'

Miss Fox appeared from the direction of the kitchen then and noting Kitty's glowing face she asked, 'How did the photographing go? Did you get to model some nice clothes?'

Kitty had a feeling that Miss Fox strongly disapproved of Richard so she answered hastily, 'It was just like a practice session today. Another one and Richard thinks that I'll be ready to start modelling properly.'

'Hmm, well, I still think that Maggie should come with you,' Miss Fox said grumpily then marched on as Kitty grabbed Maggie by the hand and hauled her upstairs.

'Richard kissed me today . . . *properly!*' she told the girl and Maggie looked anxious.

'I still think he's too old for you.'

'Oh, Maggie,' Kitty giggled. 'You sound just like Miss Fox. Surely I'm allowed to enjoy myself? We both are, and it would do you the world of good to get out and about too.' She glanced at her friend then went on more soberly, 'I know you've been through a lot, but in a funny sort of way both you and I had rather sheltered upbringings back at home. Sunday was like a mother hen, never allowing me out on my own and Mrs Dawes was very strict with you too. We deserve a little freedom now – we're both young women with minds of our own, after all. And anyway, for all Sunday's concern about my welfare, she soon forgot about me when I moved here, didn't she?' Kitty couldn't keep the note of bitterness from her voice and Maggie patted her arm.

'I'm sure she'll get in touch eventually. She always adored you, everyone knew that. She's probably just been very busy or perhaps she wants to give you time to settle in here without being seen to be interfering?'

'Well, she can please herself,' Kitty answered, disgruntled. The happy mood seemed to have flown now and suddenly she was dog-tired. 'I think I'll have a little nap. Do you mind, Maggie?'

'Not at all.' The other girl headed for the door. 'I'll go and see if there's anything I can help Cook with in the kitchen.'

Once she was alone Kitty's fingers rose to stroke her lips as she remembered how ardently Richard had kissed her. They felt almost bruised, not that she minded, and suddenly she could hardly wait to see him again. Crossing to the bed, she lay down and got comfortable, and soon she was fast asleep dreaming of Richard with a smile on her face.

Ruby was already in the dining room with Miss Fox when Kitty went down to dinner that evening and she was surprised to see that the table was set for four.

'Max is joining us,' Ruby told her. 'He has some rather exciting news for you, my dear.'

'Really?' The words had barely left Kitty's lips when they heard the sound of the front door bell.

Ruby smiled. 'That will be him now. I shall let him tell you himself.'

Max entered the room and promptly handed Kitty yet another newspaper, the *Westminster Gazette*. 'You've hit the headlines yet again,' he informed her.

'I dare say it's better than keep reading about all the unrest abroad and Emmeline Pankhurst and those silly suffragettes getting arrested,' Miss Fox snorted. 'Did you know they arrived at Buckingham Palace with a petition, and it ended up with them fighting with the police? Where's their dignity? I mean, I'm all for women having the right to vote, but the way they go about things is utterly shameless, if you ask me.' Then wagging a finger in Kitty's direction, she warned, 'I hope you have no silly thoughts about joining that unruly lot, young lady!'

'Foxy!' protested Ruby. 'Let's have no politics at the dinner table, if you please.'

Ignoring them both, Max kept his eyes trained on Kitty and went on, 'Because of this I have bookings for you right through to the end of June and still more requests coming in for later in the year. What with your singing and the modelling you'll be doing for Richard, I think you're going to be a very busy young lady indeed, my dear. I predict that by the end of this year, everyone in London will know the name Kitty Nightingale.'

Kitty beamed and tossed her head. Ruby was doing her best to look pleased, but deep down she was hurting. Max hadn't received a single request for her to appear anywhere and it seemed that she was destined to live in her daughter's shadow from now on. Still, at least it would guarantee her a good income in her retirement, and Kitty was so pliable and naïve that Ruby was sure she would do exactly as she was told, which was one blessing at least. Perhaps it hadn't been such a bad idea to finally claim her daughter, after all.

Chapter Thirty

In the blink of an eye they were into June and the heat in the city was almost unbearable. Kitty had been rushed off her feet dashing from one music hall to another and hardly knew if she was on her head or her heels as she tried to adjust to the adoration that was now heaped upon her by multiple admirers. Not that she was complaining. After each performance, she would return to her dressing room to find it full of gifts and messages from gentlemen who wished to take her out to dinner.

As it happened she had eyes for no one but Richard, and Maggie wasn't sure if this was a blessing or a curse. Admittedly she would have worried had Kitty been dilly-dallying all over the place with one admirer after another, but there was something about the photographer that she didn't like and couldn't take to. During the time they had spent together, Maggie and Kitty had become close, although they were still like chalk and cheese in both looks and nature, just as they had been as children, back at Treetops. Maggie had become very protective of Kitty, like a hen with her chick, which Miss Fox thought was no bad thing, for Ruby would not take on the role.

Sometimes, Maggie wondered why Ruby had wanted her child back. It certainly wasn't for any special mother-and-daughter time, for Ruby was very self-centred and selfish and never went out of her routine to make time to spend with Kitty. Despite the fact that

Ruby was designated her manager, it was Miss Fox who kept her eye on the girl and checked out the venues at which she was booked to appear.

'I'll not have her singing in some den of vice,' Foxy would declare. 'She's naught but a lass, after all!'

Maggie had heard her scolding Ruby one night and Maggie respected her for that. In fact, she and Foxy, as the woman had now instructed both girls to call her, had struck up an unlikely friendship. Maggie guessed it was because they both had Kitty's best interests at heart, which was just as well considering Ruby didn't seem to care what her daughter did, one way or another.

It was early one morning as Maggie was carrying the clothes Kitty had worn for her performance the evening before down to the laundry that Miss Fox stopped her on the stairs to ask, 'Is Kitty still in bed?'

Maggie nodded. 'Yes. I came home as soon as I'd helped her to get changed after her performance, but she went on to have supper with Mr Fitzherbert somewhere and I don't think she got in until the early hours so she's having a lie-in.'

'Is she indeed.' Miss Fox tutted. 'This really isn't good enough. I think it's time I had a word with Ruby. The girl isn't old enough to be staying out until all hours, as far as I'm concerned.'

Secretly, Maggie agreed with her although she didn't think it was her place to say it. Kitty was stirring when Maggie returned to her room with a tray of tea and she yawned as Maggie went over and drew the curtains, allowing the sunlight to stream into the room.

'Mm, isn't it a lovely day?' She stretched luxuriously and grinned as Maggie glared. The girl had lain awake until two in the morning waiting for Kitty to come home and felt as if she hadn't been to bed, whereas Kitty still managed to look beautiful despite the hours she kept.

'You were very late in this morning,' Maggie replied primly.

'Oh, Maggie dear, don't start. You sound like my mother!'

'Well, someone has to keep an eye out for you,' Maggie retorted as she poured the tea. 'Lord knows what Sunday and Tom would have said if you rolled in at all hours.'

She instantly felt guilty as she saw Kitty's face fall. Kitty tried to make believe that their lack of correspondence didn't bother her, but Maggie knew that it did. The couple had raised the girl as their own and had been far better parents to her than Ruby was, from what she could see of it. Already, Maggie was suspecting Ruby's motives for bringing Kitty to live with her. Kitty was now earning a very respectable sum from all her stage performances, but all she got after each one was a very measly payout from her mother. Maggie had tentatively raised this with Kitty once but the girl had defended the woman, saying, 'But you have to realise that a lot of the money I earn is going on building my wardrobe for now and paying back my mother for her expenses. Also, Max is my agent, and he needs to receive his cut of my fees.'

Maggie couldn't argue with that, although she had her own thoughts on the matter. Kitty was now doing at least three performances a week in various big music halls all over London as well as posing and modelling for Richard, who also paid her fee to Ruby.

Even so, as Kitty had pointed out, it was a beautiful day so Maggie suggested, 'Why don't we go for a walk in the park today so you can get some fresh air? It's far too nice to be stuck indoors.'

'I'm afraid I've arranged to visit Richard later this morning and I doubt I'll be back before dinner this evening.' Kitty peeped at Maggie over the rim of her delicate china tea cup. 'He told me last night that he has a whole new range of clothes he wants me to model.'

'Oh.' Maggie tried to hide her disappointment. She'd been hoping they might be able to spend some time together today. 'And what range would that be?'

Kitty shrugged. 'I have no idea. He said it was to be a surprise.'

'And would you like me to come with you to help you change?'

'No, not at all, I shall be fine,' Kitty assured her hastily. She was quite at ease with Richard helping her to get changed now, although she couldn't tell Maggie that, of course. Maggie was a little bit of a prude and wouldn't have approved at all had she known that the man had seen her in a state of semi-undress.

'In that case I shall go and help Arthur in the garden. He can give me all the news about the family.' Maggie began to select the clothes that Kitty would wear that day. Much as she disliked Richard, she would have preferred to go along to the studio with Kitty. At least that way, Kitty would be safe. There was just something about the man that gave her the creeps – not that she'd had much to do with men. In fact, the way she saw it, the only man she had associated with, her adoptive father, had almost ruined her life. And now the same gut instinct made her feel uneasy whenever she was in Richard's presence.

Kitty instantly felt guilty for leaving her alone again and reaching for her bag she delved into it and said, 'Why don't you go out and treat yourself instead? I'm sure you could find yourself a nice dress or perhaps a length of material to make one.' She held out her hand with five shiny shillings lying in the palm of it but Maggie shook her head. She was fiercely proud, as Kitty was discovering.

'Thank you, but there's no need for you to do that. I have more than enough clothes for my needs and I'm not paid to go gadding about.'

Kitty's straight white teeth nipped at her lower lip. It was still hard to think of Maggie as her maid. After all, they had been brought up together during the early part of their lives. But then the need to see Richard was strong so she didn't push the point but headed for the bathroom instead.

In Treetops at that moment Sunday and Cissie were sitting in the kitchen enjoying a glass of lemonade with the back door wide open as they tried to cool off. The younger children were all in the downstairs room that had been adapted as a classroom with their tutor, Mrs Lockett, and the older ones were at school so they were snatching a few peaceful minutes.

'Phew, I reckon I'm goin' to melt at this rate if it don't cool down soon,' Cissie commented as she fanned her face with her hand.

As usual lately, Sunday seemed a million miles away but she jerked her thoughts back to the present with a start as she asked, 'Sorry – what were you saying?'

'Oh, nothin' much.' Cissie eyed her critically. Sunday had lost weight recently and there were dark circles beneath her eyes. Cissie was aware that it was partly because her dear friend was still missing Kitty and partly because there now seemed to be a deep rift between Sunday and her husband. Treetops had always been such a happy place to live until recently but now Cissie felt as if a big black cloud was hanging over them all. The only bit of sunshine on the horizon was Lavinia's forthcoming marriage to Mr Dewhurst, although Sunday didn't even seem to be getting excited about that as yet. And now Cissie was worried that she might be about to add to her concerns when she told her what she had a mind to do – but it had been plaguing her for far too long as it was for her to put it off again, so taking a deep breath she said, 'I've been thinking that it's time I tracked down the baby that was taken away from me when I was locked away in Hatter's Hall.'

Sunday's eyes almost popped out of her head. Cissie certainly had her full attention now.

'What? But that was years ago. He'd be a full-grown man now. And what if he doesn't want to be found? Or he might not even know that he had another mother. He might not want to know you.' Then Sunday regretted her harsh words.

'I'm aware of that,' Cissie said miserably. Even now, after being married to George and having a family whom she adored, the child that had been wrenched away from her still haunted her sleep and she thought about him constantly. The staff at the asylum had told her that he had died at birth, but Cissie knew better. She had heard him cry and watched his tiny arms flailing in the air as they rushed him out of the room. It was common knowledge that the former manager there had sold illegitimate babies to childless couples and Cissie had always felt in her heart that this was what had happened to her son.

Sunday stared in shock at her old friend's bent head. She had thought that Cissie had managed to put the past behind her, but now it appeared that she was wrong.

'Are you really sure that this is what you want to do?' she said more gently. 'And have you spoken to George about it?'

Cissie sniffed as she swiped a tear from her cheek. 'Yes to both questions. It is what I want and George says if it will bring me peace of mind then I should go ahead with his blessing.'

Deep down, Sunday could understand it. Her bitterest regret was that she and Tom had never been blessed with a child of their own, but she could imagine how horrendous it would have been to have that little one snatched away from her. However, she wondered if Cissie had any idea how difficult the path she was about to take might become. For a start-off, many staff would have come and gone at the asylum by now and she doubted there would be anyone still at Hatter's Hall who remembered Cissie Burns. That would mean there were only the patients' records to go by, and it was highly unlikely the superintendent would have recorded where the baby went, even if it had survived at birth as Cissie believed.

'I suppose you think I'm mad, don't yer?' Cissie said, grieving. 'An' I know I should be grateful for the lovely childer me an' George have had . . . but I still feel as if a part o' me is missin' even after all this time. If only I could find him, even if he didn't want to know me. If I could just see him from a distance and know that he's all right, I reckon I could find a kind of peace. Do you understand?'

'I think I do.' Sunday reached out and gripped her hand. 'But truthfully, I have no idea where you should even start. Let's talk to my mother when she gets home, shall we? Perhaps she can suggest something.'

Cissie smiled and her face was transformed. She owed her freedom to Lavinia, and would do anything for her. At last she felt ready to begin her search, as she had longed to do for years, and even if that search proved to be unsuccessful, at least she would go to her maker with an easier heart knowing that she had tried to find the dear little soul she had never been able to forget. Back then, she had had no one to call her own, and so from the second she had felt the child quicken inside her she had dreamed of holding him or her in her arms. But it was not meant to be, and from the moment they had torn the little boy away from her, she had felt as if part of her was missing. Now she was ready to try to find him – because the way she saw it, nothing could be worse than not knowing what had become of her son, her firstborn child.

Seeing the conflicting emotions scud across Cissie's face, Sunday embraced her, saying, 'Don't worry, Cissie. If this is what you want, I promise we'll do all we can to help you,' and loving her as she did, Cissie knew she could believe every single word that Sunday said.

It was almost two hours later when Lavinia returned and Cissie, who had been waiting, almost pounced on her the second she set foot through the door. Seeing the agitated state the woman was in, Lavinia raised an eyebrow.

'Is something wrong, dear?' she asked as she took the hat pin from her hat and laid it on the hall table.

Lavinia Huntley had endured so many heartaches over the years but lately there was a glow about her and she was always smiling, no doubt because of the love her husband-to-be bestowed on her. William Dewhurst was the first man who had ever been truly kind to her and now everyone was hoping that from now on she would find the happiness she deserved.

By now, the younger children had finished their lessons and were scuttling about the place so Cissie whispered, 'Not wrong exactly, but I would like a private word if you could spare the time.'

'Of course I could.' Lavinia smiled apologetically at William who was close behind her and he instantly set off for the kitchen in search of a cool drink as Lavinia ushered Cissie into the drawing room.

'Out with it then,' she said with a smile. 'There's clearly something on your mind.'

And so Cissie tentatively told her of what she was hoping to do and Lavinia listened closely.

'Well, I can quite understand your reasons for wanting to do this,' she said. 'But you must realise that it's not going to be easy. It all happened such a long time ago and so much has changed since then.'

Cissie screwed her apron into a ball. 'I know that, but I don't think I'll ever rest easy if I don't at least find out if my baby lived to be adopted, and if so, where he went.'

Lavinia tapped her lip as she gazed thoughtfully from the window. 'Then we must do something about it. Will you give me a little time to think on it?'

'Of course – and thank you. You can have no idea how much this means to me.'

And with that, Cissie turned and left the room with a wide smile on her face. Suddenly it was as if she could finally see a tiny little ray of hope at the end of a very long dark tunnel.

Chapter Thirty-One

'Do you know what, Maggie, I think I might go early and surprise Richard. We agreed on three o'clock this afternoon but if I go now I might be able to persuade him to take me out to lunch.'

Maggie frowned to herself as she finished tidying Kitty's bed. 'Are you sure that's wise? He may be working and not wish to be interrupted.'

'Oh, he won't mind if it's me disturbing him,' Kitty answered airily as she began to hunt about for her bag. She had never been the tidiest of people and since she'd had Maggie to tidy up after her she'd become even worse.

Maggie stared at her enviously. Kitty had always been pretty as a child but now she was stunning. Her dark hair shone and her figure, as far as Maggie was concerned, was perfect, unlike her own big-boned frame. She only had to look at food to gain a pound in weight whereas Kitty could eat like a horse when she had a mind to and she never put on a single ounce. Kitty's waist was tiny and although she was only petite her legs were long and slender. She had developed pert breasts and her hands were tiny and delicate. But it was her face that stole everyone's heart. When she smiled, two charming little dimples appeared in her cheeks making her look incredibly young and vulnerable, which in Maggie's opinion she was. Her skin was flawless and her eyes, depending on her mood, could change from the colour of warm toffee to almost black.

The problem was, since making her debut performance onstage, Kitty had become even more aware of the effect that she had on the male sex and she was enjoying being the centre of attention, which Maggie considered to be extremely dangerous. There were so many unscrupulous men who might turn her head and take advantage of her, although thankfully at present she seemed to have eyes only for Richard and did nothing more than a little harmless flirting with the others.

Strangely enough, although Maggie was envious of Kitty she was also fiercely protective of her now, no doubt because Kitty had saved her from the streets. There was nothing that Maggie wouldn't do for her and she had come to love Kittie like a sister – which was why she was so worried about Kitty's obsession with Richard Fitzherbert. Not that there was anything she could do about it, she told herself now, apart from be there for Kitty if – or rather, *when* – he broke her heart. Kitty might think she was very grown up now in her fancy gowns, but in reality she was still very naïve.

'In that case I think I might go to see Clemency for an hour or two,' Maggie said resignedly. She often went over to see Mrs Partridge when she had a little spare time and the two had become friends. Maggie usually arrived with a few groceries for her and treats for the children, although the kindly woman always strongly objected. Maggie didn't mind spending a little of her wages on them at all. After all, she had everything she needed and she felt sorry for the family. Until she had met them she hadn't even been aware that such poverty existed. Even so, she envied the children for having such a warm-hearted woman for a mother. Mrs Dawes had always been cold and distant to her while her so-called father . . . She stopped her thoughts from going any further. She still had recurring nightmares about what Victor Dawes had done to her, and doubted that she would ever fall in love and get married now, in case the man she chose turned out to be like him!

251

'Ah, here it is!' Kitty's triumphant shout brought Maggie's thoughts snapping back to the present as Kitty plucked her bag from beneath the bed then raced over to her friend and planted a gentle kiss on her cheek.

'Have a lovely afternoon, and don't worry. I shall be back in plenty of time to get ready for this evening's performance.'

Maggie sighed and shook her head as Kitty charged from the room then went back to what she had been doing.

Once the cab pulled up outside Richard's house, Kitty gracefully hopped out of it onto the pavement feeling as if she might melt right away. The air was stifling with no breeze whatsoever, and the smells that were issuing from the gutters were making her stomach churn. Even so, after paying the driver her steps were light as she went up the steps to Richard's front door and rang the bell.

It was answered by a little maid who looked slightly flummoxed when Kitty hurried past her into the hallway without waiting to be invited in.

'Hello, Millie. Is Richard in his studio?' she asked cheerily.

'Well, err . . . yes, miss, he is – but he has someone with him. Was he expecting you?' Millie closed the front door as Kitty giggled.

'Oh, don't worry. I am a little early as it happens. Quite a bit actually, but I'm sure he won't mind me waiting until he's finished with his client. I'll just go and let him know that I'm here.'

'But, miss . . .' Millie's voice trailed away as Kitty skipped off in the direction of the studio. Once outside the door, she straightened her skirt and patted her hair into place before turning the handle but to her surprise she found that it was locked.

'Richard!' she called out, and gave the door a gentle tap. 'It's me

– Kitty. I thought I'd come a little earlier than planned. Are you dreadfully busy?'

For a few minutes, there was nothing to be heard but then Richard suddenly flung the door open, his face flushed and looking slightly annoyed.

'Are you almost finished?' she asked in her innocent way. 'If not, I can always wait out here.'

'No, I'm finished now. My client is just getting changed behind the screen. Come in.'

As he turned she noticed that his shirt-tails were hanging out of the back of his trousers and she also saw when she glanced towards the chaise longue that the cushions were in disarray. She could hear someone behind the screen and as Richard straightened the cushions a young woman appeared, also looking very pink in the face.

Kitty flashed her a smile but the woman stared back at her straight-laced. She was very pretty in a brash sort of way with blonde hair and big blue eyes and she put Kitty in mind of a china doll.

'This is Miss Melissa Hawkins. I was commissioned by her parents to take some portrait photographs of her,' Richard told her.

'Oh, I see. Then I'm sure they'll be wonderful,' Kitty said, wondering why the woman had had to change. The clothes she was wearing looked as if they would have been quite suitable for her to be photographed in.

'I'll just see Miss Hawkins to the door then. Do take a seat,' Richard said, as he took the young woman's elbow and hurriedly drew her out of the room. Once the door had closed behind them, Kitty grinned. Miss Hawkins obviously didn't like having her photograph taken if the look on her face had been anything to go by. Curious then, she crossed to the screen to see what was behind it but there were no garments in sight. *That's strange*, Kitty thought as Richard came back into the room but then she forgot all about it when he took her into his arms.

'As it happens, I think you're ready to move on to the next

253

stage of your modelling career now,' he whispered huskily when he had kissed her until her head was reeling. 'And I have the clothes here all ready to show you.' He moved across the room to a large trunk and when he lifted the lid Kitty gasped with shock and dismay.

'B-but they are all undergarments,' she said hoarsely.

Richard threw back his head and laughed aloud. 'Oh, my innocent little darling. They are still items of clothing and someone has to model them, don't they? There are magazines that advertise lingerie exclusively for ladies.'

Kitty's cheeks were burning. 'That's as maybe. But even so it would mean I would have to wear them in front of you, and that doesn't seem right.'

He pulled her into his arms again, his expression hurt. 'But surely you understand that in my job I've photographed dozens of women modelling lingerie. Don't you trust me, darling?'

'Of course I do,' she said doubtfully, but then he was kissing her again and it was so hard to think straight. He could awaken feelings in her that she had never known before and she had no idea how to handle them.

'Now,' he said, 'how about you try this on for me. They're the very latest thing, so I'm told.'

Kitty stared down at the corset in his hand and blushed an even deeper shade of red, if that were possible. Sunday had always told her that it wasn't seemly to discuss ladies' undergarments in front of gentlemen – and here was Richard asking her to parade in front of him in them! He was holding up one of the new-style corsets that were becoming popular. Ladies' fashions were changing rapidly, Kitty knew, and this particular corset was much more comfortable to wear, or so she had been told, than the heavily boned ones that had been favoured previously. It was made of a very fine woollen material with legs that she imagined would reach down to just above the knee, where they were trimmed with lace. The neckline was

254

also trimmed with lace and Kitty chewed on her lip as she imagined posing for the camera while wearing this garment.

'I'm not sure that I'd feel comfortable,' she murmured doubtfully and for the first time since she had known him Richard sneered as he stepped away from her.

'In that case I really can't see you being able to pursue your career as a model,' he said harshly. 'Models can't afford to be prudes. They must model whatever they are asked to wear and if you can't do that . . .'

Kitty's eyes were anguished as she caught at his sleeve. 'But I'm *not* a prude,' she said with a sob in her voice. 'It's just that I've never done anything like this before.'

He shrugged her hand away and crossed to his camera where he started to fiddle with the lens. 'Then that's a shame,' he said carelessly. 'There's a lot of money to be made from modelling – even more than you could earn singing, but if that's how you feel . . .'

'Perhaps I could just try it on,' she gushed, terrified of losing him and again he shrugged.

'Only if you want to. Never let it be said that I forced anyone to do anything they didn't wish to.'

Without a word, Kitty snatched the corset up and hurried off behind the screen where she fumbled with the buttons on her blouse. Her heart was pounding so hard that she was sure Richard must be able to hear it and she was all fingers and thumbs. At last she managed to get the corset on. It was a very good fit but she felt very embarrassed. No other man had ever seen her dressed – or rather, undressed – like this before, but her fear of losing Richard was greater than her self-respect, so she stepped from behind the screen with her arms folded across her chest.

Suddenly Richard was all smiles again as he advanced on her. 'Why, you look absolutely beautiful, darling,' he told her warmly. 'You have a lovely body so I really can't see why you should worry about showing it off.'

255

He gently unfolded her arms as she stared at him adoringly.

'Now, let's just make a few adjustments and then we can get started. We may as well do it now, this afternoon, and then I'll take you home. How does that sound?' He slipped the shoulder straps down, to show off her smooth, creamy skin, and tugged the front of the corset lower so that it revealed her cleavage. Her cheeks burned with shame, but she didn't try to stop him as he led her to the chaise longue and got her to lie across it before disappearing off behind his camera again.

'Now raise one knee – that's it, and let your arm dangle . . . very good. Now look towards the window with your other arm behind your head as if you are just relaxing . . . perfect. Keep that pose. Hold still . . . perfect!'

She could hear the camera clicking and after a few minutes of striking different poses she began to relax a little. It wasn't so bad really, she told herself. It wasn't as if she was lying there naked, was it?

After an eternity, Richard straightened and smiled at her. 'Well done.' He came and sat down beside her, and as his lips found hers she sighed with relief. But then the kisses were aimed at her shoulders and she felt his hand close around her breast and once again she was uneasy. Sensing that she was nervous, he sat up and said, 'Right, that's it for today. Now why don't you get changed and then I'll drop you off at home. I need to see Ruby anyway.'

Kitty's emotions were in utter turmoil, but when she was dressed again she began to feel better, and by the time they left the house to climb into his car she was smiling again.

It was mid-afternoon when Richard delivered her back to Brunswick Villa and after helping her from the car he followed her into the house.

'Right, my sweet. Good luck with your performance this evening, not that you'll need it.' He gently patted her bottom. 'Now I need to go and have a word with your aunt.' He disappeared off in the direction of the drawing room as Kitty stood there and watched him go.

Maggie was in the hallway, polishing the hall tables. After returning from her visit to Mrs Partridge she had asked what she could do to help since she hated being idle, but although they exchanged greetings, Kitty barely gave her a glance before scuttling away upstairs so Maggie continued with what she was doing. When she reached up to dust the large gilt-framed mirror that hung to one side of the drawing-room doors, she overheard the following conversation. Ruby asked, 'Well, did she do it?'

Richard laughed. 'Yes, but it took some persuading, I don't mind telling you.'

'Good. It should be easier from here on in then,' came the reply.

Maggie didn't want to be caught cavesdropping so she hurried away, but her mind was troubled. Was it Kitty they had been talking about? And if it was, what was it that Richard had persuaded her to do? After returning the polish and the dusters to the kitchen she went upstairs to Kitty's room, hoping the girl would tell her all about her day and put her mind at rest.

She found Kitty sitting in the window staring pensively down into the garden where Arthur was busy pruning the roses.

'Had a good day, have you?' Maggie asked as she entered. Kitty seemed pensive and not her usual cheery self at all.

'Yes, thanks.'

'And what things did you model today?' Maggie was struggling to get the conversation going.

'Oh, just this and that,' Kitty answered as a flush rose to her cheeks.

She clearly wasn't going to be drawn so after a few more light-hearted remarks, Maggie discreetly left the room. It was clear that Kitty needed some time alone. But what could have made her feel that way? Usually after spending time with Richard she chattered away about his many virtues fifteen to the dozen. Feeling more concerned than ever, Maggie left her to it. No doubt Kitty would come and seek her out when she wanted her.

It was after an early dinner that evening as Kitty was about to leave the table to start getting ready for the music hall that Ruby said, 'I've been meaning to have a little talk to you, darling.'

Miss Fox had just left the room and, curious, Kitty asked, 'What about?'

Reaching into the pocket of her gown Ruby withdrew some tiny sponges and a small bottle of dark brown liquid. 'Has anyone ever talked to you about err . . . the birds and the bees?'

Kitty looked confused – then as she realised what Ruby meant, she said haltingly, 'Yes, Sunday took all the older girls aside and explained to us about the monthly visitor and babies and um . . . how they were made.'

Ruby looked relieved. 'Good, then you'll know that should you be tempted to lie with a man, you could be left carrying his child?'

Wishing that the ground could just open up and swallow her, Kitty nodded numbly.

Ruby placed the bottle and the sponges on the table between them and said, 'My dear, you are grown up now. If you should ever feel the urge to make love with a man, these will prevent you from conceiving a child.' She then went on to explain how they should be used and by the time she was done Kitty was so hot and bothered that she couldn't even look her in the eye.

'I'm not saying that you *will* use them,' Ruby rushed on, seeing the girl's discomfort, 'but just in case you should need them, keep them close at hand. Your life is just beginning and we wouldn't want an unwanted baby to ruin things for you, would we?'

Like I did, Kitty thought bitterly. But her mother was still talking. 'An illegitimate child could mean the end of your career. You stand to lose *everything*, do you understand? So, better safe than sorry, eh? I know how fond you are of Richard and you are only flesh and blood like the rest of us at the end of the day.' She put the items into Kitty's hand and closed her fingers around them. 'Don't forget, it's only vinegar in the bottle so it won't harm you. But there, lecture over. Why don't you go and get ready now? Max will be here to pick us up in less than an hour and we wouldn't want to keep your audience waiting, would we?'

'No.' Kitty shook her head as she stumbled from the room and quickly closed the door behind her. She could hardly believe what Ruby had just said to her. It was almost as if she was openly encouraging her to lose her virginity, whereas Sunday had always told the girls it was something precious that should only be shared with their husbands on their wedding night. What a complete contrast the two women were.

For the first time in some while, Kitty longed to feel Sunday's comforting arms about her. Ruby had never so much as hugged her in all the time she had been here, but then Kitty had come to realise that Ruby loved herself too much to have any love left over for anyone else, even her own daughter. On legs that felt as heavy as lead, Kitty went upstairs to help Maggie pack her bag ready for her performance.

Chapter Thirty-Two

Heavy black thunderclouds hung low in a leaden sky as Lavinia sought Cissie out after breakfast one morning to tell her, 'I have decided to pay a visit to Hatter's Hall today, dear. Would you care to accompany me?'

Cissie turned alternately red and white in the face as she clutched her throat before croaking, 'Yes, I think I would. Thank you.'

Lavinia nodded. 'Good. But I can't promise anything, mind. It just seems as good a place as any to start the search for your son.'

Sunday and Tom were there and he reached instinctively for his wife's hand, but as always, she tugged it away then silently cursed herself. Why did she keep doing that? she asked herself, but the damage was done and Tom had moved slightly away from her. She was even more annoyed with him now, could he have known it, because as yet he hadn't made the time to go to London with her to try and track Kitty down. Admittedly she knew that he was always busy with jobs to do about the place but she was growing impatient and decided that if he didn't arrange a date with her soon, she would make the journey alone.

'I'll get Ben to bring the carriage around to the front in an hour. Will that give you time to get ready, dear?'

'Yes, thanks,' Cissie told Lavinia gratefully, suddenly hardly able to contain her excitement, and she scooted away to get dressed in her Sunday best hat and coat.

As the carriage rattled towards Hatter's Hall, Lavinia squeezed Cissie's hand.

'There were times when I thought this day would never dawn,' Cissie muttered thickly and Lavinia felt her pain. She knew only too well what it was like to lose a child in whatever circumstances, and was prepared to do all she could in her power to help Cissie find her long-lost son. All around them the rain was hammering down and the day was dark and dismal – and yet Cissie felt happier than she had for a very long time.

When the carriage pulled up at the gates of Hatter's Hall the gatekeeper opened them immediately and allowed them to pass through. Lady Lavinia Huntley was one of the benefactors of the Hall and was allowed entry any time she liked.

'I think you'll like Mr Wilkins, the new superintendent,' Lavinia told Cissie as they rattled down the drive towards the tall imposing building. 'He's a far cry from that dreadful Augustus Crackett, who was the superintendent here when you were admitted.'

When the carriage pulled up at the bottom of the steps, Ben jumped down from the driver's seat and helped the ladies alight. They then climbed the steps and Lavinia rang the large brass bell to one side of the entrance.

'Why hello, Lady Huntley,' the little maid who answered the door greeted them. 'Here to see Mr Wilkins, are you?'

'Yes I am, if it isn't inconvenient, dear.' Lavinia smiled as she peeled off her gloves and the girl bobbed her knee.

'I'll just go an' check if he's in his office, milady. I'm sure he'll be happy to see you.'

With that she darted away as Cissie glanced fearfully around. Just being there brought back dreadful memories.

'Why, Cissie, you've gone as white as a sheet, and you're trembling. Come and sit down.' Lavinia's voice seemed to come from a long way away and Cissie realised that she had broken out in a cold sweat. She plonked down heavily on the nearest chair as Lavinia asked another member of staff to run and fetch her a glass of cold water.

Cissie was sipping at it and trying to stop it from sloshing over the sides of the glass when she saw a rosy-cheeked man and the little maid who had answered the door to them approaching.

'Lady Huntley, what a pleasant surprise! We weren't expecting you,' he said jovially, extending his hand. 'What can we do for you on this rather dull day?'

Although they hadn't as yet been introduced Cissie took to the man instantly. He was plump and not overly tall, with a headful of thick, wavy, carrot-coloured hair, and when he smiled his eyes were kindly.

'I shall get around to that in a moment, Mr Wilkins, but first may I introduce my very dear friend, Mrs Cissie Branning?'

'I'm very pleased to me meet you, m'dear.' Mr Wilkins gave Cissie a dazzling smile before shaking her hand so hard she was afraid it might drop off. 'Now, how about we go into the day room?' he suggested. 'I've had this room especially adapted for the visitors of the patients. It's so much nicer for them than having to sit on the wards, and I'd welcome your opinion on it. There have been many other changes too,' he went on proudly. 'Many of the treatments for the patients have been stopped, since I considered them to be frankly barbaric. Only the most violent of our patients are restrained now.'

Lady Huntley nodded her approval as he led them into a large, light and airy room that had French doors leading out onto the lawns beyond. 'Normally some of the patients would be out there enjoying the sunshine but with the weather being so inclement today I'm afraid they've been confined indoors,' he explained as Lady Huntley and Cissie looked around.

Against one wall was a towering bookshelf with a very good selection of books on it, and tables and chairs were dotted here and there with various board games on them. The walls were all painted cream but some rather crude pictures that the inmates had painted added a splash of colour and altogether it was a very pleasant room indeed.

'I think it's a wonderful idea,' Lavinia told him sincerely. 'And I love the fact that you are encouraging visitors for the inmates now.'

'I prefer to call them patients,' he corrected her gently. 'After all, they are ill, and they are not in prison.'

'You are quite right. Please forgive me. But now I shall tell you why we have come today.'

As they all took a seat, the little maid brought in tea and biscuits, and the superintendent listened avidly as Lady Huntley told Cissie's sad tale, as Cissie had asked her to.

'How disgusting that the person who was there to be in charge of your welfare should abuse you,' the kindly man said chokily to Cissie when the tale was told, before blowing his nose heartily to hide his emotion, 'And now you are hoping to try and trace the child that you gave birth to within these walls?'

'Yes, please, sir.' Cissie's eyes were overly bright, and his heart went out to her. She was a middle-aged woman now but she had been merely a child then. How she must have suffered over the nearly three years she had been incarcerated here under a cruel regime.

'Then I suggest that as soon as we have finished our tea we go to the office and see if there is anything that might help us in the files,' he declared, and Cissie nodded eagerly. Soon after, she and Lavinia followed him back along the corridor to his office, which was dominated by a huge desk. Behind it was a tall bank of cupboards which was where all the files were kept.

'Now, according to what you have told me, you must have been admitted here late in 1880. That's all of thirty-four years ago, but your details should be here.' He placed a pair of spectacles on the end of his nose and began to check the dates on each of the cupboard doors. It seemed to take for ever but at last, when he was almost at the end of the wall, he cried triumphantly, 'Aha! Here we are, *Admissions, 1880.* And your name was Cissie Burns, you say?'

'Yes, that's right, Mr Wilkins.' Cissie held her breath as he began to flick through a number of dusty folders. At one point he stopped and removed one of the folders.

'I think this is it. *Burns, admitted from the Nuneaton Union Workhouse in November 1880.*' He blew on the folder, sending a cloud of dust into the air, making Cissie realise just how very long ago this had been. Her son would be almost thirty-four years old now, a grown man possibly with a family of his own. She could even be a grandma, for all she knew.

Mr Wilkins began to read the papers, his brow creased with concentration. 'It says you were a very disruptive inmate who was a threat to yourself and others. It was recommended by the doctor at the time that you should be restrained and that you should regularly undergo water treatment to calm you down.'

He carried on reading, but Cissie no longer heard the words. For a while she was back in that unspeakable world, in which she had prayed for death to come and claim her . . . *But I must stop thinking of that*, she told herself sternly. *That is not what I am here for.*

'It goes on to say that you gave birth to a boy in the following May' – Mr Wilkins glanced at her sympathetically and cleared his throat – 'and that he was born dead.'

'But he wasn't! He *wasn't*, I tell you! I heard him cry. I saw him waving his little arms, but they took him straight away from me and I never saw him again!' Cissie had leaped to her feet and there were tears on Lavinia's cheeks as she rose to put her arms about her. This was what she had feared.

'It's all right, Cissie,' she soothed. 'Try to stay calm. We believe you, don't we, Mr Wilkins?'

He nodded, his eyes sad. 'Yes, of course we do, my dear. It's an unfortunate truth that most of the babies that were born here back then were certified stillborn although some of their poor mothers swore that they weren't. After Augustus Crackett was dismissed, an investigation revealed that he had been running a very lucrative business on the side selling the little mites to childless couples. However, I'm afraid that this knowledge doesn't help us. We have nothing to go on. No way of knowing where your little man may have gone.'

Cissie began to sob then. Harsh wracking sobs that shook her frame as all her hopes turned to ashes.

'I'm so sorry, Mrs Branning.' Mr Wilkins looked so genuinely distressed that under other circumstances, Cissie could almost have pitied him.

He was strumming his fingers on the desk and then something occurred to him. 'There is just *one* person who may be able to help you,' he said. 'If she's still alive, that is. As you can appreciate, many staff have come and gone over the decades, but when I took over about fifteen years ago now there was one lady who had worked here while Augustus Crackett was in charge. She retired about five or six years ago now and must be approaching eighty. I remember her telling me once that she was responsible for looking after the babies that survived until Crackett found new families for them, but as I said . . . she may not still be alive.'

'But it would be worth finding out,' Cissie said, her voice ragged. 'Could you tell me where she lived?'

Rising from his desk, he approached another cupboard. 'This is the information I have on the staff,' he muttered. 'If I still have it, that is. A lovely woman she was, if I remember rightly. Ada Marshall was her name . . . Ah!' He held a sheet of paper up and smiled from ear to ear. 'Mrs Ada Marshall, Bluebell Cottage, Ansley Common, Nuneaton. Not far away at all, thankfully.'

'Thank you *so* much,' Cissie said as she mopped at her tears. At least there was a tiny ray of hope again now, and she would never be able to thank him enough.

She and Lavinia rose from their seats then and Mr Wilkins saw them to the front door personally. Once there, he shook hands with both of them and told Cissie, 'I wish you luck, Mrs Branning, and I will pray that you will be successful in the search for your son. Now I will bid you a very good day, ladies.'

They took their leave and once Ben had settled them in the carriage he asked, 'Where to now?'

'Ansley Common,' they said in unison and then they smiled at each other.

Suddenly a proverb that the Reverend Lockett had quoted at the Sunday morning Service sprang into Cissie's Mind:

Hope deferred makes the heart sick, but longing fulfilled is a tree of life.

Proverbs, Chapter 13 verse 12

Chapter Thirty-Three

'This is it, I think, Ben – can you stop here?' Lady Huntley shouted
through the carriage window as they rattled over Ansley Common.
They were outside a small cottage with a very overgrown garden
on the outskirts of Ansley village. Ben obligingly drew the horses
to a halt as Cissie leaned out to peer at the sign on the gate, which
read -L-EB--L. Some of the letters had faded away completely but
she was sure that this was Bluebell Cottage. The two women climbed
down from the carriage as Ben scratched his head.

'I dunno,' he said. 'The place looks deserted to me.'

His words struck fear into Cissie's heart. If the cottage was
deserted it could only mean that Ada Marshall had passed away
and with her would have gone any chance of ever finding her son.

'There's only one way to find out,' Lavinia said and pushed the
gate open. She and Cissie then picked their way down the brambly
path and Cissie found herself thinking what a shame it was that
the garden was so neglected. It must have been quite beautiful once
upon a time. Hollyhocks, delphiniums and other plants were battling
for supremacy with the weeds, but sadly it looked as if the weeds
were winning.

Once at the door, which was badly in need of a new coat of
paint, Lavinia lifted the tarnished brass knocker and rapped on the
wood – and then all they could do was wait, each with their heart
in their mouth. Just when it seemed that their journey had been in

vain they heard a tap-tapping noise from inside and then the door creaked open, the rusty hinges protesting loudly.

An elderly lady with a wizened face peeped out at them and Lady Huntley immediately told her, 'I'm so sorry to disturb you but the superintendent at Hatter's Hall, Mr Wilkins, gave us your address. He thought you might be able to help us trace a baby that was born there many years ago.'

The old woman held the door wide. 'You'd best come in then, though it's doubtful I'll remember. There were so many babbies born durin' the time I worked there, poor little mites.'

They found themselves in a large room that appeared to serve as both the kitchen and the parlour. It was very dark and so cluttered that Cissie didn't know where to look first. A huge fire was roaring in the grate despite it being summer, and a large tabby cat was curled up in a chair fast asleep at the side of it. The interior of Bluebell Cottage was a complete contrast to the outside, for everywhere was clean and tidy.

Strangely enough, despite the fact that she had aged, Cissie had recognised the woman instantly. Full of hope, she asked, 'Do you remember me, Mrs Marshall? The baby was mine and back then my name was Cissie Burns.'

Leaning heavily on her walking stick the old woman shook her head. Her hands were knobbled with arthritis and pain made her look even older than she was, although her piercing blue eyes were bright. Her hair was silver-grey and twisted into a long plait that lay across her shoulder and she was clad in a long skirt and blouse that had been out of fashion for many years. On top she wore a thick woollen shawl and a somewhat tatty but spotless apron.

'There were so many girls put in the Hall for no fault of their own,' she answered regretfully, 'and so many babbies. Most of 'em didn't survive wi'out their mother's milk, God bless 'em. But I allus did me best fer 'em, every last one of the little mites. That were

268

my job, see? Carin' fer the younger inmates an' the babbies that were born there.'

Disappointment pierced Cissie's soul. 'There was a bit of a scandal when I was admitted to Hatter's Hall,' she rushed on, praying that something would trigger the old woman's memory. 'The baby I bore was the result of me being forced by the housemaster at the workhouse, Albert Pinnegar. It was Lady Huntley here who rescued me and got me out of the asylum some years later.'

'Lady Huntley . . .' The old woman sat slowly down on the nearest chair and peered closely at Cissie and Lavinia in turn before saying, 'I do remember that case, as it happens. Didn't you give birth to a little boy?'

Cissie wrapped her arms around herself. 'Yes, but they took him away from me as soon as he was born and I never saw him again. I never even got to hold him.' Tears poured down her face. 'They told me he was dead, but I know he wasn't. I heard him cry.'

'Oh, Augustus Crackett told that to most o' the young women,' Mrs Wilkins said sympathetically. 'He sold the newborns, see, to desperate folks as couldn't have any o' their own. He were a wicked sod, so he were! But yes, I do remember you an' I also remember the babby. I don't remember where he went to though. How could I, after all this time?'

She watched Cissie's face fall and could see that this search for her long-lost son obviously meant the world to her. Cissie meanwhile was feeling devastated. Mrs Marshall had been her last chance at discovering where her baby had gone – and now that hope was no more.

'I see,' she said huskily. 'Well, thank you for at least listening to us, Mrs Marshall.' Then turning to Lavinia with her head down she said wearily, 'We'd best leave this good lady in peace.'

They were almost at the door when the old woman made a hasty decision and told her in a rush, 'I might be able to help you, Cissie

– but if I do, you must promise me solemnly that you will *never* let on that the information came from me. Can you make that promise?'

Cissie's heart almost stopped as she turned back to the woman.

'The thing is . . .' The old woman licked her dry lips. 'I sometimes used to make a note of who'd taken the young 'uns, see? It was strictly against the rules, you understand, and if old Crackett had ever found out, my neck would have been on the line an' I'd have been instantly dismissed. But if the babbies were goin' to live locally I liked to try an' keep an eye out for 'em. I got fond o' the little mites, see, an' I worried that they were goin' to good homes. O' course I didn't have time to check on all of 'em, what wi' havin' me own little 'uns to look after at home but me intentions were good. I should still have those notes somewhere.'

The two visitors waited, hardly daring to breathe, as the old woman stared thoughtfully off into space. 'Now where did I put 'em?' she wondered aloud and then she suddenly got up and began to hobble across to a large old dresser that stood against one wall. She bent with a groan and opened the cupboard beneath it, and began to sift through a mountain of paper and scraps, then eventually withdrew a battered old book.

'Here it is!' she wheezed. 'I were worried for a while there that I might have thrown it out. Now what date did you say the child was born?'

Cissie hastily told her again and the old woman sank back into her chair and began to flick through the pages.

'Here it is,' she cried jubilantly. 'It were a couple from Bedworth who took him. *Tate!* That were their name. The chap had a grocery shop somewhere in the town centre. O' course, I couldn't guarantee that it's still there, but at least it's a bit o' sommat fer you to go on.' She smiled kindly at Cissie then, who was shaking with nerves, before asking, 'But are yer quite sure it's a good idea to rake up the past, pet? Yer son would be a grown man now an' might not appreciate knowin' he ain't who he thought he was. His parents might not 'ave told him that he wasn't theirs by birth.'

'I've thought o' that,' Cissie replied. 'An' I promise you that if I do find him, I shall be careful how I approach him. The last thing I want to do is cause him any upset. But if I can just see him an' know that he's well, that will be enough even if I never get to know him.'

'In that case I wish yer well wi' yer search,' the old woman said with a sad smile. 'Yer can't begin to understand how bad it were for us who worked there who didn't approve o' the goin's-on.'

'So why didn't you do something to stop it?' Cissie asked before she could stop herself and instantly the old woman's eyes clouded.

'Eeh, if only things were that simple.' She shook her head. 'Back then we knew better than to try an' cross Augustus Crackett. The man were pure evil through an' through, an' those that did try to change things lived to regret it, believe you me. Bad things happened to them an' their families, an' I were a widow wi' a young family to support. My man were killed in a pit fall an' my kids relied on me then to put food on the table an' keep a roof over their heads, so I just did the best I could fer the babbies that were placed in my care till they were moved on, an' I'm ashamed to say I kept me mouth shut about what went on.' She wiped a tear from her eye.

'Well, we have the information that we came for and we are more than grateful for it, so I think we should be on our way now, Cissie,' Lavinia said firmly then to break the fraught atmosphere.

'Yes, yes of course.' Cissie felt guilty for confronting the woman now. After all, it wasn't Ada's fault that she had worked under such a corrupt taskmaster. It sounded like the poor soul had had little choice. She realised then how lucky she had been to have a loving husband who had been there to see their family grow up.

Reaching out, she took Mrs Wilkins's gnarled hand in hers and gently kissed it. 'Thank you,' she told her sincerely.

The woman waved her thanks aside. 'I'm only glad I could help.'

271

She hobbled to the door with them and watched while they set off, and once the carriage was trundling along, Lavinia asked, 'So what are you going to do now?'

Cissie thought for a moment before answering, 'I suppose the first thing will be to go to Bedworth and see if the shop is still there. The Tates may not still own it but whoever does may know where they went. They must be getting on in years too. I shall talk to George about it when we get home and see if he agrees.'

Lavinia thought that was wise. They had achieved a great deal in a short time, and both women were emotionally drained. The rest of the journey back to Treetops Manor was made in silence as Cissie clung to Lavinia's hand, feeling as wrung out as a wet dish-cloth.

The following afternoon, shortly after lunch, Ruby joined Kitty in the drawing room to inform her, 'Max has sent word that he has a booking for you this evening at the Canterbury Music Hall in Lambeth. The singer they'd engaged has lost her voice.'

For the first time, Kitty looked slightly dismayed at the news. 'But I was onstage last night – for the fourth show this week. I'm worn out and was hoping to rest this evening.'

Ruby lit one of the small cigars she was partial to and after blowing a plume of blue smoke into the air she gave her daughter a short lecture. 'What you need to understand is that in this business you have to take advantage of your popularity while you can. People are fickle, believe me, and they can soon shift their adoration to someone else if you don't keep yourself in the public eye.' Her voice hardened. 'You said this was what you wanted, and Max and I have worked tirelessly to make it happen for you. Surely you are not losing interest already?'

Hearing the note of admonition in her mother's voice, Kitty was quick to reassure her. 'Oh no, of course I'm not. Forget I ever said anything. I shall just go and rest now so that I'm at my best. Maggie can prepare one of my gowns.' It was the first time Ruby had ever been openly hostile to her and Kitty felt chastened as she fled from the room.

When she burst into her bedroom she found Maggie placing fresh towels in her bathroom.

'My mother just informed me that I have another booking this evening,' Kitty told her as she threw herself onto the bed.

'What!' Maggie looked aghast. 'But you performed last night after modelling for Mr Fitzherbert for most of the day. You'll make yourself ill at this rate.'

Kitty forced a smile. 'I don't mind,' she told her. 'I've got plenty of time to put my feet up this afternoon and I didn't have any plans for this evening anyway. It appears that I'm more popular than I thought.'

'That's all very well, but you can have too much of a good thing,' Maggie grumbled. Then a thought occurred to her and she asked, 'Why don't you tell Ruby that you want to take a little holiday. You could go and visit Sunday and Tom for a few days.' Although Kitty never admitted it, Maggie sensed that she missed them dreadfully. But she hadn't taken Kitty's pride into account.

'Why *should* I go and see them?' The girl reared up immediately. 'Ruby said she'd let them have my address and I've written to them on numerous occasions but they haven't even bothered to reply. I think that rather tells me something, don't you? They clearly feel that they've done their duty by me and that's an end to it – and that's fine by me!'

Maggie chewed on her lip. Despite her brave words, Kitty's lovely eyes were brimming with tears but Maggie felt powerless to help her if she wouldn't listen to advice. Kitty could be very stubborn when she had a mind to be.

'Well, it's your decision,' Maggie answered. 'And if you're

performing again this evening I'd better set to and get you a gown pressed. What about the lilac silk and Chantilly lace one? You haven't worn that this week.'

'Very well.' Kitty watched Maggie bustle over to the armoire to get the gown and once she had left the room with it over her arm Kitty turned her head into the pillow and wept, although she couldn't have said why. She had craved success and she wallowed in the admiration that was being bestowed on her. Why, only the evening before when leaving the stage and returning to her dressing room, she had found a magnificent ruby and diamond bracelet tucked in a black velvet box amongst the blooms of one of the numerous bouquets that were waiting for her from her many admirers. She had been tickled pink – even more so when Ruby had turned quite green with envy. So why then, she wondered, did she still feel so unhappy?

Chapter Thirty-Four

'Are you ready then, pet?' George gently asked his wife. They were standing outside Tate's grocery shop in the centre of Bedworth and Cissie was all of a-tremble. Tom had let George borrow his treasured car to drive her there, but now that they had arrived, for the first time Cissie was filled with doubts about whether or not she was doing the right thing.

George smiled at her reassuringly. 'You don't have to go through with this if you choose not to. But will you rest easy if you don't, knowing that your son could be so close? You've dreamed of this for a long time, my love.'

'You're right, George, of course you are,' she answered, more to convince herself than him. And then before she could give herself time to change her mind she strode determinedly forward and entered the shop. The bell above the door tinkled and she saw a woman with a large wicker basket being served at the counter by a tall man who looked to be in his late fifties. She and George stayed close to the door until the woman left and then the man looked at them and asked politely, 'May I help you?'

Both George and Cissie were dressed up in their Sunday best and just for a second she hesitated and straightened her bonnet before answering, 'I'm hoping you will be able to help me. I've come here on a very personal matter an' wondered if you'd spare me a minute of your time to speak in private.'

The man frowned. His hair must have been very dark once but it was peppered with grey now.

'May I ask what it's about?'

Cissie cleared her throat. 'It . . . it's very personal, as I say, an' it concerns both you an' your wife.'

He regarded the couple solemnly for some seconds more, then deciding that they looked respectable he said, 'Very well, I'll put the closed sign on the door for a few minutes. It's never too busy at this time of day, luckily.' He came from behind the counter, locked the door, turned the sign and then said: 'Would you follow me?'

He opened a door that led from behind the counter and they found themselves in a very cosy sitting room where a woman sat embroidering with her feet up on a stool.

'Hello, dear. It's never time for your tea break already, is—' Her voice broke off as she saw the visitors and she looked questioningly at her husband.

'This is Mr and Mrs . . .' Realising that they hadn't been properly introduced, the man glanced towards George who had taken his hat off.

'Branning,' George told him and the man nodded.

'This is my wife, Emma. Would you both like to take a seat?'

Cissie and George perched nervously on the edge of a very comfortable sofa and George gave a covert glance about the room. It was nicely furnished, and he deduced that the shop must do well. Everything here, from the curtains hanging at the window to the rugs on the floor, spoke of quality.

'So, how may we help you?' the woman asked then and Cissie couldn't help but notice that she looked rather fragile and unwell, which was borne out when she started to cough. Cissie thought she must have been a very pretty woman in her day but now her once-fair hair, which was piled neatly on top of her head, was faded, as were her blue eyes.

Her husband was instantly at her side handing her a glass of water and a handkerchief, and when the bout had passed she smiled at them apologetically. 'Do excuse me. I've been under the weather for some time and I'm ashamed to say my husband here has been marvellous and waits on me hand and foot. But there . . . you haven't come here to listen to my troubles.'

Cissie cleared her throat, wondering nervously where she should begin, but when George gave her hand a squeeze, she took courage and told them: 'What I have to say concerns your son.'

She saw the Tates exchange a worried glance before Mr Tate groaned, 'Oh dear, we had no idea he was back again. What has he done now?'

Cissie was slightly confused. What did he mean, back again? But she carried on, almost afraid to stop. 'Many years ago, thirty-four to be precise, I gave birth to a child in Hatter's Hall. He was taken away from me immediately. I can explain the circumstances of my being imprisoned there another time.' Cissie paused to dab at her sweating brow. This was proving to be even more difficult than she had imagined it would be. 'I . . . I believe that that baby, who was taken from me against my will, was the boy you took from there to bring up as your own – and I suppose after all this time, I just wanted to put my mind at rest and know that he was safe and well. I have never forgotten him, you see? So I hope you will forgive me for this intrusion. Believe me, I have no wish to upset you.'

Again, the Tates glanced at each other and Cissie saw that there were tears in the woman's eyes. This had clearly come as a shock to her, which Cissie supposed was quite understandable.

'We *did* adopt a baby boy from the asylum,' Mr Tate tentatively admitted. 'Although we have no way of knowing whether that baby was the one you gave birth to.'

'Oh, I have it on very good authority that he is,' Cissie gabbled on. 'We went to Hatter's Hall to look at the files and the super-intendent there advised us to talk to an elderly lady who helped to run the nursery there at the time my son was born. She was able to direct us to you, and if your son was born in May 1881, then there is every likelihood that he is the right one. But please believe me – I haven't come here to try and take him away from you. You are the parents who brought him up and I have no rights whatsoever over him. As I said, I just need to know that he's safe and well – and perhaps you could tell me what he's like. Is he married? Does he have a family of his own? Has he brought you joy?'

She stopped talking abruptly and flushed, and Mrs Tate smiled at her. 'We have never kept the fact that he was adopted from our son,' she told Cissie. 'And in answer to your questions, yes, he is safe and well – as far as we know. No, he isn't married and no, he doesn't have any children – not to our knowledge anyway.'

Her husband took up the tale. 'What my wife is trying to tell you is that Hugh, our son, isn't here at present. He's somewhat of a wanderer, you see,' he said, his face grave. 'Some weeks ago we had words – rather harsh ones, unfortunately – and I told him that it was time he stood on his own two feet.' The man paused and appeared to be choosing his words carefully. 'The thing is, Emma and I took him when we found that we could never have children of our own, and for a long time he fulfilled a need in us and we doted on him. Looking back, that was probably where we went wrong. Anything within reason he asked for he had, but he was such a delightful little boy that it was hard to deny him. But then when he became older we noticed a change in him. He became somewhat of a bully, I'm afraid, and got in with the wrong crowd. We sent him away to a boarding school but eventually he was expelled from there so we got him an apprenticeship with a local plumber, so that he would have a trade. That didn't last long either. Hugh wasn't one for getting his hands dirty.'

Mr Tate took a breath before he resumed. 'Then he started to gamble and would regularly disappear for weeks at a time, only coming home when he wanted money. This went on for several years until finally when Emma became ill I decided enough was enough. He is a grown man, after all, and needs to take responsibility for himself now. And so the last time he came home looking for cash to pay his debts, I refused him and we had a bitter row. And that is the last we saw of him, although I have no doubt he will return to try his luck again when he thinks we have had time to calm down.'

Cissie was shocked. This was not the picture she had painted of her long-lost son at all and yet she had no reason to doubt the couple. They seemed perfectly genuine people.

'I'm so sorry,' she said in a wobbly voice. 'I feel somehow that I am the one responsible for what you've been through.'

'Nonsense, my dear. If Hugh is indeed your birth son, no blame can be attached to you whatsoever. The child was taken from you and it was our choice to adopt him and to bring him up in the way we did. The question now is, what do you want to do? Do you want us to tell Hugh that you've been here enquiring about him, if and when he returns? I know he's always wondered who his natural mother was.'

Cissie felt her heart leap. 'Yes, I'd like that – and if he should wish to meet me, the decision will be his then. If, of course, you have no objections?' she added worriedly. The last thing she wanted to do was bring these good people yet more heartache. She fumbled in her bag then for the address she had written down and passed it to Mr Tate.

'This is where I live, and thank you both for being so very understanding. My turning up out of the blue must have come as a very great shock to you and I wouldn't want to cause any conflict between you and Hugh. After all, you have loved him and been the best of parents, whereas I never even got to hold him.' Her voice faltered for a second.

Another coughing fit shook Emma Tate's frail frame then and George and Cissie hastily rose.

'We've taken up quite enough of your time now,' Cissie said. 'Strange as it may seem, now that I know he is alive and well, I feel as if a great weight has been lifted from my shoulders, even if he hasn't turned out quite as you hoped he would. He has clearly been blessed with loving parents and I couldn't have asked for more for him, so thank you from the bottom of my heart!'

With that, she and George said goodbye to Mrs Tate then followed Mr Tate back into the shop. He shook their hands, opened the door for them and they hurried back to the car with Cissie taking great gulps of air.

Once they were on their way home, George dared to ask, 'All right, are yer, pet?'

Cissie wiped a tear from her cheek but she was smiling. 'Very all right,' she said. And as they motored on their way, Cissie spent the time trying to build a picture of her errant son in her mind.

'You mark my words, this could end in war,' Tom observed worriedly as he sat reading the newspaper in the kitchen at Treetops one morning towards the end of June 1914. Banging and hammering was echoing from the hallway where workmen were installing a telephone and everyone was very excited about it. It seemed incredible to think that soon they would be able to lift a receiver and have a conversation with someone who was miles away. George had to raise his voice to make himself heard. 'The heir to the Austro-Hungarian throne, the Archduke Franz Ferdinand and his wife were assassinated on the twenty-eighth of June by a young Nationalist while they were on a visit to Sarajevo.'

'I can't see how that would cause a war or involve us,' Cissie commented as she refilled his cup with fresh coffee, deciding that she must look at an atlas to find out where these places were.

'I just hope you're right,' Tom muttered but the headline preyed on his mind and he had a bad feeling about it in the pit of his stomach.

In the hallway, Lavinia sighed as she saw the telephone being installed. So much had changed over the years and it brought home to her the fact that she was getting older. Now there was a large airfield in Weddington in Nuneaton, and noisy aeroplanes often dotted the sky. There were trains – great beasts that belched smoke and steam and could take their passengers all over the country, and now the installation of telephones. None of these things had even been heard of when she was a child. But like George, she too had read the headlines in *The Times* that morning and she shared his concerns. It was as if great stormclouds were gathering and heading their way. The assassination of the Archduke could well herald a clash of opposing forces and then all hell would be let loose. It was such a pity, she thought to herself, when for the first time in her life she had the love of a good man and happiness was in sight, but for now all any of them could do was wait, and hope and pray for peace.

Chapter Thirty-Five

'*Must* you go out this afternoon?' Maggie asked as she looked at Kitty's pale face. There were dark smudges beneath her friend's eyes and Maggie thought she had lost a little weight. She had certainly lost some of her sparkle and now like Ruby she rarely ventured out of bed before lunchtime, unless she had singing practice or rehearsals. In the last week alone she had performed on stage five nights, and on the evenings when she hadn't worked Richard had taken her out to dinner. Or at least, that's what Kitty had told her. Maggie suspected that Kitty had probably been at his studio modelling yet more clothes, and now she was becoming curious as to why they hadn't seen any of the photographs in the magazines which Ruby read so avidly. She had asked Kitty as much only the day before and the girl had almost snapped her head off.

'Richard told me that most of my modelling shots will go into magazines in Paris and France,' she had told her tetchily and Maggie was wise enough not to pursue the subject although instinct told her something was amiss.

Over the last few weeks Ruby had given them cause for worry too. She was drinking heavily now, sometimes swallowing wine as soon as she fell out of bed in the late morning and it was beginning to tell on her. Her hair was now lacklustre and she had gained a considerable amount of weight, which was no surprise really when

Maggie considered how much she ate and drank. Her latest suitor had disappeared off the scene some time ago and it was then that Ruby had lapsed into depression. Maggie continued to be concerned about Kitty's wages. Ruby paid her surprisingly little for the number of hours she worked and Maggie wondered if Ruby and Max weren't exploiting her. Not that she would dare suggest that to Kitty. She was touchy enough as it was nowadays and nothing like her former cheery self.

Now Kitty swung her legs out of bed and yawned as she reached for her robe. 'I have to go out,' she answered in reply to Maggie's question. 'Richard will be expecting me and I can't let him down.'

Maggie nodded without comment. A few days ago, she had found the tiny bottle of vinegar and the sponges in Kitty's bag while she was changing the contents from that bag to another – and the sight of them had appalled her. Maggie knew what they were used for. Her own father had once forced her to use the same form of birth control. Thankfully, up to now the bottle was full which meant, Maggie hoped, that Richard hadn't as yet taken advantage of her friend. But how long would it be before he did, she wondered. Not that there was anything she could do to prevent it, except to be there for Kitty.

It was very frustrating and sometimes Maggie wished that Kitty would just board a train and go home to Treetops. At least Sunday and Tom had kept her safe there. She herself would be out of a job, of course, if ever Kitty did decide to do that, for Maggie knew that she would never return to her home town. There was nothing there for her but unhappy memories of the abuse she had suffered, and the constant fear and misery of life with Stella and Victor Dawes. However, since being taken on at Brunswick Villa, she had been saving her wages religiously each week, and should Kitty ever decide to go home, Maggie felt confident that she would be able to find another job in London now.

There was a tap at the door then and Miss Fox entered the room just as Kitty disappeared off into the bathroom.

'She's up then,' the woman said in her usual forthright way. 'I thought she looked a bit peaky after last night's performance and I wondered how she was today?'

'She hasn't said much,' Maggie answered as Miss Fox stepped across to the purple velvet box on Kitty's dressing table. She flicked it open and stared down at the sapphire pendant on a thin gold chain nestling inside it. It was from one of the finest jewellers in Bond Street.

'It was left in her dressing room by one of her admirers last night,' Maggie told her and the older woman shook her head.

'She must have a whole lot of such baubles by now,' she sighed. 'It's just not healthy for a young girl to have her head turned like this. Kitty might act the lady but underneath she's nothing but a young girl, and I do worry about her.'

'So do I,' Maggie confided. 'I've just asked her to stay in today and rest but she says she has to go to Mr Fitzherbert's again.'

'Hmm, he's another one I wouldn't trust as far as I could throw him.' Miss Fox snapped shut the box containing the pendant as if she'd like to shut Richard away with it. 'No good can come of Kitty spending so much time with an older, more experienced man like him. I really don't know what he's playing at, but it will end in tears, you mark my words.'

Their conversation was stopped from going any further though when Kitty emerged from the bathroom.

'Right, I'd best get on,' Foxy announced. 'Shall I ask Cook to prepare you something to eat?'

'No, thank you.' Kitty smiled at her, looking very young without her stage make-up and with her hair flowing about her shoulders like a dark silken cloak. 'I'm not really hungry at the moment.'

Miss Fox twitched her nose disapprovingly and swept from the room to check on Ruby. The latter would probably be in a rare old state as well this morning if the amount of wine she had put away the night before was anything to go by.

It was early in the afternoon when Kitty arrived at Richard's house to find him waiting for her.

'Ah!' He took her hand and drew her into the studio with a broad smile on his face. 'I have something quite exciting to tell you.'

She blinked, wondering what it could be as he settled her on the chaise longue and sat down beside her. 'A contact of mine wants to meet you. He is the editor of a very well-known fashion magazine in Paris and he hopes to be able to get some of your lingerie shots into next month's issue.'

'Really?' Kitty perked up.

'Yes. There's just one thing. He would like to be here when we're doing the shots. Would you mind that?'

Kitty looked perplexed. 'You mean he would see me actually modelling the underwear?'

'Why, of course he would. But what you have to remember is there will be thousands of people seeing you in it if he decides to use your shots, so where's the problem?'

'I suppose if you put it like that . . .' Kitty didn't like this idea at all but she was afraid of upsetting Richard again. Only the day before, she had arrived early once more – to find him locked away in the studio with the same girl who had been there before and she was feeling rather jealous. He had that closed look on his face as well. It often appeared now when she didn't do as he asked her and she was terrified of losing him.

Suddenly he was all smiles again. 'That's my girl,' he encouraged. 'I knew I could count on you not to let me down. But of course, if you *do* have serious reservations there are other models who would jump at the chance. I know Miss Hawkins would for a—'

'Oh no,' Kitty interrupted him quickly as a picture of Melissa Hawkins's china-blue eyes floated into her head. 'I'll do it – but when is the man coming?'

'This afternoon, as it happens.' He twisted a curl that lay across her shoulder around his finger sensuously and her heart began to hammer at his nearness. He always had this effect on her and she had an idea that he knew it.

'This afternoon!' Her voice came out as a squeak. She hadn't expected it to be so soon.

'Well, he was in London and in Chelsea too, and seeing as I knew you would be here, there seemed no sense in delaying.' His arm had clamped about her waist now and when he began to kiss her she felt dizzy; didn't even try to stop him when his hand began to slowly caress her breast. It was wonderful and terrifying all at the same time – and suddenly she remembered the little bottle and the sponges in her bag. Would it be so very bad to let him make love to her? she wondered. After all, he had told her he loved her a number of times now so he clearly intended them to be together. They had come close to going all the way on a number of occasions lately, but Sunday's words of warning had always stopped her so far. But then Sunday belonged to another time and another way of life now. In London, everything was so much more easy-going. Why, Ruby had had numerous lovers and wasn't ashamed to admit it. She had even provided Kitty with the means to prevent an unwanted pregnancy, so surely she wouldn't condemn her – and Kitty did *so* want to bind Richard to her for all time. Perhaps this would be the best way to do it?

Richard was panting with desire now but she managed to extricate herself from his arms long enough to gasp, 'When will the gentleman be here?'

'Oh, not for another hour or so.'

'Then I'll pop behind the screen and slip into something a little more comfortable.' She snatched up her bag and once behind the

286

screen she quickly undressed, put on the robe that Richard kept there for her and took the bottle and the sponges from her bag with shaking fingers.

When she came back to him clad in nothing but the robe and blushing furiously, he gently drew it open and moaned aloud as he stared at her naked body.

'You are quite beautiful!' He lifted her chin and looked into her eyes then asked gently, 'Have you ever done this before?' When she shook her head, he slid the robe from her shoulders and began to stroke the creamy skin of her shoulders. She was shaking now with a mixture of excitement and fear, but his voice was soft and husky as he told her, 'I won't hurt you, I promise. It will be beautiful, just like you.'

And so Kitty lay trembling as Richard slowly undressed, letting his clothes pool around his feet. She had never seen a naked man aroused before, but as he had promised he went slowly . . . and gradually her passion mounted to meet his. When he finally entered her there was a brief moment of pain but then she began to move with him as sensations she had never felt before coursed through her. By the time he rolled away from her there were tears in her eyes. She had come to his room that afternoon as a girl but she would leave as a woman and she didn't have a single regret.

'I do love you so, Richard,' she told him adoringly as she gazed up at him and he laughed and chucked her under the chin as he sat up and lit a cigarette in all his naked glory.

'That is good to hear, but now, my sweet, perhaps you should go and get ready for our visitor. He will be here soon.'

Kitty suddenly felt crestfallen. She had hoped that Richard would tell her he loved her too, but he was acting now almost as if nothing had happened between them. *Still*, she told herself, *he will when the time is right*, and so she nodded obediently and scuttled behind the screen to wash herself and put on the undergarment he had laid out ready for her. She had only just finished tidying her hair when someone rapped on the door.

'Mr Johnston to see you, sir,' the little maid shouted and Richard finished adjusting his clothing and hurried to let him in, locking the door after him.

'The young lady I told you about is getting ready for you behind the screen,' Kitty heard him say. 'Now would you like a drink while we're waiting?'

'Thank you, sir, and I suggest you pour one for the young lady too. We should celebrate the start of a long and lucrative arrangement.'

Kitty stepped out, nervously clutching the robe about her and was shocked at what she saw although she didn't know why, for she hadn't really known what to expect. Mr Johnston was a small man, almost as far round as he was high, with a balding pate and a large moustache that quivered beneath a huge red nose. His eyes seemed to bore into her soul and she felt uncomfortable in his presence.

'Here you are, my dear.' He thrust a large glass of wine at her and Kitty reluctantly took it. 'You're every bit as lovely as Ricky here told me you were. Now why don't you have a nice little drink an' relax a bit, eh?'

Kitty did as she was told and surprisingly after a few sips she started to feel much more confident.

'Ready?' Richard asked after she had finished half the glass.

She nodded. Taking her clothes off in front of this stranger didn't seem quite so daunting now. She slid the robe from her shoulders and made for the chaise longue feeling slightly wobbly. *Perhaps I shouldn't have had a drink on an empty stomach*, she thought as she settled into one of the poses that she knew Richard favoured. Today she was dressed in a very pretty white silk corset trimmed with thin red ribbons, but she had no sooner laid back than the stranger came striding towards her while Richard positioned himself behind the camera.

288

'Just a little more shoulder showing if you don't mind, m'dear.' His fat sausage fingers snaked out and smoothed the straps of the corset from her shoulders, but Kitty was feeling far too mellow to complain. In fact, she would have liked nothing more than to just curl up and go to sleep. His hand dropped to caress her breast but even then she didn't protest. She was battling to keep her eyes open for some reason and that was the last thing she remembered . . .

A gentle hand squeezing her shoulder brought her starting awake, and she found herself staring up into Richard's face. Her head was throbbing and she felt totally disorientated. And then she remembered the repulsive little man who had been present but a glance around the room assured her that he was gone. 'What happened?'

Richard smiled as he helped her into a sitting position. 'I'm afraid the wine you drank made you go out like a light so I postponed the shoot with Mr Johnston until another day.'

'I'm so sorry,' she croaked, wondering how half a glass of wine could have affected her so badly.

He waved her apologies aside. 'Don't worry about it, my lovely. I've asked Millie to make you a pot of strong coffee. Don't forget you have a performance this evening, otherwise I would have let you sleep.'

'Goodness, you're right.' Kitty felt so ill at that moment that she was wondering how she was going to manage it but once she had drunk two large cups of coffee she started to feel human again and eventually went behind the screen to get dressed.

Once she was ready, Richard escorted her outside and hailed a cab and as she sank back against the seat she felt strangely let down. In the beginning, he had always run her home in his car and after what had happened between them that day she would have expected him to be a little more gentlemanly. *But then he probably has another client to see*, she consoled herself and closed her eyes against the dull pain throbbing behind them.

'Where have you been? I've been frantic with worry,' Maggie

greeted her the second she set foot through the door and Kitty groaned. A lecture, even a well-meaning one, was the last thing she needed at present. 'We shall have to leave for the music hall in less than an hour and you haven't even started to get ready yet.' She stopped then, and peering at Kitty she said very matter-of-factly, 'You look absolutely awful. What have you been doing?'

Kitty flushed. 'I haven't been doing anything out of the ordinary,' she replied guiltily. 'I just have a bit of a headache, that's all.'

'Then we'd better get a powder down you and try to get you right for this evening.' And taking Kitty's elbow, the other girl led her up the stairs.

Chapter Thirty-Six

It was mid-July 1914 and Cissie had just returned to Primrose Cottage after spending the day at Treetops when a knock came on the open kitchen door. Humming merrily to herself she turned to see who it was and then froze on the spot. A younger version of Albert Pinnegar stood watching her and with a shock and with no need for words, Cissie knew that she was staring at her long-lost son. She had often wondered what he looked like. Had he taken after her or his hated father? And now she knew.

'Y-you must be Hugh.' Her voice came out as a croak as the man removed his hat and inclined his head and she found herself thinking that unlike his father he had manners at least.

'And you must be Cissie. My mother told me about your visit.'

Cissie had dreamed of this moment for thirty-four long years. In her mind, she had pictured a joyful reunion where mother and son would fall into each other's arms and profess their love for each other, and yet now it was here she might have been struck dumb, for she couldn't think of a single thing to say.

'May I come in?' he asked awkwardly after a time and suddenly Cissie sprang towards him and led him to George's favourite chair. It wasn't his fault if he looked like his father, after all.

'Can I offer you a cup of tea?'

'A cold drink would be lovely, if it's no trouble.'

She was pleased to hear that he spoke nicely too, no doubt down to the private education that the Tates had supplied him with. She hurried away to the marble shelf in the pantry and after pouring out two glasses of lemon barley she handed one to him and sat down opposite him with the other.

'I wasn't sure that I would ever meet you,' she said shyly and he smiled, a sad smile.

'When my mother told me that you had called, I knew I would have to come. I've always wondered who my birth mother was, you see.'

'And did she tell you how we were separated when you were born? That I had no choice?'

He took a sip of his drink and nodded, and now Cissie really studied him. He was very smartly dressed and his hair was neat and tidy. She could have taken him for a toff any day of the week, but this was her son – *her son.* In a flash she forgot all the negative things the Tates had told her about him. She wanted to judge him for herself; to get to know him.

'I want you to know that I attach no blame to you for what happened,' he said. 'It must have been dreadful for you.'

'It was,' Cissie admitted. 'I think for a while after they took you away from me that I was almost as mad as some of the poor lunatics I was locked away with.'

'But you married eventually and had more children?'

Cissie smiled now and nodded. 'Oh yes. I've been very fortunate indeed. My husband is a lovely man and we were blessed with three beautiful children. All grown up and flown the nest now, of course. But still never a day went by when I didn't think about you. You were always part of me.'

He reached out his hand to her and just for a second she almost flinched away, for he was so like his father in looks that she was suddenly remembering the feel of Albert Pinnegar's fat hands all over her. But none of what had happened was this young man's fault and he had never asked to be born.

'I felt much better after meeting your parents,' Cissie confided to him then. 'To know that you had been loved and cared for meant the world to me.'

'Huh!' he snorted. 'Is *that* what they told you? Well, it isn't strictly true. You see, I think they wanted a little puppet who would do their bidding, and because I had spirit and didn't want to take over my father's shop they disowned me. Well . . . almost. I did go to see them again a few days ago, which is when my mother told me about you and gave me your address.'

'Oh!' Kitty was taken aback. The Tates had seemed like such a nice, genuine couple. Then suddenly a shadow fell across the room and looking up Cissie saw that George had come home.

She leaped to her feet and told him joyously, 'George, you're just in time to meet Hugh – my son.'

His face straight, George held out his hand and said: 'It's nice to meet you. Cissie has always wanted to find you.'

'Thank you, sir,' Hugh answered respectfully. Then to Cissie, 'And thank you for your hospitality. I'd like it if we could meet again sometime if you felt able to, so we can get to know one another. But for now, I really should be going. I've imposed enough on you as it is.'

All the initial reservations she had felt at first sight of him melted away. He was her flesh and blood, and at last he was back in her life.

'You haven't imposed on me at all,' Cissie assured him. 'And we're both usually home at this time each evening so do call again whenever you've a mind to. You'll always be welcome.' Her maternal instincts were suddenly working overtime.

The man nodded then strode from the room and Cissie watched him go with a rapturous look on her face.

'Well, who would have thought it after all this time, eh?' she sighed. 'I must admit, I got a bit of a gliff when I first clapped eyes on him. He's so like his father, ain't he? But only in looks, mind. He seemed to be quite a charmer.'

George forced a smile. He hadn't taken to the chap at all, if truth be told. Hugh Tate had seemed to be a right smarmy so-and-so – not that he'd say that to his wife. He wanted her to keep the dream of her long-lost son intact. She'd had to wait long enough for him to come back into her life, God only knew! He just hoped that she wouldn't live to regret it.

'Pssst! Maggie, have you got a minute?'

Maggie paused on her way down to the kitchen the next morning to see Miss Fox gesturing to her from the door of the drawing room. She went to join her and once they were in the room, Miss Fox hastily closed the door and asked, 'Is Kitty all right? I went along to her performance last night and she didn't seem to be at her best.'

Maggie sighed. 'She isn't, to be honest. I think she's overdoing things but if I mention it she gets all hoity-toity with me. Perhaps you could have a word with Ruby? She could maybe talk some sense into her. Kitty can't go on like this, burning the candle at both ends.'

'Huh! Fat lot of good that would do,' Miss Fox snorted, folding her hands neatly at her waist. 'Ruby is off with the fairies most of the time nowadays. Why, only last night I threatened to tip every drop of wine I could get my hands on down the sink. If truth be told, she wants Kitty to work and doesn't care about the toll it's taking on the girl. It's Kitty's earnings that are keeping this house going at the moment.'

Maggie had suspected that Kitty wasn't being paid a fraction of what she earned and now Miss Fox was confirming it. But when Maggie tried to broach the subject with Kitty she got her head bitten off, for Kitty wouldn't have a wrong word said about Ruby.

'Ah well, don't you go fretting over it,' Miss Fox said now. 'Just make sure that she rests when she can.'

'That's easier said than done,' Maggie sighed ruefully. 'When she isn't singing on stage she's off to that damn photographer's all the time and she won't let me go with her.' The two women stared at each other for a moment, both with the same thoughts, then without another word they went their separate ways. Maggie herself was gravely concerned. The little bottle and the tiny sponges that she had found some weeks ago in Kitty's bag were now being used, which could only mean one thing. But what if they didn't work and Kitty were to find herself with child? Would her wonderful photographer stand by her then and do the honourable thing? Huh! Maggie very much doubted it. The week before, she had visited the market early one morning while Kitty was still in bed and she had seen Richard Fitzherbert strolling along bold as brass with a very pretty blue-eyed blonde hanging off his arm. Fearful of being spotted, Maggie had darted into a shop doorway until they were out of sight. From the way the girl had been gazing adoringly up at him, it had been very obvious that they were more than friends. Richard Fitzherbert was playing Kitty like a fiddle and stringing her along.

Her dilemma now was, should she tell Kitty what she had seen? After giving it much thought Maggie had decided against it, for she had a feeling that Kitty would just fly into a rage and refuse to believe her. It hurt her, though, to think that her friend was being used. But Kitty was almost eighteen years old now and Maggie supposed that she would have to learn by her own mistakes. She could only pray that, in time, Kitty would see Richard for what he was.

Only the day before, she had dared to ask outright: 'Has he ever paid you personally for any of the modelling you've done for him?' and was put firmly in her place.

'He and Ruby have an arrangement. He pays her my fee then she pays me.' Maggie had clamped her mouth shut and said no more.

Now, as she mounted the stairs with a loaded breakfast tray,

Maggie hoped that Kitty would have a quiet day at home and be able to rest. However, the second she set foot in Kitty's bedroom, she found the girl rummaging feverishly through her armoire and throwing clothes into a heap onto the floor.

'Why didn't you wake me?' she nearly screamed. 'I have to be out in half an hour!'

'I'm not a mindreader,' Maggie answered stoically as she placed the laden tray down. 'How was I to know you needed a call if you didn't tell me? And if you'll just say what you're looking for, I'll find it for you.' She sighed as she glanced at the mess. No doubt the items would all need pressing again now.

'I'm trying to find the new blue skirt and the white frilled blouse that I bought last week!'

Maggie gently nudged her aside and within seconds produced the clothes Kitty had been looking for. 'Skirts to the left, blouses in the middle and dresses to the right.'

'Well, it's not my job to know that, is it?' Kitty answered churlishly as she stamped over to the bathroom.

'So where are you off to in such a hurry?' Maggie shouted after her just as the bathroom door slammed.

'Richard's!'

Maggie said a rude word as she started to lift the clothes and place them over a chair. She might have known. And now another lonely day stretched ahead of her.

'Ah, here you are – and only just in time,' Richard scolded when she arrived at his house sometime later. Then his expression softened as he saw the dismay on her face and he stroked the tender skin on her cheek, making her legs go all tingly. 'Now just remember, all you have to do is model the clothes that the gentlemen have brought. I'll do the rest.'

Kitty's mouth went dry. 'How many of them did you say there were going to be?'

'Just the three – and don't forget they are all very important names in the fashion industry. If they like the way you model their lingerie they could well give you official modelling contracts – and then you will be in clover.'

In fact, Kitty was secretly rueing the day she had ever agreed to do this, but now it had gone too far to call a halt – and the last thing she wanted to do was let Richard down. As he was keen on telling her, there were many other models who would willingly take her place, Melissa Hawkins being first on the list.

She nodded meekly and trotted after him like an obedient puppy as he headed for his studio. The men were all there waiting for her and she noticed that the dreaded Mr Johnston was amongst them. Although it was only early in the day they all had drinks in their hands and the tallest of the men encouraged her to have one too.

Richard smiled and thanked him, saying, 'Actually Kitty doesn't like to drink too early. I have a nice pot of tea here ready for her instead.'

The cup was already prepared with milk and sugar just the way she liked it. Truthfully, Kitty really didn't want it but once Richard had poured the tea into it and given it a good stir she dutifully took it and sipped at it. He had gone to the trouble of getting it for her, after all. She thought it tasted rather bitter and while she was drinking it, Richard introduced the men to her. Mr Johnston, she had unfortunately already met, and she thought the other two looked just as unsavoury as he did. Placing the cup down, she went behind the screen to get changed to find an assortment of underwear laid out ready for her on a chair. They were by far the skimpiest garments she had been asked to model so far, but she was feeling mellower by the minute and rather light-headed. Perhaps Maggie had been right when she'd told her she should eat something. But it was too late now, she was here and she supposed she should just get it over with.

After donning a fine silk bodice and matching bloomers that barely covered her modesty, she stepped from behind the screen and took her position in front of a sheet that Richard had draped across one wall of the studio. The men were watching her intently and she felt colour flood into her cheeks as she suddenly wondered what Sunday would have thought, could she have seen her now. Then all of a sudden she felt herself sway . . . and she crumpled to a heap on the floor.

'Ah, you're back with us are you?'

Maggie's voice seemed to be coming from a long way away and Kitty groggily opened her eyes. She was surprised to find that she was tucked up in her own bed and croaked, 'What happened?' Her mouth felt like the bottom of a birdcage and she had a head-ache again.

'You fainted, that's what happened, and it's no wonder. You're trying to burn the candle at both ends,' Maggie scolded. 'Foxy has gone mad and told Mr Thomas and Mr Fitzherbert that you're to do absolutely nothing for at least a week.' She refrained from telling her that Ruby had been absolutely furious about it. Maggie had an idea that Ruby would have worked the poor girl into the ground if she could.

'But I have bookings,' Kitty objected weakly.

'Blow the bookings!' Maggie retorted. 'You're going to do as you're told for a change. Me and Foxy will see to that, so you just lay back, my lady, and make the best of it.'

Seeing that she didn't have much choice, Kitty curled up and was soon fast asleep.

Chapter Thirty-Seven

Cissie swatted a fly buzzing around her face and mopped her brow as she made her way back to the cottage early one evening in late July. The heat had been almost unbearable all day and she was looking forward to a nice cool bath and a quiet evening with George. She had decided to take the short cut through the small copse that separated her home from Treetops and was enjoying the shade of the trees when a voice made her jump.

'Hello . . . Mother.'

Startled, she glanced to the side to see Hugh leaning lazily back against the trunk of a tree, blowing smoke from his cigarette into the dusky gloom.

'Hugh.' Slowly her heartbeat returned to a steadier rhythm as she saw who it was. She had been hoping he would come again.

As he casually strolled towards her, she asked, 'Have you got time to come to the cottage for a drink? It's lovely to see you.'

He smiled as he dropped his cigarette and ground it out with the heel of his well-shod foot.

'Thank you – but I ought to warn you this isn't entirely a social call.'

'Oh?' She stared up at him and he ran his finger around the neck of his shirt as if it was suddenly too tight.

'The thing is, I'm in a bit of a pickle. You see, when Mum and Dad chucked me out I took a room in town. I was hoping to find

299

a job but I've had no luck as yet and now my landlady is breathing down my neck.'

Cissie felt relieved. She had thought he was going to tell her that there was something wrong with him.

'So I was wondering if you could see your way clear to lending me some money – just until I find a job. Ten pounds should do it.'

Ten pounds was a huge amount of money to her, and Cissie was shocked that he would ask. After all, this was only the second time they had met.

But seeing her reservations, his face suddenly turned ugly and in that instant, he looked so much like his father that her hand rose involuntarily to her mouth. The look was gone so quickly that she wondered if she had imagined it as he gushed, 'Look, if you can't manage it, it really doesn't matter. I shouldn't have asked. I just thought that being as you are my mother, you'd want to help me out of a tight spot.'

'Of course I'll help you.' She instantly felt guilty. This was the first thing she would ever have done for him in his whole life – and surely George wouldn't mind? Hugh was her flesh and blood, after all, and there was nothing she wouldn't have done for him.

'You'll have to come to the cottage with me and I'll get it for you.' She hurried on and they walked along side by side.

Once inside the cottage she left Hugh in the kitchen with a glass of lemonade while she rushed upstairs to get the money. She and George had quite a little nest egg tucked away for their retirement now. Ten pounds was going to make a sizeable hole in it admittedly, but she was certain that her husband would understand – and it was only a loan, after all. Leaning over the bed she reached into a small hole in the mattress and extracted a small bag. Inside was their life savings and she hastily counted out ten pounds before returning the bag to its hiding place.

Once downstairs she handed the money to Hugh, who took it without a word of thanks and stuffed it into his trouser pocket. He then drained his glass and told her, 'Right, I'd best be off to settle up with my landlady then.'

'What? You're going so soon?' Disappointment coursed through her. She'd been hoping they might spend a little time getting to know each other before George got home, but then she supposed if Hugh's landlady was harassing him it was best to go and pay his dues. 'Will you come again soon?' she asked hopefully and he nodded.

'You can rely on it. Thanks for this – and bye for now.' He then sauntered away whistling merrily and she watched him go, feeling strangely deflated.

When George came in sometime later he found her in a sombre mood and asked, 'What's up, pet? You look like you've lost a bob an' found a tanner.'

Slowly she told him about Hugh's visit. The couple had never had any secrets from each other and she didn't intend to start now.

'And so I gave him the ten pounds,' she finished lamely.

George frowned, not at all happy about what he had heard. In truth, he hadn't taken to Hugh at all, be he Cissie's son or not, and he certainly didn't believe the yarn the fellow had spun to them about his parents not being good to him. The Tates had seemed like kind, genuine people – whereas there was something about Hugh that raised his hackles. Even so, he could understand the dilemma Cissie was in so he told her, 'Of course you wanted to help him. But don't forget he is a grown man and he should be responsible for himself now.'

'I understand that, but I couldn't see him thrown out onto the streets, could I?'

'Well, he could always have gone back to the Tates',' George pointed out. 'It came across to me that they still loved him, and I'm sure they wouldn't have turned him away even if he has led them a merry dance.'

'We only have their word for that,' Cissie answered defensively

301

and George wisely changed the subject. He would let it go this once, but should Hugh come with his begging bowl again George decided he would take him to one side and have a quiet word in his ear. There was no way he was going to stand by and see Cissie being taken advantage of – and from where he was standing, that was exactly what Hugh had done!

In London, Kitty was also feeling the strain. For the first time that week she had a free evening, or at least an evening free from performing at a music hall. Maggie had planned for them to have a restful time staying in together, but Kitty scuppered those plans when she told her after dinner, 'Actually, I'm going to Richard's. He has some friends he'd like me to meet.'

'Oh? Who are they then?'

'How should I know until I've met them?' Kitty snapped peevishly.

'Then it might be nice if I came with you,' Maggie persevered. What could be the harm if it was going to be purely a social evening?

But Kitty quickly shook her head as she crossed to the wardrobe. 'No, there's no need to trouble yourself. You've been running about after me all day and you deserve a rest. Now will you help me choose what I should wear? Richard said I was to look my best.'

Maggie had been about to say that she never had anything *but* quiet evenings in apart from when she accompanied Kitty to the music halls. Even then the time dragged as she waited in Kitty's dressing room for her, but she bit back the hasty retort and instead began to sift through Kitty's gowns. She was getting quite a selection now.

'How about this blue one?' She lifted it from the wardrobe and Kitty nodded then sat down on the stool in front of the mirror so that Maggie could dress her hair. The chignon was becoming very popular and Maggie was a dab hand at doing them now. Kitty's long hair was given a side parting then the rest of it was drawn into a very loose bun just above the nape of the neck, which made it a perfect style for the ladies who wore hats. Once she was ready, Kitty added a long string of pearls – yet another gift from an admirer – and asked, 'How do I look?'

'Beautiful as always.' Maggie couldn't help but sigh enviously.

As Kitty drew her gloves on, she said, 'You know, I think this hairstyle would suit you.'

Maggie's hand rose self-consciously to the tight plait woven about the crown of her head. It was a severe style much favoured by older ladies, and yet she was still so young.

'I'll have a little practice on you tomorrow,' Kitty promised and Maggie shrugged. She had never been a slave to fashion. But then Kitty was ready to go and after planting an affectionate kiss on Maggie's cheek she sailed out of the room leaving her friend to face yet another empty evening. Although she was enjoying reading Kitty's copy of *The Jungle Book*, she would have preferred some company.

Once Kitty was settled in a cab on her way to Richard's the smile slid from her face. Richard had told her the day before that he was throwing a party for a few of his friends and she had suggested that perhaps she could bring Maggie along, but he had laughed aloud.

'Why would you want to bring that boring old maid along?' he'd guffawed. 'She's so prim and proper and you must admit she's not the most enticing of creatures, and that's putting it mildly. No, my darling, the friends I have invited wouldn't enjoy Maggie's company at all, I assure you. Just bring yourself.'

Kitty had wanted to protest. She and Maggie had become close and Kitty had soon discovered that beneath that crusty exterior Maggie had a heart of gold. But she hadn't dared to contradict Richard. For her, the sun rose and set with him and she lived in fear of upsetting him. She was quite surprised when she arrived outside his house to see that the lights were off in the downstairs rooms. If he was throwing a party she had expected the place to be ablaze with lights, despite the fact that it wasn't yet dark outside. However, she paid the cabbie and hurried to the front door. Millie, the young maid, let her in and informed her, 'Mr Fitzherbert and his guests are all in the studio, miss.'

'The studio?' That was rather a strange place to throw a party, but then Kitty supposed if his friends were arty types they would probably enjoy being in there and they could always spill out of the French doors into the garden if it became overcrowded. It was a lovely evening, after all.

'Here she is, the belle of the ball,' Richard said loudly when she tapped on his door, then taking her hand he drew her into the room. She saw that there were three men sitting there, each with a drink in their hands, and a little flutter of unease sprang to life in her stomach. Where were the ladies? This was hardly what she would have termed a party. The men were all avidly eyeing her up and down and she felt distinctly uncomfortable as Richard led her towards them. It reminded her of the last sitting she had done for Richard when she had become ill, although she was pleased to note that Mr Johnston himself was not present.

'Mr Travers, Mr Fulton, Mr Sutton, may I introduce my very dear friend, Miss Kitty Nightingale. As you are no doubt aware from the wonderful newspaper reviews she has been receiving lately, Kitty is fast becoming the darling of the music halls.'

The men all stood and politely shook her hand, then Richard handed her a glass of champagne in a crystal flute. She eyed it warily and couldn't help but remember how ill she had been when under the influence of the wine he had given her once before.

'Now, if you would all care to be seated, the slide show will begin.'

Kitty's head whipped around to glance at Richard. Slide show!

What did he mean? She had been led to believe that she was attending a party. She took a seat just the same and saw that Richard had erected a large screen against one wall. After drawing the dark curtains across the French doors, he went to a projector, inserted a slide – and mere seconds later, an image flashed onto the screen. Kitty instantly wanted to die of humiliation. It was of herself, in a state of semi-undress, posing on the chaise longue.

Her cheeks burning with shame, she peeped at the men from the corner of her eye and was horrified to find that their eyes were all fixed greedily on the screen. And then suddenly she was staring at some photographs that she could not remember being taken. There was one of her apparently asleep with one arm flung carelessly behind her head showing far more of her breasts than was decent.

'Richard, I don't think . . .' she objected, but her voice trailed away as he stared threateningly at her and inserted another slide.

Gulping deep in her throat, she realised that these photographs must have been taken after she had fainted. She had grudgingly agreed to model underwear, admittedly, but some of these were bordering on pornographic and she would never have allowed him to take them. They were sordid and she felt dirty and soiled, even more so when the man who had been introduced as Mr Travers put his arm about her shoulders.

'Excuse me, sir!' she exclaimed haughtily, but he merely laughed.

'You're a fine-looking little filly, me dear,' he chuckled, 'an' I'd have paid good money to be the one to break you in, but Ricky tells me he's already done it.' She pushed him away and sprang to her feet, her cheeks aflame.

'Richard! How could you?' She had trusted him and he had betrayed her.

Richard installed another slide, saying coldly, 'Oh, sit down and don't be such a prude. These gentlemen have come here tonight to see you in all your glory. And then they would like to get to know you a bit better. These fine fellows are some of the critics

305

who gave you your glowing reviews in the press. Don't you think you owe it to them to be nice to them? Remember, they can make or break you.'

Kitty's hands balled into fists. Get to know her a bit better indeed! What did Richard think she was – a common whore? Snatching up her bag, she stormed towards the door only to find it locked and she wheeled about.

'I wish to leave! Please open this door *immediately*.'

Richard was right behind her and grabbing her arm he flung her down onto the nearest chair. She stared at him in shock as she rubbed her arm where a bruise was already beginning to appear. It was only then that she realised just how much danger she might be in. And worst of all was knowing that she had been duped by him. How unwise of her, to have trusted him so blindly, but she loved him so much!

Mr Travers was advancing on her, her glass in his hand. 'Why don't you just have a little drink and calm down, darling?' he wheedled, but Kitty ignored him and kept her eyes trained on Richard.

'Look at those before you start making a fuss!' he sneered and threw some photos down on the table beside her. Kitty looked at them in horror. She was lying in some very provocative poses, and what's more, she was completely naked.

'You took advantage of me while I was unconscious!' she gasped as the knowledge of what he had done hit her full force.

He shrugged. 'You are far too beautiful to keep to myself, and believe me, there is a huge market for pictures like these. But to prevent them being seen by the wider public, all you have to do is be nice to some of my acquaintances from time to time. Believe me, it's perfectly normal, you little goose. All the models do it – it's where they earn most of their money.'

Kitty's hand flew to her mouth as her eyes filled with tears but they had no impact on Richard whatsoever.

'You can begin this evening by being nice to Mr Travers,' he rasped callously. 'Myself and the other gentlemen here will leave you both in peace. But now why don't you have a sip of that excellent champagne I poured you? It will relax you, just wait and see.'

'You – you put something in my drinks!' Light dawned. That was the reason why she had been so ill on previous occasions. The wine, the tea – they had been drugged so that she was helpless, giving him the opportunity to take these obscene photographs!

On Richard's handsome features a grin appeared, a cold, hard grin that didn't reach his eyes. 'Perhaps just a little something to make you feel more in the mood,' he leered. And then he was gathering the pictures together as she looked on numbly. Should any of these become public she would never be able to hold her head up again and she knew that she would die of shame.

'And now, my dear, I believe our Mr Travers is becoming rather impatient so the other gentlemen and I will take our leave of you for now.' In actual fact, they would be watching from a secret panel, and the two men with Richard had paid heavily for this opportunity.

He held the glass out to her again and this time she took it and drank the contents back in one go. Had he offered it, Kitty would have taken poison to dull the loathsome shame of what she was about to endure.

Chapter Thirty-Eight

'Why, Kitty, whatever is the matter?' Maggie asked as she eyed the girl's swollen eyes the next morning.

'Nothing! I've just got a bit of a headache,' Kitty said as she tugged her robe more tightly about her. Maggie had brought her breakfast up, expecting her to be still in bed, but Kitty had clearly been up for some time. In fact, the bed looked as if it hadn't even been slept in.

'What time did you get in?' Maggie asked then. 'I tried to stay awake till one o'clock this morning but I must have dozed off.'

Kitty shrugged. 'What does it matter? I'm still perfectly capable of getting myself undressed.' She knew that she was being churlish and that Maggie didn't deserve it, but how could she tell her that she had just spent most of the night in the bathtub trying to scrub away the feel of Edward Travers's hands all over her. It had been a pointless exercise. She still felt dirty; would always feel dirty now. Fresh tears pricked at her eyes and she turned her head away from Maggie. Maggie must never know what she had allowed the man to do. No one could ever know, otherwise she would never be able to hold her head up again.

Maggie's straight white teeth picked at her lower lip before she said, 'Perhaps I could get you some tablets for your headache.'

Kitty shook her head. 'No, I'll be all right. I'd just like to rest on my own for a while if you don't mind.'

'Very well.' Maggie stared at her worriedly. This wasn't like Kitty at all. 'Give me a shout if you need anything and I'll pop up later to see if you're feeling well enough to come down for lunch. Meantime, try and eat some of that toast. You need to keep your strength up.'

Kitty suddenly thought that she sounded like Sunday, who had used to say that to her back at Treetops. *You must keep your strength up, you're a growing girl!* It all seemed so long ago now and finally Kitty realised what she had lost. Sunday and Tom had loved her – *really* loved her – and treated her as their own. She had turned her back on the people who had brought her up without a second thought, sure that she would find what she had always dreamed of with her birth mother. But the woman had never shown her an ounce of love or affection from the day she had stepped through the door. And now it was too late to rewind the clock.

Just the thought of the photographs that were in Richard's possession made Kitty break out in a cold sweat. Were they ever to become public she would be ruined and no decent man would ever look at her again. She was no better than a common whore, and it was all thanks to Richard Fitzherbert. He was cruel and treacherous. Even so she still loved him and had a feeling that she always would, no matter how low he made her sink. He was like a drug to her and she couldn't bear the thought of being without him.

When Maggie left, Kitty sat at the window for a long time, staring sightlessly down at Arthur at work in the garden. A knock on the door aroused her, and Maggie poked her head around it, saying tightly, 'It's Mr Fitzherbert – for you. I've put him in the parlour. Do you want me to help you get dressed before you go down?'

'Err, no, I'll be fine like this. Thank you, Maggie.'

Maggie left and Kitty stared in dismay at herself in the mirror. Her hair was wild and her eyes were red and puffy, but then what did it matter? Richard had probably come to tell her that he didn't wish to see her again so she might just as well go down and get it over with.

She met Miss Fox on the landing, and the older woman stared at her disapprovingly. 'You're surely not going to receive a gentleman caller dressed like that, are you? It's not proper, and what's more, you look as if you've been pulled through a hedge backwards.'

'I shall only be seeing him for a few minutes.' Kitty shot past her and raced down the stairs as the woman muttered to herself before going on her way.

Once outside the parlour door, Kitty paused to rake her fingers through her hair and draw herself upright, then with what dignity she could muster she entered the room.

'Oh, darling, how are you?'

His touching look of concern shocked her.

'I can't begin to apologise enough for what happened last night, but please know that it doesn't alter the way I feel about you. Also, I want you to know it all came about by accident. You see, Mr Travers visited the studio one day and happened to see the photographs I had taken of you which I had foolishly left lying about. I know I should never have taken those particular ones without your permission, but they were meant to be for my eyes only.'

'That's not what you said last night,' Kitty accused him. '*And* you admitted to drugging me!'

'Yes, I did,' he agreed, looking shamefaced. 'But I only wanted to make you feel more relaxed. I didn't realise the drug would affect you quite so badly. Please forgive me.' He pointed to a huge box on the floor. 'Look, I bought you a present.'

She did so want to forgive him but the memory of the night before was still very fresh in her mind. 'What is it?' she asked.

He smiled and her heart skipped a beat.

'Why don't you open it and see? I'm not sure that Ruby and Miss Fox will approve of it, but I hope you will. If you don't, I can always take it back.'

She dithered for a moment but then curiosity got the better of her and she bent to lift the lid. And then she gave a joyous cry as a tiny bundle of fur launched itself at her.

'It's a Cavalier King Charles puppy,' Richard informed her as she tried to hold it at arm's length. It was furiously licking every inch of her it could reach, with its tiny tail wagging fifteen to the dozen and Kitty's heart was lost.

'Oh . . . it's quite beautiful. Is it a boy or a girl?'

'A girl – well, I suppose I should say a bitch really.'

Kitty laughed as the little body snuggled into her. 'I shall call her Tallulah,' she declared as she and the pup surveyed each other. 'Thank you. We had dogs back at Treetops but I never had one of my very own before.'

'So, am I forgiven then?'

Staring at him over the dog's head she said, 'If I say yes, what will happen now?'

'Unfortunately, we – or should I say you – will have to continue to be nice to Mr Travers and his friends from time to time. We will lose everything if you don't. Your music-hall bookings, your modelling assignments . . . But it won't be so bad. You'll get used to it and I assume Ruby has explained how you can prevent—'

Kitty flushed and nodded rapidly. 'Yes, she has.'

'Good, then let's try and put what happened last night behind us. You must know how much I care about you and how jealous I was to have to let Edward . . .' He came to a halt. 'But let's not go into that, eh? Just know that whatever happens from now on, you are my girl forever.'

Kitty stared at him reproachfully for a moment. Half of her urged the other half to walk away right now. And yet she couldn't begin to imagine her life without him in it any more. And he had finally said that she was his girl! Her heart sang. He had finally said it straight out. She was his. It could only be a matter of time before he asked her to marry him – and then she wouldn't care what happened to her career. She would be his wife and they could put all this behind them for ever.

She nodded, too full to speak, and as he hugged her and the puppy to him he grinned slyly to himself over her shoulder. Just as he had planned, she was now his to use and abuse as he liked, and what a little earner she was turning out to be already! Edward Travers had paid him generously for her favours the night before. Of course, he would have to give some of that to Ruby, that was part of their agreement. But this was only the beginning. Kitty Nightingale was like putty in his hands.

'What the *hell* is that?' Miss Fox asked a short time later when Kitty was standing in the hallway with the puppy in her arms.

Kitty giggled, more her old self again. 'Richard bought her for me. I'm going to call her Tallulah. Isn't she lovely?'

Miss Fox looked positively horrified. 'But it'll be messing and piddling all over the place,' she groaned. 'We'll have to get a kennel outside for it. I can't see Cook allowing it in her kitchen. And who will look after the dratted mucky little thing when you're out?'

'She will *not* live outside, she will stay in my room with me,' Kitty told her forcefully. 'And when I'm out, Maggie will keep her company.' With that she sailed past the woman with her nose in the air and Miss Fox stifled a grin. The girl had been down in the dumps for a time now but the puppy seemed to have perked her up no end. She just hoped this Tallulah wouldn't start chewing up everything in sight. Puppies had a habit of doing that.

Turning her attention to Richard, Miss Fox treated him to a glacial stare and he beat a hasty retreat to the drawing room to see Ruby before he left. Noticing that he had left the door slightly ajar, Foxy made towards it with the intention of closing it. However, as she reached out for the handle she saw through the crack Richard hand a wad of notes to Ruby who immediately pushed them down her cleavage, which seemed to be increasing by the day. No wonder, Miss Fox thought, the amount of food and chocolate she put away.

'So, it all went as planned then?' Miss Fox heard Ruby say.

'Absolutely! Travers was thrilled with her though she took a bit of persuading.' Richard laughed as he sank into a chair. 'I had to resort to a touch of blackmail. But I bought her a puppy this morning so I think I'm back in favour. It will be easier next time, I've no doubt.'

'A puppy!' Ruby sounded appalled. She couldn't abide the nasty little things, but then if it kept the girl quiet it would be worth putting up with it, for now at least.

Unable to control her rage, Miss Fox flung the door open and marched into the room. She didn't like the sound of this at all.

'Just what is going on?' she demanded as two pairs of eyes turned to stare at her.

'Going on? I don't know what you mean, Foxy.' Ruby fluttered her eyelashes, the picture of innocence. 'Richard here was just saying that Kitty didn't seem so keen to do her modelling last night, that's all, and after he's worked so hard to set it all up for her and get such important contacts too.'

'In case you had forgotten, Kitty is not yet eighteen, she's still just a child,' Miss Fox rapped out. 'And if I find out that either of you are trying to force her to do something against her will—'

'Oh, don't be so silly,' Ruby interrupted with a wounded look on her face. 'As if I would do anything to hurt her. You should give me more credit, Foxy darling.'

Miss Fox wavered. Ruby was very convincing so perhaps she had just got the wrong end of the stick?

Richard meanwhile beat another hasty retreat. 'It's time I was off,' he said and after nodding towards the two ladies, he disappeared. Miss Fox shut the door behind him before rounding on Ruby.

'I reckon it's about time you put your daughter's interests first,' she said. 'The poor lass must wonder why you ever bothered uprooting her – and if I find out that you only want her for the money she can earn—'

'Oh, Foxy, there you go again!' Ruby dramatically ran her hand across her forehead. 'You're giving me a headache by keeping going on at me. Of course, I love Kitty dearly. It's just that I'm having to learn how to be a mother and it isn't easy.'

Miss Fox felt slightly mollified. Admittedly, it couldn't be easy for her. After all, until Kitty had arrived, Ruby had never had to think of anyone but herself and she had been used to being the centre of attention.

'Well, just think on what I've said!' With that Miss Fox sailed from the room like a ship in full rig. No doubt she should go and sort out some sleeping arrangements for the latest addition to the household before she had the housekeeper moaning about it. As if she didn't have enough to do!

Chapter Thirty-Nine

Finally, late in July 1914, Sunday and Tom left the children at Treetops in the capable hands of Lavinia and caught the train to London. Sunday had given her husband no peace since seeing the newspaper report on Kitty, and at last they were on their way to search for her. Tom also hoped that a few days alone together would allow them to regain the closeness they had once shared and he was in good spirits, but Sunday's thoughts were all focused on tracking Kitty down. After all, she reasoned, if the Kitty she had read about in the paper was indeed *their* Kitty, it shouldn't be so hard, surely?

Once they had alighted from the train at Euston, they booked into a small but comfortable hotel in Marylebone.

'I was thinking we could have a nice meal in the hotel this evening and start our search in the morning,' Tom said with a hopeful sparkle in his eye but Sunday quashed his hopes immediately.

'The sooner we find her, the sooner we can return home,' she told him coldly, and so the search began in earnest that very evening as they began to tour the sites of the music halls to examine the acts that were advertised on the billboards outside. It was late in the afternoon on their second day when they at last found what they were looking for. They had hired a cab to take them to Wilton's Music Hall in the East End, halfway between Whitechapel and the Tower of London.

Almost before the hackney cab had stopped, Sunday leaped down, pointing excitedly to the billboard.

'Tom – it's Kitty. Look!'

Kitty's picture was plastered across a large billboard and even in her fine gown with her hair piled in curls high on the crown of her head, there could be no doubt that it was her.

Tom stared at it in wonderment. Kitty looked so grown up compared to the young girl he loved and remembered so well. For the first time in weeks Sunday was smiling and hopping from foot to foot in her excitement.

'She's not performing here until tomorrow evening,' he pointed out, but Sunday didn't care, she was so thrilled to have found her.

'You must go in and book our tickets immediately,' she ordered him. 'Then when the performance is over we'll ask if we can go backstage to see her.'

Almost as excited as his wife was, Tom strode away to do as he was told. For the rest of that evening and the whole of the next day, Sunday paced about their hotel room like a caged animal, wishing away the hours until she could see her beloved Kitty again. They left their room just the once when Tom persuaded her to go shopping for something special to wear to the performance. Although music-hall audiences came from all walks of life, including those who didn't have two ha'pennies to rub together, Sunday wanted to make an effort. She chose a pretty green satin gown that belied her forty-four years and showed off her still-slim figure to perfection.

At last it was time to set off for the music hall. Kitty had star billing and would be the final act on stage, so once again Sunday had to quell her impatience as she and Tom sat through several variety acts before the interval. It was then that, rising from her seat, she said, 'I'm going backstage right now. I shall burst if I have to wait much longer to see her.'

Tom looked uncertain as she snatched up her cloak. 'Look, pet, is that a good idea? She'll no doubt be busy getting ready.'

'I don't care,' Sunday retorted with a toss of her head. 'I'm sure she'll make time to see us when she knows we're here.' And with that she was off and Tom had no choice but to follow her.

Eventually, after explaining to various people that they were Kitty's family they were directed backstage and found themselves in a long corridor with dressing rooms on either side of it.

Sunday skipped along, studying the names on the doors until she stopped at one, exclaiming, 'This is it! KITTY NIGHTINGALE!' she told Tom, and without even giving him a chance to reply, she rapped on the door and threw it open.

The young woman sitting at the mirror applying her greasepaint spun round to see who it was and at sight of Sunday a million different emotions flitted across her face.

'*Sunday!*' Her first reaction was to race across the room and throw her arms about her, but she stopped herself just in time. She wasn't the same girl that Sunday had known. She carried dark secrets – and she knew that she would not be able to bear it if Sunday or Tom were ever to find out what she had been forced to do. 'How are you?' she asked instead, forcing her voice to remain steady as she turned back to the mirror.

Sunday looked at Tom in bewilderment before answering, 'Well, better now that I've seen you, pet. We were worried sick when we didn't hear from you.'

Kitty didn't believe her for a second. She had written letters which had been ignored – and they couldn't have *all* have got lost in the post. 'Well, as you can see, I'm perfectly all right and making rather a name for myself,' Kitty answered coolly.

'Yes, that's how I found you, I saw a piece about you in the paper.' Sunday was bemused and finding Kitty difficult to talk to, when she had been expecting a joyful reunion. 'And how are you enjoying living with your mother?' Sunday asked then.

317

Kitty glanced at her in the mirror. 'Very much,' she lied. How could she admit that she missed Sunday every single day and the happy life they had once shared?

'Oh . . . good.' Sunday gazed at the girl, thinking how very much she had changed. She was harder now and more brittle somehow, although she looked well enough. 'I err . . . was thinking that after your performance we might meet, go out for dinner and have a catch-up,' she suggested. 'Or if you're too tired this evening we could perhaps make it tomorrow morning?' she ended hopefully.

Kitty steeled herself. 'I'm afraid that won't be possible,' she managed to say. 'I'm being taken out to supper this evening immediately after my performance and I have plans with my mother tomorrow. But it was very nice to see you.'

For the first time, Sunday felt a flicker of annoyance. She and Tom had come all this way to surprise the girl but she was acting as if they were being dismissed.

'So when *will* you be available?' she asked sarcastically.

Kitty swallowed then and answered, 'I'm not sure without consulting my diary.'

'*Consulting your diary!*' Sunday was appalled at her flippant attitude. 'I thought you would be pleased to see us,' she went on, and there was a wobble in her voice now. Tom, who had said nothing, held her hand – and for once, Sunday didn't pull away.

'I am, of course – but I'm so busy, you see? But it was very good of you to call.' Kitty felt as if her heart was being ripped out but she knew that it was time to let them go once and for all now, for their own sakes. They must never be besmirched by what she had become, and the things she had done. She loved them too much to let that happen.

Sunday's shoulders sagged as she realised that Kitty was truly gone from her now. She and Tom were no longer needed – or even wanted, if Kitty's attitude was anything to go by.

'So,' Sunday said, 'I suppose we'd best be off then.' She desperately wanted Kitty to ask them to stay but the girl merely nodded as she returned to applying her greasepaint.

'Yes, I mustn't hold you up,' came that artificial voice. 'Goodbye then. Have a safe journey home.'

Blinded by tears, Sunday turned and allowed Tom to lead her from the dressing room and only when she was sure that they had gone did Kitty allow her emotions to bubble to the surface. That night, when she sang the tragic song by Irving Berlin, called 'When I Lost You', she gave the words such meaning that the audience wept with her.

One overcast day early in August, Sunday descended the stairs at Treetops to find Tom waiting for her in the hallway. The adults always rose before the children to enjoy a hot drink and ensure that the preparations for the children's breakfast were well under way and that the fires were lit, for although it was August the early mornings could be chilly in the big house.

'Good morning,' Sunday greeted him, much as she would have a stranger. She had grown even more distant since her encounter with Kitty in London, as if it was somehow his fault. Then when there was no answer she noted his grave face and asked, 'Is something wrong?'

'I'm afraid there is. Would you come into the day room with me?'

Sunday followed him, closed the door and looked at him questioningly.

'There is news from Nuneaton. As of eleven o'clock last night, Britain is at war with Germany.' There seemed no easy way to tell her, so he had just come out with it.

'Surely not! You must be mistaken.' Her face paled as she thought of what this might mean to them.

'I'm afraid there is no mistake,' he told her soberly. 'Our Prime Minister, Herbert Asquith, issued an ultimatum to Germany requesting that they get out of Belgium by midnight on August the third – and when they failed to do so he felt that he had no alternative but to declare war. People are already gathering outside Buckingham Palace in London to state their allegiance to the King and Queen, who have appeared on the balcony.'

'So what will happen now?' Sunday asked in a wobbly voice.

'Recruitment centres are springing up all over the country – no doubt there will be one in Nuneaton too – and all young men are being encouraged to join to go and fight for their King and Country. I should tell you that I have just spoken to Ben and he has told me that he intends to enrol this very day.'

'Oh no! Surely not.' Tears sprang to Sunday's eyes. Now, too late, she realised how estranged they had become since they had learned about his birth mother and the fact that her own husband was his father. None of it was Ben's fault, and yet she had treated him abominably, holding him at arm's length and denying him the affection he had always known. No wonder he wanted to enlist.

'But he's too young to go off fighting a war,' she objected. 'Perhaps we can encourage him to change his mind?' She stared at Tom hopefully but he shook his head.

'His mind is made up. And I should also tell you that I intend to enlist too.'

Sunday clutched at the back of a chair as her head wagged from side to side. 'B-but your leg! Surely you are not well enough to fight.'

He shrugged. 'There are many people involved in fighting a war apart from those who go to the front. They need stretcher-bearers and men to care for the horses. I could do either of those jobs.'

'But I don't *want* you to go! I need you here!'

He gave her a sad smile. 'We both know that you haven't needed me for some time,' he said, but there was no recrimination in his voice, only hurt. 'I think the time apart might do us both good. The way we have been living isn't natural for a man and wife.'

'And that's all *my* fault,' she wept. 'Oh, Tom, I *so* wanted to bear your child and then when I heard that Ben was yours and that some other woman had given you what I was unable to, I couldn't bear it.'

He sighed. There had been so much pain, so much sadness. 'Somewhere along the way I think you lost sight of the fact that the only one I ever really wanted was you. A child would have been a bonus but it never affected my feelings for you. The trouble is, I don't know if we can ever go back to the way we were now.'

She wanted to rant and rave, to throw herself at him and plead with him not to leave and yet somehow, she knew that he would not change his mind. And so she simply stood there as the only man she had ever loved quietly left the room, closing the door behind him.

When Ben and Tom drove into town they found queues of young men standing outside the hastily improvised recruitment office in the town centre. There was almost a party atmosphere amongst them, as if they were going off on some big adventure. 'After all,' Tom heard one young chap say, 'they reckon it will be all over in no time so we'd best get in while the goin's good.'

He and Ben joined the back of the queue and as Tom glanced at his son he wondered if they would be shipped somewhere together. He hoped so. Once they had given their details, birth date, address, et cetera the young men in front of them were being shown in to see a doctor for a hasty medical, to check whether they were fit enough to enrol. From the brief amount of time each of them spent in there with the medic, Tom could only surmise that the examination must be a very cursory affair. At last he and Ben reached the desk and after giving the required information Ben was ushered into the doctor. When it was Tom's turn he went in to find an elderly, harassed-looking little man in a white coat with wire spectacles perched on the end of his nose, sitting at a desk with a mountain of paperwork teetering at either side of him.

'Name?' he barked, then paused with his pen mid-air and frowned as he saw Tom limping towards him. 'No disrespect intended, my man, but aren't you a little long in the tooth to be here with the youngsters? And I can't help but notice you have quite a pronounced limp.'

'I'm intending to enrol as a stretcher-bearer or a groom to care for the horses,' Tom answered calmly.

'I see, and apart from your limp are you healthy or are there any other medical conditions I should know about?'

'None. I'm fit as a flea except for my leg.'

The doctor wrote for a while then, coming around the desk, he looked into Tom's eyes, throat and ears and listened to his chest.

'You'll do,' he said. Then issuing Tom with a pass he waved him away, saying, 'You will receive information as to where you will be stationed to receive your training within the week. Next!'

Tom limped away to rejoin Ben who was waiting outside for him smoking a cigarette. It was done, there could be no going back now and he prayed that God would have mercy on their souls.

Their faces anxious, Lavinia and Sunday were waiting for the men when they got home.

'So . . . did they accept you?' Sunday asked, her eyes trained on her husband. When he nodded, she let out a deep sigh. She had been praying that they would turn him away because of his limp but her prayers had gone unanswered.

Cissie and George were also there, and William who was listening gravely.

Lavinia spoke up. 'William and I should inform you that because of the latest developments we have decided not to wait until Christmas to get married. I want *all* my family present for this event, and that includes you and Ben, Tom. William has been to get a special licence this morning and we shall be married in two days' time. Let us hope it is before you both have to leave to start your training.'

'But I thought you wanted a big affair?' Cissie queried.

Lavinia shook her head. 'It wouldn't seem right now in view of what's happened. How could we enjoy our day, knowing that young men and our loved ones were away fighting for our country? No, William and I will be quite content with a nice quiet affair. I was hoping that you would give me away, Tom.'

Tom flushed with pleasure. 'It would be an honour. But now I must go and see to the horses if you'll all excuse me. From what I heard whispered in town it won't be only the men that are going to be shipped off to war. They intend to take all the healthy horses too.' He left then without looking so much as once at his wife as she stood there tearing at the handkerchief in her hands.

Cissie and George drifted away too then. George had decided that for now he would remain at Treetops to try and keep the place running, although he couldn't promise that he would never enlist if hostilities didn't end as quickly as everyone was forecasting. There was no way he wanted to be branded a coward.

'Why don't you go and persuade Cook to make us all a nice cup of tea, darling?' Lavinia suggested to William and he obligingly went off to do as requested although he wondered if he would get any sense out of Mrs Cotton. Her loud sobs had been heard echoing all along the hallway for most of the morning, for her grandson had enlisted too and she was already worried sick about how he would fare. Even the children were subdued; they had picked up on the uneasy atmosphere and were drifting about the house like silent little ghosts.

Once alone with her daughter, Lavinia told her, 'William and I have also decided that due to the circumstances we shall live here rather than in his townhouse after the wedding. With Ben and Tom going you will need all the help you can get, but I'm sure we shall manage between us.'

Still stunned at the developments, Sunday merely nodded and deciding that it was time she spoke out, Lavinia said: 'Don't you think it's time you and Tom were friends again? Do you *really* want him to go away to war with things so strained between you? I don't want to interfere between husband and wife, sweetheart, but this estrangement has gone on for long enough. How will you live with yourself if anything should happen to him, knowing that you sent him away feeling unloved and unwanted?'

For a moment Sunday merely chewed on her lip as she blinked back tears. But suddenly they gushed from her eyes and poured down her cheeks. 'But I *do* still love him and want him,' she sobbed.

'Then *tell* him before it's too late,' her mother advised and drawing her into her arms she held her convulsing frame close to her.

That afternoon was unbearably hot and even when darkness cloaked the landscape there was no escape from the humidity. There was not so much as a hint of breeze, and Sunday's wide-open bedroom window did nothing to ease the heat. The house was quiet as she lay on her bed thinking on her mother's words. She was very aware that Tom was only yards away along the landing, but it felt as if they were miles apart, and now at last she allowed herself to admit how much she had missed his nearness. Soon she would miss him even more. He would be gone, possibly for ever, and the thought was unbearable.

She tossed and turned for some time, eventually clambering from the bed and going to the window to look out across the moon-washed grounds. Beyond the copse she could see the lake glistening like liquid silver and somewhere an owl was hooting. Everything looked so peaceful that it was hard even now to believe that they were at war. And then finally she knew what she must do and she prayed earnestly that she hadn't left it too late. On bare feet, she left her room and tiptoed along the landing to the room where Tom now slept. Then mustering every ounce of courage she had, she gently tried the door. It was unlocked so she slipped into the room, closing the door softly behind her. She had expected to find Tom in bed but was surprised to see his silhouette in the window. He was quite naked and as he turned to stare at her questioningly, she suddenly started to cry.

'Oh, Tom, I've been such a fool,' she said with a catch in her voice. 'I've punished you for having a relationship with someone you knew before we were even together, and I've punished Ben too. Do you think he will ever be able to forgive me? Can *you* forgive me? I'm so, so sorry . . .'

There was a prolonged pause and she was so terrified that her husband had gone from her for ever and her eyes were so blinded by tears that when his arms came about her, she started in shock.

'You silly little goose,' he whispered into her hair. 'Of course I forgive you. You must know by now that you are the only girl I've ever loved.'

'But – but you'll be gone soon.' Her voice held a note of panic.

'Aye, I will, pet. But now I'll have someone to come home to again, so you can be sure I'll be careful.'

And then his lips tenderly found hers and as he lifted her and carried her to the bed she forgot all about the war; all about everything but the man she adored.

Chapter Forty

'I'm afraid the fact that we're now at war is going to affect Kitty's bookings badly,' Max told Ruby as he sat poring over the newspaper in her drawing room.

'Why is that?' Ruby asked, selecting another sugar candy from the large box at the side of her.

'Well, for a start, half of the young men are flooding into the recruitment offices, and without them it's doubtful their young ladies will want to visit the music halls alone.'

Ruby licked her lips. She couldn't see what all the fuss was about or why Britain had volunteered to enter the war in the first place. Why should something that was happening hundreds of miles away affect them? But then Ruby had never been very politically minded.

'Will you have to go?' she asked then.

Max shook his head. 'Not immediately. They'll be looking for younger men to start off with and I'm well into middle age now.'

'There you are then,' Ruby replied smugly. 'They're saying it will all be over by Christmas, aren't they?' Privately, she wasn't too concerned about Kitty's singing career taking a dive. The girl was earning far more now entertaining Richard's wealthy friends, although she couldn't tell Max that, of course, and Kitty had no idea how much money was changing hands either. Ruby was raking it in, thanks to her beautiful daughter, and Kitty was now so besotted with Richard that Ruby was sure she would have jumped off Tower Bridge had he told her to.

Max stared at her thoughtfully for a moment. He could have told her that he thought everyone's life would probably change because of the war. If there was an invasion, no one would be safe and it seemed certain that shortages of food and clothes would occur. But he didn't bother. He had finally realised that Ruby's whole world centred around Ruby – and sometimes now he wondered how he had ever thought her attractive. There had been a time when he would have walked through fire for her. She had been one of the best-loved music-hall singers in London, but then her looks had begun to fade and she had blamed him for the decline in her career. His thoughts were interrupted then when the door suddenly burst open and Kitty's puppy came gambolling into the room.

'*Ugh!* Get that disgusting creature out of here before it wees all over my carpet,' Ruby cried. She well and truly hated the dog, and she and Kitty had exchanged more than a few harsh words when Ruby had ordered that Tallulah should live outside.

'She most certainly will not,' Kitty had said indignantly, standing up to her mother for the first time since her arrival. 'She will sleep in my room with me and that's an end to it! Otherwise I shall have to look for somewhere else for us to live where we can stay together.'

Ruby had instantly backed down. She couldn't afford for Kitty to leave now; the girl was paying for her to carry on drinking, eating expensive chocolates and treating herself to anything she fancied.

Max laughed as Tallulah rolled onto her back for a nice old belly-rub and seconds later Kitty pounded into the room and came to a skidding halt when she saw her pet.

'Sorry,' she apologised as she bent to scoop the wriggling pup into her arms. Knowing how much Ruby disliked dogs she did try to keep Tallulah away from her, but was not always successful, as now.

'Can't you take her out into the back garden?' Ruby enquired peevishly.

'I was just about to, but she was too quick for me.' Kitty smiled at Max, then quickly departed. She took Tallulah out into the garden every day to see young Arthur now and like Kitty he was besotted with the little dog.

Once they had gone Ruby frowned as a thought occurred to her. 'Do you think Richard Fitzherbert will go to war?'

'I think it's highly unlikely that he'll volunteer – let's put it that way,' Max answered sceptically.

Ruby breathed a sigh of relief and they went on to speak of other things until Max left to keep an appointment with one of his clients.

Kitty was outside with Arthur by then and the two of them were laughing as they watched Tallulah bounding about the garden. She was like a little spring lamb and Kitty couldn't imagine being without her now. Tallulah had become her confidante, for as close as she was to Maggie there were some things that Kitty just couldn't confide to her. Late at night when she had been entertaining one of Richard's friends she would lie on her bed and pour her heart out to Tallulah, who seemed to understand the deep sense of shame that Kitty was experiencing. The little dog would lick away her tears and snuggle close to her as Kitty sobbed into her soft fur.

'But I know he loves me really, despite what he makes me do,' Kitty would whisper to her, trying to convince herself. 'And someday soon he'll ask me to marry him and I'll be able to put all this behind me.' She loved Richard so much that she had to tell herself this, otherwise she feared that she might lose the will to live.

Maggie joined them then to inform Kitty, 'The dress you ordered yesterday has just been delivered. I've unpacked it and hung it in your room.'

'Thank you, Maggie.' Kitty had treated herself to a dress in the very latest fashion, with a dropped waist and a straight skirt that reached to the ankles. However, the new dress was the last thing on her mind at present. Like Ruby, she was concerned that Richard might think of joining the Army. The Secretary of State for War, Field Marshall Earl Kitchener, had had posters stating YOUR COUNTRY NEEDS YOU plastered all across the city, and in central London alone the response at the recruiting offices had been so successful that mounted police had been deployed to hold the crowds in check. What if Richard were to take it into his head to join? She decided she would speak to him about his intentions that very night. He had promised her that this evening would be just for the two of them and she was looking forward to it. However, just before six o'clock Richard telephoned and left a message with the maid telling Kitty that he had been unexpectedly called away for the night and so unfortunately would have to cancel their arrangement.

The maid passed it on to Maggie who was secretly pleased when she delivered it. Kitty was looking tired and she thought a quiet night in would do her the world of good. They were few and far between at the moment, although now that Maggie had Tallulah to keep her company while Kitty was out, she didn't get nearly so lonely.

'Oh!' Kitty was disappointed at first, but soon decided that it would be nice if she and Maggie had an evening in together. She felt guilty for abandoning her friend so much, but she had been so busy that she hadn't really had much choice. Now suddenly the thought of a long leisurely soak in the bath and an early night didn't seem so bad after all.

Kitty left the door to the bathroom open while she bathed and she and Maggie chatted through the door.

'I was reading that there's going to be a terrible shortage of nurses and doctors as well as young men,' Maggie remarked. 'A lot of them are going to be shipped over to the field hospitals they're erecting in Belgium and France by all accounts.'

Kitty sighed. She was heartily sick of hearing about the war. It seemed to be the main topic of conversation on everyone's lips.

'And they reckon that women will be called on to take over men's jobs as well,' Maggie chattered on.

'Doing what?'

'Factory jobs, driving – anything the men did, really. Someone's got to do them, haven't they, otherwise the country will grind to a halt.'

Kitty frowned. She couldn't quite imagine such a thing. A woman's place had always been in the home, keeping house and bringing up her family, and it was hard to imagine a woman doing a man's job. But then she supposed that time would tell. If what Lord Kitchener had forecast came true, the war would be over by Christmas and the men would all be returning home again.

She came out of the bathroom eventually to find Maggie staring broodily from the window down into the garden and she asked, 'Are you all right, Maggie?'

'What? Oh yes – yes, thank you. I was just thinking . . . I wonder what's happening back in Nuneaton. Do you think anyone we know will have joined up?'

'I should imagine so.' Kitty began to rub her wet hair with the towel. 'Ben may well have done, although I'm not sure if Tom, George and your father would be too old?'

As the closed look came down in Maggie's eyes at the mention of her father, Kitty could have bitten her tongue out. Maggie very rarely mentioned the Daweses; it was if she had closed the door on that chapter of her life.

'Perhaps you should write to Sunday and Tom to see what's going on there?' Maggie suggested, but now it was Kitty who stubbornly clamped her mouth shut. 'Why should I?' she said. But it hurt her to say the cruel words.

Maggie shrugged, at a loss as to what to say. It truly felt that she and Kitty had only each other left from their former life now, but that suited her just fine. It was such a wonderful relief, not having to lie awake fretting about whether Victor, her adopted father, would sneak into her room during the night to do unspeakable things to her. Sweat broke out on her brow just thinking about it and she hastily said, 'Why don't we go for a nice stroll? We could take Tallulah, she'd like that. Then we can come back and you can catch up on some of the sleep you've missed.'

It sounded very appealing so Kitty nodded and began to get ready. Sometime later with Tallulah on her lead they set off, strolling arm in arm. It was a beautiful evening with a light breeze, and Kitty felt herself relaxing as they meandered along the streets of Chelsea. Kitty bent at one point to untangle Tallulah's lead from around her leg and as she did so, Maggie saw Richard's car cruising towards them. She frowned. He said that he had been called out of town – so what was he still doing here in the area? More to the point, where was he going?

He passed by without noticing them and Maggie was relieved. This was a case of least said soonest mended as far as she was concerned. She was enjoying having Kitty to herself for a time and didn't want anything to spoil it. Even so, once again she had to question Richard Fitzherbert's commitment to Kitty.

'There, that's better, isn't it?' Kitty straightened and smiled at Tallulah. 'I shall be so pleased when you get used to walking on a lead.'

The dog merely wagged her tail and tugged ahead again. Everything and everywhere was so new and exciting, and she wanted to go everywhere and see and smell everything all at once. In fact, people seeing her and Kitty might wonder who was taking whom for a walk.

Maggie linked arms with Kitty and they went on their way with Kitty blissfully unaware that Richard had been caught out in yet another lie. The evening was drawing in a little when they returned to Brunswick Villa to find Ruby entertaining her latest gentleman friend in the drawing room.

'Ah, Kitty darling,' Ruby cooed as the two girls walked past the open door. 'Do come and meet Mr Wallace.'

Kitty reluctantly passed Tallulah's lead to Maggie and entered the room.

'Teddy, dear, this is my niece, Kitty Nightingale. You must have heard of her. She's making quite a name for herself around the music halls. Voice like an angel, darling – nearly as good as mine.'

The smarmy little man bent and kissed the back of Kitty's hand. She suppressed a shudder. His hair was plastered to his head with Macassar oil and he reminded her a little too closely for comfort of some of the 'friends' that Richard insisted she should entertain.

'It's very nice to meet you,' she said politely, tugging her hand from his. 'But now if you will excuse me, I was hoping for an early night.' Without giving Ruby a chance to object she quickly slipped from the room, closing the door firmly behind her.

Ruby's cheeks had been rose-red, and Kitty feared it wasn't just down to the amount of rouge she wore. Her drinking was out of control now; she would drink wine with her breakfast and continue for most of the day, but then shame-faced, Kitty knew that she was hardly in a position to criticise. She herself had taken to having a stiff drink on the evenings when Richard wanted her to entertain. She had found that it calmed her nerves and helped her to relax as she lay in the men's arms. Every time, she would close her eyes and try to pretend it was Richard. That was the only way she could endure what they did to her, although she had to admit that the gifts they bestowed on her were nice. She had a drawer full of expensive jewellery now and a selection of the very finest French perfumes, but none of them really meant anything to her. All she cared about were the times when she and Richard were alone together. Sighing, she took the stairs two at a time to find Maggie and Tallulah waiting for her in her room.

'Why don't you treat yourself to an early night too?' Kitty suggested as she scooped Tallulah into her arms.

'Actually I think I will, if you're sure you don't need me.' Maggie covered her mouth with her hand to hide a yawn, then after pecking

Kitty's cheek she went away, leaving the other girl alone. Kitty's thoughts turned to Richard and her stomach started to churn. Would he feel the need to sign up and go to war? She wasn't sure how she would cope without him if he did. And now, because he had cancelled their date, she would have to pass a sleepless night before she found out what his intentions were. With a sigh, she began to take the pins from her hair, blissfully unaware of Tallulah, whose tail was wagging furiously as she systematically chewed up yet another of Kitty's satin shoes on the floor behind her.

Chapter Forty-One

With a heavy heart, Sunday stood at the drawing-room window at Treetops watching Tom galloping down the drive on one of the stallions he had reared. Astride a horse his limp was unnoticeable and he cut a dashing figure. When he wasn't helping George with jobs that needed doing about the house or gardens he spent most of his time in the stables now, and Treetops had become known as one of the finest stud farms in the country. Tom had bred most of the horses stabled there and Sunday knew that he was devastated to learn that the majority of them would be taken to war and would probably never return.

It was heart-breaking too, when she thought of all the time and effort he had invested in them. When a horse was due to foal he had been known to spend whole nights in the stables with the mare, to ensure that all went well, but there was nothing to be done now but accept the situation. In the field to one side of him she could see Ben talking to George, and guilt sliced through her again. She had been so cold to them both for so long, and now she would have only a very short time to try and make it up to them. It seemed so unfair. Why did this damn war have to go and happen anyway? She was continually whipping herself. Perhaps if she and Tom had not been estranged he would never have felt the need to go away. With his lame leg he would certainly have been classed as unsuitable for fighting but because she had been so stupid he would now still be at risk in his role as a horse handler. But there was no turning the clock back now. What was done was done and they would all have to make the best of it.

She was still standing there a few moments later when her mother entered the room and Sunday forced a smile to her face. Lavinia was due to be married the following day and Sunday wanted to make sure that it was as pleasant an event as it could possibly be, even with the shadow of war hanging over them all.

'Cook is running herself ragged in the kitchen,' Lavinia informed her with a grin. 'There was really no need for you all to go to the trouble of a party. William and I would have been quite happy to just catch the train to Brighton for a few days after the ceremony.'

'It's the least we can do.' Sunday planted an affectionate kiss on her cheek. 'It's just so sad that you won't have the big wedding we'd planned at Christmas and the honeymoon in the South of France.'

Lavinia waved her hand airily. 'My dear girl, I am about to marry the love of my life. What more could I ask?'

'Just think,' Sunday chuckled as something occurred to her. 'After tomorrow you'll be plain Mrs Dewhurst and no longer Lady Huntley.'

'That's fine by me,' Lavinia answered. 'In fact, I can hardly wait. But now have you sorted out what you're going to wear? I do wish you would have let me buy you a new outfit.'

'It doesn't matter what I wear. You are the bride and it will be you everyone is looking at, which is just as it should be,' Sunday pointed out. 'And besides, I really don't need any more clothes. But now will you excuse me? If Cook is getting in a flap I ought to go and give her a hand. She still has your wedding cake to ice. You just relax, I want you feeling all rested for your big day.'

'I just wish that I could have seen William today,' Lavinia said wistfully and as she left the room Sunday wagged a finger at her.

'You know it's bad luck for the bride to see the groom the day before the wedding.'

'I'm hardly some young filly, I can't see what difference it would have made at our age,' Lavinia grumbled, but Sunday was not going to budge on this one.

'Just settle down and read a magazine or something,' she suggested in a no-nonsense kind of voice and then with a last grin she went off to the kitchen.

Lavinia Huntley's wedding day dawned sunny and bright and Treetops was a hive of activity as Cissie and Sunday helped the children who now lived there into their Sunday-best clothes. Lavinia had been like a grandmother to them and they were all keen to be a part of the special occasion. Treetops was their home, and they loved, and were loved by, everyone there.

'Goodness knows when we'll have time to get ready ourselves,' Cissie muttered as she brushed a little girl's hair before tying it back with a blue ribbon. 'There you are, Susan. Run along now.' And the child went to join the others.

It was so unlike Cissie to grumble that Sunday peeped at her from the corner of her eye. Now that she came to think about it, Cissie hadn't seemed to be herself for a few days. Normally they confided everything to each other but Cissie hadn't said that anything was wrong.

'Right, that's the last one done,' Sunday said then as she eyed her charges with satisfaction. 'It's your turn now, Cissie. Go and get changed while I help Mother with her hair. I've only got to slip my dress on so I shan't be two minutes.' She wagged a warning finger at the children then. 'And mind you lot don't go getting up to mischief and getting dirty.'

The children giggled and skipped happily away as Cissie slowly made her way to the room where her clothes were laid out ready. They had decided it would save time if she didn't have to rush off

336

back to the cottage. Once inside the room she closed the door behind her and her chin sank to her chest as she sniffed back a tear. Her son had paid her the third visit in as many weeks only days ago and once again he had played on her sympathy and gone away with yet more of hers and George's savings tucked in his pocket. Cissie had tried to tell him this time that she really couldn't spare any more, but he had become quite abusive with her and it had almost broken her heart.

'I should have realised you wouldn't want to help me,' he had whined. 'You never wanted me in the first place so why should you want me now?'

'But I *do* want you . . . I *always* wanted you!' Cissie had objected as he sat with a fierce look on his face. Then when he had risen to leave, she had panicked. What if he turned his back on her and she never saw him again? She had dreamed for so long of finding him and now she finally had – and yet, deep down, she was ashamed to admit that although he was her own flesh and blood, she didn't like him. He had soon shown himself to be like his father in nature as well as looks, and being no fool, Cissie understood that he only wanted to keep a connection with her so that he could bleed her dry of money. Now, too late, she believed every word his adoptive parents had said about him – but her savings were almost gone. What was George going to say when he found out? Never in their entire married life had they had secrets from each other, but she was too ashamed to tell him what she had done.

With a sigh she put the thoughts to the back of her mind. Now was not the time to dwell on them. Tomorrow would be soon enough when the wedding was over and the newlyweds were enjoying their honeymoon. Swallowing a sob, she hurriedly changed her dress and tried to focus on the day ahead.

Downstairs, George was waiting to take the bride to church in Tom's car when there was a tap at the door. All the staff were frantically rushing about trying to get the food laid out in the dining room for when the happy couple returned so George answered the door to find the postman on the step.

'Morning, George.' Bill Day touched his cap. 'Big day today, eh, for Lady Huntley, God bless her. And not afore time. I reckon she's overdue a little happiness. But hark at me rabbitin' on. I've a couple o' letters here for you.' He frowned as he handed them over, wishing he had a shilling for every such letter he had delivered in the town and surrounding villages that week.

George frowned too when he saw the official-looking envelopes. 'Thanks, Bill.' They were undoubtedly the letters telling Ben and Tom when they were to report for training, but what a time for them to come. Hastily making a decision he stuffed them deep down into the pocket of his jacket just as Sunday appeared on the stairs.

'Anything for me, George?'

'Nah, just a bill for me.' He felt no guilt whatsoever for the lie. If Sunday were to see the letters before they left for the church, the day would be ruined before it had even begun. He would leave them where they would be found late that evening.

The day was a huge success from beginning to end. Lavinia looked beautiful in her blue dress and matching blue picture hat trimmed with silk roses, and she was so happy that she positively glowed and looked far younger than her years. William looked handsome too and when he saw his bride walking down the aisle towards him on Tom's arm, little Susan and her twin Becky clutching a posy each and trotting behind, his chest swelled with pride. The Reverend Lockett's service was touching, and by the time he pronounced them man and wife there was hardly a dry eye in the church. Outside in the sunshine the newlyweds were showered with rice and rose petals before being ushered into the car by George, who then drove them back to Treetops Manor.

'If only Kitty had been here it would have been just perfect,' Sunday said sadly as she was driven home in the trap by Tom. It was a sturdy old contraption pulled by their faithful nag, Meg. She at least would be safe when the Army requisitioned their war horses, for she was certainly too old to be of any use in the war.

Unsure how to answer, Tom shrugged. He too still missed Kitty although he rarely mentioned her for fear of Sunday bursting into tears again. 'She's young and impressionable and I've no doubt she's having the time of her life in London.' He reached over to gently squeeze his wife's hand. 'I'm sure she'll be in touch again when the novelty wears off. But come along now; we won't have sad thoughts today.'

'No, you're quite right!' Sunday stuck her chin in the air and smiled at some of the children who were seated behind them. 'Let's go and get this party started!'

That afternoon, the house rang with laughter and thoughts of war were pushed to the back of everyone's mind. Lavinia and William had eyes only for each other, which Sunday thought was just as it should be. For the first time in her life Lavinia had a man who truly loved her and her daughter was sure she had never looked more radiant.

Mrs Cotton had produced a banquet fit for a king. There were cold joints of beef and pork, pies and sausage rolls, pickles, sandwiches, salads, fresh baked bread and rolls and all manner of treats, and the children took full advantage of it. So much so that one little boy who had overindulged in the quivering jellies and blancmanges had to be whisked away to the lavatory, where he was heartily sick. Mid-afternoon, after they had all eaten, Lavinia seated herself at the piano to play some well-loved tunes and soon everyone was dancing, including Sunday and Tom.

'Eeh, pet, I'm that glad we're on good terms again,' he whispered huskily into her hair.

When she stared up at him, all the love she felt for him was there in her eyes. 'So am I. I just wish I'd come to my senses sooner. Before you—'

He quickly pressed a finger to her lips. 'I've told you, this is a happy day so we'll have no more of that sort of talk.'

At tea-time, Lavinia and William disappeared upstairs to get into their going-away outfits and when they came back down they were showered with yet more rice and confetti. The children were enjoying themselves immensely and the house echoed with laughter.

'Let's be having you then,' George said with a broad grin. 'The car is all ready and waiting for you outside, and if you don't get a move on you'll miss your train.' He hoisted their suitcases and took them outside to stow in the boot while the happy couple said their hasty goodbyes.

Sunday got quite tearful and Lavinia chuckled as she hugged her close. 'Now then, what's all this? We're only going away for a few days. I'll be back before you know it.'

'I know,' Sunday sniffed. 'But I shall miss you so.'

Lavinia planted a gentle kiss on her forehead, then her groom said, 'Now then, Mrs Dewhurst,' took her hand and hurried her out to the car. William could hardly wait to have her all to himself for a few days.

Everyone stood on the steps waving and throwing the last of the rice, and the children howled with laughter as the car rattled off down the drive with all the tin cans they had tied to the bumper jogging along behind them.

'Crikey, they'll hear them coming from a mile away,' Cissie chortled, then linking her arm through Sunday's they went back into the house. The party was over and now it was time to get the children ready for bed and start the tidying up.

'Phew, let's put our feet up an' have a cuppa for ten minutes before we start on the cleanin',' Cissie suggested an hour later as she filled the kettle at the sink and everyone agreed that was a very good idea.

They were still all there when George returned from the railway station ten minutes later.

'Did they get off all right?' Sunday asked as she peeped at him over the rim of her cup.

'They certainly did and will be on their way to Brighton by now, lucky devils.' He glanced at Cissie then. She'd been looking a little tired and agitated these last few weeks and he wondered if he should ask Sunday whether they could have a few days off for a little break somewhere, just the two of them. They could afford it if he pinched a bit out of their savings, and as their own children had all flown the nest now there was nothing to stop them. He then remembered the letters in his coat pocket and the happy feeling faded away. Much as he hated to do it, he couldn't withhold Ben and Tom's mail for any longer.

'Ah, these came just before we went to church,' he said with a forced smile. 'Everyone was in such a dither to be on time that I stuffed them in my pocket and forgot all about them.'

He handed them to the two men and as Sunday saw the envelope over Tom's shoulder the colour drained from her face.

'It's asking me to report for training the week after next,' he said solemnly.

'I'm to go at the beginning of next week,' Ben told them and a silence descended on the kitchen.

It was broken when Tom said in a falsely jovial voice, 'Well, it stands to reason you'll need more training than me. I'm only going to be tending the horses and stretcher-bearing. Where have you got to go, Ben?'

'Warwick.'

'Oh!' Tom was quietly disappointed. He had hoped that they might be able to stay together. 'I'm to report to a training camp in Worcester. Still, I dare say we'll both get leave when the training's done before we get shipped out, so we'll no doubt see each other again after you've gone.'

As Sunday stared at the two of them, she saw the deep love that had grown between father and son, and once again she was ashamed at how she had behaved, and she ran to put her arms about them both and gather them to her. Now the nightmare was about to begin.

Chapter Forty-Two

'What do you mean, they're closing down some of the theatres and music halls?' Ruby snapped.

'Exactly what I say,' Max answered patiently. 'And don't snap at me. It wasn't my decision.'

Ruby was vexed. And just when Kitty was earning really good money as well, she thought. Still, it wasn't all doom and gloom. At least Richard would still keep her busy, 'entertaining'. The girl was in great demand now.

'I dare say everyone thought that as most of the young men are going to war there won't be a call for such places now,' Max said.

'Hmm.' Ruby took a long swig of the sweet sherry she had become partial to and Max stared at her disapprovingly. Lately her shapely curves had turned to rolls of fat and she was looking her age. Easy to see why she was no longer in demand. The same was not true for Kitty, of course. The public loved her, simply couldn't get enough of her, so it was very unfortunate that this should happen now. Oh well. He heaved a sigh. Everyone was saying that the war would be over in no time, so hopefully it would only mean a temporary break in her career.

Max took his leave soon after and Miss Fox entered the room to stare disapprovingly at the glass in Ruby's hand.

'I've said it before and I'll say it again! It's no wonder you're putting so much weight on, my girl. Drinking at this time of the day and all those chocolates you eat!'

When tears started to Ruby's eyes the woman's voice instantly softened. 'I don't mean to be harsh on you,' she said as she placed the stopper back in the sherry decanter and moved it out of reach. 'But you really should start to take a little better care of yourself. Get out in the fresh air for a nice brisk walk. Kitty could come with you. You spend nowhere near enough time with her.'

'Oh, here you go again,' Ruby said spitefully. 'Why don't you just lock her in her room where you can keep a constant eye on her and have done with it? I sometimes think you worry more about her than me,' she sulked.

'Now you know that's not true,' Miss Fox chided, taking a seat at the side of her. 'But she's so young and naïve, I just worry that she could be taken advantage of. It's so easy for a pretty girl like her to have her head turned, as you know to your cost.'

'I'm sure Kitty won't make the same mistakes that I did,' Ruby said as colour flooded into her cheeks. 'And it didn't turn out so badly for me, did it?'

Deciding that enough had been said for now on that subject, Miss Fox withdrew a number of envelopes from the pocket of her skirt. 'These are all bills that are outstanding,' she said. 'Can we afford to pay them?'

'Of course we can.' Ruby rudely snatched them and began to glance through them.

'But how?' persevered Foxy. 'How can we pay them?'

'Kitty earns a very good wage,' Ruby answered shortly. 'And I as her mother handle her finances for her. Such a young girl would probably waste it all.'

'Then surely you could put the money away for her?' Miss Fox said tentatively. It didn't seem right to her that Kitty's money was now paying the lion's share of running the house as well as keeping Ruby in the manner to which she had become accustomed. 'We

344

could always look round for a smaller house and do away with some of the staff.'

'We'll do no such thing!' Ruby bristled at the very idea. 'Kitty is given more than enough for her needs. Have you heard her complaining?'

'Well no, but—'

'Then I suggest you leave that side of things to me – and now, if you don't mind, I can feel a headache coming on. I think I'll go back to bed for a little lie-down.'

As Ruby heaved herself up from the sofa Miss Fox opened her mouth to protest but then clamped it shut again. She had been about to say that Ruby had only just got up – but it would only cause yet another row and they had been having far too many of them lately. She watched the woman wobble from the room then with a sigh she began to tidy the cushions.

Upstairs, Maggie was also feeling worried. Kitty was in the bath in the adjoining room and when Maggie opened a drawer to put some clean handkerchiefs away, she came across the sponges and the small bottle of vinegar. It was almost half empty again – and Maggie knew that it was time to express her concerns. She had put it off for too long but the way she saw it, Kitty was playing with fire.

When Kitty emerged from the bathroom wrapped in a large fluffy towel she found Maggie sitting on the end of the bed with her hands folded primly in her lap.

'Oh dear, I know that look. What have I done now?' she asked.

Without a word Maggie rose and went to the drawer, and when she withdrew the offending articles, colour flamed into Kitty's cheeks.

'What do you think you are doing, snooping amongst my private things!' Jumping up and running over to Maggie, she wrested them from her hand.

'I wasn't snooping, I was putting your clean handkerchiefs away,' Maggie answered reasonably.

Kitty was quivering with humiliation and indignation but suddenly her shoulders sagged and a tear slid down her cheek. 'It – it's not what you think,' she hiccuped as Maggie put an arm about her shoulders.

'Then perhaps it would help if you talked to me about it,' she said comfortably.

For a moment, she thought that Kitty might refuse, but the girl could keep it to herself no longer. 'I . . . I have to . . . to entertain certain of Richard's friends for him.'

'*What*?' It was even worse than Maggie had imagined. 'You mean you . . .'

'Yes.' Kitty nodded miserably.

'But *why*?' Maggie felt it was completely out of character for Kitty to lower herself to such levels.

'Because Richard took some photographs of me when I was . . . Well, I'd had a drink and wasn't really aware of what was happening and I was – shall we say in a state of undress?' She shuddered. It sounded even more sordid when she said it out loud. 'Richard promised me that he only took them for himself to look at, but the men saw them somehow and stole some without Richard knowing – and now, if I don't do as they ask, they'll expose them to the public, so I really don't have a choice, do I?'

'Richard took photographs of you in a state of undress while you were powerless to stop him?' Maggie said, her voice incredulous. 'Did you willingly undress for him?'

'Well no,' Kitty admitted, then seeing the look on Maggie's face she hurried to defend him. 'But he only undressed me so that he could take the pictures for his eyes only. I'm not sure how the other men got to see them. They must have visited him when he wasn't expecting them.'

'Yes – and I just saw a purple pig fly past the window,' Maggie snorted before she could stop herself.

Kitty instantly pulled away from her. Even now she couldn't bear to hear a wrong word about Richard.

Maggie looked at her imploringly. 'Surely you can see that you're being blackmailed into doing something you don't want to do,' she said. 'And if Richard loves you so much, how can he bear to let other men paw all over you. It just doesn't add up!'

'He doesn't have any choice, like me,' Kitty muttered. 'But one day it will all stop and we'll be married then.'

'And has he actually *asked* you to marry him?'

'Well, not in so many words – but he's implied that we'll always be together,' Kitty answered in a wobbly voice.

'Oh, Kitty, this has to stop. It can't go on.'

'It has to go on for now.' Kitty dropped onto the stool in front of her dressing table. 'Richard has promised me that it won't be for much longer, and then the men will return the photos and that will be an end to it.'

'But . . .' Maggie hardly dared voice her fears. 'What happens if you fall with child before then?'

'That's what they are for – to prevent that happening.' Kitty nodded towards the sponges. 'Ruby gave them to me and told me how to use them.'

'She *what*!' Maggie was appalled. 'But Ruby is your *mother*! Surely she should be discouraging you from losing your virginity before marriage?' *Not like me*, she thought bitterly. *Victor Dawes made sure o' that.*

Kitty smiled sadly. 'Ruby lives a different life to the ones we led,' she pointed out. 'She's far more daring. Why, Sunday and Tom would have murdered me if they thought I'd even contemplated

347

being intimate with a man before I was married. But Ruby lives for pleasure.'

'Hmm, well, there must be something we can do to stop this going on,' Maggie muttered. 'You're being used and abused against your will – and it isn't right.'

'It's not so bad as you think.' Kitty laid a gentle hand on Maggie's arm. 'I always have a good drink before I have to do it and that takes the edge off anything. Why, sometimes I can't even remember it afterwards. I sort of block it from my mind.'

Now Maggie understood the half-empty bottles of wine she had found hidden about the room and she shivered with revulsion.

'Perhaps we should get right away from here,' she said. 'Go where nobody knows us. I'm sure we'd be able to find jobs and somewhere to live, especially now there's a war on. They reckon women will be having to do men's jobs while the men are away fighting. Or perhaps we should tell Foxy what's going on? I know she's been worried about you for a while and she might be able to stop this.'

'You really don't understand, do you?' Kitty said. 'You mustn't tell *anyone*. It would only make things worse – and anyway, I don't want to leave. I could *never* leave Richard. If this is the only way I can be with him, then I'll put up with it for as long as it takes.'

Maggie stared back, feeling at a complete loss. It appeared that Richard Fitzherbert had bound Kitty with invisible threads, and until the girl could see him for what he really was, there was nothing Maggie could do to help her. The trouble was, by then it could well be too late. Far too late.

Chapter Forty-Three

'George?' Cissie gulped to clear her throat. Her husband looked up from the newspaper he was reading in their kitchen. It was a beautiful balmy evening and through the open doorway they could hear the sound of the birds in the trees.

'Yes, pet, what is it?' He'd known for a while that something was troubling her, and was relieved that she now seemed ready to speak about whatever it was.

Cissie meanwhile was trying to choose her words carefully, and as she thought of their depleted savings, guilt gnawed away at her like a hungry woodworm.

'I, err . . . I was thinking about what you suggested earlier – about us taking a little holiday. I think it's a lovely idea, but the thing is . . . I've used some of our savings.'

Relief flashed in his eyes. 'Is that all? Well, you're entitled to, my lovely. What did you spend it on – a nice new dress or hat?'

'No, nothing like that.' Cissie twisted the piece of huckaback she had been drying the dishes with into a knot. 'The truth is, I helped Hugh out – again.'

George frowned. Since meeting the man, he'd been making enquiries about him in the town and nothing he had learned was good. No one had a kind word to say about him. He was workshy, a drunkard, a bully and a gambler. George, however, had not shared any of this information with Cissie. She clearly adored her son, and after all the years of being apart she was determined to see only the good in him. George secretly doubted that there *was* any good, but he would not have hurt her for the world so he had kept his own counsel. Now, however, he asked, 'How much have you helped him out?'

Cissie licked her dry lips. 'About twenty-five pounds up to now and he called by yesterday to say that he needed more.'

'*Twenty-five pounds!*' George was horrified. 'But why the hell would he need that amount of money?'

Cissie's eyes were brimming with tears. She would not admit that she was a little afraid of her own son, but she was. 'Well, he's been kicked out of his lodgings by all accounts and he has to live, doesn't he? He says that his adoptive parents won't help him any more – and I am his birth mother, after all.' She faltered to a stop as George shook his head.

'I'm sorry to say this, Cissie, but I think he's playing you for a fool. He knows you feel guilty for not being there to bring him up – through no fault of your own, may I add – and he's out to bleed you dry. Well, it's gone quite far enough now. If he comes back asking for more money I shall deal with him next time – whether he's your son or not!' Then as Cissie's hot tears brimmed over and spilled down her cheeks, his voice gentled. 'Look, pet, you must realise that this can't go on? Hugh is young, fit and healthy. He could work for a living if he had a mind to, or even enlist in the Army. God knows he's the right age, but he won't make any effort while you keep supporting him, will he?' George was secretly devastated that Hugh had milked them of such a huge portion of their life's savings, and yet he could understand why Cissie had indulged him. He would probably have done the same had he been in her shoes, but enough was enough and now he intended to put a stop to the man's sponging. It would be interesting to see if Hugh still bothered with Cissie then, when he had nothing to gain from her but her love.

'But what shall I say if he comes asking for me?' Cissie was wringing her hands together. 'He usually comes when he knows you will still be over at Treetops.'

'Just tell him that I've moved the rest of our money and you don't know where it is,' George advised. 'Then he'll have to come and ask me for it – and believe me he'll get short shrift. Will you do that for me?'

She nodded. 'Of course, but I'm hoping he won't come asking again.' She pottered away to put the kettle on then as George pretended to go back to reading his newspaper.

It seemed no time at all before the day of Ben's departure dawned, and after saying tearful goodbyes to everyone at Treetops, Sunday and Tom drove him to the Trent Valley railway station. Their hearts were heavy. However, they were surprised when they arrived there to find an almost carnival atmosphere. A brass band was playing outside and young men with happy smiling faces were enjoying being the centre of attention. They looked as if they were going on holiday or on some great adventure rather than to fight in a war, and were clearly relishing being treated as heroes.

The platform was teeming with all the newly enlisted boys, some looking not old enough to be going, Sunday secretly thought. And then suddenly they heard the train chugging into the station, belching smoke and steam, and the faces of the women fell and tears began to spill as they hugged their menfolk to them. Who knew if they would ever come home again.

'Please take care of yourself,' Sunday implored as she threw her arms about Ben. 'You must know that I love you.' She so bitterly regretted the way she had treated him when she had discovered that he was Tom's son, but it was too late to turn the clock back and she could only pray that he would return safely so that she could prove to him just how very much he meant to her.

He nodded as he gave her a hug. He had forgiven her for the cold way she had treated him when she discovered that he was her husband's son. It had been no hardship, for in truth Sunday was the closest thing to a mother he had ever known, and until then she had doted on him.

'I'm only going to do my training,' he teased her as he gently wiped a tear from her cheek. 'I shall no doubt be back for a short while on leave in a couple of weeks' time.' He turned to Tom then and shook his hand.

'Stay safe, son,' Tom muttered thickly and then Ben was throwing his kitbag on board and clambering into the train after it. The platform began to empty as the other young men followed suit and then the air was filled with shouts of, 'Goodbye, stay safe!' as the train began to pull away. Sunday and Tom stood there waving until it was out of sight then sadly made their way back to the car, missing Ben already.

That evening, Cissie finished her chores at Treetops and set off for Primrose Cottage, leaving George to help Tom stable the horses. She strode through the copse thinking that she wouldn't be able to take this short-cut for much longer. Once the nights started to darken there was far more chance of tripping over a tree root or something and hurting herself, so she tended to skirt the woods then. She had gone about halfway when Hugh suddenly appeared like a spectre from behind a tree. Her heart sank into her boots. He must have been waiting for her, and she cursed herself silently for coming this way. Even so she greeted him with a smile.

'Hello, son. How are you?'

He fell into step beside her. 'Not too bad as it happens although I do have a favour to ask of you.'

Cissie thought she knew what was coming although she remained tight-lipped.

'The thing is,' Hugh went shamelessly on, 'I have this friend who I borrowed some money off some time ago and the long and the short of it is, he needs it back. I wouldn't ask normally but this chap can cut up a bit rough, if you know what I mean. Anyway, I was wondering if perhaps you could see your way clear to giving me another loan. Just until I find another job, of course.'

'Oh, Hugh, I'm so sorry, I'm afraid I can't,' Cissie told him nervously.

His face darkened. 'Do you mean you can't – or you won't!' he asked, and he put Cissie in mind of a spoiled child. Suddenly, she understood that George was right. This had gone quite far enough.

'I mean I can't,' she answered levelly. 'I told George about the money I had already lent to you and he wasn't too pleased, so he's moved it and I have no idea where he's put it.' Then as guilt swamped her again, 'But I could let you have the few shillings I have in my purse . . .'

'A few *shillings*! That's no good to me. I need some real money,' he snarled, then to her shock he caught her arm and swung her about. 'I find it hard to believe your husband would hide your own money from you. Are you sure you're telling me the truth?'

Her anger suddenly rose to match his then as all the dreams she had harboured about him slipped away.

'I am, as it happens, but even if I did know where it was I wouldn't give you any more,' she stormed back. 'Do you realise that you haven't even asked me how I am – if I've had a good day; if everything is all right! And why haven't you? Because you don't really give a damn about me, that's why. I'm just the mug that's been handing you money left right and centre. Well, it stops now. If you want to build a mother-son relationship with me, I'll welcome you with open arms. But if you only want me as a means of getting money, then I'm sorry I ever came looking for you!'

She watched his lip curl and was transported back in time. He was so like his father, she wondered if there was any of herself in him at all. But then she decided that she should give it one last try and she reached out to him. 'Hugh, you're young and healthy. Surely you could get a job somewhere, and if you've nowhere to live you could always come to me. I would never see you out on the street.'

'Live with you?' he ground out mockingly. 'A common whore? No, thank you very much. I'd rather sleep in the gutter.'

She recoiled as if he had slapped her and as he turned to leave she took hold of his sleeve in desperation, to stay him, begging, '*Please* don't go like this!'

The next thing she knew, a fist was flying towards her and when it caught her squarely on the chin, the blow lifted her momentarily off her feet. And then as she flew backwards, she fell awkwardly and heard a loud snap before pain sliced up her arm. Her forehead connected with a large rock hidden in the grass, and instantly she felt something wet and sticky running down her cheek. 'Hugh . . . help me,' she implored weakly. She could vaguely see the outline of him leaning over her, but now darkness was rushing towards her and as she sank into it she knew no more.

Hugh stood towering over her as his heart pounded with panic. She looked in a bad way and the ground beneath her head was rapidly turning scarlet red. Her arm was at an unnatural angle too, and he didn't think she was breathing. God damn it!

Swiping the sweat from his forehead on the back of his sleeve, he tried to steady the rhythm of his heart. If she was dead, he would be tried for murder and he didn't fancy ending his life dangling from a hangman's noose. What should he do? He couldn't go into town without the money he owed. The bit about the man he owed it to being a bad lot had been true at least. It never occurred to him to run for help – he only cared about himself. But what to do? *What to do?*

354

And then it came to him. He'd get as far away from here as he could with whatever money he had in his pocket, and then first thing in the morning he would enlist in the Army and be shipped abroad. Rather that than be hanged. Rummaging in his pocket with shaking fingers he withdrew the contents and hastily counted the coins there. Not a great deal but he'd go straight to the railway station and get on the first train that pulled in. Then without giving his mother another glance he set off as fast as his legs would take him, leaving her lying there in a pool of blood.

'I'm home, pet,' George called wearily as he arrived at the cottage that evening. He was later than usual as he'd stayed behind to do some of the jobs that Ben would normally have done, and now all he wanted was a nice hot cup of tea and his bed. He was surprised to find the kitchen empty. Normally the kettle was singing on the hob by the time he got back and Cissie was bustling about the place, but tonight only silence greeted him. He checked the upstairs, thinking that she might have gone up for a lie-down, but the rooms up there were deserted too so he came back into the kitchen and scratched his head. He knew that she had left Treetops some time ago. She should have been home long since.

After filling the kettle he placed it on the range and stood in the window looking for her, but by the time he had measured the tea-leaves into the pot and the kettle had boiled, there was still no sign of her. With a resigned sigh, he lifted the kettle from the range and placed it on the trivet. Perhaps Sunday had called her back for something. Oh well. There was only one way to find out, so he set off back the way he had just come.

'No, I haven't seen her since she left after we'd got the children tucked into bed,' Sunday told him with a worried frown. 'Perhaps she just decided to go for a walk?'

'I doubt it. Look up there.' George pointed to the heavens where angry black clouds were scudding across the sky. 'I reckon we're going to have a storm afore long an' Cissie hates thunder an' lightnin'.'

'I'll come with you and we'll have a scout round for her. She can't have gone far,' Tom volunteered.

'I'll come too.' Sunday moved towards the door but Tom shook his head. 'No, you stay here, lass. One of the little 'uns might wake up an' need you.'

Seeing the sense in what he said she nodded, but a knot of fear had formed in her stomach. 'She might have taken the short-cut through the woods,' she said then, and George scowled.

'I've asked her not to go that way but you could well be right,' he agreed and he and Tom set off. Because of the approaching storm it was unnaturally dark and by the time the men reached the edge of the woods they were wishing they had thought to bring a lantern.

'You take that side o' the path an' I'll take this,' Tom suggested, and straining their ears for any sounds they set off below the trees, calling Cissie's name. They were almost halfway through the woods when George said, 'What's that ahead? There's somethin' lying at the side o' the path.'

They hurried forward and Tom was appalled to realise that it was a body. Whose he couldn't tell, for it was far too dark by now and thunder was rolling above them . . . but it was definitely a woman. George was immediately in a terrible state, because he feared it might be his wife.

'You get the top half and I'll get the legs,' Tom called to George above the crash of the thunder. 'We have to get her out of here and we may as well head back to Treetops, that's the nearest.'

Between them they lifted the dead weight and laboriously retraced their steps, but they had gone no more than a few yards when a sheet of lightning filtered through the trees and George gasped.

'My God, it's Cissie,' he rasped. 'And she's covered in blood. She looks in a bad way, God help her.'

'Just keep going,' Tom answered breathlessly as a torrent of rain poured out of the black clouds and dripped through the trees onto them. 'We need to get her back to the house as soon as possible. She must have tripped and fallen.'

Somehow they managed to get out of the woods without incident, their burden becoming heavier by the minute. They could see the lights of Treetops shining through the gloom now and redoubled their efforts to get their precious cargo out of the rain.

Before they had even reached the door, Sunday flung it open. 'Bring her into the drawing room,' she ordered. 'Then you fetch the car and go into town for the doctor, Tom.'

Dripping water over the floor the two men did as they were told and once Cissie was laid gently on the sofa Tom shot away to get the doctor as George dropped to his knees at the side of his wife.

'Is . . . is she . . .' He found that he couldn't say the words.

After feeling for her pulse, Sunday gave a small sigh of relief. She knew what he had been thinking and she had feared the same.

'There's a pulse but it's thready,' she told him in a shaky voice, then pulling herself together with an enormous effort she ordered, 'Go and fetch me a bowl of hot water and some towels. We must get her out of these wet clothes and cleaned up a little. And while you're in the kitchen ask one of the maids to run up to my room and fetch one of my clean nightgowns.'

George was trembling so much that he barely heard her and she had to bark the orders at him again before he sped away to do as he was asked.

'Who could have done this to her?' he groaned miserably as later he helped Sunday to strip the sodden clothes from his wife's inert body.

'She might just have fallen over a tree root or something and banged her head,' Sunday pointed out. 'But never mind that – we must stop this bleeding. Hold that towel over the gash while I wash her.'

Sunday gently undid Cissie's blouse and slid it down her arms – and it was then that they both saw the bruises forming there, black and purple against her pale skin.

'That's a hand-print if I'm not very much mistaken,' George ground out as anger coursed through him. 'She's been attacked, the poor lass! And look at her chin! Someone has thumped her, I can tell. There's another bruise forming there and her lip is split. She'll be black and blue in a few hours' time.' He wept, and didn't care who saw him.

'But who would want to hurt Cissie?' Sunday asked him. 'She never did anyone any harm in her whole life, bless her.'

George clamped his lips together as a thought occurred to him. *Hugh!* Could it be that he had waited for her yet again – and turned nasty when she refused to give him any more money? *If it* was *him I'll find him and kill him with my bare hands, and sod what happens to me*, George silently vowed. Then he and Sunday, having done all they could for her for now, sat and built up the fire, waiting for the doctor as George prayed for his wife to survive.

Chapter Forty-Four

'Next train leaving is bound for London, sir,' the ticket clerk told Hugh as he stood before the booth at Trent Valley railway station. He was soaked to the skin and shivering with fear and cold, but there was no time to think of that now. He must get away. Pushing the wet coins across the counter, he waited impatiently while the clerk got his ticket.

'Should be here in ten minutes or so,' the friendly clerk informed him. 'You timed that nicely, sir.'

Hugh ignored him and strode away, intent on getting onto the platform. He had literally a few pence left in his pocket now, not even enough to buy a meal let alone anywhere to stay when he got to the capital. Still, it was only for one night, he consoled himself. He'd book into a hotel then slip away without paying first thing in the morning. It wouldn't be the first time he'd done it and he doubted it would be the last.

Meanwhile the clerk was watching him go with an offended look on his face. *Some people have no manners*, he thought to himself, then lifting his newspaper he settled back in his seat and forgot all about the rude fellow as he became immersed in the news again.

359

In London, Kitty was preparing to go out although Maggie couldn't help but notice that she didn't seem too enthusiastic about it. Maggie couldn't blame her. The things Kitty had confided to her were haunting her and she desperately wished that she could help her friend, but Kitty had been adamant that the secret must remain between just the two of them.

All of a sudden she blurted out, 'Why don't you let me come with you? Nothing could happen if I was there, and we could tell a white lie. We could say that Ruby had decided that you weren't to go out on your own again.'

'It wouldn't work.' Kitty sighed. 'I know you mean well and I'm grateful for your concern, really I am, but I think it would only make things worse. The men I'm entertaining have told Richard that if I don't do as they wish, they will send the photographs to the newspapers.' She shuddered at the thought of it. 'Can you imagine the shame of it? If you really want to help, Maggie, will you pour me a large glass of wine? It relaxes me and dulls what lies ahead. Still, it won't be for ever. Richard says the men concerned will soon tire of me and be off in search of fresh prey, and then we can become a real couple and start to plan our lives.'

Maggie reluctantly poured the drink and handed it to Kitty, who knocked it back in one go. 'Ugh! It wouldn't be so bad if I actually liked the stuff,' she said afterwards.

Something else then occurred to Maggie. 'What if Richard decides to enlist in the Army?' she asked. 'What will happen then?'

'He won't do that.' Kitty shrugged her arms into the sleeves of her coat. 'I was concerned that he might, but he informed me that he has no intentions of doing any such thing.'

'But what if they make it law that every man under a certain age has to go?' Maggie pressed.

'Richard assures me that his father has friends in very high places so that isn't likely to happen. As he often tells me, "money talks" and Richard's family have plenty of that.'

Maggie was secretly disgusted. Had she been a man she would certainly have gone to fight for King and Country, but it seemed that Richard wasn't quite as brave as he tried to make out. Why should he be exempt from the war when thousands of other young men were marching off to fight?

Kitty reluctantly headed for the door then, with Tallulah close on her heels. 'Now you stay with Maggie and be a good girl,' she said as she scooped the little bundle of fluff up and kissed her soundly on her wet nose. She then passed her over into Maggie's arms and without another word left the room, deciding that she might just as well go and get whatever lay ahead over and done with.

As Kitty left the house in London, the doctor was just about to leave Treetops.

'Is she going to be all right?' George asked desperately.

'Well, I've splinted her arm and I've sewn up the gash on her forehead as neatly as I could, although I fear she will bear a scar,' the doctor answered, snapping his black bag shut. 'But there is nothing much I can do about the blow to the head. Mrs Jenkins could be unconscious for some time, there again she could wake up within minutes, or . . .' He shook his head gravely. 'I should warn you that she may not wake up at all. We have no way of knowing what damage may have been done so I'm afraid it's all down to waiting now. Would you like me to get her transferred into the hospital?'

'That won't be necessary,' Sunday said quickly. 'I'd much sooner nurse her here. Do you agree, George? She'd be distressed if she woke up to find herself in unfamiliar surroundings – and she will wake up... I *know* she will! Cissie is a fighter. I'll get her carried upstairs and we will all care for her. My mother and her new husband will be back from their honeymoon in a few days' time and I know they'll want to help, so between us we'll manage just fine.'

'Very well.' The doctor then changed the subject: 'You would be well advised to inform the police of what has happened. I'm quite sure that this was a vicious attack and whoever did it to her should be caught. I shall call again first thing in the morning but should you need me before then, don't hesitate to send for me.'

'I'll do that. Thank you, doctor,' George responded grimly then he settled at the side of Cissie to stroke her hand and whisper to her as Sunday saw the doctor to the door.

Another hour passed before he set off for the police station with Tom after ensuring that Cissie was safely tucked up in a comfy bed in one of the spare rooms with a blazing fire in the grate, a soft lamp alight in the corner and Kitty sitting at the side of her.

The officer on the desk at the police station listened as George told him of the attack and wrote everything down before asking, 'Do you have any idea who may done this, sir? Did your wife have any enemies?'

'No, she doesn't have any enemies. My Cissie wouldn't hurt a fly,' George ground out. 'But yes, I *do* have an idea who did it. I think it was her son, Hugh Tate.'

'Her own son?' The officer looked shocked and George quickly went on to tell him of how Hugh had been taking money from his wife.

'I told her that the next time he turned up, she was to refuse him,' George went on. 'And if she did, I think he probably turned nasty.' It was all his fault, George thought. No amount of money was worth Cissie getting hurt.

'That's a very grave allegation to make. Do you have any evidence that points to it being him?'

'N-no,' George admitted reluctantly. 'But who else could it be? I want you to bring him in for questioning and if he can't tell you where he was this evening then I'd say we had our man, wouldn't you? Who else would want to attack my Cissie?'

'Leave it with me, sir,' the officer told him. 'We'll start an investigation straight away and rest assured, we will keep you fully informed.'

George thanked him and left the station with his hands clenched into fists with rage.

'You surely don't believe that Cissie's own flesh and blood would do that to her, do you?' Tom asked as he drove George home. It was late now and the streets of the town were almost deserted save for the odd man staggering out of the doors of an inn.

'Aye, I do.' George was keeping his eyes peeled for a sight of Hugh and it would be God help him if he clapped eyes on him. 'I'm tellin' you, Tom, he's a bad 'un. I've only met him a couple o' times but I didn't take to him at all. He's the double of his father inside and out from what I can make of it, though I've never said that to our Cissie. I didn't want to upset her, like.'

Tom nodded sadly. He had known Cissie for many years and was all too aware of how deeply she had longed to find the son who had been stolen from her arms at birth. 'Well, you've reported your suspicions to the police now, so best let them handle it, eh? Our time will be better spent taking care of Cissie.'

Seeing the sense in what Tom said, George lapsed into silence, but inside he was afraid. If his suspicions turned out to be true, the knowledge of what her son had done to her could well kill his beloved wife, even if her injuries didn't!

George and Sunday sat with Cissie for the rest of the night, insisting that Tom should get some rest. 'The staff will need someone to help them with the children in the morning and there's no sense in us all sitting here. Go and get some rest,' Sunday ordered with a tired smile.

Tom knew that she was right and eventually made his way to bed, but sleep evaded him as he thought on what George had told him. First thing in the morning, as soon as it was light, he was up and dressed. Thankfully the house was still sleeping as he slipped out of the back door and made for the woods. It had been too dark to see anything the night before and he wanted to check the area where the attack had taken place.

The birds were singing their dawn chorus as he picked his way through the dew-laden trees and he found the place where Cissie had been knocked down quite quickly. The light that filtered through the trees made the blood on the ground stand out against the soft green grass and he shuddered involuntarily then paused to look around. At first glance there appeared to be nothing untoward but then his eyes were drawn to something white at the side of the path. For a start, he thought it was a piece of paper that had blown there, but when he bent to pick it up he found that it was a hand-kerchief. A very fine lawn man's handkerchief, as it happened. And then he saw in one corner of it, the embroidered initials *H. T.* – and his stomach turned over. *Hugh Tate!* It had to be. George must have been right. But the question now was, what was he to do with it? This would provide very damning evidence when the police came to investigate the crime scene. Personally, he hoped that they could catch the fellow, lock him up and throw away the key. But what would that do to Cissie? As George had done with the letters on the day of Lavinia's wedding, he hid the handkerchief deep into his coat pocket, but this time, it would never see the light of day.

Turning about, he made his way back to the house where he prepared a tray of tea to take up to George and Sunday. No doubt they would be grateful of a cup by now. But when he got upstairs he found there had been no change in Cissie's condition whatsoever.

'She hasn't made so much as a murmur,' Sunday informed him as she crept towards the door, leaving George holding his wife's hand fast in his.

Tom placed the tray down and gave his wife a cuddle. 'She'll survive, she's a strong lass,' he told her with a confidence he was far from feeling and Sunday leaned against his chest, enjoying the closeness of him. It had been a trying few days, one way or another, what with her mother's wedding, Ben's departure and now this terrible accident! All she could do was pray that Tom was right.

Chapter Forty-Five

When Maggie entered Kitty's room the next morning and drew the curtains aside, she was shocked to see the bruise on Kitty's cheek as the girl pulled herself up onto her pillows.

'What happened?'

Kitty self-consciously fingered her cheek. 'Let's just say I wasn't as compliant as a certain gentleman expected me to be,' she murmured. It was such a relief to be able to talk frankly at last. 'No one will notice when I perform, thanks to rouge and Max Factor.' She tried to make a joke of it.

'Oh, Kitty, this has *got* to stop!' Maggie hissed in great distress. 'Why on earth is Richard allowing you to be treated like this if he loves you so much?'

Kitty instantly sprang to his defence and Maggie realised that she had said entirely the wrong thing.

'Richard doesn't know,' she answered. 'He went out and left me to . . . Well, he went out to meet a client, but it's nothing really. As I said, I can soon cover it with a little rouge. Now do stop fussing and pass me that tea.'

Maggie did as she was told, then tucking Tallulah beneath her arm she carried her downstairs and out into the back garden to do her morning toilet before the little puppy deposited it on the bedroom floor. Arthur was there, hoeing the vegetable patch, and Tallulah raced towards him. She and Arthur were firm friends now and he often entertained her in the garden if Kitty went out during the day.

'So what's up wi' you, this lovely mornin' then?' he asked brightly, noting Maggie's downcast expression. 'Are you all right, Maggie?'

There was nothing she would have liked more than to confide in him, for she loved all the Patridge family and would never forget their kindness. Instead, however, she forced a smile and lied, saying, 'Nothing, I'm fine,' and satisfied with her answer Arthur went back to fussing the dog.

When she returned to Kitty's bedroom, Maggie found she was already in the bathroom so she started to tidy the bed.

'What are you going to tell Foxy about your face?' Maggie asked through the bathroom door, which was slightly ajar. 'She doesn't miss a trick and she's no fool, you know!'

'I shall tell her I had one glass too many and tripped and fell,' Kitty replied. 'That's believable, surely?'

'I suppose so. Just so long as I know what you're going to say, so we can have our stories matching.'

Later that morning, Kitty wandered downstairs into the drawing room. Ruby had just risen and staring at her daughter she asked, 'What happened to you?'

Kitty told her the story she had told Maggie, and Ruby shrugged though she didn't believe a word of it. She'd had more than one rough gentleman handle her over the years and you soon got used to it. So long as Kitty continued to bring the money in she wasn't much concerned.

'Max just called by to say that he's managed to get you a booking next week,' she told Kitty then and the girl brightened considerably. Most of the bookings had dried up as if by magic the instant war had been declared, just as Max had prophesied. Kitty still took her classes, however; it was important to be professional and to keep her voice as tuneful as ever. Ruby then showed her an illustration in one of her fashion magazines of a dress that she wanted to have made and the conversation turned to safer topics. When Ruby went upstairs for her bath, Kitty remained, staring glumly from the window. Her hand absently rose to her breast, which felt full and tender. She was being sick in the mornings too and had missed two courses. It all pointed to one thing: she was having a child and the thought terrified her. The baby's father could be any one of the awful men she had slept with, and the knowledge of that made her feel utterly worthless. She had longed to confide in Maggie – but she was too ashamed and now she hoped that she wouldn't have to, because for the last two days she had been having terrible stomach cramps. She wondered if it was the onset of a miscarriage and prayed that it was. Better that, than to bear an illegitimate child, father unknown. She dreaded to think how Richard might react if he found out. He would leave her, she was certain.

Once again, she yearned to see Sunday and feel her motherly arms around her, but after the way Kitty had treated her and Tom when they had come to visit her at Wilton's Music Hall she could hardly blame them for wanting nothing more to do with her. But it didn't stop Kitty missing them.

She was still standing there when a stomach cramp made her bend double and she felt something warm and sticky between her legs. It was blood! Kitty waited until the pain had passed before hobbling to the bathroom and locking herself away.

Two hours later, when Maggie returned to Kitty's bedroom, she found her lying pale on the bed. It was all over.

Maggie eyed her suspiciously before asking, 'What's wrong? You look awful!' Kitty's eyes seemed to have sunk into her head and she looked as weak as a kitten.

'I think I'll get the doctor,' Maggie decided, and when Kitty loudly protested, her worst suspicions were confirmed. 'You're having a baby, aren't you?'

Kitty shook her head. 'I was,' she admitted – and then the tears came, hot tears that threatened to choke her. Maggie quickly got on the bed beside her and put her arms around the other girl and there they lay, drawing what comfort they could from each other as Kitty grieved for the innocent child that would now never be born. And it was all due to her own wickedness.

The joy of Lavinia and William's homecoming a few days later was somewhat marred by Cissie's predicament, but just as Sunday had expected, the newlyweds went to their room, unpacked their things and pitched in to help wherever they could.

By the time the doctor had called and carried out another examination of the patient Lavinia had already got the children washed, fed, clothed and off to school, or into the schoolroom for the little ones.

When he had finished, the doctor folded his stethoscope, shoved it into his bag and beckoned Tom onto the landing.

'It's not good, I'm afraid,' he told him, rubbing his face tiredly. 'The longer she stays unconscious, the more chance there is of her just slipping away from us. She could have brain damage, you see?'

Tom nodded as his stomach churned. He himself was due to leave in a few days' time to start his training and he hated to go with this tragic situation hanging over them. But what choice did he have? If he didn't report for training he would be classed as a deserter.

He saw the doctor out and the man promised to return later in the day. He then went to relieve Sunday for a time, insisting that she should go and get some rest even if it was only for an hour. George, understandably, wasn't so easy to shift. He refused to budge.

'I'm not leaving her,' he told his friend. 'I want to be here when she wakes up.'

'Have it your own way, man,' Tom soothed and shortly after he noted that George had laid his head on the bed at the side of Cissie and was snoring softly.

Shadows were creeping across the lawn that evening when George suddenly felt a gentle pressure on his fingers.

'Cissie just squeezed my hand,' he said elatedly as Sunday and Tom crowded around the bed, and sure enough minutes later they saw her do it again. Then as they watched with bated breath they saw her blink and soon after she groggily opened her eyes.

'Oh, Cissie, my little love. *Thank God,*' George sobbed as he kissed her fingers and cried unashamedly. 'I thought I was going to lose you for a time back there.'

'Wh-where am I?' she asked as the room swam into focus.

'You're in one of the bedrooms at Treetops and you're safe. Something happened to you in the woods on the way home the other night. Do you remember?'

Her mouth was dry and her head felt as if it was about to split in two as she tried to think, but everything was just a blank. She then tried to shake her head but the pain of moving it was too great and her arm was hurting her too; in fact, the pain was excruciating. 'N-no I can't remember anything,' she whispered.

'Well, it doesn't matter for now. The main thing is that you're back with us again. Now we've just got to get you well again, my lovely.'

Smiling at each other, Tom and Sunday joined hands and tiptoed from the room, leaving the couple behind them in peace.

Cissie remained in blissful ignorance as to what had caused her injuries even when questioned by the police, and all too soon the day of Tom's departure arrived. Following Cissie's attack, George had written to their grown-up children asking them to come home, and now Primrose Cottage felt as if it was bursting at the seams, but at least Cissie had taken the first painful steps towards her recovery and everyone was grateful for that.

George was waiting in the car to drive Tom to the station and Sunday was tearful as they stood on the steps, saying their goodbyes.

'I had hoped that Ben would get leave before I had to go so that I could see him one more time,' Tom fretted, and a pain pierced Sunday's heart.

'You *will* see him, I know you will. You're talking as if you'll never see him again,' she scolded fearfully, then throwing herself into his arms she began to sob. 'Please promise me that you'll be careful.'

He planted a kiss on her sweet-smelling hair. 'Of course I will and I'll be back on leave before you know it. You just look after yourself and everyone here for me. I don't want to be worrying about you lot.' Then putting her firmly from him he limped down the steps and clambered into the car.

'I want to come to the station with you,' she shouted, longing to delay their parting but he shook his head as he blew her a kiss.

'No, it's better we do it here. You go back inside now and know that I'll be thinking of you every minute.' He nodded to George then and the car drove away as Sunday stood there sobbing helplessly.

Three days later, things improved somewhat when the front door opened as Sunday was sorting through the mail. She knew it was too soon for Tom to have had a chance to write and yet she still found herself waiting for the postman each morning. She glanced over her shoulder then dropped the letters as she saw Ben standing there, looking handsome in his uniform.

'Oh, sweetheart . . .' Sunday flew into his arms and he was thrilled at her welcome. Now he knew that, at last, they were back on their old footing. Laughing, he picked her up and swung her round as Lavinia hurried from the day room wondering what all the commotion was about.

371

'Ben!' She too rushed to greet him and there were tears of joy on the women's faces when they finally drew apart.

'You look such a fine young man in uniform,' Lavinia teased and Ben blushed. 'Come on, you must be starving and longing for a drink.' Lavinia linked her arm through his and hauled him towards the kitchen.

'Now don't start feeding me up,' he chuckled. 'I've only been gone a couple of weeks.'

'Even so, you look thinner,' Sunday commented, eyeing him up and down.

Soon he was seated at the kitchen table with them all fussing over him. 'So how was the training?' Sunday asked as she poured him a second cup of Cook's home-made ginger beer.

Ben's smile vanished. 'It was all right. We were taught how to use our rifles and spent half the time stabbing sandbags and shooting at targets. That was fine, though I'm not so sure how I shall feel having to stab or shoot a human being if it comes to it,' he admitted. This gave the others pause for thought.

They had a good old gossip then as Sunday told him all about what had happened to Cissie.

'Has she remembered yet who it was that attacked her?' Ben was horrified. The womenfolk wouldn't be safe with a maniac like that about.

Sunday shook her head. 'No. The last thing she remembers is leaving here that evening to go back to the cottage . . . and then everything after that is a blank. George is convinced that it was Hugh, her son, who did it – but seeing as he's disappeared off the face of the earth we'll never know. It does look rather suspicious though, him clearing off like that, don't you think?'

'I hope it wasn't him,' Ben commented. 'It would break Cissie's heart. She was so thrilled when she finally tracked him down. And at least she's recovering now, which is the main thing.'

'Hmm.' Sunday frowned. 'I'm afraid you may be rather shocked when you see her next. Her arm is still splinted, of course, and the doctor has warned her that it will always be weak now. It was a very bad break – and her face is badly scarred too. She's very conscious of it, although George – in fact, all of us – has assured her that she's still lovely and it doesn't matter to us in the least. We're just grateful we didn't lose her. But of course, it matters to her. Cissie has never been a vain person but now she can hardly bear to look in a mirror.'

They reverted to talking of Ben's training then and he had them roaring with laughter as he described some of the characters he had met and the conditions they were forced to live in.

'We're in big tents,' he said, 'which is fine in the warm weather, but I dread to think what it will be like in the winter. And the beds are made of wood! Not very comfortable at all, I can assure you. But the food is the worst thing! It's some sort of stew most days that we wouldn't feed to yon Barney. I shall waste away,' he sighed dramatically, and once again they all fell about laughing.

'So how long are you home for?' Sunday asked, wiping her eyes.

'I've got a week's leave then I report back to camp and we all get shipped out.'

'I see, and have they told you where you'll be going?'

'Belgium or France I should imagine, although it's all very hush-hush.'

Sunday's stomach dropped at the thought of it but she kept her smile firmly in place as she told him, 'Then we shall have to make the most of every second we have with you until you leave.'

She gave his hand a loving squeeze, and as she stared at him she found herself wondering when he had changed from a boy into such a handsome young man.

Chapter Forty-Six

'I wonder why Hugh hasn't been in touch,' Cissie said thoughtfully as she and Sunday sat enjoying elevenses in the kitchen at Treetops in mid-August. The police had closed the investigation into Cissie's attack. As they pointed out, there was no evidence to suggest that anyone else had been involved. She might just have fallen badly and as she was still blissfully ignorant about Hugh's part in it she hadn't argued with them. Sunday hoped it would stay that way, for there was nothing to be gained from yet more heartache – although she and Tom had their own thoughts on the matter.

'It could be that he's enlisted and been sent off to train before he could come to say goodbye to you,' Sunday suggested, hoping to make Cissie feel better.

'Eeh, I'd be that proud of him if he had.' Cissie smiled. 'An' if that's the case, I might well get a letter from him, mightn't I?'

'There's every chance.' Sunday personally doubted it but she wouldn't have hurt Cissie's feelings for the world. She was still recovering and already it was evident that her arm would never be the same again. Every time Sunday looked at her badly scarred face, anger bubbled inside her, directed towards the person she and Tom were convinced was responsible.

She herself had been very down in the dumps since Tom had been home on embarkation leave before being shipped off. The house wasn't the same without him and Ben, and now with Cissie unable to do much, a lot of extra work had fallen on her and George's shoulders.

During the last two weeks, three of the children she had cared for had gone to new homes. One little girl had gone to live with a couple in Leamington, and Bobby and Wilfred had been taken by an elderly couple who owned a farm out Kenilworth way. Now there were only three children left in her care – the youngest, the twins Sarah and Becky, and a girl of eleven, and Tom had requested that until he returned from war, there should be no more. It was too much work for Sunday without him there to help.

Seeing the sense in what he said, Sunday had agreed – but now she was missing the children who had left Treetops as well as Tom and Ben. It seemed to be all very depressing at the minute, the only bright spot being that everyone was still forecasting that the war would be over by Christmas. Sunday prayed that they were right, then perhaps they could all get back to some sort of normality.

The two women were still sitting finishing their elevenses when the postman stuck his head around the kitchen door and gave them a cheeky grin. He usually managed to time his visits to scrounge a nice cup of tea and sometimes a hot buttered scone off Cook, but today he told Sunday, 'I reckon you'll give me two cups o' tea today when you see what I've got for yer!' He waggled an envelope in the air and Sunday's heart began to beat faster.

'It's from the mister if I ain't very much mistaken,' he told her. 'I'm deliverin' no end o' these here brown envelopes now.'

Sunday flew across the room so quickly her feet barely touched the floor, and snatching it from his hand in a most unladylike manner she headed for the hall door, telling Cissie over her shoulder, 'Get Postie a cuppa would you, pet? I want to see what Tom has to say.'

She then went and locked herself away in the drawing room where she joyfully tore the envelope open and withdrew two sheets of thin notepaper. Much of what Tom had written had been crossed out, no doubt by the censor, but she read the rest eagerly.

My darling girl,

I hope you and everyone at Treetops are well. I just wanted to let you know that I have arrived safely in France and we are now on our way to xxxxxxxxxx

The next two lines had been crossed out.

The sea journey here was a bit dicey. The ship we travelled in was tossed about like a feather on the wind on the way across and most of the men were seasick. Not pleasant as we were packed in like sardines in the bowels of the ship with nowhere to escape the smell. Even so the men were in good spirits and we finally landed in Boulogne to a wonderful welcome from the French people. They were waiting at the end of the gangplank to greet us and shake our hands and then eventually we were loaded into lorries and taken to our barracks, which proved to be no more than a sea of tents set in fields of mud, hardly what we were all hoping for, I have to admit. From here we can hear gunfire and screaming and it's like landing in hell. The food is pretty dismal too and most of the men are in pain. Their boots are ill-fitting so their feet are covered in blisters and the uniforms while looking smart are itchy after you've worn them for a while.

Three more lines had been scribbled out at this point so Sunday hurried on to the final page.

I'm sorry if I sound miserable. Remember it's not so bad for me as the other chaps so please try not to worry. I'm only to be a groom whereas the young men will be going to the front when they receive their orders. Some of them look like they are still wet behind the ears and nowhere near old enough to be here. Have you heard from Ben, my love? I pray every day that he is safe. Please give everyone there my love and take care of your-self. I can hardly wait until we are together again, and I am living for that day. Please write to me when you can and tell me all that's going on at home.

Your loving husband,
Tom xxxxxx

Tears slid down Sunday's cheeks as she folded the letter and slipped it back into the envelope. It sounded truly dreadful out there – and if what the papers were reporting was true, many of the young men who Tom had mentioned might never return to their families again. A cold finger crept up her spine as she offered up a silent prayer, asking God to keep Tom and Ben safe.

In London Miss Fox's thoughts were also gloomy as she pored over the newspapers. She liked to keep abreast of what was happening in the war and read the papers from cover to cover every day now.

Ruby entered the room as she was still sitting there and asked brightly, 'What are you looking so glum about, Foxy?'

Miss Fox raised an eyebrow. 'In case you'd forgotten, we are at war. Isn't that reason enough?'

Ruby waved her hand airily. 'Oh, I swear you need something to worry about. How can what's happening all that way away possibly affect us?'

'There's none so blind as those who will not see,' Miss Fox said tightly. 'I wonder if you'll be singing the same tune if the Germans send those Zeppelin airships over here, emptying bombs on us. And there's talk of their warships coming over here, and all. London will be a prime target, what with all the docks. Perhaps we should think of renting somewhere in the country till all this is over? We could do with somewhere smaller now anyway, now that you're not earning. I've said it before and now I'll say it again: if we had somewhere smaller, we wouldn't need so many staff.'

Ruby had been preening in the gilt mirror that hung above the fireplace but now she turned, looking appalled. 'Move from Brunswick Villa? Live in something smaller? Why ever would we want to do that?'

'For all the reasons I've just stated – and because we have a young girl upstairs who needs protecting and looking out for. Surely you wouldn't want to put Kitty at risk? In case you've forgotten, she's your daughter – though no one would guess it, the way you treat her.'

Ruby's face turned ugly as she placed her hands on her ample hips and glared back at the older woman.

'First of all, we can still perfectly well afford to live here.'

'How? If you've no money coming in?' Miss Fox spat.

Ruby's eyes sparked with malice. 'Never you mind. It's enough for you to know that we are very comfortable! And as for Kitty, how do you think she would react if we were to try and move her away from Richard? She's totally besotted with him!'

'True, I'll agree with you there, but what bothers me is where all the money we need to stay here is coming from? These so-called modelling shoots he's got her doing? There's something fishy about those sessions if you ask me. Why don't we ever see any pictures of her in the fashion magazines?'

'Because she appears in magazines abroad,' Ruby blustered, but she knew that Foxy could tell she was lying. The woman had always been able to read her like a book. And then when her companion continued to stare at her suspiciously Ruby lost her temper and waggled a finger at her. 'How dare you question my care of my daughter! I think it might be a good idea if you remembered your place if you wish to continue living here. I could always get another maid, you know!'

Miss Fox visibly flinched as if she had been slapped, then drawing herself up to her full height she rasped, 'You wouldn't last two minutes without me behind you. Look at you! But at least I know where I stand now.' With that she sailed from the room with what dignity she could muster.

Upstairs, Maggie and Kitty were discussing the war news too, oblivious to the row that had just taken place downstairs.

'I nipped to the market yesterday,' Maggie told Kitty conversationally as she dressed her friend's hair. 'And I was shocked to see how few young men there are about now. It's frightening, isn't it – to think what might happen to them, I mean. And it's no wonder that they've closed most of the theatres and music halls down now. There aren't that many young couples about any more.'

Kitty nodded. 'Foxy was telling me that they're digging trenches for the men to shelter in, in France, and they say the conditions they are existing in are appalling.' Out of the corner of her eye she saw Tallulah disappearing off under her bed with yet another of her shoes then and she immediately chased after her. This was the second pair her puppy would have ruined in a week if she didn't manage to rescue it.

'Naughty girl,' she scolded as she retrieved the shoe, undamaged this time, but she then followed up the telling-off with a kiss on Tallulah's silky head. She loved the little dog unconditionally now and couldn't imagine being without her no matter what damage she caused.

'You spoil that dog,' Maggie commented, although truthfully she was just as guilty of doing the very same thing.

'That's what you have dogs for, to spoil them,' Kitty replied philosophically. For most of the time they avoided speaking of what happened on the nights she entertained Richard's acquaintances now. Kitty knew how much it upset Maggie and tried to avoid the subject.

'Do you think we might end up with certain things being rationed?' she asked Maggie then.

Her friend nodded. 'I can't see how it can be avoided. Once the German warships start patrolling the British coast, lots of things that come in from abroad are not going to be able to get through, are they? I think clothing might be hard to find too. Most of the clothes factories have already pledged to sew uniforms for the forces for the duration of the war, so it stands to reason that there aren't going to be so many fashionable outfits available in the shops.'

The girls lapsed into silence then, until Kitty took Tallulah down into the garden to see Arthur and have her usual runabout.

She found the lad in a sombre mood and asked, 'Where's that cheeky smile then? Is something wrong, Arthur?'

He looked up and bit his lip before admitting, 'I've gone an' upset me mum, though I didn't intend to.'

'Really? What have you done that's so bad?'

'I, err . . . I went and joined up yesterday an' she's bin cryin' her eyes out.'

'You did *what*?' Kitty gasped. 'But you aren't old enough to enlist.'

'I am . . . nearly,' he answered sullenly. 'I just told 'em a bit of a white lie about me age, that's all. But a few months is neither here nor there, is it?'

'Oh, Arthur.' Kitty stared at him. He was at that curious age where he was neither a boy nor yet a man, but all arms and gangly legs, and Kitty felt almost as upset at his news as his mother was. She looked forward to seeing his happy smiling face each day and knew that she would miss him. Tallulah would too.

'Is there no way you could get out of it?' she asked then and he looked horrified at the suggestion.

'I don't want to get out of it, Miss Kitty. I *want* to go an' fight for me King an' Country,' he told her with his chin in the air.

'Then in that case I'm very proud of you – but promise me you'll try to stay safe. It won't be the same here without you and we'll all look forward to you coming back a hero. When do you have to go?'

'They're sendin' me for trainin' next week,' he informed her. 'So today I shall have to go into the house an' tell the missus I won't be able to come any more after the end o' this week.'

Kitty nodded. Despite Ruby's loud protestations that the war would not affect them at Brunswick Villa, it appeared that it was doing so already.

Chapter Forty-Seven

Throughout August, Miss Fox continued to read the newspapers avidly. The British troops had been engaged in a bitter struggle alongside their French and Belgian comrades for the town of Mons, but despite their best efforts it was becoming clear that the fighting skills of their enemy were proving too much, and on 23 August the Allies began to retreat. There had been a great many casualties but the battle raged on in an ever-shifting line from Belgium in the north, to Alsace and Lorraine in the south. In under a month the Germans had swept over most of Belgium and crossed the Sambre and the Meuse, forcing the French to retreat to the Somme, the last barrier before Paris.

'So much for it all being over by Christmas,' Miss Fox sighed as she stared at the photographs of wounded soldiers in the paper. 'If you ask me, this is only the beginning.'

'Oh, stop being so pessimistic!' Ruby said, her voice peevish as she studied her face in a hand mirror while plucking her eyebrows. 'I'm more upset about the shortage of clothes in the shops. They're getting hardly any new stock in – it's all hands on deck for sewing uniforms for the troops. Of course, I understand that the men will need them – but what about the women who are left behind? Are we to walk around in our drab old things until this stupid war is over?'

How selfish! Miss Fox tutted to herself, wondering how anyone could even think of something so trivial and frivolous at such an awful time. These were dark days. Men were dying on the battlefield and all Ruby cared about was where her next new outfit was coming from. Maybe if she stopped eating so much and lost weight, some of her beautiful gowns could be adapted to suit the latest slimline designs, intended specifically to save on precious fabric. But then Phyllis had learned long ago that Ruby was thoroughly selfish, with no thought for anyone but herself. Sometimes she wondered why she stayed with her; why she didn't just clear off and make a life for herself instead of waiting on Ruby hand and foot all the while, but the truth was she loved her and was loyal to her despite her many faults and couldn't bring herself to do it, even when Ruby pushed her patience to the limit.

Pushing the newspaper aside, she rose from her seat, saying only, 'I'd best go and give Maggie and Kitty a hand with the cleaning. Now that the maids have left to work in the factory, the house won't clean itself, will it?'

Ruby was too absorbed in her grooming to even answer so Miss Fox left the room to find Kitty mopping the hall floor while Maggie polished the banister rail. Both girls had been marvellous in that respect now that she only had Mabel left, although Maggie did the lion's share of the housework if Kitty was off to Richard's, which was far too frequently for Foxy's liking.

The older woman padded off to the kitchen to make sure that Cook had all she needed for the main meal. Certain foods were becoming harder to obtain, but thankfully their cook had a canny knack of being able to produce a meal from the most meagre of supplies, so up to now they had continued to eat well compared to most, although Phyllis wasn't sure how they would fare when the produce that Arthur had grown in the garden ran out. A mental picture of him in his uniform, looking ridiculously young and vulnerable when he had come to say goodbye to them all, flashed in front of her eyes and she had to swallow the lump in her throat.

Miss Fox was not a sentimental woman, but the thought of that young lad going off so bravely to fight for his country had touched her deeply, and she prayed that one day he would return safely. It was also only now that he had gone that she realised just how hard he had worked about the place.

Miss Fox suspected that the cook only stayed on because she was rather too old to change her ways, which was one blessing for them at least. Foxy dreaded to think how they would have fared if the cooking had been left to her, for she openly admitted that cooking had never been her strong point. In fact, long ago when she had been just a child herself she could remember that her mother, Katherine, had used to tease her and tell her that she was the only one she knew who could burn water if left to her own devices.

Downstairs, she found the cook chopping a large cabbage for dinner, and after checking that all was well she went off to the laundry room to do some washing. It certainly wouldn't do itself, and now that the girls were busily engaged in the cleaning it was a case of all hands to the pump! Thank heavens for the hot weather, thought Phyllis Fox, as she soaked their drawers in the copper and fed sheets through the mangle before pegging them onto the line. War or no war, the washing had to be done.

As the year crept on, news from the front did not improve. The soldiers were dropping like flies in their thousands – mass slaughter – and being forced to live in atrocious conditions. The battlefields were a sea of mud, and corpses sank into it, some never to be seen again. When the Prime Minister broadcast that yet another half a million men were needed, once again there was a surge to enlist. Training camps were springing up all over the country and the women left behind raced to work in the armament factories.

'It's not looking likely that it will be over by Christmas like they forecast, is it?' Sunday asked George one day and he shook his head. He too desperately wanted to enlist now, although he was no longer a very young man – but he was torn. With Ben and Tom already gone, the majority of the hard work at Treetops Manor now fell on his shoulders and with Cissie still not being completely well yet he didn't know how they would manage without him.

Sunday had been hoping that the menfolk might get leave in the near future but that hope was fading now. It appeared that only those who had been badly injured were being shipped home, so in a way she hoped that they were not amongst them. Every day, families were receiving telegrams informing them that their loved ones had been killed in action, and now she watched the drive leading to the Manor apprehensively each day, praying that she would not see the boy on the bicycle whose unfortunate lot it was to deliver these missives of death. It felt as if the world had gone mad and she dreamed of the way things had once been and wondered, like many others, if those happy days would ever return.

Far away, Tom was also thinking of the comforts of home as he rubbed the horses down before making them as comfortable as he could for the night in the makeshift shelters that had been erected for them. He had placed deep layers of straw down on the floor for them to lie on and was almost ready to bed down for the night himself when he heard a couple of young soldiers, new recruits, sniggering outside the tents.

'What have you got there then, lads?' he asked affably and the two young privates jumped nervously.

'It's just a magazine that's goin' round,' the youngest-looking of the two told him guiltily, then with a grin at his mate he passed it to Tom.

Tom began to flick through the pages, which were covered in photographs of young women in various stages of undress. 'Dirty young devils,' he chuckled. After all, they weren't doing any harm and he had been young himself once, although it seemed like a long time ago now. 'You'll be giving yourselves wrist ache if you keep looking at these.' And then suddenly the smile froze on his face as his eyes fastened on one particular photo. It was of Kitty, there could be no denying it, and the photograph left little to the imagination.

Shock and anger coursed through him as he thrust the magazine back at the young private and strode towards his barracks, his mind in turmoil. What could have made her stoop to such levels? he wondered. He had thought that she was making a name for herself on the stage, and the Kitty he remembered would never have done anything like this. Sunday must never find out about it. He paused to light a cigarette and think. *Just as soon as I get home I'll persuade Sunday to come to London with me one more time*, he decided, but he was all too well aware that this might be some long time away. What could happen to their lass Kitty in the meantime?

Late that evening, Kitty returned from Richard's and carelessly tossed a small black velvet box towards Maggie, who had waited up for her.

Maggie sprang the lid of the box and gazed down at a beautiful ring, a sapphire surrounded by sparkling diamonds. 'Why, this must be worth a small fortune!' she exclaimed.

Kitty shrugged. 'Throw it in the drawer with the others,' she said, her voice dead.

Maggie did as she was told, putting it in amongst the collection of expensive-looking boxes. There were bracelets, rings, necklaces, brooches – so many of them now, and yet she had never seen Kitty wear any of them.

'One day I'll take the lot to the pawnbroker and get rid of them,' Kitty said scornfully. Only she could know what exactly she had had to do to earn these baubles, and she resented them as much as the men who had given them to her.

'Do you know, the silly old sod I entertained this evening actually offered to make an honest woman of me?' she snorted as she started to remove the pins from her hair.

Maggie was aware that Kitty had changed lately. She'd become harder somehow. Noticing that her friend was watching her closely, Kitty confided, 'I don't think about any of it any more, so what does that make me?' Then she held her hand up before Maggie could answer. 'You don't have to say it – I already know what I am. I'm a whore, or as good as.'

She stared at her reflection in the mirror, her eyes dull. 'Like mother like daughter, eh?' Then when Maggie looked shocked she went on, 'Oh, I admit I was very naïve when I came here. I thought my mother had brought me here because she loved me and she finally wanted to be with me. I dreamed we would live happily ever after but I worked out some time ago that she only saw me as a means of making money.' She laughed, a harsh sound that made the hairs on the back of Maggie's neck stand on end.

'She thinks I don't know that she and Richard get paid for the favours I give to the men,' Kitty said bitterly. 'But what can I do about it? At the end of the day, she *is* my mother and the truth is, I would do anything for Richard. I'm still sure that he'll marry me one day so until then I'll just have to keep on doing what I'm doing. In the meantime, I've discovered that it isn't so bad. The men, most of them, treat me well and spoil me – and I suppose I enjoy that side of it.'

Maggie gulped deep in her throat. She wanted to tell Kitty that they should both get right away from there, and yet she knew that she would be wasting her breath. Some things were better left unsaid – and until Kitty had realised that Richard had no intentions

387

of ever marrying her, all Maggie could do was be there for her. She hurried across to undo the buttons on the back of Kitty's dress, and help her with her hair.

At that moment, Tom was sitting on the camp bed in his bitterly cold tent quietly smoking a cigarette and thinking of home and his wife, so he decided to write to her. He always felt closer to Sunday somehow when he put his thoughts on paper, although he had no idea if his letters were getting through. Sometimes it was weeks before he heard from her, then suddenly a glut of letters would arrive all together. He kept every one beneath his pillow and throughout the day he always put the latest one beneath his jacket, close to his heart. Now he lifted his pen and began as his breath floated like lace around him in the freezing cold air.

My dear love,

I pray that this letter finds you and everyone at Treetops safe and well. I have just finished my shift with the horses but wanted to write before I attempt to sleep. It's always so hard when you have the sounds of the big guns in the distance, although I am getting used to it now. I have not had a good day. Earlier this afternoon I was forced to shoot one of the beautiful horses that had broken its leg in battle. We have little or no medication left for them now, and even straw and hay are becoming scarce so I am just having to do the best I can for them in this bitter cold weather. I don't mind telling you, as I took the gun to this magnificent animal I was openly crying at such a waste of life. I send them off each morning with a heavy heart knowing that some of them won't make it back. I feel the same every evening when I watch young men being stretch-

388

ered off the battlefield with horrific injuries or dead. When will it all end?

I just had a meal in the dining tent. It was some sort of greasy stew with a few over-cooked vegetables floating around in it, but I ate it anyway as I know I have to keep my strength up, but how I long for one of Cissie's delicious dinners!

A new batch of young men arrived in the camp this afternoon. I haven't met them as yet but I dare say I will as once again there are empty beds in my tent. Know that you are the first person I think of in the morning and the last one I think of before I close my eyes at night. Pray God we will be together again soon, my dearest love. Until then take care.

Your loving husband,
Tom xxxx

He had barely finished signing his name when a few new faces drifted in and he nodded towards them.

'All right, lads?' he greeted them. They reminded him of the incident with the mucky magazine earlier, and he knew his decision not to tell Sunday was right.

They smiled, looking utterly terrified. It had felt like they were embarking on a great adventure when they left home, but they weren't feeling quite so brave now that they were faced with the stark realities of war. Most of them looked to be little older than babies, barely old enough to shave, but then his eyes were drawn to one older chap – and his stomach churned.

It was Hugh Tate, Cissie's son – and he was the double of his father.

Once the initial shock of seeing him had worn off Tom was consumed with anger. If the handkerchief he had found at the scene with Hugh's initials on were anything to go by, he was the one who had attacked his defenceless mother and left her for dead. He was a coward, just as his father had been before him.

As yet, Hugh hadn't noticed Tom watching him and was gazing about with a hunted expression on his face, clearly terrified of what lay ahead of him. And so he should be, Tom thought, but he felt no sympathy for this chap; he deserved everything that was coming to him – and more. The young men quickly claimed the empty beds, nodding towards Tom in a friendly fashion, but Hugh kept himself to himself, which suited Tom just fine. The least he had to do with him the better as far as he was concerned.

He watched as Hugh unpacked his kitbag and stuffed the contents into the bedside locker. He then withdrew a bottle and took a hefty drink from it just as the sergeant strolled in and barked, 'Right, you lot, let's have you outside. You aren't here for a holiday. I want to go through the drill of what will be happening first thing in the morning with you. You'll be up at five and over to the dining tent then back here and kitted up before you're taken to the trenches. You'll do twelve hours on and twelve hours off – if you're lucky enough to come back, that is. Now look lively and line up and *try* and look like soldiers, eh? We've no time for nancy boys here, and any of you that decide you've had a change of heart, forget it. Once the shout goes up for you to move out of the trenches and attack comes, any of you that decides to do a runner will be shot for the coward that he is!'

The pasty-faced youths and Hugh were lined up along the side of the tent now as the sergeant strolled along inspecting them, but Tom couldn't hear what was being said now because some of the chaps who had just finished their twelve-hour shift were stumbling inside and heading for their beds. They were all covered in mud from head to toe but were so traumatised and exhausted that they simply dropped onto their blankets as they were, the only colour showing on them being the whites of their eyes. Tom quietly crept amongst them shaking their blankets out and gently covering them before retiring to his own bed. His day would begin at five the next morning as well and he intended to get as much sleep as he could before the nightmare started again. It was easier said than done with the sounds of explosions and gunfire echoing all around him, but he had learned to cope with it now and soon he slept.

Chapter Forty-Eight

The clanging of a bell had the men tumbling out of their camp beds the next morning and as one they surged towards the wash tents, for what good it did them. They were confronted with tin bowls full of freezing cold water beside which stood a scratchy towel and slivers of soap. Tom wondered how long it had been since he had felt properly clean and couldn't remember. He couldn't even take his boots off to wash his feet because the layer of mud on the duckboards only ensured that they would be as filthy by the time he put them back on. Many of the men were suffering from infected blisters and trench foot so he supposed he shouldn't complain.

When they were done, the men trooped off to the dining tent, their teeth chattering, and Tom found himself watching Tate, who was already sweating profusely at the thought of what was ahead. Had it been any of the other young chaps, he would have sympathised with them, but he couldn't feel an ounce of pity for this man.

Breakfast consisted as usual of lumpy porridge and slices of cold toast and Tom forced some down, noticing that Tate barely ate anything. They all returned to the tent then to collect their rifles while Tom went off to the stables.

The horses whinnied and tossed their heads when they saw him, and he went along the line of them whispering in their ears and stroking their noses. The next hour was taken up with saddling them ready for the officers and trying to keep them calm as they stamped their feet and pulled on their reins.

It had been quiet since early that morning but by now Tom knew that this could change at any moment. And then the shout would go up: 'Forward!' and the men would surge up out of the trenches and charge towards the barbed-wire fences that marked the enemy line. That was when the real nightmare would begin, as the Germans opened fire and he was forced to stand and watch the young men fall. Only when the all clear sounded would the stretcher-bearers venture out to retrieve the wounded and the dead who hadn't already been swallowed up by the foul-smelling mud.

It was no wonder the rats were so huge, he thought. The sight of them gorging on the corpses was seared on his mind and would haunt him for ever. The soldiers in the trenches were plagued with them too; the damn filthy things seemed to be everywhere but there was little anyone could do about it, they were all too busy trying to kill the enemy to have time to try and kill the plague of vermin. Those men who had been there for a while and still survived had come to accept them, while the new recruits were horrified at their presence.

He was still stroking the horses when the dreaded shout went up: 'Forward!' and all hell broke loose. The soldiers rose from the trenches like spectres in the early-morning mist and from his vantage point he watched as they waded as best they could across the field. Within seconds the air was filled with the sound of gunshots. He could see the Germans approaching from the other side of the field and then the two sides were locked in combat as men dropped like stones. It was sickening and he glanced away, only to see one soldier hovering on the lip of the trench. With a little shock, he recognised Hugh Tate. He was shaking uncontrollably until an officer suddenly came behind him and pushed him forward with the butt of his rifle.

'Get a move on, or I'll shoot you where you stand!' the officer roared. 'We won't stand for cowards here!'

As Tate moved forward, his head down and his whole body quivering, Tom found himself thinking, *There's one I wouldn't be sorry to see shot!* Then he felt ashamed. Tate was still Cissie's son at the end of the day and she would be distraught if anything were to happen to him. She still had no idea that it was Hugh who had attacked her and left her for dead, and with luck she never would remember. But then the officers arrived and started to mount the horses and Tom had no more time to think of anything but the poor beasts who were about to go into battle.

As the war raged on, Kitty's first Christmas away from Treetops approached but this year there was little for the people of Britain to celebrate. Ruby was in a drunken stupor for half the time now despite Miss Fox's constant attempts to pour away any wine or gin she found about the house. Many of the music halls had closed but Kitty was still very popular at the ones that remained open, although her bookings were fewer and further between than they had been before war had been declared.

She was at Richard's one afternoon when the maid came to inform him that there were some women at the door asking to see him.

Richard frowned as he asked, 'Who are they? I'm not expecting anyone.'

'I've no idea, sir, they wouldn't say.'

'Then you'd better show them in.' No doubt they were new clients, he thought.

'Right you are, sir.' The little maid bobbed her knee and hurried away, to reappear a few moments later with four ladies following her.

'Mr Richard Fitzherbert?' The older of the ladies, who was beautifully spoken, stared imperiously down her nose at him.

Richard said smoothly, 'Yes, how may I help you? If you wish to have photographs taken I'm afraid you will have to book an appointment.'

'Believe me, I would never appoint *you* to do anything for me,' the woman replied, then without another word she handed him an envelope as the other ladies looked on.

Bewildered, Richard slit it open and as he did so, a lone white feather fell out and drifted to the floor. It was then that Kitty realised who they were. They were part of the Suffrage movement and were making it their business to hand out white feathers to any gentleman whom they considered fit enough to be away fighting for their country.

'You are a *disgrace* to your sex, sir,' the woman told him coldly. 'Shame on you for your cowardice.' And with that she turned and walked away with a look of pure disgust on her face as the other women trotted behind her.

Kitty was deeply distressed and tears sprang to her eyes, but Richard appeared to be unmoved.

'Stupid old harridan,' he muttered angrily as he ground the feather into the carpet with the heel of his shoe. 'It's a shame they can't find something better to do with their time!'

'The trouble is, they're saying that soon all men under forty won't be given a choice about enlisting,' Kitty told him tremulously. 'They will be sending for the ones fit enough to fight whether they wish to go or not. What will you do then?'

'I shall simply go to ground until it's all over,' Richard answered icily and, for the first time, Kitty felt ashamed of him.

Despite all of Miss Fox's efforts to make Christmas Day a special time, it fell flat. In spite of the food shortages she had managed to produce a very good-sized goose, which had been cooked to perfection, and there was also a large and spicy plum pudding that had been soaked in brandy for weeks, yet for different reasons, none of the residents of Brunswick Villa had much appetite.

As usual, Ruby was pleasantly merry by lunchtime, Maggie was quiet and Kitty couldn't help but remember the happy Christmases she had spent at Treetops Manor with Sunday and Tom. Even Miss Fox was sad as she thought of little Arthur and wondered how he was faring. They had received one very heavily censored letter from him only the week before, telling them that he was now in Flanders, where she knew from the papers the fighting was fierce.

After dinner, they all opened their presents. Miss Fox had bought Ruby, Kitty and Maggie very pretty silk scarves and Ruby had bought Kitty a charming little gold bracelet, which Kitty suspected had been chosen by Foxy. They exchanged all the presents politely and made the necessary noises then Kitty and Maggie volunteered to clear up while the kindly cook, who had put together a large basket of Christmas fare for Arthur's mother and her offspring, put her feet up by the fire to enjoy a glass of sherry and a mince pie. In truth, the girls were glad of something to do. Kitty had thought she would spend the day with Richard, but he had disappointed her the week before when he had informed her that he would be travelling to his family's home on Christmas Eve to spend the holiday with them in their country home.

'So why didn't he invite you to go with him?' Maggie had asked in her usual forthright manner. 'If you are a couple, surely it's time he took you to meet his parents?'

Kitty had simply shrugged. She had hoped that would be the case too, and the hurt went deep. All in all, it was turning out to be the worst Christmas ever, Kitty thought as she fingered the gold locket that hung around her neck and thought of Sunday.

At that moment, could they have known it, the soldiers were enjoying a break from fighting. A truce had been called for Christmas Day and the men were making the best of it. In the morning, they had attended a service given by the hospital chaplain and they had sung Christmas carols as they thought of their loved ones back at home. The Christmas dinner was the best meal they'd had since enlisting and when it was over they were shocked to see the Germans warily crossing the field waving white handkerchiefs.

Seeing the hesitation on the faces of the young privates who shared his tent, Tom told them, 'Go to meet them, lads. Enjoy yourselves. I don't think they wish us any harm.' He would have liked to go with them but his leg was paining him today so he stood on the edge of the muddy field and watched as the young men met in the middle of the field and shook hands. Tom was choked. Soon an unlikely game of football was taking place between the two sides on any bit of solid ground they could find. It was a time for peace, a time for them to come together as mere men rather than enemies, and it brought home to each and every one of them how pointless the war was. Each one of the Germans was someone's son, husband, lover or brother – and just for this one special day they and the British troops could be friends. As the day drew to a close they parted, all too aware that the very next day they would be killing each other again, and that yet more telegrams would be sent out to grieving relatives, telling them that a young man they loved had died in battle.

It was early in January 1915 that young Arthur sat in the trenches reading over again the letter he had received from his mother shortly before Christmas. He had read it so many times that he knew every word by heart now but he never tired of it. It seemed to bring his family closer somehow.

Dear Arthur,

I hope you are well, son. Miss Fox come to see us yesterday wiv Miss Kitty an she bourt us the luvliest basket of goodies fer Christmas. I've had a rare old game keepin the little uns from eating everyfin before the day. We are all well, cept little Cedric whos had a cold, you know he always suffers wiv his chest in the winter an its been right bitter here. The frosts been so fick I swear yer could cut it wiv a knife come morning. Yer dad is bein kept busy on the river an ive joined a knittin circle. Weve been knittin socks fer the troops. I hope you are bein as careful as yer can, son. We speak about yer all the time an though I was angry wiv yer fer joinin up before yer had to I'm right proud of yer an longin to see yer home safe an sound again. Yer can be sure on Christmas day we'll all be thinkin' of yer. I pologise fer the spellin. Yer know I've never been a skolar.

May God kepe his eys on yer, my dear boy.

Yer luvin mum xxxxxxxxx

Arthur flicked a tear from his cheek as he folded the precious letter and tucked it down the front of his battledress next to his dog tag. The duckboard he was sitting on with his back pressed against the cold earth wall of the trench was slowly sinking into the mud but Arthur was so cold that he didn't care any more. Men were pacing up and down blowing on their hands and stamping their feet as they waited for the order to advance. This was the part he hated the most; the waiting. Funnily enough, once the shout came and he was up and over on the field, he had got into the habit of blocking everything else from his mind. It was do or die up there – although he often had nightmares now as the faces of some of the men he had rammed his bayonet into paraded before his eyes in their death throes. A huge rat suddenly ran across his foot and

Arthur shrieked as he kicked it with all his might. The loathsome creature sailed through the air, hit the other side of the trench, dropped to the ground then scurried away with its prize – someone's finger – still in its mouth as Arthur shuddered and tucked his hands under his arms. And then the shout came and pandemonium broke loose as the men grabbed their rifles and surged towards the ladders propped up the sides of the trenches.

Once up on the field, Arthur positioned his rifle in front of him and plodded along. He could see the enemy advancing and started to fire then suddenly he felt as if someone had thumped him in the chest before he hit the mud with a sickening thud. He had dropped his rifle and he lay there staring up at the sky before raising his hand to his chest where he found nothing but a gaping hole with something warm and sticky spurting out of it.

That's strange, where's me jacket gone? he wondered, then suddenly a picture of his mother's face flashed in front of his eyes and he smiled. He lifted his arm, for the vision was so real that he felt she was there with him. The sounds of the battleground receded and he felt strangely peaceful. 'I love yer, Mum,' he whispered through the blood that was bubbling from his lips and then his eyes gently closed and he knew no more.

It was four weeks later when Arthur's mother was scrubbing the doorstep that the boy on the bicycle braked beside her.

'Mrs Partridge?'

She nodded numbly. Her mouth had suddenly gone dry and no words would come out of it. He handed her the brown envelope then touching his cap respectfully he pedalled away as she knelt there staring down at it. She had no need to open it, for she knew what it would tell her. She had felt it for some time. Her son was gone from her for ever. Arthur would not be coming home.

Heaving herself up, she staggered inside leaving the bucket and scrubbing brush exactly where they were. And then she sank down onto the nearest chair and slowly slit the envelope open.

It is with deep regret that we write to inform you that your son, Private Arthur James Partridge, was killed in battle . . .

The telegram fluttered to the floor and tears rained down her face as she thought of her beloved boy, her firstborn, so smart in his Army uniform, and her chest swelled with pride. Her son had died a hero.

Chapter Forty-Nine

June 1915

'I sometimes think this war is never going to end,' Sunday said mournfully, as she stood staring from the drawing-room window at Treetops Manor.

'Well, at least we are safer here than most places,' her mother remarked, looking up from her sewing. 'According to the newspapers, those Zeppelin airships are causing havoc and death all over the country. And that new poisonous gas the Germans are using can blind you or send you mad by all accounts.'

She instantly wished she could retract what she had just said as Sunday burst into tears. She knew that her daughter worried about Tom and Ben all the time. There was no chance of either of them being granted any leave in the circumstances.

'What you must think is that no news is good news,' Lavinia said, trying to inject some lightness into her tone.

'But I haven't heard a word from either of them for months,' Sunday fretted.

Lavinia raised an eyebrow. 'You should know by now how long it's taking for everyone's mail to get through. You'll probably get a glut of letters when they do arrive.'

Sunday nodded, knowing that her mother was right. Somehow she just had to get on with things and continue praying that the war would soon be over. Compared to many of the families in town who had received the dreaded telegrams informing them that their loved ones would not be returning, she knew that she was very fortunate. But it was so hard . . .

In Chelsea, Kitty was also feeling depressed. Maggie had gone to visit Mrs Partridge with a basket of goodies as she often did these days, since they had received news of Arthur's death. It was so hard to believe that the lad had been killed when he'd had his whole life ahead of him – but then the war was wicked.

Since being presented with the white feather, Richard had kept out of sight although Kitty still regularly visited the studio to entertain his friends. She had thought that the shame of being exposed as a coward would force him into enlisting, but that hadn't been the case. If anything, he was even more adamant now that he would never go to fight. Rather than have an end in sight the war seemed to be escalating and it appeared that no one was safe now, be they on land or on the sea. But life went on with many women in Britain now taking on the men's roles full time. It was common now to see women driving buses, working in factories or as clerks or farmhands. Kitty sometimes wished she could do something to help and she mentioned it to Richard.

'I'm sure I could drive an omnibus if someone taught me,' she said. She quite liked the idea but he grew so angry at her suggestion that she abandoned the idea and like everyone else simply prayed that the conflict might soon be all over.

One morning in early December 1915 as Tom was preparing the horses, he noticed Hugh Tate standing at the edge of the trenches smoking a cigarette. For now, all was quiet but Tom knew that this could change at any moment and he watched Tate from the corner of his eye. An early-morning mist floated above the frost-coated field and all that could be heard was birdsong, so Tom was making the most of the peace. But it didn't last long and all too soon the shout went up and the men began to pour out of their hiding places and march towards their enemy with their rifles raised as the sound of gunfire filled the air.

Tom saw Tate hesitate as an officer drew alongside him. 'Well, go on then, man!' the officer roared as he nudged Tate with his rifle. For a second Tate hovered, then suddenly he turned and ran in the direction of Tom as fast as the cloying mud would allow.

'*Halt*, I say, or I shall fire!' the enraged officer screeched but Tate was beyond reason now and was in a blind panic. And then Tom could only watch as the officer raised his rifle and aimed it at the would-be deserter.

'This is your last chance, Corporal Banks. Stop now or I shall fire!'

So . . . he's using a false name is he? Tom thought.

Completely disregarding him Tate ran on until suddenly the officer pulled the trigger. Tate jerked like a puppet on a string, a look of pure shock on his face, then with a grace that would have done justice to a ballet dancer he slowly dropped to his knees before falling face first into the stinking mud.

Greatly shocked, Tom gulped deep in his throat. It wasn't the first time he had seen this happen with other young men who had lost their nerve, but knowing that this was Cissie's son affected him badly. She would be devastated to learn that her firstborn had died a shameful death. But then the officers were all around him, mounting their horses, and he had no more time to dwell on it until the last of his charges had been ridden away. When he next looked towards Tate's body it was to see a huge rat feasting on the hole in his back, and turning quickly from the sight, Tom emptied the contents of his stomach into the mud. It was an image that would haunt him for the rest of his life, along with all the other horrendous things he had been forced to witness.

Late that night, as he lay shivering in his tent, he wondered what he should do about it. The authorities would not be able to write and inform Mr and Mrs Tate of Hugh's death if he had been using a false name. At least it would spare them the shame of knowing that the man they had raised as their own had died a coward's death. Should he write and tell Cissie about Hugh's death – would it be better to let Sunday break the news to her? Thoughts of home brought a lump to his throat and he had to blink very hard to stop the tears from falling. It seemed so very long ago since he had seen his loved ones now and he wondered if he ever would again. Was his son all right? Had Ben survived so far? The worry never left him. He had seen hundreds – maybe thousands – of young men lose their lives needlessly. The sound of the chap in the next bed coughing interrupted his thoughts. Many of the soldiers had ailments now – how could they not have, when forced to live in these atrocious conditions? But then he supposed they were the lucky ones. At least they were still alive for now – although who knew what the morning might bring?

The days wore on. It was shortly before Christmas 1915 that Tom was admitted to the field hospital. He was suffering from frostbite, and when the nurses managed to get his boot off and then soak off his sock, the smell was overwhelming.

'Those two toes in the middle of that foot are going to have to be amputated, otherwise you could lose the whole leg,' the doctor told him as he examined his feet. 'Sorry, old chap, but as soon as this is done you'll be sent home to recover on the first boat available.'

Tom grinned despite the pain. Two toes seemed a small price to pay if it meant him spending Christmas back at home.

'Ah well, at least they're on the lame leg,' he said bravely as a young harassed nurse began to gently wash his feet in a bowl of warm water. It was the first time they had been out of his boots for months and the warmth seemed to be climbing up his leg. For the last two months Tom had also been helping the stretcher-bearers at the end of each day as well as tending the horses, and as he laid back against the pillows he suddenly realised how completely exhausted he was. Tom secretly thought the stretcher-bearers had the worst job of all. They would cross the field each time there was a ceasefire, collecting the dog tags from the corpses and bringing back to the hospital tent as many of the wounded as they could. For months, there had been a terrible shortage of medical supplies, and the overworked doctors and nurses were forced to do the best they could with what little they had. The worst-affected patients died, and many of the ones that were left had suffered horrific injuries.

He glanced to either side of him. The beds were rammed in close together in regimentally straight lines along both sides of the hospital tent. It was hard to determine how old the man was in the bed to the right of him. His whole head, even his eyes, was heavily bandaged with only his lips showing and he was lying so still that he might already have died. Burns probably, Tom thought with a sick feeling in the pit of his stomach.

The young chap in the bed to the left of him was shouting feverishly, and once the nurse had prepared Tom for theatre and taken away the bloody bowl of water, Tom tried to comfort him. Poor lad, he couldn't have been any older than eighteen or nineteen and the wire cage across his legs told its own sorry story.

'Calm down, old chap,' Tom said kindly. 'Shall I call the nurse for you? Are you in pain?' He was suddenly ashamed that his own complaint seemed so trivial.

'I've lost me legs,' the boy sobbed. 'An' yet I swear I can still feel 'em.' He turned tortured eyes towards Tom, whose heart went out to him. 'What'll I do now? My girl back at home won't want me like this, will she?'

'She will, son, if she truly loves you,' Tom tried to reassure him but the lad's head wagged from side to side.

'No. My Molly's a looker, a little beaut. She'll not want a cripple! An' I . . . I want my mum!'

Stretching his hand out as far as it would go, Tom managed to stroke the boy's arm. Words seemed so inadequate.

The discomfort in his foot was getting worse now. Strange, that – he hadn't felt anything while his feet were freezing but now that he was becoming warmer for the first time in weeks, the pain was setting in.

When he awoke the next morning to the sounds of the big guns booming, he blinked, wondering where he was. Then a young nurse's face swam into focus and she smiled at him tiredly.

'Your op went well,' she told him as she tucked the covers around him. 'And you're one of the lucky ones. There's an ambulance due here today to take the injured to the nearest port so's you can be shipped home.'

Tom returned her smile groggily then glanced towards the bed on the left to see that it was empty and neatly made with clean sheets and blankets.

'The young chap that was there last night – where is he?'

The nurse sadly shook her head. 'He didn't make it. It was the shock, you see?'

Turning his face into his pillow, Tom sobbed. When was this bloody senseless war going to end? And how many more young lives would it claim before it did?

The voyage back to Blighty on the hospital ship was appalling. There were no painkillers available and now Tom's heavily bandaged foot felt as if it was on fire. He quickly became hot and feverish. As the boat was tossed about like a cork he began to vomit and a nurse fetched a doctor to him.

'Infection has set in,' the doctor informed him. He wasn't really surprised. The conditions surgeons were forced to cope with in the field hospitals were far from ideal and infections were rife. 'Never mind, old chap. Just try to hold on in there. Soon as we land we'll get you transported home and then I've no doubt your wife will give you the best of care.' Even though Tom was gravely ill, his injuries did not warrant a bed in one of the military hos-pitals. These were reserved for the more serious wounds and even then, there were nowhere near enough beds.

'I'm all . . . all right.' Pains were shooting up his leg but thoughts of home made him grit his teeth bravely.

'That's the ticket.' The doctor patted his arm approvingly and moved on to the next patient as Tom tried to sleep. When he did eventually manage to drop off, his dreams were weird and mixed. Sunday was there, and Kitty and Ben, and his lips curved in a smile. But then he was back on the field watching Cissie's son fall into the mud and he began to thrash about. He had just told her that Hugh had died a coward's death and she was inconsolable.

'Wake up, Corporal Branning. We're in port now and going to transfer you to an ambulance. Can you hear me?'

He started awake, his face drenched in sweat and found himself staring up into the face of a nurse with a kindly smile. He nodded dizzily, and then he was being lifted onto a stretcher and once more sleep claimed him.

It was late that evening when the transport he was in turned into the drive of Trectops.

'Very nice home you've got here, matey,' the jolly stretcher-bearer remarked as he peered through the trees. 'This is goin' to be a wonderful surprise for your missus. She'll have you right as rain in no time, no doubt.'

Tom felt a surge of joy as he nodded weakly and then they were pulling up at the bottom of the steps and the driver hopped out to run up and knock on the door.

It was Cissie who opened it and when the man told her why they were there she squealed with delight and ran back into the house, all of a flap, to find Sunday.

'*Tom!*' Suddenly his wife was there, and strangely the pain didn't feel quite so acute. She clutched his hand as the driver told her the extent of his injuries and gave advice for the treatment and then Tom was stretchered inside and up to their bedroom. Once the transport men had left, leaving strict instructions for her to get their own doctor to see him as soon as possible, Sunday made sure he had a cup of tea and hot buttered toast first before washing him from head to toe, with many changes of warm water and using her own soap, before drying him, rebandaging his wound and helping him into a clean pair of pyjamas. As he settled back onto the feather mattress and pillows, enjoying the warmth of the roaring fire, Tom felt truly as if he had died and gone to heaven.

Cissie then fetched him a small bowl of hot stew, thick with gravy and chunks of tender meat, and Sunday spoonfed it to him. There had been times when she had feared she would never see him again, but her husband was home, and now she was determined to get him well and fit again.

'I love you and I've missed you *so* much,' she whispered to him as she held another cup of hot sweet tea to his mouth.

'I missed you too.' And then with his belly full and a smile on his lips he sank into a deep and healing sleep. The only problem with getting him well again, Sunday thought to herself as she sat and watched over him, was that he would then be recalled to rejoin his unit. But she decided that she wouldn't dwell on that for now. Christmas was just a whisper away and thanks be to God she would be sharing it with the man she loved.

Chapter Fifty

'You're going to spend Christmas with your family *again*?' Kitty couldn't hide her dismay from Richard, who had just told her of his plans.

'Why wouldn't I?' he answered curtly.

She wanted to scream at him, *Because I thought you would be spending it with me!* But the words seemed to lodge in her throat.

'I dare say you'll be happy enough spending it with Ruby and Maggie,' he said dismissively. He had been nowhere near as attentive to her of late and Kitty was beginning to wonder if their relationship was ever going anywhere. She knew that Maggie would be happy to see her away from Richard for good, but there was something about him that she found impossible to resist. He only had to crook his little finger and she came running. She only wished that she could have the same effect on him.

Suddenly tired of everything, she collected her bag and after walking to the door of the studio she told him, 'I think I'll go and get an early night. I have a headache coming on.'

He didn't even look up from the newspaper he was reading but simply nodded. 'As you wish. I'll see you tomorrow before I leave for the family seat in the country.'

Kitty plodded through the hallway to the front door on feet that felt like lead. Why wasn't he asking her to go with him? She knew that she was well spoken, Sunday had seen to that, so surely it couldn't be because he was ashamed of her? But then she thought of the evenings she spent with Richard's so-called friends and wondered if this was the reason why he wanted to keep her a secret. Now he had used her for his own purposes, she was no longer a desirable prospect.

She pushed the idea away as she stepped out into the chilly night to hail a cab. Richard didn't even trouble himself to hail one for her and see her safely inside it – nor had he done so for some months, now that she came to think about it. She stood there shivering as a cab pulled up beside her. The weather was so cold that already her teeth were chattering and added to that it was raining, fine needle-sharp spits of rain that made her cheeks sting. The month before had been reported as the second coldest November on record and December hadn't been much better. Kitty wondered briefly if they might have a white Christmas but she doubted it. The weather was too wet and cold for snow, and as she settled into the cab she found herself remembering the happy Christmases she had spent at Treetops with Sunday and Tom.

Blinking back tears, a wave of homesickness and despair washed over her. Only now could she admit to herself that she deeply regretted Ruby ever sending for her. The dreams she had secretly harboured of being reunited with a mother who had been forced to give her up because of genuine hardship had long since died. If truth be told, Ruby had no time for her and sadly Kitty knew it. And yet, something made her stay and it wasn't only Richard. She actually felt sorry for Ruby. There was a certain vulnerability about the woman now that made Kitty feel protective of her. She supposed that was what made Miss Fox stay with her too. It certainly wasn't because of the way she was treated, that was for sure, for Ruby could often be heard bellowing at her from all over the house.

With a sigh, Kitty stared at the rain-lashed windows.

It was mid-January 1916 when Tom received a letter asking him to report for a medical to see if he was fit enough to return to his unit. It sent Sunday spinning into a panic.

'But your foot isn't properly healed yet,' she objected.

Tom smiled at her as he stroked her hair. He was sure she grew more beautiful with each passing year and the thought of leaving her again was like a physical pain, but he knew that every man was needed.

'You know I have no choice,' he told her softly. 'If I don't report for the medical I shall be classed as AWOL and we wouldn't want that, would we? I may be many things, sweetheart, but I'm not a coward.'

The words made his thoughts turn to Hugh Tate and he glanced at Cissie who was dusting her way around the drawing room. Up until now he had shied away from telling her about her son, but now he decided that she deserved to know that he was dead.

'Cissie, come and sit with me for a moment, would you?' He patted the seat at the side of him and Cissie did as she was told, wondering what it was that he wanted.

'The thing is,' he began, finding this much more difficult than he could ever have imagined. 'Before I was injured I noticed that your son was stationed in the same place as me.'

'*He was?*' Cissie clasped her hands together as she beamed at Kitty. 'Didn't I tell you he would have gone to fight?' She looked at Tom again then with hope shining in her eyes and suddenly he knew what he must do.

'He, err . . . I don't quite know how to tell you this, but he – he was killed in battle. Your son died a hero, Cissie, and before he died he asked me to tell you that he was sorry for any trouble he'd caused you, and about the money he had borrowed from you. He intended to pay it back just as soon as he could.'

Every word was a lie. He better than anyone knew that it was Hugh who had attacked Cissie that night in the copse. But how

411

could he have told her that? He was glad now that he had destroyed the incriminating evidence, the handkerchief Hugh had dropped at the scene, and he prayed that God would forgive him for lying.

He held his breath as he watched a mixture of emotions flit across her face then a solitary tear ran down her cheek and she managed to smile.

'I always knew he was a good lad deep down,' she breathed. 'And at least I can be proud of him now. Thank you for telling me, Tom.' She rose then and quietly left the room to tell George and to grieve in private. *I'll tell Mr and Mrs Tate the same thing when I'm able to save their heartache as well*, Tom promised himself.

'Knowing you as I do, I think there is more to this than you're saying,' Sunday told her husband. 'But bless you for sparing her feelings. At least she has something to hang on to now.' And then she went into the safe shelter of his arms, determined to make the most of every precious second they had left together.

A week later, George drove Tom into town in his freshly laundered uniform with his kitbag slung across his shoulder, for his medical. The goodbyes at Treetops had been tearful but Tom was grateful that he had managed to see his home again for a few weeks at least.

'I'll wait here for you, man,' George told him in a thick voice when they arrived.

'No, you get yourself away. I'll probably be catching a train,' Tom advised.

'Aye well, I'll wait all the same till yer come out again,' George insisted, and knowing better than to argue Tom nodded and went inside to meet the Army doctor. His limp had been much more pronounced since losing his toes to frostbite and his foot still pained him, but all the same Tom walked in with his back as straight as he could hold it.

Once shown into the doctor's office he found the man poring over his records. 'Ah, Corporal Branning?'

'Yes, sir.' Tom stood to attention as the doctor came around the desk to him.

'Right, let's have a look at you then, shall we? Hop onto the couch.'

Tom proceeded to take his boot and sock off and the doctor then examined him before saying, 'Could you walk a straight line for me?'

Tom did as requested as the doctor watched him with a thoughtful expression on his face before saying, 'You know what, man, I reckon you've done your bit now. That leg and foot of yours are in a pretty bad way. I'm going to give you a medical discharge on the grounds of being unfit to fight any more.'

Tom was astounded. 'What? You mean I don't have to go back?'

'That's exactly what I mean.' The doctor sat back down at his desk and began to scribble on his pad. 'It's all credit to you that you enlisted at your age before you were asked to in the first place, so hold your head high and go home to your family. I shall be sending my report to your commanding officer so this is an end to it for you.' Then his manner becoming official again, he barked, '*Next!*' as Tom staggered from the room with his sock and his boot still in his hand.

He found George waiting outside for him and dropped into the passenger seat of the car, looking dazed.

'Railway station is it then?' When Tom shook his head, George frowned. 'Where then?'

'Home,' Tom told him with a broad smile. 'I've been classed as unfit so this is the end of the war for me. I just wish to God that it was for the rest of the chaps still fighting, God bless them!'

'Amen to that,' George agreed with all his heart as he turned the car towards home.

413

It was in August 1916 that Sunday saw the sight everyone dreaded: the telegram boy cycling up the drive. Her heart turned over. It had to be news of Ben – who else could it be? Feeling slightly sick, she went to the door to meet him and once the brown envelope was in her hand she stood staring at it as if it might bite her.

Cissie found her still standing there in a state of shock some minutes later.

'Where's Tom?' Sunday asked in a wobbly voice.

'He's helpin' George scythe the grass – but give that here,' her friend ordered. 'Best see what it says before we fetch him, eh lass?'

She took it from Sunday's shaking hand and quickly split it open, then breathed a huge sigh of relief. Like Sunday, she had thought the worst. 'It *is* about Ben but he ain't dead.' She gave Sunday, whose face had drained of colour, a quick hug. 'He's been injured in Flanders and now he's in a military hospital in Portsmouth.'

'Does it say what his injuries are?' Sunday asked tremulously.

Cissie shook her head. 'No, but there's a telephone number to ring. We'd best fetch Tom now an' let him do it. An' let's just thank God that he's still alive, even if he is wounded.'

She scuttled away then as Sunday stood gripping the edge of the banister rail. They had all been reading the war reports religiously and she knew of the terrible conditions the troops had been forced to fight in at Flanders. The men were wading waist-deep in stinking mud made deeper still by the relentless rain that had been lashing the battlefield. Men who were unfortunate enough to slip off the duckboards that had been thrown down on the morass were reported to be drowning in the sludge, dragged down by the weight of their equipment. Guns and horses were being sunk irretrievably. Sunday wept as she thought of what Ben must have endured. He was alive, admittedly – but would it be the same Ben they had known who came home to them, if or when he did? Common sense told her that he couldn't be the same. He had seen things that no one should ever see and the experience was bound to have affected him. But then she knew that they must all cling on to the fact that he was alive whatever his injuries were. Somehow when he came home they must help him to recover.

In a slightly more positive frame of mind she waited for Tom to join her.

It took Tom almost two hours to get through to someone at the hospital in Portsmouth who was able to tell them what was wrong with Ben – and it wasn't good news.

'Severe burns.' The strain showed on his face as he dropped the receiver back into the cradle. 'They're all down one side of his face and one arm, apparently.'

Cissie and Sunday held hands tightly as they both remembered what a handsome chap Ben had been.

'Will he be badly scarred?' Sunday breathed.

Tom nodded, his face set in grim lines. 'It sounds like it. They've already done a number of skin grafts – but I'll know more tomorrow. I'm going to catch the first train out in the morning and go down to Portsmouth.'

'May I come too?'

He stared into Sunday's anxious face. 'Of course, if Cissie here can manage on her own.'

'She won't have to, I'll be here to help,' Lavinia said as she joined them. 'You two just shoot off and pack an overnight case. It's too far to travel there and back in one day. We'll be fine, won't we, Cissie, my love? You just go and give Ben what comfort you can and tell him we're all longing for the day when he can come home.'

Tom had a lump in his throat that prevented him from speaking. It was so unfair, he thought. Why couldn't it have been him? Ben was so young to have to bear something so horrible. He had his whole life in front of him. But that was war for you. It was no respecter of age or circumstance, and Ben was just one of hundreds of thousands of young men who had suffered the same fate or worse.

Raising a grateful smile for Lavinia and Cissie he limped away to get out his travelling case, and Sunday went with him.

Chapter Fifty-One

May 1918

'Right, m' ladyship, get your arse out of that bed right now!' Miss Fox stamped across the room and swished Ruby's curtains aside. 'It's halfway through the afternoon and it's high time you got up!' Her eyes rested on the empty sherry bottle at the side of Ruby's bed. Things had been going steadily downhill for months, with Ruby sinking into a deep depression. No doubt they should be grateful that as yet they had escaped the Zeppelin raids. Many other areas in London had not been so lucky. But that wasn't the only worry she had now. Earlier that morning the cook had presented her with a pile of unpaid bills.

'The butcher is saying he won't deliver any more meat till this is settled,' she'd fretted. 'And most of the other tradesmen are putting their foot down, including the dairy, the grocer's and the coal man, though that's not so important now the weather is changing for the better. I'm sorry to trouble you with this, Miss Fox. The mistress usually sees to all the bills, as you know, but she hasn't been well of late, has she.'

'Leave it with me,' Miss Fox had told her, taking the bills from the woman's hand, and she had then closeted herself away to go through them. She'd been appalled when she'd seen how much

417

they amounted to, and how many months old they were, and now it was time to have it out with Ruby.

She waited until Ruby had dragged herself up onto the pillows, looking, Miss Fox thought, like death warmed up, but she had run out of sympathy. Taking the pile of bills from her pocket she waved them at her, saying, 'What's going on here then? The tradesmen are refusing to deliver to us any more until these are settled. Why haven't they been paid?'

Ruby rubbed her forehead, which was throbbing. 'Oh, Foxy, go away, I can't be doing with things like that right now.'

'I'm going nowhere till I've had an explanation,' Miss Fox retorted sternly. 'Just look at the state of you! You should be ashamed. Kitty and Maggie are doing all the housework since the maids left. That's saved on wages for a start, so what's the problem? And where is the money coming from now anyway to keep us afloat?' It was clearly Kitty who was bringing the money in, but it was what she might be having to do to earn it that concerned Miss Fox.

Ruby snapped, 'Why don't you mind your own business? Give the bloody bills here and I'll see that they're paid.'

'Better still, you can give *me* the money and *I'll* pay them.' Miss Fox stood hands on hips as she glared at her and sensing that the game was up, Ruby played for time.

'Very well. But I can't give it to you this minute, can I? At least have the grace to let me get up.'

'Very well. I'll see you downstairs in ten minutes,' Miss Fox answered waspishly and turning about, she stamped from the room.

She found Maggie downstairs in the drawing room polishing the sideboard and fixing a smile to her face she asked the girl, 'How is Kitty today?'

Maggie shrugged. Kitty had been giving them both some cause for concern for a while now. All her sparkle had gone and she looked tired and drained all the time.

'Oh, no better no worse.' Maggie paused to look at Miss Fox, then making a decision, she said in a rush, 'I think Mr Fitzherbert treats her diabolically.' There, it was said even if it wasn't her place to say it.

Strangely enough the older woman nodded in agreement. 'I think you're right, Maggie, and I wish we could get her away from him. But he seems to have some sort of hold on her.'

Maggie flushed. She knew exactly what that hold was. While Richard and his friends had possession of the photos that Kitty was ashamed of, he would always have her in his power, but Maggie had promised her friend that she would never tell Miss Fox about them and up to now she had kept her promise. They heard Ruby lumbering down the stairs then, and lifting the cleaning rags, Maggie hastily left the room and went in search of Kitty. She found her in the bathroom looking grievously ill and asked, 'What's wrong? Have you been sick?'

Kitty nodded as she swiped the back of her hand across her mouth. 'Yes, I think I must have eaten something that disagreed with me. I'll be fine now though.'

'Hmm.' Maggie wasn't so sure but she left her then and went about her chores.

Downstairs, Miss Fox and Ruby were in the middle of another heated argument.

'What do you mean, you haven't enough to pay them all?' Miss Fox demanded angrily. It looked like she was going to have to dip into her own savings yet again. 'You don't seem to object to paying the wine bills and they're sky high!'

'Oh, so you even begrudge me a drink now, do you?' Ruby whimpered pathetically. 'Even though that's the only pleasure I have left.'

It hit Miss Fox like a blow then just how far Ruby had sunk. The music-hall bookings and her suitors had long since disappeared and now she looked a total wreck. She didn't even bother to get dressed or brush her hair most days and her skin had taken on a curious yellow tinge, as had the whites of her eyes.

'Just look at the state of you.' There was anguish in Miss Fox's voice. 'If you carry on like this you're going to kill yourself!'

Ruby shrugged. In truth, she didn't much care. She was used to being pampered and adored, but now her lifestyle was slowly catching up with her and she couldn't cope with not being everyone's darling. Ruby thrived on attention but that was long gone and her only comfort now was found in a bottle.

'Who would care if I did?' she said and Miss Fox was enraged.

'*I* would, for a start! And what about your daughter? She isn't well herself but you haven't even noticed, have you? You're too wrapped up in self-pity to care for anyone but yourself and you should be ashamed.' She took a deep breath then and tried to calm herself. This futile arguing was getting them nowhere. 'Right, now let's go through these bills together and deal with the most urgent ones first, shall we? Give me the key to the safe and we'll see how much money is in there.'

The safe was positioned behind one of the gilded pictures on the wall and once Miss Fox had the key she unlocked it and withdrew what money was in it. She quietly counted it out before seeing what the bills amounted to, then turning to Ruby she told her, 'We're going to have to pawn or sell some of your jewellery.'

'What!' Ruby was clearly horrified. 'Oh, Foxy, *no*, not my jewels!'

'Do you have a better idea?' Miss Fox said. 'I can help out a little with what I have left of my savings, but it will be nowhere near enough to clear this lot.' She spread her hands to encompass the bills scattered across the table. 'And that safe is fair bulging with baubles – far more than you need.'

Ruby pouted like a spoiled child and just for an instant Miss Fox spotted the lively young woman she had once been and she softened. 'Come along, we'll go through them together and that way you can keep your favourite pieces,' she suggested encouragingly. 'Then we're going to have to cut our cloth accordingly even if it means moving to a smaller house as I originally suggested. We've obviously been living above our means and we rattle around in this place anyway now.'

Her face set in a sullen moue, Ruby watched as the older woman carried a number of small boxes to the table and began to open them. There were rubies, diamonds, sapphires, emeralds and pearls – all bought by Ruby's one-time admirers.

'See?' Miss Fox sighed. 'There are far more here than you could ever wear anyway, so choose the ones you like most and want to keep.'

Ruby's hand shot out like a greedy child's and within seconds the majority of the boxes were piled up in front of her.

'I'm sorry, love, but that's too many,' Miss Fox said patiently. 'Let's try again.' Eventually she had a number of very high-class jewellery items selected and rising with her booty, she told Ruby, 'There's no time like the present, is there? I'm going to the pawn-shop right now to see what I can get for them.'

Ruby was clearly very far from happy. 'Then can you at least just pawn them? Please don't sell them.'

'And what would be the point in that? You and I both know that the chances of us ever being able to afford to redeem them are slim now. No, it will be far better if I sell them, but don't worry, I'm no fool and I'm not about to let them go for a pittance.' She then gathered the bills together too and sailed from the room as Ruby watched her go with a deep frown on her face. *Interfering old cow!* she thought, then crossing to the decanter she poured a generous measure of brandy into a glass and tossed it back in one go.

By the time Miss Fox returned almost two hours later, Ruby was merry again. 'Did you get a good price for the jewels?' she immediately enquired, holding out her hand for the cash before the other woman had barely had time to enter the room.

Miss Fox removed her hat and patted the sparse grey bun perched at the nape of her neck. 'I most certainly did, but it's no use asking for the money. I've paid all the bills up to date on the way back, so there's precious little left, and from now on we're going to count our pennies like everyone else is having to do. I shall be responsible for the household expenses in future, and the first thing I shall be cutting back on is the wine bill. That was the highest of them all. You're actually paying a great sum of money to kill yourself!'

When Ruby looked as if she was about to throw a tantrum Miss Fox then turned and calmly left the room, but could Ruby have known it her stomach was churning. She had managed to avert a crisis this time – but what would they do when the jewels were all sold? Perhaps they could sublet some of the rooms to lodgers? And Cook had been saying for a while that she was thinking of retiring to the country to live with her widowed brother. That would save another wage, although it would mean yet more work for Maggie and Kitty, not that they ever complained. Heaving a lengthy sigh, Phyllis Fox hurried off to find somewhere quiet where she could think things through in peace.

That same day at Treetops, Sunday and Tom were welcoming the first of their evacuees from London. A few families had written to them asking if they would be prepared to take their children into a safe place for the duration of the war. Their fathers were all away fighting and their mothers were now working, so Sunday was happy to oblige. She could only imagine how terrifying it must be to have bombs dropping out of the sky so close to them, and her maternal instinct rushed to the fore as George delivered the children to her after picking them up from the railway station.

There was another set of twins, Henry and Harry, as alike as two peas in a pod, and then two little girls from two different families, Jenny and Nancy. The twins were five years old, the girls six and seven and they were all from the East End of London.

'Cor blimey, missus, this place is *massive*! I reckon it's as big as Bucking'am Palace!' Harry greeted her, and Sunday grinned. She had an idea she was going to have her work cut out with these four. They certainly weren't shy. Ben chose that moment to wander around the corner of the house then and immediately all four pairs of eyes turned to him and the children openly had a good look at the disfigured side of his face. Sunday cringed. Ben was so self-conscious of his scars and still refused to venture outside the grounds of Treetops for fear of people staring at him and whispering. Even so, he had come a long way. When he had first returned home he would not even come out of his room.

'You copped it there good an' proper didn't you, mate?' Harry chirped and Ben seemed to shrink before her eyes. Turning about, he beat a hasty retreat without even bothering to answer.

'So what's up wiv 'im then?' Harry enquired. 'He's an 'ero, ain't he, so why should he be ashamed?'

Sunday had been about to scold him, not the best of starts, but saw then that Harry hadn't meant any harm. He was just a very chatty five-year-old who saw things as they were.

'Ben is very sad about the way he looks now,' she explained instead. 'So perhaps you could avoid staring at him or mentioning his scar, eh? Could you do that for me?'

Harry shrugged and glanced at his brother. ''S'pose so,' he muttered, wondering what all the fuss was about. But then Tom, who Harry was sure was yet another war hero because he was leaning heavily on a stick and limping, was leading him inside, and in his excitement to see his new home he forgot all about Ben, for now at least.

'Something tells me we're going to have our hands full with our new charges,' Sunday told Tom with a twinkle in her eye that evening when all the children were tucked safely in bed.

He nodded and grinned, thinking again what a shame it was that he and Sunday had never been blessed with a child of their own, although she had been a wonderful mother to so many others. But then he knew he should be grateful for what they had. Ben was home, thank God, even if it wasn't the same Ben they had waved away to war. At one time, Tom had hoped his son might marry and produce grandchildren for him and Sunday to love, but the chances of that happening were slim now. Since he wouldn't go past the gates of Treetops, how was he to meet any young ladies? So many young chaps had war wounds and permanent injuries, so he was not alone and had nothing to be ashamed of. On the contrary!

'You don't think the children will make Ben feel worse about his scars, do you?' Sunday asked then.

Tom shook his head. 'Not at all. I don't wish to sound cruel but he's got to come to terms with it sometime and the children might just help him do that. The boys think he's a real hero!'

Sunday hoped that he would be proved to be right.

It had taken them months and months to nurse Ben back to health once he had come out of hospital, and his outer healing was almost as good as it would ever get. His inner healing, however, Tom feared would never take place. Ben still suffered from terrible nightmares where he was trapped in the trenches, covered in flies and rats, or of thrusting his bayonet into some young German's heart on the battlefield. He had seen and suffered too much for a young chap his age, as had thousands of other young men, but that sadly was the cost of war and those who had so far survived it must pay that terrible price.

Chapter Fifty-Two

On a gloriously sunny morning in mid-June, Maggie found Kitty being sick into the lavatory yet again, and this time she had to voice her fear.

'Kitty,' she began tentatively. 'You do know that you've missed another course, don't you? How many is that now?'

'Three,' Kitty answered dully, before rinsing her mouth.

'Then perhaps it's time you went to see a doctor?'

'No,' the girl replied. 'I think it's time I spoke to Richard.'

'Perhaps you should,' Maggie agreed as she helped Kitty to sit down in her bedroom. Her friend had lost weight and there were dark circles beneath her lovely eyes. Maggie had suspected for some time that Kitty might be carrying a child but hadn't dared to mention it, but now it could be ignored no longer.

'What do you think Richard will say?'

'There's not much he can say, is there?' Kitty sighed. 'He'll just have to marry me, won't he?' It was many weeks since she had lain with anyone apart from Richard; the war had seen her suitors sent to fight or to live very different lives from before.

Maggie didn't answer although she couldn't really see him doing that unless someone held a gun to his head. Her greatest fear was what would happen to Kitty if he abandoned her. Even now she still thought the sun rose and set with him, and would not have a bad word said against him.

'Then if that's what you plan to do, perhaps it should be done as soon as possible?' Maggie said sensibly. 'You must be about three months pregnant already, which means you'll be showing soon, so best get it over with and see what he says, eh?'

Kitty nodded. She had tried to convince herself that she'd missed her courses simply because she was a little run down, but she couldn't deny the truth any longer. And although the last pregnancy had ended in miscarriage, she longed for this child, as it was Richard's. They had been together now for several years; surely it was time for them to settle down? 'I'll do it today – in fact, I'll go round there this very morning,' she said resolutely and began to get ready.

It was only half past ten when she arrived at Richard's house feeling rather apprehensive. How would he react to being told that he was going to be a father? she wondered.

The maid looked at her askance when she answered her knock on the door and muttered, 'Oh . . . good mornin', miss. I don't reckon the master's expectin' you. He's still abed. Would you care to come back later?'

'No, that's all right. It's important that I see him. I'll wait in the studio. Just pop up and tell him I'm here, would you?' Kitty said as she began to take her gloves off. She hurried along the hallway, let herself into the studio to wait for Richard and made herself at home, leaving the door open behind her.

Some minutes passed before he appeared in his dressing robe with his hair standing on end and looking none too pleased.

'What's brought you here so early?' he said rudely as he stomped past her to reach the cigarettes, and she could have sworn as he passed that she got a whiff of perfume. *It's probably just his cologne*, she told herself as he lit a cigarette and blew a plume of smoke into the air.

'Well?' he repeated.

Kitty gulped, then taking a deep breath she blurted out, 'I had to see you, Richard. You see, I'm going to have a baby – *your* baby!'

She watched the horrified expression on his face and felt like crying. It wasn't the reaction she had hoped for, but then she had been shocked too. He just needed time to come to terms with it, that was only natural.

He began to pace up and down, then stopping abruptly he barked, 'Are you sure? And how do you know it's mine?'

'Of course it's yours,' she said. 'For the last few months I have only been entertaining your two most elderly friends and they . . . Well, let's just say that neither of them are capable – if you know what I mean.'

'And what are you going to do about it?'

She stared at him aghast. He looked so cold and aloof. 'Wh-what do you mean?'

'I mean there are people you can go to. Women who will get rid of it for you.' All the while he was speaking he was glancing nervously towards the door but Kitty was so distraught that she barely noticed.

'But I don't *want* to get rid of it.' She was crying now. 'It's *our* baby! I want us to get married and to be a family.'

'And what about the photos, if the men turn ugly and decide that they will sell them to the newspapers?'

Her chin rose. 'Then let them. We'll go and live somewhere far away where nobody knows us. I'm tired of being used and I want to lead a normal life now.'

Seeing how distressed she was becoming he ran a hand distractedly through his hair as he commenced his pacing again. Then suddenly he stopped in front of her and, taking her hands in his, he smiled – the smile that could still turn her to putty in his hands.

'Of course, you are quite right, my darling,' he said. 'Let them do their worst and we will be married. How does a month from now sound to you? That should give me time to arrange everything. But can we have a quiet wedding, perhaps at the registry office? I don't think the circumstances warrant a grand affair, do you? If you're happy to leave everything to me, I shall go ahead and make all the arrangements. You just find yourself a pretty white outfit.'

Suddenly her face was radiant. She would have married him in a shed had he asked her to because finally all her dreams were coming true. They would be wed and live happily ever after just like in the fairy stories Sunday had used to read to her.

He gently led her back towards the door. 'And now, darling, I really must go and get ready for the client who is due shortly.'

Once he had hurried her out of the door, she felt as if she was floating on a cloud. She hastened back home to tell Maggie the good news, although she wasn't looking forward to telling Ruby. Still, it couldn't be helped and her mother would just have to accept the situation, Kitty decided.

'You're what?' Maggie gasped when Kitty burst into her bedroom to tell her the news.

'I'm going to be married – in a month's time!' Kitty was beaming from ear to ear. 'Richard has promised to make all the arrangements. It will be a quiet wedding though. We don't want a big fuss although I will need a new outfit, of course. Just think what fun you and I will have choosing it. And there must be one for you as well, Maggie dear. I want you to be my bridesmaid.'

Maggie was so flabbergasted that she was rendered temporarily speechless. She had feared that Richard would turn his back on Kitty once she had told him about the baby, but it appeared that he had come up trumps.

'And where will you live?' she asked eventually when she found her voice again.

Kitty shrugged. 'I don't know, to be honest. We haven't looked that far ahead yet, but wherever it is I shall want you to come with me. I shall still need a maid because once the war is over I shall take up my singing career again and I'll need someone to help with the baby.'

'But I don't know anything about babies!'

'Neither do I,' Kitty giggled. 'But we'll learn together. Oh, Maggie, I can't tell you how happy I am, although I dread telling my mother.' A frown wiped the smile from her face then as something occurred to her. 'I wonder how she will manage without my money coming in? I'm not entirely stupid and I know that Richard gives her money and so does Max when I get a booking, and I doubt I ever see a fraction of it.'

'You shouldn't worry yourself about that,' Maggie said stoically. Personally, she found it appalling that any mother could treat her daughter as Ruby had treated Kitty, but for the sake of her friend's feelings she had never said as much. Kitty had already sold all her jewels to help out with the bills and the money that Sunday had once given her had gone, too. The only item of jewellery Kitty had kept was the locket that Sunday had given her on the day she left Treetops.

'Hmm.' Kitty went to stand and stare thoughtfully out of the window. 'Well, I know Richard is very rich,' she said quietly, 'so perhaps if Ruby and Foxy move to somewhere slightly smaller he might still help them out financially?'

I wouldn't bet on it, Maggie thought, but again she remained silent. This was all happening a little too quickly and easily for her liking. Richard had shown no signs of wanting to marry Kitty before, during the years they had been together.

Kitty whirled about then, the smile once more in place. She was so excited that nothing could worry her for long. Lifting Tallulah into her arms she kissed her silky head and told her, 'We're going to live with your new daddy soon, sweetheart.'

And seeing her friend so happy, Maggie couldn't help but smile too. Everything would work out, she decided. It usually did.

Kitty had planned to tell Ruby her news that evening after dinner but her plans went awry when Miss Fox informed her that Ruby was ill in bed with a tummy upset.

'Then perhaps I should tell you,' Kitty said solemnly. 'The thing is, Richard and I are going to be married – in a month's time.'

Foxy's mouth dropped open and she reminded Kitty of a gold-fish she had seen at the fair she'd gone to with Sunday and Tom once, back in Nuneaton.

'That's a bit sudden, isn't it?' the woman managed to say eventually.

Kitty didn't want her to know about the baby yet, not until after the wedding. 'Not at all,' she said. 'I've known him since shortly after I came to live here, and we can't see any reason to wait any longer.'

'I see.' But Miss Fox didn't see. In fact, she was knocked for six. Richard Fitzherbert was a renowned lady's man, and many young women had tried to snare him before Kitty and failed miserably. Deep down, she was actually quite relieved, especially if this was what Kitty wanted, which judging by her animated face it certainly was. She hadn't approved at all of the way Ruby had treated her daughter and could only hope now that her husband-to-be would make up for it. 'Then I wish you both all the very best,' she said sincerely and once again Kitty glimpsed the soft heart behind the no-nonsense exterior.

'There's just one thing,' Kitty said, serious again. 'Will you and my moth . . . Ruby be all right for money when I'm gone?'

Miss Fox nodded. 'Of course, why wouldn't we be? I've already put plans into motion for us to move to a smaller house. Lord knows, this place is far too big for us now and it will be even more so once you and Maggie have gone. I take it Maggie is coming with you?'

When Kitty nodded, Miss Fox smiled. 'Right, so where is the wedding to be then?'

'I don't know yet, probably at his local register office. Richard said it wouldn't seem right having a big do, what with the war and everything.'

'Then I shall do you a wedding breakfast back here,' Miss Fox told her.

'Oh, but you don't have to—'

'I insist.' Miss Fox suddenly did something that she had never done before and, leaning forward, she gave Kitty a tender hug. Inside, her heart was breaking. This lovely girl deserved to have someone to love her, and if that someone turned out to be Richard Fitzherbert, then she would force herself to try and like him for Kitty's sake. Perhaps things would start to improve for the girl now?

'Right!' She turned towards the door. 'I shall have a word to Cook about getting some extras in for the big day.'

Kitty watched her go in amazement. Miss Fox had been perfectly lovely about her forthcoming nuptials. She just hoped her mother would react as well.

It was almost a week before Kitty saw Richard again. She had been waiting for him to telephone or call by, but when he didn't she went to visit him and found him at work in his studio.

'I was getting worried,' she told him truthfully. 'I expected you to call and see me and when you didn't . . .'

'I've been run off my feet organising the wedding and I was going to come and see you this evening.'

'Oh.' She instantly felt guilty and he was forgiven. 'And how is everything going? Do we have a venue and a date yet?'

'We do, as it happens.' He lit a cigarette and leaning against the back of a chair he stared at her. 'We're to be married in the registry office in Westminster at eleven o'clock on the fourteenth of July. How does that sound?'

'It sounds wonderful.' Crossing to him she flung her arms about his neck. 'And afterwards Miss Fox is organising a small reception back at Ruby's. Will you be inviting many people?'

'Not that many.' He gently untangled her arms. 'I thought we'd just have it quiet and select.'

'But your family will be coming, won't they?' She sighed with relief when he nodded. Secretly she thought it would have been far better if she had been able to meet them before the wedding day but she supposed it was too close to worry now, only three weeks away.

'And where shall we live afterwards?'

'Ah, now that's a secret.' When he tapped the side of his nose she giggled. It was all so exciting. She had supposed that they would live here, but perhaps he was planning to surprise her with a new house somewhere? He hadn't been spending a lot of time here lately, she suddenly realised.

'And what about . . . your friends?' Her face was anguished now. 'Have they agreed that I won't have to entertain them any more?'

'Yes, of course. Everything has been concluded most satisfactorily. I even have the photographs in my possession now so you can stop worrying and concentrate on getting ready for the big day. Unfortunately, I heard from my mother that my father has been ill, so I will be going away tomorrow to spend a few days with him. I hope that he'll be well again in no time, but don't fret if you don't hear from me for a while. I shall be back in plenty of time for the wedding, never you fear, and then it would be better if I popped over to see you at Ruby's when I get back, as there's a lot of packing up to be done here.'

Kitty felt a tingle of excitement. He had just confirmed what she had suspected – that he had found a new house for them to live in. Otherwise why would he be packing? But she didn't wish to spoil what he obviously wanted to be a surprise so she simply nodded sweetly. Inside, her heart was singing. She would never have to kowtow to any of Richard's colleagues again, and very soon now she would be Mrs Katherine Fitzherbert. She was a little disappointed that Richard had to go away, admittedly. And again, she was also a little miffed and hurt that he hadn't offered to take her along, but the knowledge that she would soon be his wife, for better or for worse, and with their child on the way, outweighed every other emotion and she would have laid down her life for him if asked.

Chapter Fifty-Three

Richard called in to see Kitty the week before the wedding and she flew into his arms. 'I've missed you,' she told him, the soft mound of her tummy pressing into him.

He smiled. 'Sorry. I was away longer than I expected to be, but everything is booked for the wedding now. I shan't be seeing you again before the big day though. Lots to do, you know? And it's bad luck anyway.'

Kitty pouted. 'But that only applies to the night before the wedding.' There were still four days to go until they became man and wife.

'Even so, I'm very busy but just think – after Saturday, we'll have all the time in the world together.'

Slightly pacified, she nodded. In truth, she would be glad to be away from Brunswick Villa now. Her mother hadn't taken the news of the forthcoming wedding at all well and had barely spoken to her since.

Now Kitty took Richard's arm, intending to take him into the day room where they could have some privacy, but he gently put her from him, saying, 'I just need a word with Ruby. You run along and I'll catch you before I go.'

Slightly crestfallen, Kitty watched him stride off down the hallway before hurrying upstairs to her room where Maggie was busily packing their cases.

'I thought I might as well make a start,' she told Kitty. 'But do you have any idea where all our things have got to go to?'

Kitty shook her head. 'Not yet, Richard hasn't said. I dare say he'll arrange for them all to be collected in due course.'

'Hmm, well, perhaps he ought to get a move on,' Maggie answered fractiously. 'It would be nice to know where we're going to be living after Saturday! This is all a bit disorganised, if you ask me. I mean, all we know is what time to turn up for the ceremony.'

'That's all we need to know,' Kitty chuckled. She went over to stroke the new outfit she had chosen to wear for her wedding, which was hanging on the wardrobe door. Their choice had been severely limited because of the shortages of clothes but she and Maggie had finally found it in a little shop off Bond Street and Kitty loved it. It was a gown in a lovely summer blue colour, trimmed with cream satin ribbon all around the handkerchief edge and neckline. The lining was a heavy satin, the overlay a thin floaty material that swayed about her with even the slightest movement. And they'd even managed to find an adorable little hat in the same colour to go with it. A pair of cream satin shoes and a matching bag completed the bridal outfit, and they had then decided that her bouquet should consist of tiny cream rosebuds and gypsophila. It would be a long way from the fairytale wedding that Kitty had always dreamed of, when she would float back down the aisle of the church in a froth of tulle and lace on Richard's arm, but she didn't mind any more. All she cared about was becoming his wife, and very soon now her wish would come true. Kitty had even managed to persuade Maggie into a new outfit in a very pretty pale green that complemented her colouring.

Maggie had not been at all happy about what she termed as unnecessary expense. She had saved almost every penny she had earned since coming to London, but she hadn't wanted to disappoint Kitty. After all, the wedding was going to be a very quiet affair, so if her having a new outfit pleased Kitty then it was worth every penny. And she could wear it again. Glancing up from the packing she saw that Kitty was still fingering the material of her wedding dress and she bit down on her lip. No matter how she tried, she couldn't rid herself of the feeling that there was something not quite right about this wedding. On the odd occasions when she had seen Richard and Kitty together she got the distinct impression that Richard was far less enamoured of Kitty than she was of him. In fact, Maggie had been frankly disbelieving when Kitty had informed her that he had agreed to marry her. But perhaps she should give him credit for that at least? Now Kitty's child would be born in wedlock, which was something to be grateful for.

She closed the bag she had been packing and told Kitty, 'I think it's time we had a tea break. I'm going down to make some, shan't be a tick!'

She had almost reached the bottom of the stairs when she became aware of raised voices coming from the direction of the drawing room. Richard and Ruby were clearly having words. She knew that she should carry on, but instinct made her creep closer to the door to try to hear what the row was about.

'You can't expect me to do that!' she heard Richard say, but she couldn't hear Ruby's reply, and was so afraid of being caught eavesdropping that she hurried on her way. She was deeply concerned. What was it that Richard didn't want to do? If it was about the wedding, she knew it would break Kitty.

The smell of cabbage met her as she entered the kitchen. The summer cabbages in the garden were on every menu because they were plentiful and Cook had been baking pies for the wedding feast for days now. Far more than they would ever be able to possibly eat, Maggie secretly thought, but she didn't say so.

'So how is the bride-to-be bearing up?' Miss Fox asked cheerfully, looking up from the bread she was kneading at the opposite end of the table to Cook. The latter had been giving her cooking lessons as she intended to retire soon after the wedding.

'Oh, she's fine.' Maggie filled the kettle and placed it on the range then asked cautiously, 'Are you and Ruby going to manage all right when we've gone?'

'Why, bless you, of course we will, pet.' Miss Fox wiped a floury hand across her forehead. With all the baking that was going on it was uncomfortably hot in the kitchen even with the back door and the windows wide open. 'I've actually found quite a nice little house nearer to the river in Wandsworth that I'm thinking of renting for me and Ruby,' she confided. 'Cook here has informed me that she's finally going to retire and I can't say that I blame her. The house I've got my eye on will be much cheaper to run and with no wages to find each week I shall go out to work. Probably in one of the armament factories.'

'But why can't Ruby go out to work instead? She's younger than you,' Maggie objected.

Miss Fox raised her eyebrow. 'Can you really see that happening? I'm afraid Ruby is used to being waited on.'

'So why don't you take the house for yourself then and leave her to get on with things?' Maggie had been longing to say that for some time, but now the words had slipped out before she could stop them. 'I – I think Ruby takes advantage of your good nature,' she blustered on as colour flooded into her cheeks. 'And I really don't know why you stay with her, the way she treats you!'

She expected Miss Fox to shout at her but instead the older woman smiled sadly as she rested her knuckles on the table. 'I don't know why I stay either if I'm honest,' she confessed. 'I suppose it's because we've been together for a long time and I know she needs looking after.'

A silence settled between them then until the kettle began to sing on the hob and Maggie bustled away to make the tea. Once it was all ready and the tray was laid, she carried it off without another word. The way she saw it, she had said far too much already.

Saturday morning dawned bright and clear, and as Kitty stared excitedly from the bedroom window she saw that it looked set to be a beautiful day.

'Just think, in a few hours' time I shall be Mrs Fitzherbert,' she giggled as Maggie pressed her onto a chair and placed a tray of tea and toast across her lap. And then suddenly she was up and running towards the bathroom with her hand clamped to her mouth. It was the same every morning and Maggie wondered how much longer this sickness was going to last. She also worried about how Kitty would fare at the birth. She was so tiny, but all she could do was hope that when the time came, all would go well.

Eventually, Kitty did manage to nibble at the toast and take a few sips of tea, and then it was time to start getting ready. Maggie slipped away to get into her own new finery then came back to help Kitty with her toilette and her hair. She was almost ready when a tap came at the door and Miss Fox appeared.

'The florist just delivered these,' she told them and they smiled as they saw the beautiful teardrop bouquet for Kitty and the smaller posy for Maggie. There were also four very pretty corsages fashioned in the same flowers as the bouquets. One for Kitty, one for Maggie, one for Miss Fox and one for Ruby.

Maggie fastened hers to her new dress immediately and as Miss Fox fixed Kitty's to her dress for her, she told her tentatively, 'I'm afraid that Ruby isn't well enough to attend the service, my dear. But never fear, she'll be here when we get back for the wedding breakfast.'

Tears welled in Kitty's eyes. 'At this rate, there'll be no one there,' she said sadly. 'Richard's father can't come either because he's still poorly and I don't even know who Richard has chosen for his best man!'

'Just so long as the groom arrives on time,' Miss Fox told her with a twinkle in her eye. Along with Maggie she didn't much like Richard but he was Kitty's choice, so as long as he made her happy she could live with it.

Kitty rose then and when Miss Fox had passed her the bouquet the older woman had to wipe a tear from her eye.

'Why, I swear you're easily the most beautiful bride I've ever set eyes on,' she said throatily and she meant it. Kitty's face was glowing with happiness and Miss Fox just wished that Ruby could have taken the trouble to get up and see just how radiant her daughter was. But then there was no more time to lose. The car had been ordered and would be outside waiting to take the bride-to-he to the wedding venue now.

'Come along now, girls!' Miss Fox clapped her hands then, making both girls smile. 'It wouldn't do for the bride to keep the groom waiting. Well, not for too long anyway.' She then ushered them down the stairs like a mother hen and just as she had thought they found the car waiting outside.

The elderly driver jumped out and helped the ladies to get in, and soon they were on their way. Maggie had expected Kitty to be nervous, she herself certainly was, but Kitty appeared to be almost serene, in fact.

When they arrived at the steps of the registry office they saw a young woman and a soldier looking very smart in his uniform posing on the steps for photographs. A large crowd of family and friends all throwing rice and rose petals surrounded them, and just for a second Kitty felt a stab of pain as she thought of Sunday and Tom and wished that they could have been there. But they were part of her past now and within the next few minutes she would start to build a new family with Richard.

Calm again, and skirting the newlyweds, she and the others made their way inside. At once her eyes began to search for Richard but he was nowhere to be seen.

'Perhaps he's already gone in?' Miss Fox suggested, striding towards the room where the marriages took place. They found the room quite empty and a surprised registrar looked up at them from his desk.

'Good morning, ladies. May I help you?'

'Yes, we are here for the Fitzherbert wedding at eleven o'clock,' Miss Fox informed him.

The man reached for his diary and began to scan the page.

'I'm terribly sorry but I have nothing about that in here. My next marriage isn't until one thirty this afternoon. Are you sure that you've come to the right place?'

'Of course we have!' Miss Fox was indignant. What did he think they were – a load of idiots? 'Here, give that to me, my man, you must be mistaken,' she said hoarsely as she snatched the diary from his hands. And then after running her finger down the page she visibly paled. 'I . . . I'm afraid he's right, Kitty,' she said. 'There's nothing about this wedding in here.'

Kitty clutched at the back of a chair as the room started to spin. What could this mean? She knew that she was in the right place. Richard had written the address and time down for her. And where was he anyway? Wasn't it usual for the groom and his party to arrive before the bride?

'I . . . I don't understand,' she breathed as the registrar lowered his eyes, clearly embarrassed.

'Perhaps you should go and see your fiancé?' It was the only thing he could think of to say.

Kitty nodded numbly as Miss Fox and Maggie each took one of her arms and led her from the room. She felt sick at heart and very confused.

It wasn't until they were all standing outside on the steps again, which were deserted by now, that Miss Fox steeled herself to say, 'I'm afraid it's beginning to look like you've been stood up, Kitty.'

Kitty's eyes flashed. 'Richard would never do that to me!' she said vehemently. 'He loves me – I know he does!'

'Then let's get around to his house to sort this out straight away.'

Miss Fox was already risking life and limb after running into the road to wave her arms frantically at any cab that was passing, while Maggie was chewing on her lip, looking as pale as lint. What had started out as such a happy day was fast turning into a nightmare – but surely Richard would not be so cruel? There must be a logical explanation for what had happened, and the sooner they got to the bottom of it the better.

When the cab pulled up outside Richard's smart townhouse they were all surprised to see a large van outside and men trailing in and out of the house carrying furniture. Kitty tossed her bouquet onto the seat and before anyone could stop her she hopped out of the cab and sprinted breathlessly up the steps and into the hallway.

Richard's little maid was there but dressed in her own clothes rather than her uniform and she looked shocked to see her.

'What's going on?' Kitty gabbled and the girl looked acutely embarrassed.

'All the furniture is goin' to the auction house, miss,' she said quietly. 'This is the men from there collectin' it now.'

'And where is Mr Fitzherbert?' Kitty demanded.

Millie squirmed as she tried to avoid Kitty's eyes. 'He, err . . . he ain't here, miss.'

'So where is he then?' Kitty's eyes were flashing now and the young maid took a deep breath.

'The master left two days ago. He's gone to live abroad, miss. His ship sailed on the tide last night.' Millie could have added, 'With that Melissa Hawkins, as you'd know if you'd kept your eyes open,' but couldn't bring herself to be so cruel.

Kitty recoiled. 'B-but there must be some mistake. We were

441

supposed to be getting married this morning. Has he left a forwarding address?'

'Not with me, miss, I'm so sorry. He's paid me up to date, and when the men have finished here I'm to lock up and hand the keys in to the landlord.'

'The landlord? But I thought Richard *owned* this house.'

'No, miss, Mr Watson only rented it.'

'Mr Watson? Don't you mean Mr Fitzherbert? His family have a mansion in the country, don't they?'

The little maid sighed. 'That's what the master liked everyone to think, but in fact he came from the slums of the Whitechapel Road. It just suited him to build up an image so he could attract wealthy clients, see? I'm so sorry. It seems like you've been sucked in good and proper. But if it's any consolation, you ain't the first. Now if you'll excuse me, I must get on.'

Kitty stood for some seconds as she tried to digest what she had just been told then very gracefully she sank to the floor in a dead faint as all her dreams shrivelled and died.

Chapter Fifty-Four

Well-known London Photographer Exposed as Fraud proclaimed the headlines on the front page of the *Daily Mirror* the following week. Maggie saw a copy on the newspaper-stand and, for a second, her heart stood still with shock. Hurrying into the shop, she quickly bought a copy and once outside again, she read the article there and then.

Society photographer Richard Fitzherbert, who professed to be the son of a lord, has been exposed as a fraud. His real name is Harry Watson and he was born and raised in Whitechapel in the East End. Watson is being sought by the police for recently inveigling large sums of money from various wealthy women under the pretence of investing those funds to produce a huge profit. When no profit was forthcoming, several of his victims came forward to lodge a complaint with the police, but Watson has since disappeared. It has also come to light that he had run up heavy gambling debts and also owes money to many other traders and his landlord. He also evaded conscription and played no part in defending our great country in times of peril. The man is a scoundrel. A warrant for his arrest is in place but it is believed that he is with his lover, Miss Melissa Hawkins, and that they may have tried to escape abroad. The police are asking anyone who might know of his whereabouts to come forward to assist with their inquiries.

Maggie flinched. Kitty must never see this article as it might endanger the baby; she was in a bad enough state as it was. So after arriving back at Brunswick Villa, she left the newspaper in the kitchen for lighting the range. Unfortunately, a few days later, Kitty was getting the fire going – and there it was right in front of her. The poor girl was inconsolable as she realised what a fool she had been, and ever since that day she had sunk into a decline. Nothing Maggie did or suggested elicited any kind of response.

It was early in August and Kitty's pregnancy was beginning to show. Maggie knew that she had no choice but to tell Miss Fox and her employer Ruby about it. It was only the fact that Kitty rarely got dressed nowadays that the two friends had managed to hide the situation for this long.

Cook had retired two weeks ago, and now Maggie and Miss Fox were keeping the house running between them. Many of the ornate gilt mirrors and pictures had disappeared to the pawnshop, along with some of the more expensive knick-knacks, for there was no money whatsoever coming in now. Sadly, the small house that Miss Fox had hoped to rent had been flattened by a Zeppelin bomb, and only the day before she had hinted that she was thinking of going to work in one of the armament factories. Maggie had strongly objected, pointing out that if anyone should go out to work it should be her. She was the youngest, after all, but Miss Fox wouldn't hear of it. 'You'll have your hands full looking after Kitty and Ruby, and seeing to the running of the house,' she had insisted.

Ruby was now very unwell and only the week before, Miss Fox had called the doctor in to see her. He had given the woman a thorough examination and then gravely informed Miss Fox that he feared that Miss Smith's liver was failing: the amount of alcohol she had consumed over the years had done its worst and caused irretrievable damage. Miss Fox was devastated. Even so, she was determined to make sure that whatever time Ruby had left would be as comfortable as she could possibly make it. Maggie had been touched at her loyalty. Personally, she didn't feel that her employer deserved such kindness although she didn't say as much to Miss Fox. And now here she was about to add to her troubles – but what option did she have?

She found the older woman rolling pastry at the table for an apple and blackberry pie, and taking a seat beside her, Maggie took a deep breath before saying, 'Foxy, I'm afraid I have to tell you something. It's about Kitty. You see, she's—'

'Having a baby?'

The woman's words shocked Maggie so much that her mouth gaped. And here she'd been thinking that they'd managed to keep it from her.

'I guessed even before they set the date for the wedding,' Miss Fox told her. Then leaning heavily on the table, she sighed, 'I suppose I should tell Ruby now. She'll not be best pleased – not that there's much she can do about it. When is the baby due?'

'To our reckoning, late December.'

'Very well. Pour a glass of that ginger beer for Ruby, would you, pet, and dig out a couple of arrowroot biscuits to go with it, eh? I'll have a chat to her when I take it through. No point in putting it off any longer, is there?'

As Maggie did as she was told, the woman lined a pie dish with pastry and added the bottled apples, and the blackberries they had picked in the orchard that morning, sprinkled some precious sugar on top, then added the lid and popped it in the hot oven. Removing her apron, Foxy picked up Ruby's snack and muttered, 'Wish me luck. I'm not at all sure how madam is going to take this latest blow.'

As usual, Ruby was reclining listlessly on the chaise longue in the drawing room. Placing the plate and tumbler on a table beside her, Miss Fox told her quietly, 'I think you ought to know . . . you're going to be a grandmother.'

'*What!*' Ruby sat bolt upright in her chair, her face a mask of horror. 'You mean Kitty is with *child*?'

'Well, who else could it be?' Miss Fox said peevishly.

Ruby glowered as she strummed her fingers on the arm of the chaise longue. And then she shocked Miss Fox when she snarled, 'She will have to get rid of it! There's a woman I know of round the corner in Fulham who will do it for five pounds.' She knew this because she herself had visited her on more than one occasion, but she couldn't reveal that.

Miss Fox's chest swelled with rage. '*Get rid of it?*' she spat. 'But this is a baby we're talking about – your own flesh and blood. And what about the risk to Kitty? I've read about what's happened to some of the poor girls who go to backstreet abortionists. She's your daughter, don't you care?'

Ruby waved her hand airily. 'It's worth the risk. Think of the scandal if she tries to keep it, Foxy. Once the war is over she can return to her singing career, but not with a baby hanging around her neck. The public would shun her and say that she was a fallen woman.'

'Even if she'd consider it, it's too late now,' the other woman said tersely. 'She's too far gone.'

'So?' Ruby's eyes flashed. 'It just means the procedure will be slightly more unpleasant, that's all. Send the girl to me immediately and I'll tell her where to go.'

Miss Fox stared at her incredulously. She had always known that Ruby was selfish and self-centred, but she had never dreamed that even she would sink to such depths.

'I'll do no such thing,' she ground out. 'Kitty will have this baby so you'd better get used to the idea.'

'Then she and Maggie will have to leave,' Ruby said heartlessly.

'Neither of them are any good to me if they're not bringing money in.'

'You would turn your own daughter out onto the street?' Miss Fox shook her head. 'I've never said this before but I'm ashamed of you.' And with that she turned and quietly left the room. She hadn't expected Ruby to be pleased at the news, but never in her wildest dreams had she imagined that the woman would be so callous.

After climbing the stairs, she entered Ruby's bedroom and sank onto the side of the bed. As usual, it was just as Ruby had left it, with clothes and dirty glasses strewn all over the place. Even now that they had no servants she still expected to be waited on hand and foot. After a time, Miss Fox rose and wearily began to tidy things away, and it was as she was placing some handkerchiefs into a drawer that she noticed something tucked beneath them. She investigated, and withdrew a number of sealed envelopes addressed to Treetops Manor in Nuneaton. After opening the first one, she gasped. These must be the letters that Kitty had written to Sunday and Tom when she had first arrived at Brunswick Villa at the age of fifteen. No wonder Kitty had been so dismissive of them when they had gone to see her at Wilton's Music Hall. The poor girl must have thought that they had been ignoring the letters she had written to them. But Ruby had deliberately never posted the letters so her family would have no forwarding address. And all this time the poor girl must have been thinking that they had abandoned her. This was the worst act of all and suddenly Foxy realised what she must do. She made her way to her own room and after some thought as to what she should write, she quickly jotted down a letter then hurried away to post it while she still had the courage.

A few days later as Sunday was sifting through the mail at Treetops, she came across a small packet with handwriting that she didn't recognise. Carrying it through to the drawing room she settled into the window seat, smiling when she saw Ben playing with the evacuee children outside on the lawn. Despite her initial fears about how he would react to them, they had done him good and accepted him exactly as he was.

Ben had come a long way since his return home when he had refused to leave his bedroom. He had been so ashamed of the damage to his face that he couldn't bear anyone to look at him. The livid scars on his arm could be hidden with a shirt, but the same couldn't be said for those on his face – yet very slowly he was coming to terms with the fact that he was just going to have to live with them. In truth, they had healed a great deal in the time he had been home. The angry redness had faded, but one side of his face was permanently disfigured and he still wouldn't leave the grounds of Treetops despite all their best attempts to persuade him to do so. Ben had resigned himself to a life alone. As he'd pointed out, who would want him now, looking like this? *Someone who truly loves you*, Sunday had gently told him but this was something he found impossible to believe.

Now with the sounds of laughter echoing from the lawn, Sunday returned her attention to the packet and after withdrawing a sheet of notepaper, she began to read. And then she systematically went through the rest of the contents, which consisted of several unopened letters addressed to her and Tom. Seconds later she was on her feet and racing through the house, shouting, 'Tom! *Tom!*'

'All right, all right, pet! Where's the fire?' He appeared from the direction of the kitchen and she thrust the letter into his hand. 'Read this!'

After quickly doing so, he stared at her. 'Isn't this Miss Fox the servant who came from Kitty's mother to take her off to London?'

Sunday nodded. 'Yes, and she's saying that Kitty is in trouble and in dire need of our help and will we please take her back? What shall I tell her?'

448

'Tell her that of course we will!' Tom lifted his wife off her feet and swung her about. 'And there's no time like the present. Write back now, and I'll get straight off and put it in the post.'

Ten minutes later he was heading for the post office in Nuneaton with a broad smile on his face. Of course he and Sunday were concerned about what sort of trouble Kitty might be in – but whatever it was, they would help her through it.

One day soon afterwards, Miss Fox called Maggie into the kitchen to make an announcement. 'My dear, you and Kitty are going home – to Treetops. It's all been arranged. You will see that she gets there safely for me, won't you?'

Maggie paled. Treetops was very close to the Daweses' home in Witherley and she was terrified of bumping into the man who had abused her – but even so, for Kitty and her unborn baby's sake, she would risk it. Miss Fox pressed some money into her hand. She had pawned the rest of Ruby's jewellery, her own savings having dried up long ago.

'There's a train leaving for Nuneaton at seven o'clock this evening,' she said, 'and I want you, Kitty and Tallulah to be on it. This should be more than enough for the tickets, and Sunday and Tom will be meeting you at the station.'

'Oh, Foxy, I shall miss you,' Maggie cried in a rare show of emotion, and she was shocked to see that there were tears in the older woman's eyes.

'It's better for Kitty this way,' Miss Fox told her huskily. 'But now go and get packed – and not a word to Ruby, mind. There will be a cab calling for you at six and I want you to be ready. There's something else you need to know, but I want you to promise to keep it to yourself until you get back to Treetops. Will you do that?'

Maggie promised, and just for a second Miss Fox's chin drooped to her chest. But then with an enormous effort she explained about the letters that had never been sent. Sensing her pain, Maggie embraced her, and not another word was said.

Upstairs, when Maggie told Kitty the news, she was astounded.

'I can't go back to Treetops,' she argued. 'I was so horrible to Sunday and Tom when they came to see me at the Wilton's Music Hall. They won't want me back there.'

'Ah, well that's where you're wrong.' Maggie smiled. 'Miss Fox has written to them and they're already expecting us. You're going home, Kitty.'

For the first time in many months, Kitty raised a smile. She was going back to where she belonged. But first there was something she must settle so she went in search of Miss Fox and found her sitting in her bedroom, having a little rest.

'Ah, here you are, Foxy.' Kitty gave her an affectionate smile. 'Maggie has told me the news, and I can't even express my thanks for everything you've done for me. But before I go, there's something I must ask you. Something that I've been longing to know, ever since I first heard about him. Won't you please tell me who my father was now? I promise to keep it a secret. All you've ever told me is that he was a politician.'

The older woman's mouth opened and closed as she wrestled with her conscience. She had tried so hard to avoid heaping any more hurt onto Kitty but now, at this time of endings and new beginnings, the girl deserved to know the truth.

'The truth of it is, there never was a politician.' Phyllis Fox lowered her eyes in shame. 'I just made him up to make you feel better about yourself.'

Kitty stared at her steadily for a moment as she digested her words then she said, 'Ruby didn't even know who my father was, did she?' When Miss Fox mutely shook her head, Kitty turned and left the room with no further comment. Could she have known it,

450

Miss Fox had only confirmed the suspicions she'd had for some long time. Why else would she have changed the subject every time Kitty asked her about him?

After pulling herself together, Miss Fox went downstairs, where she found Ruby with a bottle in her hand just about to refill her glass. As Foxy entered the room, Ruby tried to hide it down the side of the chair, but to her surprise the older woman took it from her and filled the glass for her.

'You have a drink, sweetheart, if that's what you want,' she encouraged and Ruby was shocked although she didn't argue.

Miss Fox spent the rest of the afternoon pacing up and down, thinking everything through. She'd had such high hopes when she had fetched Kitty from Treetops, daring to believe that Ruby would change once she had her own flesh and blood to love, but sadly it hadn't happened. Ruby had loved only herself for far too long to have room in her heart for anyone else now.

By the time six o'clock rolled around and the cab arrived, Ruby was so drunk that she had passed out, so after checking on her Miss Fox accompanied the girls to the door. The driver immediately began to load their luggage on board as Miss Fox took Kitty's face between her two hands and stared deep into the girl's eyes. Kitty was surprised to see that she was crying.

'I'm so sorry things didn't work out for you here, my dear,' she whispered brokenly. 'But go back now to the people who really love you and make the best of your life. It's all before you, although you may not think so now.' She kissed her tenderly on the cheek then turned her attention to Maggie, who was also looking tearful.

'And you!' Miss Fox squeezed her hand. 'You're a good girl, Maggie, and one day you're going to make some young man very happy.'

'Huh, I doubt that,' Maggie snorted but Miss Fox put her right.

'There's more to a person than looks, my girl, and you've got a big heart and a good head on your shoulders. But now just one

451

more thing. Ruby and I will be leaving here this evening too, so there'll be no keeping in touch. But go knowing I thought the world of the pair of you. Now be off before I start making an exhibition of myself! Believe me, this is for the best. If there were any other way, I'd keep you both close for ever.'

Once the cab door had closed behind them, Phyllis waved until the vehicle was out of sight. Then drawing herself up to her full height she went back into the house to put the final part of her plan into action.

Ruby had woken up on the big sofa and grinned at her lopsidedly as Miss Fox entered the room. Phyllis stood looking at her for a long time before taking a tiny bottle from her pocket. A sob caught in her throat, then turning her back on Ruby she tipped half of its contents into a large glass of wine and quickly stirred it.

'Here you are, my lovely.' Her hand was trembling as she handed the glass to Ruby, and tears were rolling down her cheeks. 'Get that down you and your troubles will all be over, God willing.'

Ruby took it greedily and knocked it back, and within seconds her head began to loll. Swiftly moving to her side, Miss Fox lifted Ruby's feet onto the sofa and placed a pillow beneath her head before sitting close beside her and taking her hand.

'There, my lovely girl,' the older woman crooned. 'You just trust your old mum to know what's best for you, eh? I'm just sad that I had to send my granddaughter away. You never really took to her, did you? But then that was my fault – I see it now. When she was born and you told me you wanted rid of her, I couldn't bear it, so I paid all those years to know that she was safe and sound at Treetops. Oh, I admit I wasn't happy about the way you exploited her when I fetched her home, but then I shouldn't have expected any better of you. It was me, Katherine Smith, who made you as you are, through spoiling you, so it's me who should take the blame.'

She sighed deeply, and her tears fell on Ruby's hand, clasped between her own. 'I can remember the day you ran away from home seeking fame and fortune, and I told you I'd washed my hands of you. But I couldn't keep it up, could I? I soon came back with my tail between my legs, but you were a star by then and all I could be to you was a servant. I even became Miss Phyllis Fox for you. It wouldn't have done for all your fancy friends and admirers to know where you came from – a rented room in Tooting with no man about the place – would it? I know how unhappy you are now that your looks are fading and you're ill, so I'm doing this for the pair of us. At last we can be mother and daughter again, without you being ashamed of me and your beginnings.'

Lifting the bottle of wine, she poured another glass and added the remaining contents of the small bottle. Raising it to her lips, she took a long swallow. Ruby's breath was coming in little shallow gasps now, so Miss Fox quickly drained her own glass and climbing up to lie beside her, she wrapped her arms protectively about her daughter.

'Sleep tight, my darling girl, and please forgive me, God,' she whispered as the poison began to work. For a time, there was nothing to be heard but the sound of their breathing . . . then shortly after, there was nothing but silence.

Chapter Fifty-Five

Kitty sat as if she had been turned to stone all the way back on the train clutching Tallulah on her lap as she tried to imagine what sort of a homecoming she might receive. She had been so cruel to Sunday and Tom when they had come all the way to visit her, and she was no longer the same innocent girl she had been when she left Treetops. Would they ever be able to forgive her?

She also had very mixed feelings about leaving Ruby and Miss Fox. She'd been so thrilled when her mother had sent for her, but her dreams had come crashing down when she realised that Ruby only valued her for the earning power that she might possess. *Still,* she consoled herself, *at least I got to meet her so I won't have to spend the rest of my life wondering what she was like.*

Maggie seemed to pick up on her fears, for she squeezed Kitty's hand reassuringly. 'It'll be all right,' she promised, and Kitty prayed that she was right.

Sunday and Tom were waiting on the platform for them when they steamed into Nuneaton and Kitty's fears vanished the second she stepped from the train to be hugged by Sunday, who was crying unashamedly.

'Oh, my darling girls,' she sobbed as she tried to cuddle both Kitty and Maggie at the same time. 'Welcome home.' The letters from Kitty had explained how Maggie had come back into her life, much to the joy of all at Treetops. Everyone had worried about Maggie since her disappearnce some years ago.

Kitty began to cry too as Tom rushed about collecting their luggage and Sunday led them out to the waiting car.

'You do know that I'm going to have a baby, don't you?' Kitty asked tremulously when they were finally driving through the familiar town.

'Of course I do, and it will be very welcome just as you two are,' Sunday assured her as she sat between them on the back seat holding their hands.

She turned to Maggie then and told her gently, 'But I'm afraid I have some rather bad news for you, pet. Mr Dawes died of a massive heart attack shortly after you ran away and your mother Stella passed away too within months of him going. Their solicitor has been trying to find you ever since. You're quite a wealthy young woman now. Your parents left you their house and everything they owned. The solicitor had tenants living in The Gables and has kept the money for you.'

Maggie shuddered. 'I will never go back there,' she declared. 'That house holds too many unhappy memories for me.'

'I see.' Sunday stared at her curiously. Maggie obviously had a lot to tell her – since she wouldn't have run away for nothing – but all that could come in her own good time. For now, Sunday was just content to have both girls back with her, where they belonged.

Over the next few weeks, Kitty unburdened her heart and told Sunday everything. She held nothing back – but never once did Sunday condemn her.

'You are young and you were exploited,' she told her gently. 'And Richard was a cad.'

'But he didn't really *force* me to do anything,' Kitty defended him.

Sunday stroked her hair. She blamed Kitty's mother as much as anyone for what had befallen the girl, but she wouldn't tell her that. 'You might not be able to see it now, but he did so in a roundabout way. He played on your naïvety. But put it all behind you now. You have this precious little one to think of now.'

Kitty bowed her head and cried bitter tears at the mistakes of the past but miraculously Sunday still loved her despite the degrading life she had been leading, and somehow now that she had confided in her she began to feel a little better.

It was much the same with Maggie when she eventually broke down and conquered her shame to tell Sunday about the terrible things her adoptive father had done to her.

'You should have come to us and told us what was going on,' Sunday said, as she wept with her. 'That evil man should have been punished for what he did.'

'But he was, wasn't he?' Maggie gazed at her through a veil of tears. 'I think it must have been me running away that brought on his heart attack. He would have been terrified that I was going to tell someone.'

Sunday saw the sense in what she said. Perhaps Maggie was right? If she was, then Victor Dawes had paid the ultimate price for his wickedness. And now that Maggie no longer had to live in fear of seeing him again, she, like Kitty, could start to put her sorry past behind her.

'It's over! I just heard on the wireless that the war is finally over!' Ben announced joyously as he burst into the drawing room on the blustery morning of 11 November 1918.

Everyone began to hug each other and shake hands; even Kitty, who was normally so quiet, raised a smile. Then Ben suddenly grabbed Maggie and began to waltz her about the room, much to everyone's amusement.

'What a Christmas this is going to be,' Tom cried as he hurried away to fetch a bottle of wine. 'I think we should drink a toast to peace at last!'

By the time he returned, the church bells all over the land were ringing and Tom hastily filled some glasses and passed them around. They were all aware that the war had cost millions of lives and that today would be filled with sadness for those whose loved ones would not be returning. The empty stables also told a story. Even so, it was a time for rejoicing.

For the people at Treetops, the last few weeks had been eventful to say the least. First, they had welcomed Kitty and Maggie home with open arms. Somehow Maggie's confession to Sunday had brought them closer than ever. The Daweses' house had been put up for sale on Maggie's instructions and was now sold, and for now the proceeds were sitting in the bank until Maggie decided what she wanted to do with all the money. Until then, Sunday and Tom had promised her that she had a home with them for as long as she wanted. Their little evacuees had returned to their families the month before, and ever since then, the household had been adjusting to the new peace and quiet. The remaining young people that Sunday and Tom had cared for had also grown up and left, and the twins had been adopted, and for the first time in years Treetops had no children racing along its corridors. But Sunday knew it wouldn't be like that for long. Kitty's baby was due soon and she could hardly wait for it to be born. Kitty had come out of the terrible lethargy she had sunk into after Richard's betrayal, but there was a kind of ethereal quality about her that worried Sunday. Despite all their best attempts to get her to eat, her body was painfully thin while her belly was so enormous that Tom often teased her that he was afraid she might pop.

457

When Kitty had first come home to a royal welcome, both Sunday and Tom had been touched to see how devoted to her Maggie was, and it did Sunday's heart good to see how close the two young women had become. Sunday had also noticed how kind Ben was to Maggie and how the girl seemed to glow when she was in his company. She had quietly hoped that a romance between them might develop but up to now there had been no sign of it. She lived in hope that it might still come about, and for now she was content with the way things were going, especially with the wonderful news that Tom had just given them, that this war to end all wars had itself come to an end.

'Things are finally working out,' Sunday told Tom with an ecstatic smile on her face. 'Kitty and Maggie are home and the best of friends. Who would ever have thought it, eh? When you look back to how jealous Maggie was of Kitty when she was little, I mean.'

Tom grinned. 'They were just children,' he pointed out. 'And do you know what? I think Maggie loved Kitty even then. It's just that she so desperately wanted a family of her very own to belong to. It's heartbreaking how things turned out with the Daweses, but at least we can make sure she feels loved from here on in.'

That afternoon, Big Ben in London struck one o'clock after four years of silence and suddenly everywhere was a blaze of colour with flags of every Allied nation flying from hastily erected flagpoles on hundreds of rooftops. The King and Queen attracted huge crowds as they took an informal drive through the centre of London to Hyde Park, and thousands of people crowded into Downing Street to cheer the Prime Minister, Lloyd George, and his cabinet. Blackout curtains were ripped down, and suddenly all the shop windows were ablaze with light. It was truly a day to rejoice and by the time they went to bed that night everyone, even Kitty, was in a happy frame of mind.

'I'm going to make sure that this will be the best Christmas that Treetops Manor has ever seen,' Tom told his wife as he took her in his arms and kissed her tenderly and she didn't doubt him for a minute.

Two weeks before Christmas, Tom and George drove into Nuneaton market and returned home with an impressive specimen of a Christmas tree. Despite the weather, which was grey and dismal and very, very cold, nothing could dampen their spirits.

'But wherever shall we put it?' Sunday asked as she stared in awe at the giant tree.

Kitty, who was now well overdue for the birth of her child, and Maggie had come from the drawing room to see it and Maggie giggled. 'I reckon it will have to stay right here in the hall,' she declared. 'It's far too tall to fit in any of the other rooms – unless you want to chop some off it.'

'I will *not* chop any off, young lady,' Tom retorted. 'And I think it will look splendid in the hall. Ben, be a good chap and go and find a good sturdy bucket for it, will you?'

Ben shot off to do as he was told as Kitty waddled back into the drawing room, closely followed by Maggie, who was becoming really concerned about her. Only the night before, Kitty had suddenly said, 'You *will* keep an eye out for the baby, won't you, Maggie?'

'You'll be able to do that yourself,' Maggie had told her, but it had worried her all the same. Was Kitty trying to tell her in a roundabout way that she didn't expect to survive the birth? But that was nonsense! Kitty might be small and fragile, but thousands of women her build had given birth with no complications – so why should she be any different? Sunday and Tom already had the best doctor and midwife in the district on standby and now Maggie just hoped that the birth would soon be over.

Later that day, Maggie and Ben decorated the tree as Kitty sat on a chair and watched. Ben was perched on a ladder doing the top half while Maggie attended to the lower branches.

'No, don't put that one there,' Maggie scolded him. 'Just a bit further along . . . yes, that's better.'

Kitty smiled. 'You sound like an old married couple,' she told them and was tickled when they both blushed and hurriedly got on with what they were doing. So that was how the land lay, was it? She'd noticed how well they were getting on and the way Ben's eyes would follow Maggie about, and Kitty hoped that something would come of it. Maggie had been so good to her, she deserved a little happiness herself now.

Verity and Edgar Lockett, the reverend from Chilvers Coton Church, came to supper that evening and Lavinia and William were there too, and so the happy atmosphere continued.

'Are you sure it's big enough?' Edgar teased as he stared at the giant Christmas tree when they arrived.

Tom playfully punched him in the arm before dragging him off to enjoy a pre-dinner cigar and a glass of port with the other men in the library while Cissie and Sunday pottered about the kitchen putting the finishing touches to the meal.

They were halfway through it when Kitty said rather faintly, 'Would you mind excusing me?'

'Of course not, love,' Sunday said immediately. 'You're not in pain, are you?'

Kitty shook her head. 'No, nothing like that. I think it's just the weight of all this.' She patted her gigantic abdomen, then rising she lumbered away as Maggie watched her go anxiously.

'Perhaps I should go with her?'

'No, pet. Finish your dinner first,' Sunday said. 'I'm sure she will call us if she needs us.'

'How long has she got to go?' Verity asked as she helped herself to another slice of the succulent roast pork.

'According to Maggie, it should have been at the end of November

460

– but then babies have a habit of coming when they're ready, don't they?'

Verity nodded and the subject was changed.

The day before Kitty's birthday, when Sunday came across her staring pensively from the window, she asked, 'Are you all right, love?'

Kitty nodded. 'Yes, but I'd be glad of a little chat if you have the time?'

'Of course.' She took a seat at the side of her and waited for Kitty to begin. The girl clearly had something on her mind.

'I just wanted to say thank you for the way you've welcomed me home without making a fuss about . . . you know?' She stroked her stomach and flushed.

'Don't be silly, why should I make a fuss? A baby is a blessing at the end of the day and it will be welcomed and loved. It isn't your fault that you find yourself in this position. It's that no good—'

Kitty held her hand up as she saw the raw yearning on Sunday's face. She had always known how much Sunday had wanted to bear her own child and thought it a crying shame that it had never happened for her.

'Stop, please,' she said. 'It isn't quite what you think. What I mean is, Richard *did* blackmail me in the beginning into entertaining his friends – with my mother's encouragement, of course – but truthfully, once I got used to it I found there were benefits to being an old gentleman's darling. I suppose that must be some of my birth mother coming out in me,' she said quietly. 'I liked being pampered and spoiled, just as I loved the adoration I got from the crowds when I was on the stage. Does that make me a bad person?'

Sunday took her hand. 'Not at all. It just makes you human. You were a young girl who had her head turned, that's all, by people

461

who were much older than you and should have known better.'
Sunday was under no illusions.

'Well, it's kind of you to say it, but do you feel sad that I'm no longer the young innocent who left here?'

'Stop this right now,' Sunday told her sternly. 'You are just our Kitty. You will *always* be our Kitty, so let's have no more of this silly talk.'

Kitty clamped her lips together and eventually Sunday went about what she had been doing, but for some reason a chill had settled in the pit of her stomach and she couldn't seem to shake it.

Kitty's labour pains began early the next day when they woke to find the world coated in a thick frost. As a weak wintry sun rose in the sky above Treetops Manor, everywhere looked as if it had been sprinkled with diamond dust but Sunday flew into a panic as soon as she realised what was happening and hardly noticed anything.

'Tom, go and tell the doctor and the midwife that we need them as soon as possible,' she ordered. 'And you, Maggie, will you and Cissie get some boiling water on the go and fetch some towels – lots of them, please. Oh – and could you carry in the crib from the nursery? I have it all ready for the baby. Warm the sheets before you make it up.'

Maggie duly pottered away and returned with the crib which was placed at the side of the bed ready for the new little life that would soon be sleeping inside it. The tiny sheets and baby garments were airing by the fire. At that point Sunday's stomach began to churn with excitement.

The midwife huffed her way up the stairs almost an hour later. She was a portly woman who had delivered hundreds of babies in her time and Sunday knew that Kitty would be in safe hands. 'There

I was, just about to start icing me Christmas cake when Tom raps on the door.' She winked at Kitty then to show that there was no hard feeling. 'Let's have a look at you then, pet. Hopefully this will be over in no time an' we can all enjoy getting ready for Christmas then, eh?'

As Sunday drew back the bedclothes and revealed Kitty's enormous stomach the midwife's eyes stretched wide. 'Good grief,' she gasped. 'I ain't in all me years seen such a little 'un wi' such a huge bump. I reckon this is goin' to be a big baby.' She felt around gently then sent Sunday and Maggie out onto the landing while she examined Kitty more thoroughly.

Her joking manner was gone when she joined them and she confided, 'I'm a bit troubled, I have to admit. The lass is huge an' her only a little thing. This ain't going to be easy. Have you sent for the doctor? I've a feeling we might need him afore the day is out.'

Sunday nodded. That sick feeling was back in the pit of her stomach again but then they heard Kitty groan and they all rushed back in to her.

As the morning lengthened into the afternoon, every minute began to feel like an hour. The doctor had arrived by then and he sent Sunday and Maggie downstairs to join the others who were all gathered in the day room waiting for news.

Cissie floated from there to the kitchen making endless cups of tea until they all felt that they might drown in it, and then mid-afternoon, the midwife appeared to tell Maggie, 'She's askin' for you, pet. She's insistent that she sees you.'

Maggie flew past her, taking the stairs two at a time to find Kitty looking deathly pale on the bed. Even so she managed a weak smile when she saw her friend, and when Maggie clasped her hand she breathed, 'I just wanted to say thank you – for everything. I . . . I don't know what I would have done without you.'

She pressed something into Maggie's hand then but the girl was so distraught that she merely shoved it into the pocket of her dress before saying, 'Give over, will you, and concentrate on getting this baby here.'

Kitty gasped then as a pain gripped her and she arched her back. Once it had died away she panted, 'Be happy . . .' But then the doctor was ushering Maggie from the room again and the midwife was back so Maggie went away leaving them to do their job.

As the afternoon progressed darkness fell and Sunday and Tom went quietly about the house lighting the lights.

'Should it be taking this long?' Tom asked, nodding towards the ceiling.

'First babies have a habit of taking their time,' Lavinia assured him but deep down she was very worried too by now. The doctor had informed them some time ago that Kitty was having a bad time of it, but all they could do was wait and pray that all would go well.

The evening wore on and gradually the screams that had echoed from upstairs faded to dull whimpers but still there was no baby and Sunday was feeling frantic now as she paced up and down.

'You'll wear a hole in the carpet at this rate, my darling,' Lavinia told her gently but Sunday was beyond reasoning. Every instinct she had told her that something was seriously wrong, but there was not a thing she could do about it. And then suddenly the noises stopped. As one, Sunday and Maggie started across the room, almost colliding in the doorway, and then they were racing up the stairs side by side. Without even bothering to knock, Sunday flung Kitty's bedroom door open just as the doctor was handing a tiny blood-covered infant to the midwife.

Maggie's hand flew to her mouth as she realised that the child, a little boy, wasn't breathing and then the midwife was hanging him upside down and smacking his bottom soundly. When it became clear that this was having no effect she laid him on the end of the bed and began to blow gently into his rosebud mouth but after a few minutes the doctor shook his head and laid his hand on her arm.

'You can stop now.' His voice was grave. 'I'm afraid he was dead before we managed to deliver him.'

Sunday held each other and began to cry. Poor Kitty, all that effort and nothing to show for it! And he was such a bonny little boy.

Chapter Fifty-Six

Once the midwife had wrapped the baby in a blanket and laid it silently in the crib, Sunday crossed to Kitty whose eyes were feverishly bright in her waxen face.

She clutched at Sunday's hand before saying on a sigh, 'I love you, Sunday – never forget it. You've been more of a mother to me than my real mother ever was. And you, Maggie, I love you too.'

And then she was drifting away from them again and the midwife was shooing them out of the room. They found Tom and Ben waiting like expectant fathers on the landing for them and it felt like the most natural thing in the world for Ben to wrap his arms about Maggie as Tom hugged Sunday.

'I-it was a little boy, but he was stillborn,' Maggie sobbed, and then suddenly becoming conscious of their closeness she hastily stepped away from him and her cheeks began to burn. Ben would never look at a plain Jane like her, she knew. At the same time, Ben's face set in hard lines as he cursed himself for a fool. How could he ever have allowed himself to believe for a minute that Maggie would ever look the side that he was on? She was a grand lass and bonny, the sort that any man would take for a wife, but she must find the sight of him disgusting, just as he himself did every time he glanced in the mirror.

'That's a shame.' He nodded at her then turning abruptly he

466

made off down the stairs with a speed that would have done justice to one of Tom's racehorses.

Seeing the look of bewilderment on Maggie's face, Sunday gently chided, 'You shouldn't have pushed him away like that, lass. Not when he cares so much about you.'

'Cares? About *me*?'

It was Tom who answered when he said, 'You women can be blind as bats sometimes, I swear. If you care for him at all, go after him and tell him afore you miss your chance.'

Lifting her skirt, Maggie did just that, finally finding Ben leaning heavily on the edge of the deep stone sink in the kitchen. Suddenly shy she stuttered, 'Ben . . . I didn't mean to push you away up there. I just thought that—'

'I know what you thought.' His voice was laced with bitterness. 'You didn't want me to get the wrong idea and think that you might be interested in me! Why would you be, with me looking like this?'

Taking his arm in a firm grip, she swung him about with a strength she hadn't realised she had, and now her eyes sparked fire as she said, 'Isn't it time you stopped feeling sorry for yourself? You're home all in one piece and even with your scars you're still the most handsome man I've ever seen whereas I'm . . .' She flushed and her anger died. 'I'm just a plain Jane.'

Now it was his turn to look stunned. 'You plain? *Never!* Why, you're bonny inside and out. I've watched you looking after Kitty, running around doing whatever you can to make her more comfortable, and I've found myself feeling jealous of her.' He couldn't believe he had said that! 'Aye, I have.'

Suddenly they smiled at each other.

'Do you know what,' Maggie said timidly. 'I don't think now is really the time for this while Kitty is going through so much, but if you still feel the same when it's all over . . .'

Taking her hand he said huskily, 'You're on, lass.'

Upstairs, Tom and Sunday were still waiting for news of Kitty when the bedroom door opened and the midwife stuck her head around it to tell them, 'There's another baby coming. Pray to God that this one survives.' With that she closed the door again as Tom and Sunday stared at each other in amazement. No wonder Kitty had been so enormous; she had been carrying twins! Soon after they spotted Maggie and Ben coming back up the stairs to join them and Sunday was pleased to see the way they kept glancing at each other. *There's two that will be all right from now*, she found herself thinking. *Now I just have to worry about Kitty!*

It wasn't long before a thin wail pierced the air and Sunday's eyes lit up. The second baby had been born and if the noise it was making was anything to go by, this one was healthy. The midwife bustled out with the tiny child wrapped in some of the warm bedding and she thrust the bundle towards Sunday. 'Can you see that she gets a bath?' she asked. 'I need to be in there with the doctor doing what we can for the mother. And yes, it's a little lass by the way, small but she seems healthy enough, she's certainly got a good pair of lungs on her.' Then her eyes solemn she said, 'I ought to warn you, it's not looking good for the mother.' Then she was gone as Sunday stared after her with stricken eyes.

'Come on, pet, we've been given our orders,' Tom told her gently and with a jolt Sunday realised that he was right. Once downstairs, everyone crowded around them and as Sunday slowly unwrapped the coverings from the tiny body they all gasped. The baby was beautiful, a perfect little replica of her mother with violet-blue eyes and soft dark downy hair.

Cissie hurried away to fetch a bowl of warm water and a towel and once the child was washed and dried they dressed her in some of the tiny clothes they had laid out all ready.

'She's just so gorgeous,' Cissie sighed. 'Enough to make you feel broody.' They all fell silent then, their thoughts centred on the soul who was fighting for her life upstairs. Very soon the infant was crying for her first feed and Cissie warmed some milk and fed her with the glass bottle they had ready in case of emergencies.

It was just before midnight when the drawing-room door opened and the doctor appeared looking tired and despondent. 'I'm so very sorry,' he said quietly. 'I did all I could but she just slipped away.'

It was well past midnight when Cissie had washed and changed Kitty and laid her stillborn son in her arms. They all walked noiselessly, one by one, into the bedroom to say their goodbyes. Strangely, Kitty looked more peaceful than she had for a long time and Sunday prayed that she was destined to go to a better place. Soon, the undertaker came to take her and the babe to the Chapel of Rest. Weary and heartbroken, no one wanted to go to bed. Instead, they congregated in the kitchen for yet another cup of tea.

Cissie and George had finally gone back to their cottage and the new baby was fast asleep in Sunday's arms when Maggie suddenly remembered that Kitty had given something to her earlier on.

'This is for you.' She fished an envelope out of her pocket and handed it to Sunday. After passing the baby into Tom's waiting arms Sunday slit it open.

Dear Sunday,

I have had a strange feeling for some time that I will not survive my baby's birth and so I am writing this letter to hopefully secure his or her future just in case.

Should anything happen to me I humbly request that you and Tom will bring the baby up as your own child. I know how much you have always longed for a baby so in the event of my death this little soul will be my final gift to you. I know he or she will receive the love you showered on me and I hope that when you think of me in the future you will remember me fondly. Would you also kindly ensure that the locket that you gave to me on the day I left Treetops is passed on to my baby, please? It is my most treasured possession.

With love always,
Kitty xxxx

As tears began to stream down Sunday's cheeks Maggie and Ben stole away hand in hand, leaving Tom and Sunday to say a proper hello to their brand new baby daughter.

'My poor Kitty,' Sunday sobbed. And then, with the baby still tight in the crook of one arm and well wrapped up, Tom opened the back door briefly and pointed up at the sky. It was ablaze with stars that twinkled down on the frosty trees and lawns, transforming them into a winter wonderland.

'Look up there, my darlings,' he whispered as he kissed the sleeping baby and then his wife. 'This Christmas morn, our Kitty will be the brightest star you can see. She'll always be close to us – and what a precious legacy she has left us. Now at last we have our very own little girl and through her Kitty will live on.' He closed the door and embraced them both in the warm, protective circle of his arms.

Sunday blinked back her tears and murmured in agreement as she bent to gently kiss the tiny little angel in her arms. Tom was right – Kitty had left them the greatest gift of all, and while they had her, Kitty would always be just a heartbeat away.

'You're right,' she whispered thickly. 'But I ought to tell you now that in about another six months' time, this beautiful child will have a little brother or sister.'

It took a second or two for her husband to grasp her meaning. Then his mouth gaped. '*What!* You mean that you're . . .'

Sunday nodded and smiled as tears slid down her cheeks. 'Yes. I didn't want to tell you until I was sure. We've been disappointed *so* many times, and I'm past the normal childbearing age, as you know. But the doctor confirmed it yesterday. I was going to tell you then, but with Kitty . . .'

'I know,' he soothed. Neither of them would ever forget their beloved Kitty, but now, despite her loss, they had a future to look forward to, with their brand new little family.

THE END

Acknowledgements

Firstly I'd like to say a big thank you to my brilliant agent, Sheila Crowley for all the hard work she's done on my behalf and for all her help and support, not forgetting Abbie, her lovely assistant.

Secondly an enormous thank you to Eli, Kate, Sarah, Tara and all the brilliant team at Bonnier Zaffre, also to all of my lovely readers who helped to make the first of this series, *Mothering Sunday*, into a *Sunday Times* Bestseller.

Thank you all so much! I feel very blessed to be surrounded by such wonderful people.

Welcome to the world of *Rosie Goodwin*!

Keep reading for more from Rosie Goodwin, to discover a recipe that features in this novel and to find out more about what Rosie Goodwin is doing next . . .

We'd also like to introduce you to MEMORY LANE, our special community for the very best of saga writing from authors you know and love and new ones we simply can't wait for you to meet. Read on and join our club!

www.MemoryLane.club

A Christmas Message

Hello everyone,

I can't believe that as you read this we will be racing towards Christmas once again! Where does the time go? It doesn't seem more than the blink of an eye when I was writing to you all in March to celebrate the publication of the first of my Days of the Week collection, *Mothering Sunday,* and now here we are with the second of the series, *The Little Angel* on the shelves.

It's been a bit of a roller coaster year for me. It began in the New Year with the death of our lovely aunt in Wales. Special thanks to Christine, a family member who lived close by who made Auntie Doreen's final days as good as they could be. You are such a star Christine and we are all very grateful to you!

On a happier note, we are now eagerly awaiting the birth of a brand new little granddaughter. I am writing this early in August and she is due the second week of September so by the time you read this she will be here! We can't wait to meet her now! Her birth will be closely followed by my daughter's wedding early in October. I don't mind telling you my office and the top bedroom in my house looks like a bridal shop. I have tiaras, a wedding dress, flowers, table decorations, bridesmaids' dresses etc. all over the place. So; a birth, a death and a marriage all in the space of one year! The circle of life.

Then before we know it Christmas will be here. I love Christmas! It's a time when we can forget work for a few days and spend a little special time with our families. We all lead such busy lives so it's nice to be able to gear down for a while with the people we love most. In December the work begins: we raid the loft and down come all the Christmas decs. The first thing to go up is the big tree in the dining room. It usually takes me and the children a whole afternoon to dress it, then we tackle the trees in the other rooms along with all the other decorations. Next day, hubby gets the ladder out and begins to put up the outside lights and by the time he's finished it usually looks like Blackpool illuminations! That's not to mention all the shopping, and sometimes you think; *phew is it worth it?* The answer to that is, **yes it is**, the minute you see the children's excited faces on Christmas Eve. Our family always celebrates with a traditional Christmas dinner – turkey and stuffing, roast potatoes, the whole works followed by Christmas pudding, crackers and party poppers! Then the children go into one lounge to play with their toys while the adults relax with a good old-fashioned Christmas film in the snug curled up by log burner in the inglenook. We then all get together again on Boxing Day and do the whole thing all over again, bliss! And of course, the day after Boxing Day is the day that the girls and I hit the sales, there's nothing better than a bit of retail therapy, especially when there are bargains to be had!

The new book was written with Christmas in mind and as soon as I saw the cover of *The Little Angel* I fell in love with it as I hope you will. It's so Christmassy that I could almost feel the snow on my face and it portrays the main character in the book so well that it really brought her to life! In this book we meet Kitty, Monday's child, who is fair of face. She is such a character: beautiful, self-centred and vain yet deep inside she has a kind heart and I truly grew to love her as her character developed. I do hope you will care for

476

her as much as you loved Sunday in *Mothering Sunday*. Within days of it hitting the shelves it had gone into the *Sunday Times* Bestsellers list and myself and my wonderful team at Bonnier Zaffre were absolutely thrilled. I have now completed *A Mother's Grace*, due out next spring where we meet Tuesday's child, Grace, and I am now busily working on Wednesday's child. No peace for the wicked! But I am loving every second of writing this series. Each one will be a completely stand-alone book focused on a different character although as it goes along you may recognise some characters from the previous books. Thank you all *so much* for the lovely reviews and the feedback you gave for the first book, please keep them coming for *The Little Angel*. A writer's life can be very isolated at times. We spend most of it locked away in our office with our imaginary characters so to hear from all of you makes it all worthwhile.

Finally, now I have told you all my gossip, I would just like to take the opportunity to wish all of you and yours a very Merry Christmas and a Happy New Year. Have a good one!

Much love,

Rosie
xxx

Very Rich Fruit Christmas Cake

You will need:

1lb	450g	Currants
11oz	300g	Sultanas
6oz	175g	Raisins
4oz	125g	Glacé cherries, halved
4oz	125g	Almond flakes or chopped blanched almonds
4oz	125g	Mixed peel, chopped
Grated rind of 2 lemons		
3 tbsp	75ml	Brandy (and more to feed the cake)
11oz	300gr	Plain flour
1½ tsp	75ml	Mixed spice
½ tsp	2.5ml	Nutmeg
3oz	75gr	Ground almonds
9oz	250g	Butter
10oz	275g	Soft brown sugar
1½ tbsp		Black treacle
6 large eggs		

Method:

1. Put the dried fruit (and almond flakes) in a bowl and pour the brandy over them. Leave to soak for at least 30 minutes, stirring occasionally.

·MEMORY LANE·

2. Preheat your oven to 275F/140C/gas mark 1. Prepare either a 10 inch square tin or 9 inch round tin by double lining it with baking parchment.
3. Place all of the dry ingredients – flour, mixed spice, nutmeg, ground almonds – in a bowl and mix well.
4. In another bowl cream the butter and sugar together, using a wooden spoon, until light and fluffy. Slowly beat in the treacle. Add the eggs individually, adding a tbs of the flour mixture with each egg.
5. Fold in the remainder of the flour mixture and the fruits, half at a time. Mix thoroughly but gently to be sure not to break up the fruit too much.
6. Place your mixture in the prepared tin. Leave slight dip in centre of mix.
7. Bake for 3 hours then test with a skewer, it make need more time.
8. When cooked, remove from oven but leave in tin for at least 15 minutes.
9. When cool, turn out on to a wire cooling rack and remove the paper.
10. Poke holes in the cake, using a skewer and spoon over 2 tbsp of brandy.
11. When quite cold double wrap in greaseproof paper and place in air tight tin.
12. Do not eat for at least 3 weeks. During this time unwrap cake regularly and brush with Brandy about 1½ tbs each time. Don't feed the cake for a week, before icing so that the surface can dry.
13. Ice and decorate. Once iced the cake should be sealed and can be kept for a long time, maturing.

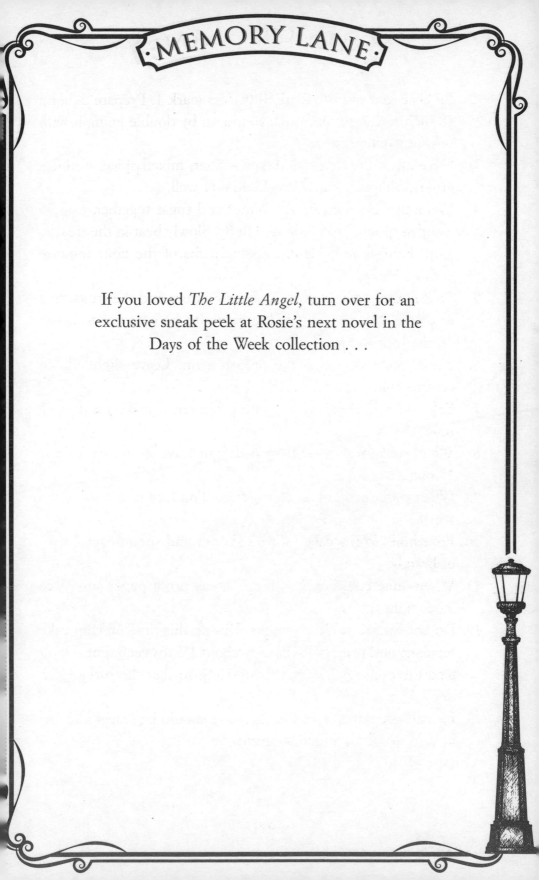

If you loved *The Little Angel*, turn over for an
exclusive sneak peek at Rosie's next novel in the
Days of the Week collection . . .

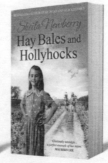

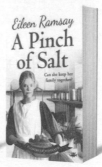